Will Morgan

George E. Meuser

DEDICATION

Dedicated to my wife Judy, and my friend Sandy,
class of '55, CUHS

1

CAPTURED

Shifting around so that the crook of his arm was under the emaciated chin, he took a deep breath, closed his eyes and squeezed tightly. His friend struggled for several seconds, grabbing at his arm, but he had promised that he would not stop, that he would see it through. Once the body relaxed, and the hand falling limp, he forced himself to look down into the still face, the half shut eyes that were already glazing over. He was filled with a deadly resolve. Someone was going to pay.

Reveille sounded, but Sgt. Will Morgan had been up for almost an hour preparing for the coming march. He had always been an early riser, even as a kid. He found this time to be the most fulfilling time of day. It was just he, his horse and no distractions. At the sound of the bugle, he ordered his troops to *Fall In*, and took his place for the report of absences. Today, there were none. The men then fed and tended their horses, checking legs, hooves and shoes for any problems. Morgan had already finished that chore. He walked along the picket line, seeing to his men. The company cooks had also been up early and had a hardy breakfast ready as the men formed lines past the mess tents. It was his opinion the troops would have eaten just about anything that morning, after the long cold ride of yesterday.

As *Boots and Saddles* sounded, Morgan buckled on his saber and pistol. The extra hour had also given him time to rub off the light film of rust that had covered his weapons since yesterday. Noticing Jimmy Compton had done the same., he wished he had more troopers like him. He usually made an effort to curb his personal feelings towards his men. It made their deaths easier to stomach if he didn't know too much about them. He had made an exception regarding Jimmy, who watched everything he did and copied his every move. He, too, was always up early, preparing for the day. When Will put an extra poncho over his horse at night, so did he. Will made it a habit to never slouch in the saddle, and Jimmy always rode ram-rod straight. When a battle charge sounded, he knew that Jimmy would be at his side, and never let him down. He led Pops into line and stood by his head. When the CO gave the command *To Horse* he placed his left foot in the stirrup then swung up into the saddle at the command *Mount*. After all the times he had gone through this procedure, it still gave him a feeling of satisfaction to hear three hundred butts hitting the saddles at the same second.

Looking at the dull gray sky, he knew that it would rain again. It had rained every day for the last eight days. In that time they had not seen one Reb, not that he minded that much. Why wars were fought during the winter months was beyond his comprehension. With so many units, on both sides, pretty much holed up in winter camps, it made little sense to have the cavalry out roaming around the countryside. Not only was it hard on the troopers, but also hard on the horses and mules. Regrettably, no one had ever asked him for his opinion on the subject.

Reigning to his left, he took his position with the other sergeants between the officers and the men of lower rank. *Right! Forward! Fours Right!*

He nudged Pops but the horse had already started moving into position. Will smiled. Hell, he thought, Pops knows the commands as well as I do. They left the encampment at a walk and within the hour it started to rain. First a few tentative drops, then the sky opened up, drenching the men, and he could see no more than fifty yards. He pulled the brim of his hat down and re-arranged his scarf to cover his nose and mouth. His eyes stung from the cold. He slid his right hand under the poncho and placed it under his arm. Although Jimmy was behind him, he knew that he was doing the same. He smiled at the thought. For all the discomfort of long rides in the rain and the occasional terror of racing into cannon fire, he enjoyed the companionship of military life. He had never felt more close to people as he did in the army, and being a Sergeant gave him a sense of responsibility that he had never had riding the range chasing cattle. They had each other's backs, and he had theirs. He took this responsibility very seriously.

They stopped for noon rations, but no fires were built. The rain was still pouring down and no one wanted to have to struggle getting a fire going.

"Mighty fine day for a ride, don't ya think, Sarg." Jimmy had walked over to Will, who was hunkered down under the limbs of a large tree. Not waiting for an answer, he took up a position beside Will and leaned back against the trunk. He never called him anything but Sergeant Morgan, unless they were alone and out of earshot. Morgan always addressed him as Cpl. Compton.

"Great day for a ride in the country. Don't ya' think?" He repeated, with a grin.

"Can't say as I've ever seen a better one. Horses seem to be enjoying it too. Saw a few flounderin' around in the mud, just for fun." He paused. "Glad to hear you're enjoyin' it. We aim to please," Will drawled. "Sure beats sittin' around a fireplace with nothin' to do but soak up the warm and watch the flames."

The exchange brought a feeling of loneliness for his childhood home, and evenings with his family, enjoying the warmth of the fire and good conversation with his Father. He had learned so much from him. "Do the right thing, stand for something and don't back down when challenged. Folks that don't have convictions don't amount to much. You figure out who you are, and stick to your principles."

Will had tried to follow this advice. He hoped that his dad approved of what he was.

"Ah, the life of a cavalryman. Course, it sure beats walkin', and that's a fact. Danged glad to git out of that outfit," Jimmy said with a grin.

"Yeah, me to. Looks like they're gittin' ready to move out. Good thing, cause my cold, wet butt was startin' to freeze to the ground."

By early afternoon, the rain slackened and then stopped. The temperature dropped and small icicles formed on the brim of his hat. Within minutes, spikes of ice pushed their way up from the frozen mud. The wet needles on the trees began to turn to ice. Will wanted to hunker down in his saddle to conserve body heat but he didn't. If truth be told, he was starting to hate being cold and wet.

On a rise three hundred yards ahead a lone Confederate, concealed in a small group of trees, looked down at the approaching soldiers. After observing the length of the column, and guessing at their number, he mounted his horse and rode away at a gallop. He was smiling at the thought of doing battle with these Yanks, especially when they would be taken by surprise. It was gratifying to come across them after riding for four days and not seeing any sign of the enemy. The thought of a long night ride in the freezing weather ceased to bother him; not with news like this. He bent forward, pressing his face into the mane of his horse, as he sped down the hill.

They traveled about twenty miles that day. On a good day they could have traveled thirty or more. During the ride, Will had let his mind return to the situation he thought they were in. Of course, he wasn't told anything, but his opinion was that they were in big trouble. He was dismayed that Gen. Burnside had sent them this far south and now east over the Cumberland Gap into more heavily populated southern territory. The supply line from Camp Nelson in Kentucky was stretched to the breaking point. He figured the length to be well over a hundred and fifty miles. He felt sorry for the men, horses and mules that had to make that dangerous trip continuously, to keep them supplied. Everything the Company needed to survive depended on them. Any miscalculation or mishap and the entire command would be stranded. There was no way this many men could survive living off the land for long. Although he wouldn't admit it out loud, his confidence in Burnside was minimal, at best. Having conducted a running war with Indians down in Texas, he sure knew how a war should be waged, and this wasn't it. Wars should be waged with cunning and deception, and a minimal loss of life. Marching into cannon fire was plain stupid.

At last, Maj. Beer held up his hand and pointed to an open space in the trees. Within minutes, camp was set up and small fires started.

Once Will had set up his tent, he took his spare poncho, walked over to the picket line and draped it over Pops. He was a large horse, standing seventeen hands, and being coal black with one white foreleg, he stood out from all the rest. He noticed that Jimmy's horse, Rover, was already covered. Some thought him a little crazy for pampering his horse this way, but Pops had never let him down. With the smell of blood and the roar of cannon, Pops had never flinched or wavered and putting a cover over him, in weather like this, was the least he could do. He gave him an extra ration of oats and wiped the wet from around his eyes. If he had an extra hat, he would have cut ear holes in it for him. He checked the animal's shoes one more time and with a final slap on his rump, returned to camp. On entering his tent he first took out his diary. Taking pencil in hand, he wrote. *Sept. 23, 1863, Rode all day in the rain.* With that terse entry he called it a day.

Jimmy watched Will cover Pops. He thought of inviting him over to share his small fire, but before he could catch his attention, Will had crawled into his tent. The ride had been long and miserable and Jimmy was sure that the Sarg was as tired as he. He thought of him as he hunched by the weak flames. In his eyes, they didn't come any better and he had never seen anyone as brave. When engaged in combat, Morgan was an awesome sight to see, and that was a fact. They were the same size, about five foot six or seven, and slim. The similarities stopped there. Where his own hair was blond and eyes hazel, Sarg's hair was coal black and he had the darkest eyes Jimmy had ever seen. Only nineteen, the boy hoped, maybe, he could be a man like the Sarg some day. He'd never asked, but thought him to be about thirty, or so. It was hard to tell. He smiled as he remembered watching Sarg in the last few battles. He seemed to be everywhere, shouting his battle cry as he urged his troops onward, his arm waving his saber over his head, standing tall in his stirrups. He was damn glad that Morgan was on his side.

The following morning, the sun was out and the trees were returning to normal. The smell of wet leaves filled Morgan's nose and the cold air felt good in his lungs, reminded him of Thanksgiving at home. As Will was drinking his morning coffee, he overheard two officers discussing plans for the day. He was pleased to hear that the 3rd Battalion was being assigned to protecting the supply line in a few weeks. "None too soon." He said, under his breath.

Unknown to them, the Confederate scout had ridden all night and at that moment a rebel force was within fifteen miles and closing.

Later in the morning a fog settled in, casting an eerie pall over the column. Sounds of hooves slogging through the mud, jingling bridle chains and an occasional cough from the men, drifted around Will, their sources, unseen. For no apparent reason, it brought a feeling of foreboding to Will. He couldn't seem to shake it. Maybe it was the realization that they could walk right into the enemy without warning that made him tense. He moved his head back and forth, eyes squinted, trying to penetrate the fog, but it was no use. He knew that if trouble was lurking out there Pops would know before he did, and let him know. He wondered, from time to time, just how much his horse actually understood beyond his more acute senses of scent and hearing. It could be his imagination, but in battle Pops seemed to be aware of everything that was going on and was able to anticipate Will's directions. When the war was over, he knew that if there was any way of keeping him, he would do it.

By early afternoon, the fog was lifting, and Will was hungry. His thoughts of food were interrupted by the sounds of gunfire from the forward scouts. The column, stretching back over a quarter of a mile compressed and came to a halt. Major Beer, riding near the front, galloped up to the crest of a small hill ahead and stopped. Will watched him as he peered into the thinning fog, then turning in his saddle, he cupped his hands and yelled "*Company Fours! Left in line! March!*".

The column, resembling a giant snake, moved into position and began to trot. Sabers were drawn and pistols were exposed. They moved steadily forward, waiting for the command to charge. Will could feel the excitement in Pops. He had to keep a firm grip on the reins to prevent him from breaking into a run. When the command came, horses lunged forward, kicking up mud on those that rode behind. Some went down, slipping on the icy mud, and their riders were urging them up. Will could feel the unsteadiness in Pops's gait, but he stayed up and pressed forward at a dead run. As always Will was filled with sheer exuberance tinged with fear as the horses and men flung themselves toward the enemy.

A hundred yards ahead, the Confederate line stretched clear across the gap between the hills, and Will could see the glint of carbines in the weak sunlight. Battle flags were waving as flag bearers raced back and forth behind their front lines. Smoke from the enemy fire billowed all along the line, and the familiar whine of bullets cut the air, as well as the sound of them hitting flesh.

The screams of dying men and horses sounded on both sides, as he guided Pops towards a gap in the enemy line. Extending his saber as high as he could reach, he waved it in circles and then pointed it toward the enemy. He took a deep breath and sounded his war cry.

Others took it up behind him and then they were crashing into the enemy. Swinging the saber, he took down three Rebs before he was through their lines. Then he turned Pops in a tight circle to come around for another pass. Sheathing the saber, he drew his pistol and re-entered the fray. Two more went down, then two misses. Dammit, he thought, make 'em count. Slowing down he shot a man trying to get control of his horse. The man was driven sideways and the frightened animal bolted into two other riders, sending their mounts to the ground. Will glanced at the fallen trooper, hardly more than a boy. He pushed the image from his mind.

The rebel force broke and retreated towards the town of Jonesville in the near distance. An officer tried to rally his troops, but was shot off his horse by someone to Will's right. A quick glance told him that Jimmy had gotten off the shot. Those men who were still mounted urged their horses after the fleeing Rebs with a fresh battle cry. They overtook them at the outskirts of the town. There was wild confusion on both sides as horses galloped helter-skelter many without riders. Within five minutes, the Rebs were either walking out with their hands raised to be rounded up or disappearing into the fog along the hills. As things settled down Will was able to estimate they had taken about a hundred prisoners. It had been a good day. He grinned, as Jimmy rode up.

"Danged if isn't a fight to crow about. I seen a few of our boys wounded, but none dead and look at all those Rebs a givin' up." Jimmy exclaimed, with gusto.

They heard later that twelve troopers were killed and nine wounded. Three later died. It took some of the joy out of the day's battle.

For the next six weeks, the 16th patrolled first south along the east side of the mountains and then back again. Unlike the first day, the Rebs never again fought a frontal attack, but were like pesky bees, keeping up a continual harassment, sniping from cover or ambushing troopers they found separated from the main body. One had to be on guard, twenty-four hours a day. Will was impressed with their methods but did not like being on the receiving end. If given the choice, he would have liked to confront the enemy in the same way. None of this march into the cannon fire stuff. Sneaking around, looking for the good shot instead. Trying to out-think them and beat them at their own game. Yup, that was the way to fight.

Will liked the looks of the countryside, with tall timber and a mixture of smaller growth covering the hills. He liked it better than his home in Iowa. He tried to picture these hills in spring, with the new growth, and leaves covering the hardwood trees. Must be plumb beautiful, he thought. Might come through here some spring if I live through this damn war. He looked around to make sure that he would always remember it. Small water falls cascaded from unseen places up in the hills, splashing down through the rocks, then rushing down beside the road. He could imagine a hundred shades of green on the barren branches and could picture a small cabin in the clearing, up ahead, with a few cows and chickens. Make a man proud to have a place like this for himself. Beers located a small clearing for a base camp early on and for the first time in two weeks they were able to get there tents set up with proper drain ditches. It was a time to organize their equipment, get some fires going and get dried out. Will was feeling good about it until he overheard the officers discussing the existence of a small town about a mile down the road. Thought of the houses and barns that would have provided them excellent shelter made him shake his head in disgust. Anyway they would be patrolling from this camp for a while and that was better than cold camps any day.

Two nights later, the weather turned ugly. Will could feel the temperature dropping by the minute. A thin layer of ice formed from the thickening fog and entire trees were turning to ice. Limbs snapped and came crashing to earth. Men were frantically moving their tents out into the open. The next morning, two sentries were found frozen to death near the picket line. When the frozen bodies were brought in, their poncho's broke apart as they were laid out.

They were breaking camp and Will was up early attempting to fold his tent when he received word that the two men had died in the night. He walked over to find out which two of his troop he had lost. It was Pvt. Johnson and Pvt. Edwards, stretched out on the ground, faces a pale blue, coated in a thin layer of ice. Their unseeing eyes stared up at the dull gray sky, their fingers still clutched the carbines which were frozen to their gloves. Will felt the sense of guilt he always experienced when one of his men died. For them to die other than in battle was even harder to take. Both good boys. He returned to his tent, and although his body warmth had kept it from freezing through the night it was stiffening up fast. He folded it up, as best he could, without breaking the fabric and rolled up his blanket. He noticed several of his men trying to deal with the frozen material, and went over to help. Jimmy had arranged his gear and was no where in sight until, peering through the trees, he saw him with his horse Rover and Pops, at the picket line. He had to smile at the boy's dependability.

Suddenly a trooper burst through the trees shouting "Turn out! Company L! Turn out!"

Will ran to his kit, grabbing his carbine from under his blanket and ran towards the frantic trooper. His heart sank as he saw Rebs pouring out of the trees behind him. He changed course and ran to the picket line. Jimmy, hearing the shouts had quickly buckled the cinches on both their horses. It was times like this that Will appreciated the standing order that no horse would be unsaddled, just a loosening of the cinches.

Jimmy heard Sarg running towards him as he bridled Pops. Turning, he caught the look of urgency in his face and felt a small stab of fear. Gripping the tether ropes, he jerked both of them loose and handed the Sergent his reins.

"All set, Sarg." He tried unsuccessfully to keep the fear out of his voice. Then he caught sight of the number of enemy soldiers charging towards them with so few defenders in position to protect the line. He was struck with a bolt of sheer panic. Shifting his glance to Sarg's determined face showed him his fear was not shared, and that steadied him.

They swung into their saddles amid a flurry of confusion as men frantically attempted to bridle, cinch and mount their horses. It would have been hard enough under normal conditions but frozen fingers and gear made it almost impossible. Perhaps fifteen, out of the fifty horse picket line achieved a rider in time to join the fray.

"We got to git around them," Will yelled. "Git around 'em!" The mounted men managed to obey the order and swung in behind Will and Jimmy. They put spurs to their horses and crashed through the undergrowth in a wide circle. Will could see the enemy, to his right and managed to get off three shots. He thought he got a hit, but wasn't sure. Other small groups of riders and those left on foot were rallying, and the rebel forces began falling back down the road towards the town. He resented the fact that Maj. Beers had insisted that they set up camp a mile away. Now it looked like they would have to flush the Rebs out from among the buildings, and that would surely increase casualties. The enemy was not in a rout, but was pulling back in a systematic retreat that seemed to have been well planned.

Will glanced around at his small group of riders. Damn, he thought. Not enough to make a charge. Another five minutes of warning, and they wouldn't be in this fix. With limited resources and no game plan, he decided to attack anyway before the Rebs could hide.

"Let's give 'em hell, boys. Follow me!" With a roar of enthusiasm, they formed a line and rushed towards the cluster of buildings comprising the town. Suddenly near the first outbuildings Jimmy's horse went down. It's head snapped backwards from the impact of the bullet, striking Jimmy in the face, before jerking to the left and down. Blood sprayed out of the animal's gaping wound as Jimmy flew over its head, so startled that he still gripped the reins. Unable to let go in time, the reins jerked him backwards and flipped him sideways. He landed hard.

In passing Will could hear the woosh of air that went out of Jimmy as he hit the ground. He reined Pops in and made a tight circle back to the fallen boy. He reached down and grabbed him by the wrist but could not lift him off the ground. Cold fingers and wet gloves prevented a good grip. He could sense the panic in Jimmy as he tried to run along side Pops, making a valiant effort to keep from falling, but it was no use.

"Damn!" he shouted as he lost his grip, ran two long steps and fell.

Will swung Pops around for another try, but Jimmy was on his knees dazed. Kicking loose from the stirrups, he dropped to the ground and ran to the young soldier's side.

"Get out of here, Sarg! Save yourself!" Jimmy's eyes were wide with shock. Blood spattered face and he was obviously having a problem focusing.

Will didn't answer. Grabbing Jimmy by the back of his belt he dragged him up on his feet and pushed him toward cover in a tumbled down smoke house. "You hurt bad?"

"I don't think so, but I gotta catch my breath a minute." He was gasping for air and rubbing his shoulder. It felt as though his arm had been ripped out and his whole face was numb. "Damn, Sarg, those bastards killed Rover. Best horse in the world, and they killed him." Tears were in his eyes. He sat for a moment, rubbing his sore chest and nose and lifting his arm up and down. "That is the worst spill I have ever taken off a horse, and that's for sure." He wiped at the mud and blood on face with his sleeve. He checked his pistol that, by some miracle, he had managed to hang on to, and took several deep breaths. After a moment he managed a weak grin at Will, then he stood and turned towards the door. " Let's go git us some Rebs." He burst out of the door and was gone.

Will, caught by surprise, followed, but Jimmy was already out of sight. He pulled up beside a delivery wagon and crouched down so that he could see under it and use its broad side for protection. Men were rushing back and forth three blocks away, but none close enough to distinguish friend from foe. He looked for Pops, but he was nowhere to be seen. He sure didn't like the idea of being afoot. Crouching over, he sprinted to where he'd dismounted and retrieved his carbine. He ran back to the smoke house and checked for mud in the barrel. Reloading, he peered out the door but did not see any enemy within gunshot range. He ran down the street, ducking behind a wooded barrel in a doorway. He squatted there for few minutes getting his wind back and wondering where the hell Jimmy had gone. Then taking a deep breath he started down the street, sweeping the area with his eyes, hoping to see Jimmy or his horse. He saw neither. Gun fire from an upstairs window temporarily drove him back. He could see dozens of Rebs entering the street two blocks away and he had to fight off a feeling of shock at their number. He knew the best defense was sometimes an offense, and the idea of running away from a fight sort of went against the grain. He got off one round from the carbine, but there was no time to reload. Drawing his pistol, he charge forward. He fired. A miss. He cursed himself for wasting a shell. Kneeling, he aimed and fired. The Reb fell in a heap and didn't move. Finding another target, he fired, but the man ducked behind a house. Another miss. A hail of bullets, which seemed to come from every direction, changed his mind about the idea of an offense. He ran into a narrow alley. Trying to jump some boxes but tripped and fell. He was shocked to realize that he had fallen on someone. Leaping up, he looked into Jimmy's startled face.

"Jesus! You scared the hell out of me," Jimmy exclaimed, visibly shaken.

"Well, you scared the hell out of me too" Will blurted out. "What are you doin' in here anyway? Let's go git those Rebs you were talkin' about."

"Got to reload. Not too many shells left. Things are gittin' a little frantic out there. Ain't this just one hell of a mess?"

"You sure got that right. Runnin' a little low myself." Will replied, checking his cartridge belt. "You ready?"

Jimmy nodded. "Lets have at 'em."

Once they left the alley, they realized the approaching forces had dispersed and the street was now empty. Noticing stairs leading to the upper floor of a hardware store, Will whispered, "This way." as he took the stairs two at a time. They burst through a door into sudden warmth. An old man was cowering in the corner, wide eyed, with his hands straight up in the air.

"Don't shoot me!" he pleaded. Will could see the man's lips tremble.

"Don't you worry about that." Will replied. "Can we have a couple of those biscuits on the stove?"

"The old man nodded." His fear was not diminished one bit. He was clearly sure they would kill him when they finished.

They left several minutes later, having eaten the biscuits and taken a few minutes to warm up in front of the pot bellied stove. As Will was shutting the door, he glanced back at the old man who was still cowering in the corner, hands straight up. "Thanks, old timer."

"Could'a spent the whole day there." Jimmy said, with sincerity. "That stove shore felt good." They had returned to take refuge behind the barrel.

"What do we have here? Looks like a ladder to the roof." Jimmy was peering upwards. Seconds later, they were crouched on the roof behind the façade.

"Thought the old guy was gonna die of fright. We're bad lookin' hombres, I guess."

"Just you, Sarg. Ain't nobody scared of me."

From their vantage point on the rooftop they were able to get a panoramic view of most of the action. On establishing the base camp the company's field cannon had been pulled up a small hill overlooking the town under the cover of darkness. Regrettably, their attempt to hide it had not been particularly successful. It wasn't a large cannon, as cannons go, but out here in the sticks, it was the biggest thing around, and was mighty impressive in close quarters. At the Rebel attack movement by the gun guards had attracted the enemy's attention. They managed to achieve a good field of fire from an adjacent hillside and within minutes, their sharpshooters had picked off most of the contingent of guards. The Rebs were now attempting to take over the hill and gun. Two tries had been made, but they had been driven back by a withering fire from the cavalry who were, for the most part, afoot. Again, they saw a chance of gaining control of the deadly weapon and seven Rebs headed for it in a broken run. At the same time, the gun crew, which had been bedded down in camp, was coming in from the direction of the road. Realizing what was happening they sprinted towards their gun, but the Rebs managed to get there first.

Will watched the Rebs from his vantage point as they zig-zagged, through the trees, crouching, attempting to make smaller targets of themselves. Just like ducks in a pond, Will thought. They sure made interesting targets. Too bad the distance was so great. No sense in wasting ammunition. He watched, with dread, the fight over the gun. If it was lost to the Rebs, his men would be in big trouble.

Although the Rebs were first to the gun, they had no time to turn it clear around and fire it. The crew managed to overwhelm them in a fierce hand-to-hand battle. Once the scattered rebel forces realized that they had lost control of the cannon they began to retreat to regroup in the town. Within seconds, the gun was loaded and swinging around in their direction, but most of the departing Rebs were below the arc of the gun's fire. They were taking no chances and were soon nearly out of sight of the gun crew who got off one round at a small knot of them attempting to take cover down a side street. Piles of trash cluttered their narrow escape route, allowing only those in the front to make it to safety. Bodies went flying and a silence fell over the area at the sound of the cannon.

A rebel officer, riding a white horse, broke from the trees a half mile away, and galloped over to the harried lieutenant of Company L which, through no fault of their own, had been stranded on foot, except for the officer in charge in a small clearing. He seemed to be demanding their surrender. The lieutenant drew his pistol and pointed it at the Confederate officer. He must have squeezed the trigger but nothing happened. He looked down at the weapon as if he couldn't believe its treachery. The rebel officer's bullet struck him in the head, driving him off his horse. His men dropped their guns and surrendered. Will, wondering just where this mounted officer had come from, wished he were closer to the action. Though this had all taken place in a matter of minutes it was born in on him that it was past time to make a move. He would have loved to have shot that officer off his horse, but the range was too far. He hated to see any of his fellows surrender, and he guessed that they had just lost twenty or more. He wondered why they didn't put up a good fight. He would learn later that they were within twenty bullets of being weaponless. No sense in dying for nothing. Leaving the rooftop, they worked their way through town. Small gunfights erupted, as troops from both sides managed to run into each other. The two made their way to a small feed store where they could see nearly everything and decided it was a good place to make their stand.

Over the next hour, the cannon kept up a spaced shelling of various targets and sporadic shots were heard around the town, but eventually a lack of ammunition silenced the weapon and the troops were also running low. Will and Jimmy made every shot count picking off passing Rebs. Fewer and fewer shots were heard, and then silence.

"I'm out," Jimmy exclaimed. He had spent five minutes searching the floor for extra shells. He had searched the store from top to bottom for shells, but found none.

"Me too." Will muttered. He had checked his cartridge belt three times, hoping that extra shells would magically appear. "I guess it's up to Beer, now. I suggest we just wait it out and see what he does. Sure don't like the idea of surrenderin' but I like the idea of fighting with no ammunition even less. Dammit to hell!"

Another detachment of the enemy hidden in the hills watched and waited. When the firing stopped, they emerged from the woods and charged the town.

Major Beers watched in horror as the fresh Reb troops swept down from the trees. He had almost decided they had a chance. What to do? He could order his men to attack with sabers and bayonets, but to what end? Certain death. He knew that they would follow his command, but he couldn't say the words. Reaching down, he picked up a pole with a piece of tent material tied on the end and waved it back and forth. It was done. He took out his sword and studied it, as he had studied it a thousand times. Such a beautiful weapon.

Will saw the waving flag of surrender, and felt a sense of relief mingled with dread. "Well, looks like the war is over for us, Jimmy. Let's head on over." His heart was beating fast, as he saw the mass of gray uniforms swarming down towards him. No way out of this, he thought. Keep your damn head up. They may have caught us, but they sure as hell haven't beaten us. No sir, not by a long shot. Jimmy was actually strutting. Will had to smile.

The firing had stopped at the first sight of the flag of surrender. Riding out from the line, an officer and two privates approached the Union line where the defeated troops were now congregating.

"Who's in charge of this force?"

"I am." Major Beer replied with a stiff bow.

"Then Sir, I demand your sword."

Major Beer unfastened his buckle and handed the sword to the officer, along with his pistol. Again, he bowed, stiffly. He thrust out his jaw and stood smartly at attention. At that moment, Will felt proud to have had him as his commanding officer.

Humiliation swept over Will like a blanket. Reluctantly, he unfastened his belt and let the saber fall. He had left the carbine in the feed store, but drew his pistol and dropped it onto the thawing mud. He looked down at it, and regretted having to drop it on the ground. It had saved his life over and over again, and it seemed like an insult to end up throwing it on the ground. He had seen hundreds of men surrender to the Union, but had never thought of what it was like. Now he knew how it felt and he didn't like it one damn bit. He realized that his troops were probably watching him, so with effort, he dismissed his pistol and snapped to attention, jutting out his jaw, and gave the rebel officer a smart salute. Caught off guard, the man returned it.

Major Beer and the other officers were rounded up and marched off. Will never saw them again. It was a strange feeling to realize that he and the other sergeants were now in charge. How many had survived? He felt the weight of responsibility. He wouldn't let them down.

2

LIBBY PRISON

Over the next four hours every building was searched from top to bottom. Haystacks were poked with hay forks, while squads crawled under every structure, even out-houses. Will and the other prisoners watched from the field where they were being held. It was amazing how many were rounded up, brought in two or three at a time, from where they had been hiding. It became a source of great merriment to find out where some had hidden. Several came in with shit up to their knees. No one had to ask where they had taken refuge. Two were wearing dresses. The fact that they both wore mustaches as well, seemed to have slipped their minds.

Later that evening, the non-coms were issued a few sacks of corn meal to be distributed among the troops. Will took the small sack and poured out a ration for each of his men. It was a short ration for men who had been working so hard that day.

"How they expect us to eat this stuff? Raw?" Someone growled with disgust.

After some discussion, someone suggested using their hats as mixing bowls. After dipping some water from a bucket provided by a Reb private, they each worked their meal into a pasty dough. Then they flattened it as best they could into a patty about half an inch thick. A small fire was started and, a few at a time, they cooked their patties on a piece of metal that someone borrowed from a guard. Disheartened, hungry and filled with dread, they silently ate their first meal in captivity.

Will looked across the fire at the familiar faces of his troops. He was saddened by those faces that were missing. He guessed that he had lost over a quarter of his men. He could see defeat in some of their faces. That bothered him.

"Well boys, looks like we're out of the fightin' for a spell. I guess they'll take us down south where the sun shines hot. Can't say as I'll miss this cold." He forced a smile. They were not impressed.

Slipping into a Texas drawl, he went on, "Rode down in Texas for a spell. Some strange fellers live in Texas. Hot down there, terrible hot. Causes all kinds of problems, you know." He paused. Some were listening. He continued. "Yep, that heat will cause a man to do some strange things. Why, one day Clyde and me, we was out a chasin' cows. Well, after a bit Clyde says, Whoa up! So's I whoa up. Clyde gits off his horse, juts out his chin and marches around to it's back end. He lifts up the tail and stands there lookin' at its ass for a spell. Then he leans forward and kisses it! Yessir, by God. Well I don't say nothing', not wanting to get betwixt a man and his horse. Well, we rides on for quite a spell and he hollers Whoa up! again! So's I whoa up again. He gits off and does the same danged thing. By this time, I jist gotta ask. I says, "Why you a doin' that? You like the taste?" Hell no. he says, That there is the whole reason. I got a bad case of chapped lips, and this keeps me from a lickin' 'em."

23

First a few giggles, then the entire group started laughing. It pleased Will to see them finally relax some.

"That is the dumbest joke I ever heard," one man exclaimed, in disgust.

"Then why the hell are you tryin' to keep from grinnin?" Another replied.

"Danged if I know," the man exclaimed.

The following day they marched till almost dark stopping only for a few crackers at midday and a drink from a creek a few times.

That evening, they were gathered together in a clear space with a rope around the perimeter. Will looked at the distance from the enclosure to the closest trees and decided that the chance for escape rated from poor to none. For every prisoner, there were at least two armed Rebs, and he had no idea how many more lurked out there in the woods. He followed directions. There might be better circumstances for escape later.

A Reb Sergeant strolled out and took a position of importance. He spread his legs and crossed his arms over his chest. "You Yanks stay inside this here rope. You touch it we goin' to kill ya. You stay on the ground. No standin' up. You stand up, you dade. Now git down on the ground."

Sleep came hard, not knowing what tomorrow had in store, especially on the icy ground without blanket or poncho. Curling up with his back against Jimmy and wrapping his arms around his knees, he managed to conserve some body heat. He thought, with longing, of his bedroll and tent out there somewhere, and he wondered who had taken possession of Pops. He resented the fact that some Reb was free to read his diary. He hoped that the new owner was illiterate. Maybe then he'd just use it to clean his butt. With that thought, he dozed off.

Sometime in the night one of the prisoners stood up. Everyone awoke at the crack of a carbine. The man fell, clutching his chest. He tried to speak. "Had to take a leak. Just standin' to take a leak. You tell my Agnes what......."

No silly joke would relieve the gloom that settled on them with the firing of that carbine.

Jimmy fumbled for the small metal case in his pant pocket. He didn't have to open it, but he had to hold it. On lonely nights he often held it. Sometimes he whispered his love to the smiling face inside. He needed her strength tonight.

The next four days they walked. More prisoners were added to their ranks along the way. Every man wanted to tell the story of his capture. Many had similar stories and eventually the talking tapered off as putting one foot in front of the other became their prime concern. Each man trudged along with his own thoughts. Will circulated among them when he could, letting them know that he was available if they needed his help. He thought about mentioning the hope of being exchanged but knew that if they weren't, it would make it worse to have put it into words. Two of his fellow Sergeants had been killed leaving him in charge of their men along with his own. They had been good soldiers and good friends. He would have felt much better if they were here to share the decision making.

As they approached each small hamlet along the way the folks there would line up to watch them pass. For the most part they seemed content to just watch, but from time to time verbal confrontations took place between them and the prisoners. Will had admonished his men to refrain from taking parts in these exchanges. It just stirred everybody up.

By the look of most of the townsfolk it wasn't worth the trouble. They were a rough and sorry lot. Poorly dressed and ill equipped for scratching out an existence in this rugged land. The soil seemed to be fine for growing trees and weeds but the winter ravaged gardens were unkempt and overgrown with wild plants. The houses, for the most part, were as poorly built as a pig barn at home, with cracks in the walls big enough to spit through. Many had no chimney on the house itself but had a kitchen of sorts outside with just a makeshift roof to keep the rain off the cook. What a way to live, Will thought.

"Hell of a thing to make a cavalryman walk. If I'd a liked walkin' I would a stayed in the infantry. Feet don't like this one bit," Jimmy growled. "I wonder where the heck we're goin. You figure we might be exchanged?" His voice sounded hopeful.

"Lots of prisoners have been. It would sure please me to be back in the saddle again. Just have to keep a thinkin' positive. This damn war can't last forever." Will replied.

The muddy roads were littered with small rocks that made walking hard and the sticky gumbo stuck to their boots building up on the soles so thick that it threatened to pull them off their feet. Within a short time most of the men had managed to obtain a stick of some sort to scrape the mud off, but it was a continual process. By the third day some complained of boot soles falling off or wearing through.

Will could feel blisters on both his feet. A man could do just about anything, as long as he was mobile, but once his feet were done, so was he and this was getting brutal. He was greatly relieved when they saw a train waiting for them in the small town of Bristol.

It wasn't much of a train. As a matter of fact, besides being small it seem to be held together mostly with rust. The locomotive sounded like it had more leaks than a tin can at a shootin' match. It was pulling four flat cars and four cattle cars. Will ushered Jimmy toward the cattle cars. "Might have a little more protection from the cold," he said. Jimmy nodded.

"Hey, Sarg. There's Pops!" Jimmy pointed to a group of men on horseback, standing in the road a hundred yards away.

"Damned if it isn't !" Will replied, with a smile. He motioned to one of the guards.

"What you want, Yank?" It was obvious that he didn't give a rat's ass what Will wanted.

"See that rider over there on the black with the white foreleg?"

"What about 'em?"

"That used to be my horse, and I would sure like to talk to his new owner, if that's possible."

"Yer hoss?" The guards attitude subtly changed. "I reckon I can do that." He motioned to another guard. "Ya'll keep an eye on these Yanks." He walked to where the horsemen were assembled and talked to the man on Pops. The rider looked in their direction then reined away from his comrades riding toward them.

Will knew that Pops recognized him when he shook his head and snorted. Will ran his fingers along the horse's head as Pops stuck his muzzle under Will's arm. The rider seemed to be excited to meet Will.

"This here is one fine animal, Yank. What you call 'em?"

"Pops," Will replied, chocking back a tightness in his throat.

"I'll call him that," the rider replied. He patted the horses neck. "I want ya'll to know that I'll damn sure take good care of him for ya."

"I appreciate that. Best horse I ever sat. You take care of him and he'll never let you down."

The guards started pushing them towards the waiting train. He rubbed Pops between the ears and looked up at the rider. The Reb gave him a genuine smile and saluted. "Good luck Yank. Don't ya'll worry, 'cause I'll treat him right." He reined Pops around and rejoined the other riders.

As the men boarded the train they scraped the mud off their boots one more time on the metal step. Then they lifted their weary bodies up into the car. Will and Jimmy found a corner and sat down. When the car was half full, the men that were still standing started pushing towards the sliding door, complaining that there was no more room. The guard rolled the door shut and locked it. After the guard had moved down to the next car, everyone took advantage of the extra space. "Those boys don't have any idea about countin'," one trooper observed.

It was soon evident to Will that this was a universal weakness in the lower ranks of the Confederate Army. Time after time this casual attitude toward mathematics made it possible to manipulate the food counts to gain an extra portion or two for every fifteen or twenty of their actual number.

As the engine wheezed and hissed its way to life, beginning its lumbering progress, everyone groaned. The wheel bearings had not been greased in months, maybe even years. The screeching and grinding pierced into their brains and scraped their nerves bringing hands over battered ears. As the miles went by they learned to ignore the clamor, as much as something like that could be ignored. The rail beds were also in poor shape and every few minutes the wheels would cross a wider gap between the rail sections that slammed the floor boards against the backsides of the sitting prisoners. To protect themselves they took to squatting against the rough walls until their legs went into spasms.

Sometime in the first couple of days they crossed into the back country of Virginia. They stopped briefly in Lynchburg to take on more prisoners. From time to time, the little engine would jump the rail, but the crew was well versed in prying it back into place. Will, as well as every man on the train, looked forward to these little setbacks, because those were the only times they got to stretch their legs and relieve themselves outside. The condition inside the stockcars was getting unpleasant to say the least. The men on the flat cars, could defecate off the side, but those in the enclosed cars had no way to get their waste outside. The stench had become almost unbearable.

Rations were minimal and hunger was becoming a fact of life. Some handled it better than others. Will could never understand the need to complain about things over which he had no control. If complaining had a positive outcome, he would be up there leading the band. That these complaints fell on deaf ears was pretty clear. If the Rebs had much to eat they weren't about to share. Eventually, the whiners gave up.

If there was a train station in a settlement along the way the name of the place was on the station. If there was no stop there was nothing to identify it. Will realized that, if truth be told, he didn't give a darn. He didn't see anyplace here that he would like to call home.

An older man taking up a space nearby couldn't get up off the floor one morning. As Will leaned over him he could see the old soldier had reached the end of the line. The dying man reached in his shirt pocket and took out a harmonica.

"You take this. Ain't much, but it helps to pass the time."

He seemed to sleep then. Will stayed near him until he died a few hours later. He regretted that he never asked the man his name. He remembered hearing the music from time to time when there was a lull in the train's racket but hadn't paid much attention to who was producing it. The old man had been pretty good, though. Some of his songs were enough to bring a lump to his throat, and for that space of time Will was able to close his eyes and be conveyed to the vast open ranges he had ridden in bygone days. It reminded him of the sounds of the wind through tall grass.

Over the next few days, Will and Jimmy repeatedly attempted to play a tune on the thing, but the sounds they made merely brought groans. It was definitely harder than it looked. At last one comment from the back of the car succeeded in halting their concerts, at least inside the closed car.

"Will you boys stop that infernal noise? I can't hear the damn wheel bearings."

The seventh morning produced some interest in where they were. They were entering a real town. They crossed a long bridge over the Appomattox and crept toward the station. The sign on the building said Richmond. The old engine screeched to a stop with a last gasp, as the steam was released from the patched and blackened boiler. The sigh that echoed throughout the length of the train was one of infinite relief.

As they climbed down they were formed into lines of four and marched into the commercial area of town. Will was glad to stretch his legs now his blisters had healed. He squared his shoulders and walked proudly down the street. Jimmy, alongside him, was doing the same.

They passed a multitude of large, stately buildings on brick paved streets. Along their route Jimmy noticed a sign for an up-coming slave sale. It sent a shiver through his body. My God, it was true. And he was right in the middle of it. He had seen black men working along the track, but being enclosed in the boxcar, he had only glimpses of them through the cracks. These pieces of paper brought it home to him in a way those tantalizing looks had not. He could see a number of white men standing in front of these businesses, and a feeling of disgust washed over him. These were the traders he had heard about. Those that bought and sold black men, women and children. He thought of John Henry, the only black man he had ever known. At one time he had been a slave. Maybe sold right here in that building. Up until now, the fact of slavery had been just something to talk about. Sure, he had seen some at a distance, sometimes up close, but seeing the poster was a shock. Thinking of John Henry brought on a wave of homesickness that almost overwhelmed him. He struggled, inwardly, to shake it off but was only partially successful. He gripped the smooth silver of the case.

Most of the buildings they passed were related to the sale and storage of tobacco or cotton. After about a half hour's march they were ordered to halt in front of a brick warehouse. A large painted sign above the door read:

Libby and Sons, Ship Chandlers and Grocers

The building was huge. Will studied the impressive architecture with appreciation. Though he didn't know it then, for the next four months, this was to be their home. The worst drawback to their stay, as with the boxcar, was sanitation. There were four hundred prisoners in this one building, with nothing other than one hole in the floor. A steel grate prevented anyone from using it to escape. Within a short time Will did not see that that would be a problem. They were desperate, but not enough to pry up the grid and drop down into that steaming mound. As the smell got worse, the men moved further and further away until they were all crowded against the outer walls. Although the building was divided into several large rooms, the smell was everywhere.

Will and Jimmy claimed a spot along the back wall and near a corner. A crack in the wall allowed a small draft of fresh air in from the outside. It wasn't much, but better than nothing. They took turns pressing their faces to the opening, when the stench became too thick.

"Don't look like we'll be back in action soon, so I suggest you start callin' me Will. We have too many *Sarges* around here already."

"I'll sure try to remember that, but after calling you Sarg for all this time, I might make a mistake now and again."

Rations were served once a day and consisted of the usual half brick of meal, a pint of vinegar, and a small piece of meat, which Will could not identify. After some thought, he decided he really didn't want to know what it was. A colony of large rats, evident at their arrival, was no longer anywhere to be seen.

One thing they seemed to have an abundance of was tobacco. Everyone got a plug with their ration and as Will and Jimmy had never taken to that habit they were able to make some advantageous trades. It seemed a shame, to Will, to see men trade away food that would prolong their life for something that had no redeeming value he could see, but he wasn't forcing them. Weakened by malnutrition, they would be among the first to die.

Boredom was the hardest obstacle for Will and many of the others to conquer. His life was going by and he wasn't living it. Sleeping was a means some took to avoid it. After several deaths occurred among those that devoted most of their time to sleeping, Will and Jimmy decided on a routine of walking the floor in turns, followed by a brisk and sometimes contentious discussion. The topics were wide ranging. Milking cows, training horses, the color of the sky that they could not see, and most often food and women. Mostly food.

After one of these talks, Jimmy took out his treasure. He carefully opened the hasp and handed it to Will. Will had seen Jimmy looking at it from time to time but had never asked about it. He held it in a shaft of light from the small upper windows and studied the face of the young lady within. She was obviously sitting down, her hands in her lap. She faced the camera at a slight angle and smiled at something over the shoulder of the photographer. Her face was nicely shaped and her long hair draped over her right shoulder covering her right breast. She was wearing a high necked dress with lots of buttons and frills. If the lady was as pretty as the picture made her out to be she was definitely a looker. Will took one last look and handed it back. Jimmy carefully closed the cover and returned it to his pocket. "That's Twyla. She's my girl, back home."

"Well, she sure is a nice looking young lady. You're a lucky man." As he spoke the words, he realized that he really meant them. He had no one to miss him except his folks. On the road for years after leaving home, he had become attached to no one. Times like this he wished that someone special was thinking of him and looking forward to his return. He was beginning to feel sorry for himself so he forced his thoughts back to food.

As the days dragged by, tempers flared from time to time. It was to be expected. Several fights broke out, mostly a few punches, nothing serious. It became evident that one particular man was usually involved. He was wearing Sergeant stripes like Will and was from a group that joined them at the train station. Will decided to keep an eye on him. He wasn't huge but big and broad, perhaps five-ten and a hundred-eighty pounds, and it was apparent that he liked to throw his weight around. After a week, Will decided that he had the fellow pretty well sized up.

Will was ready when the bully intentionally pushed a fellow prisoner into one of the large support posts. The man fell to the ground, blood running from his nose and mouth. Dazed, he looked up at the sergeant.

"Run into me again, I'm going to do more than that. You keep out of my way." He looked around to make sure that everyone in the area heard him.

Will had seen enough. He believed a sergeant was supposed to look after his men, not abuse them, and he followed his beliefs to the letter. The big man caught sight of Will who was making his way through the crowd followed belatedly by Jimmy and some others. He waited with a swagger and a leer until they faced off, at about two feet distance.

"You want some of this?" he grinned, looking down at Will. "You got anything to say, just spit it out."

"I'm going to say this once, so I suggest you listen real good. You have the size on me, so there is an off-chance that you might be able to lick me in a fight, but before you do, you better decide if it's worth it, because I don't fight fair and I don't quit. If I get on you I'll rip off your ears, gouge your eyes out, bite off your nose, or anything else I can get my teeth into. You might win, but you'll never look in a mirror again, and the sight of you will make the ladies puke. If I see you bothering any of these men again, I'll find you and we'll have it out. Do you understand?" The words were spoken low and direct with no hint of bravado, just a statement of fact.

The man just glared at him.

"One last time, do you understand?" This time Will barked out the question.

The man still glared, but there was a look of caution in his eyes. "Yeah."

Will turned and walked away.

The stranger hated to admit it, even to himself, but there was something in the eyes of the smaller man that sent a chill down his back. He was relieved when he left. He looked around to see what the reaction was from the crowd, and was irritated to see that they no longer looked at him with apprehension. He jutted out his chin and strode over to the far end of the building where a few of his friends sat who hadn't seen him put down. He knew that before long what had happened would be known by all. He sulked in impotent rage.

When they were out of earshot Jimmy sputtered, "Jesus, Will, did you mean all that? I think he was about to wet his pants."

"Unless he does it again, I guess we'll never know for sure. But I sure meant it when I said it." Will slapped him on the back. "That tired me out. Guess I'll rest a spell." They returned to their corner.

By the middle of the second month, prisoners began to die in numbers. Among these were older men who were less able to cope with the riggers of confinement, those that deprived their bodies of even the scant rations for tobacco, and of course the sleepers. Will noticed that one of the dead was wearing Sergeant stripes and looking closer, recognized the fellow he had threatened.

Other prisoners had been filtering in, in groups of between ten and fifty, as close as Will could guess. It was becoming crowded right up to the sewage pit, and many had given up even trying to get to it to relieve themselves. The wide board floors were slick with excrement. There was no way to get away from it. The coarse meal was irritating to the intestinal tract and brought on acute diarrhea and vomiting to many of its victims. Once started, it seemed to bring on a chain reaction throughout the building.

Towards the end of the third month, Will guessed that several hundred had died. Although the food wasn't adequate to really satisfy the appetite and the meal tore up the innards, Will figured that the majority had just given up hope of ever getting out alive, and at that point, had faded fast. Once their spirit gave out they were gone in a few days.

It was an early morning in the middle of February when they were ordered outside. It was a cold morning with a dull overcast sky. It had rained that night and the streets were wet and muddy. To a man, they breathed in the cold fresh air until their chests practically burst. The dreary sky looked magnificent. The mud smelled good and clean as they wiped their hands and boots through it to rid them of the filth they had just left. Many danced a little jig just to get their blood running properly. Will put his arm around Jimmy's shoulders.

"By God, we beat this place," he murmured, as tears of relief ran down his face. They grinned at each other. One of the prisoners asked a guard where they were being taken. The guard just shrugged his shoulders. "Gonna put Yankee officers in here."

The guards didn't waste any time getting them started down the street. Some, who had spent long hours laying down, had a hard time loosening up the knee joints. A few had to be carried to the waiting train. The sight of the engine brought a chorus of groans and curses. Every man hoped that the wheels had been greased, but they were disappointed. At their first turn it was evident that they had not seen a drop of grease and were probably a little worse than before.

In the back of everyone's mind was the hope that they were going to be traded. No one dared speak his thoughts out loud on the possibility that it might jinx their chances. Within the hour the train took a south-westerly route. There would be no trade. That evening they pulled into Gaston, North Carolina. They were given a few tasteless crackers, and changed cars. The lack of maintenance was the same, except the track was a little more smooth. The next day they were in Raleigh. Another brief stop before continuing.

As the train meandered aimlessly through the back country, the land, to Will, took on a bleak and sterile look. Many of the trees were stunted as if starved for water and nutrients. Most everything else seemed just plain wore out. The few people that came to watch them pass seemed to have the same deficiency. Thin as the train's passengers, with long arms and legs and narrow chests. Will had seen better clothes on his father's scarecrow back home. Bib overalls seemed to be the attire of choice. Most were without shirt or shoes. These were the people they were fighting. It hardly seemed worth the sacrifice. He had to remind himself that, if these folks could afford it, they would all own slaves.

They stared hopelessly at the small towns that they passed through, hoping for a name sign, but at best they were just numbered. They seemed to be going in circles first one direction then another and some of these little burgs looked awfully familiar.

Sometime in the seventh week of this ordeal, someone yelled "Macon."

Where was that? Will wondered.

Before he could ask, someone muttered, "Georgia. Right dab square in the middle of the Confederacy."

Without stopping, the little engine made a left turn and headed south. The next morning, the engine sputtered to a stop. The steam from the old boiler was released and a great many guards were on hand to escort them off the cars.

"Welcome, ya Yankee busturds. This heeah is yo new home." He pointed to the long row of vertical logs that made up one side of a stockade about a half mile away. "This heeah is called Andersonsville. Yonder is Camp Sumpter, your new home. Hope ya'll enjoy it" he giggled.

3

GATES OF HELL

The five hundred men formed lines of four and marched away from the ugly little town. Sullen town folk glared at them. Some threw clods of mud. Will was relieved to see the prisoners ignore them.

Jimmy marched slower and slower as they neared the fifteen foot tall gates. He would have stopped if not pushed forward by those behind.

"Oh Will, I'm a gittin' a real bad feeling about this place." Jimmy whispered. "Don't know why, exactly, but I got a bad feeling." His face had lost some of its color. He gripped the metal case in his pocket.

Will put his arm around the younger man. "Don't you worry about it. No damn Reb prison can beat us. Trust me." He wished that he felt as confident as he talked. He looked up at the tall squared off logs towering fifteen feet into the blue sky and felt a wave of despair. There would be no escape over the top. He wondered how far down they were sunk in.

The gates opened and they were herded into a large enclosure. Spotting a small iron skillet tied to the backpack of a guard trying to make his way through the crowd Will deftly pulled the twine that held it and caught the skillet as it dropped. He slipped it into his shirt. The guard went on, unaware of his loss.

"Holy cow, Will, you could'a been caught."

"You're right, but I wasn't." Will replied smugly. "Anyhow, I figure we need it more than he does."

A second gate opened and they entered the main stockade. The gates closed behind them with an ominous thud. The prisoners fanned out glad to get away from the confinement of the last few months. It felt good to just have space in which to walk.

"Well, the idea of charging the gate is out. Might make it through one, but not two," Will observed. "Let's take a walk around this place and see what we're up against." The enclosure seemed huge. Would they find a weakness?

"Sounds good to me. Let's start over there." Jimmy pointed to the last section of wall that was still under construction. The sound of slaves singing, as they labored on the wall, had caught his attention. They took up a spot as close as they dared, without getting shot, and sat down. The slaves, numbering close to a hundred, were cutting, squaring and standing in place the perimeter logs. Twenty feet long, they were sunk in a five foot ditch. The leader, a robust fellow with a deep voice, would sing the words and the others would repeat them. It was music like Jimmy had never heard. Heads would sway to the sound, and upper torsos would bend. Those prisoners sitting around him were also taken by the rhythm and were swaying back and forth.

"Those fellows sound pretty darn good. Don't think I've ever heard anything just like it before," Jimmy exclaimed with a grin. "We have a black man in Willow Creek, but John Henry is more like family.

He sings pretty good too, but he mostly just hums." The thought of John Henry brought an ache to his chest. God, he missed home.

"Well, I've seen a quite a few in Texas," Will replied, shaking his head.

"Were they slaves?"

"Yup. Don't recall seeing any that weren't. You can always trust a field hand like these fellows if you need help or getting information, but you have to watch out for those house slaves."

"What's the difference?"

"I can't say, exactly, but I reckon those that work close to the Master either try to curry favor or in some cases are afraid to take a chance on gettin' demoted to field hand. Anyhow, that's the way it was in Texas. This is interesting, but we need to check the whole place out. Let's look around and come back later. They'll be here a while yet."

As they were standing up, Jimmy picked up a piece of leather, half buried in the mud.

"What are you planning for that?"

"Figure to make a pouch to carry Twyla and your harmonica in. My pockets are just about shot and my pants are starting to rot off." He tugged gently on his pant leg and it seemed likely to come apart in his hand. He looked at Will and shook his head. "Hell, I'll be naked in a week."

They paced off the stockade while they looked for any weakness. They found none, but determined that the size was one thousand feet long by eight hundred wide. The longer distance ran north and south, with a small stream crossing at mid-point, flowing from west to east. The original creek was about a yard wide and ten inches deep. However, during construction, the area had been stirred into a quagmire of ooze which spread out ten feet or more on either side. To the west on either side of the stream was a gate. A plank walk crossed the bog near each end and on the west it was wide enough to accommodate a wagon coming through one gate and leaving through the other. Small wooden signs designated the upstream third to drinking water, the center area to washing and the east to the latrine, where a long wooden bench along a slit trench stretched a third of the way parallel to the stream. Both ends of the enclosed area rose to the north and south, slanting upwards from the creek in the center. Two large pine trees had been left standing towards the middle of the north slope. Positioned along the top of the wall, about thirty yards apart, guards were posted. Umbrellas protected them from the sun and rain.

They returned to the construction site to listen to the slaves sing. After three months of confinement the deep mellow sound of the singing was a real treat. Will took out the harmonica and played along, as best he could. As the songs were made up as they went along, it was a hopeless endeavor but he enjoyed the challenge. Jimmy looked quickly at the picture of Twyla and then started fashioning a pouch from the leather. He had managed to hide his small folding knife from inspections. Although prisoners had been allowed to keep their belongings, he hadn't trusted them to leave him a potential weapon, and now used it to shape the stiff material.

"Take a real good look at those black fellows, Jimmy. By their looks, they have about as much smarts as a bucket of dirt, but you watch careful. See? When the Rebs look away, they slow down. Those boys are sly as foxes. You catch them when they think no one is lookin' and you can see the difference."

After a few minutes, Jimmy grinned. "You see that one with the red shirt? Well I think he's the head man. They all follow his lead. Don't know why those Rebs don't notice it."

"Because they're the ones that are as dumb as a bucket of dirt. Now let's go get some of those reeds and make us a she-bang."

Reeds were plentiful in the slimy ooze and within a few minutes they had their arms full and headed up into a corner of the stockade. It was during the search for the best reeds that Jimmy found a weak point in the prison wall. As they headed up the hill, he told Will of his discovery.

"I found a way out of here, Will," Jimmy exclaimed, excitedly. "Where the water comes in under the wall, it looks like there is a gap of about a foot. I think we can go under the logs. Be a tight fit, but most of the guards will probably be lookin' at the open space. The guards probably can't even see us once we git up close to the wall."

Within five hours they had dug a hole three feet wide, six feet long and two feet deep. They had buried the ends of the larger reeds in the pile of dirt around the hole like hoops on a covered wagon. They then wove the smaller reeds through these for the roof. When finished they were impressed with their handiwork. So was the guard, watching from his perch.

"Gawl damn, if'n that ain't the damndest thing I ever seen." The guard, a thin man with a short beard was leaning out and looking down at their handiwork. He shook his head in amazement, then sent a stream of tobacco in their general direction.

"Damn right it is," Will spoke softly to Jimmy. "Fool wouldn't even think about building some shelter, let alone actually figuring out how to do it."

The North Gate opened and the ration wagon was pulled in by a pair of mules. Both looked forward to getting something to eat, no matter what it was. They took their time walking down, to let most of the prisoners go first. Something about standing in line again, even to get food, was more than they wanted to do. This would probably be the only time food was handed out this way. By tomorrow, if their escape was unsuccessful, Will and the other Sergeants would be receiving and distributing the rations in the prescribed way.

The first meal consisted of a quart of meal, a sweet potato, a few ounces of salt beef and a half quart of vinegar. Both were excited about having something else with their ground corn meal. Several minutes were spent scrounging material for a fire from the slash left from clearing the area and building the stockade. Their skillet was a blessing and made a fine hash from their combined rations. They forced themselves to eat slowly, and savor each morsel. Sitting back they smiled contentedly at one another. Filling their stomachs made them feel things weren't going to be as bad as they had imagined. The food was a definite surprise.

After eating they buried their skillet under the she-bang. It might make a noise or hang up going under the wall, and if they didn't succeed, they would need it here, inside the prison.

Will looked at the darkening sky and wondered just how much darker it would be in another hour. Jimmy was straining at the bit to get going.

At last, he was satisfied and they sauntered down to the slit trench near the west wall. They sat on the board and waited a few more minutes. The guards' apparent lack of interest in their activities was encouraging. Slipping over to the small opening they took a deep breath and submerged their bodies face down in the water. Pushing with the toes of his boots and gripping the ooze with his fingers, Will pulled himself under the logs. Jimmy followed.

Within a minute, the two were on the outside and slithering upstream. Twenty yards ahead, where the stream looped slightly to the left, was the Reb mess tent right on the bank on the outside of the loop. Leary of getting too close, they cut across the loop, crawling slowly to avoid sudden movement which might draw attention. They then re-entered the relative safety of the water. Moving steadily, they soon passed the outside perimeter of the rebel encampment. Once out of sight of the last lantern rays they crawled out, and after taking a good long look-see, stood and walked away. The stench from the creek water clear through the Rebel camp had been almost enough to bring up their dinner. The little stream had been used as a garbage dump by the cooks and overflow from slit trenches that lined it for twenty yards had finished the job of turning its clean water into a sewer. They were glad they were out where they wouldn't be expected to drink from it, as it was the only source of water inside the prison.

"Which way do we go, Will?" Jimmy whispered. He was wiping the muck from his face with the sleeve of his shirt. They removed their water laden boots and emptied them. Wiping the excess mud out they put them back on.

"Either north, and hope we run into our lines, or south and hope we make the coast. If we can get there we can probably find a way to get out to one of the blockade ships."

"I say we head south, then, what do you think?" Jimmy asked. Will's mind was racing, trying to think of how they were going to travel hundreds of miles in hostile territory. He had to force it to the immediate problem of getting away from the vicinity of the prison.

"South then, let's go." Will whispered back. He took one last look at the distant glow from the rebel camp and hoped that he would never see it again.

Within minutes it was darker than Will could have imagined possible. A light rain was also not in their plan. Branches struck his face as he forged ahead. Limbs and rocks tripped him. Panic gripped him. This was going to be harder than he thought. He could hear Jimmy cursing behind him.

"Here, grab my hand. No sense in gittin' separated." Will reached back and fumbled for Jimmy's outstretched hand. Jimmy gripped his hand like a vice. Fear of getting separated was uppermost in both their minds.

"Hope you can see better than I can. Dark as the inside of a cow." Jimmy whispered.

No sooner had he spoke the words than Will tripped and dragged Jimmy down with him. "That answers my question," he said with a low laugh. "You're one hell of a guide."

"Hey, this was your idea. I'm just along to keep you company," Will retorted. "Damned fool idea, if you ask me."

"It's my plan, if it works and we get home. If we don't make it, you can take the credit," Jimmy retorted, with feigned disgust.

Occasionally the clouds parted and the moon shone through. During these short moments, they ran like they had never run before. Unfortunately, their bodies were in such bad shape that within twenty yards, they were hunched over, trying to get more air in their lungs. Their legs were in pain and going into spasms. Long periods were wasted as they sat to rest.

The rain stopped in the faint light of pre dawn, and for the first time they could try to get some idea of where they were. For all the good it did them, they still had no idea. The sunrise only told them they sure weren't heading south. They were headed west. They turned south and strode briskly for the next hour. It was during a much needed rest stop, that they heard the first, far off, sound of bloodhounds. They looked at each other, then were up and running away from the sound. However hard they ran the dogs were getting closer. There was no way they were going to outrun them. At last, Will fell to his knees. Jimmy slumped down beside him. "It's a lost cause," Will croaked. "I'm beat."

"You and your damn escape plan. I could be tucked in our she-bang, sleeping like a baby," Jimmy wheezed. He forced a grin through clenched teeth.

"We have to get away from those dogs. Look for a tree to climb." Will ordered, as he jogged on looking for something left that was big enough to shinny up. Any sizable trees for miles around were now part of the prison walls. He saw Jimmy climbing up a tree that didn't seem big enough for a possum, but they couldn't be choosers. Spotting a fairly good one, he climbed up until he was ten feet off the ground. They didn't have to wait long.

Within minutes, two large bloodhounds were at the base of their trees, calling the other dogs in the pack. Seven broke through the trees and tried in vain to get to their prey. Unlike the bloodhounds, who were well fed and good looking animals, these mongrels were stick thin and terrifying. They obviously planned to eat what they had treed. The bloodhounds, having done their job, sat in the shade and waited. One rolled on his side and slept.

Three riders on mules came into view and seeing the yapping mongrels, rode to where they could see Will and Jimmy. They looked as if they were related. All three had long faces and no chins to speak of. Their eyes were large and somewhat dull green. Long shaggy mouse colored hair hung below their shoulders. They had ears that stood out like bat wings. They also looked mean, like boys about to pull the wings off a fly. They wore nothing more than bib overalls and tall peaked hats with wide floppy brims. The overalls were almost all patches and too short. Their lower legs were thin as sticks. Will thought that they looked stamped out by the same cookie cutter. Obviously not some of the South's finest.

"Ya git yerselfs down atta tham thar trees, an' ya better be quick 'bout it," the obvious leader drawled, with a yellow toothed grin. He dismounted and stretched his arms out, then hooked his thumbs in his overalls, and spit a huge hunk of tobacco towards the tree that Will was perched in. His eyes caught Will's and did not blink. Neither did Will. The man stared for a good minute, then looked away. Irritation showed on his face.

"We sure will do that. We sure will, but would you mind calling off your dogs before we do?" Jimmy asked, politely.

One of the other men barked an order and the dogs retreated to the side of the mules. Will was rather impressed. The dogs were well trained. Both Will and Jimmy climbed down and faced the three riders.

The riders smirked and moved in closer. Suddenly the leader made a clicking noise, and the dogs charged. Both men tried to run but the dogs were all over them. They fell to the ground and curled up in a fetal position, protecting their faces with their arms. Will could feel fangs sink in to his legs, and was suddenly aware that he was screaming in pain and terror.

At a word of command the dogs retreated. Will could feel blood running down his left leg. A gash ran four inches up his left arm. He was afraid to look further but a glance at Jimmy's bloody legs and he knew what his own looked like. On his second attempt, Will was able to stand. On the third, Jimmy was up. They looked at each other, then their captors. There were no grins. This was damn serious. The leader walked over and glared at them, trying to decide whether to steal their boots. Looking at their small size he grunted and swung his leg over the back of his mule.

The three were leering at them, enjoying the show. "We's headin' back now. My dawgs like the taste o' Yankee blood. Ya'll give us trouble, we'z gonna let 'em eat ya rat down to da bone. They pretty hongry. Eat ya down to a skelten in no time. Fact is." The leader drawled as one of the riders got down and tied a rope around Will's neck and then Jimmy's. He swung a leg over his mule and wrapped the rope over a stub of wood where a saddle horn used to be, and they all headed out. They had a hard time keeping up with the mules even though the pace was moderate.

Will was shocked to see how few miles they had covered in all that running. He doubted that they had gotten four miles away. The riders laughed and made comments about them but neither Will nor Jimmy gave them the pleasure of a retort. They were too disappointed to respond.

As they approached the gate, they could see twenty prisoners being yelled at by a black haired rebel officer. He spoke broken English, and Will had a hard time understanding the ranting.

While Will and Jimmy were making their escape these twenty other men had gone over the wall. Cutting strips from their tents they had made a rope, and with a rock tied to the end, had managed to sling it over the logs. They were unaware that they were being quietly rounded up as soon as they dropped to the ground beyond the wall. After the twenty had gone over, the Rebs put a stop to it. The twenty later found out that they were caught because one of the other prisoners had revealed their plan. They were lucky that they only had to listen to this old captain's harangue. It was evident he was a person of importance, though like so many officers on both sides, he had let himself go to pot. His uniform looked like it had been continually slept in and a sagging gun belt holding an immense pistol, almost brought a smile to Will's lips. He managed to refrain.

The officer glared at them as they were led towards the prison gates by the three riders. Motioning with his hand to one of the guards, he took him aside and gave him instructions. The scowl on his face and the cold eyes removed any notion that this man was ridiculous. He held their lives in his hands and they both knew it. He marched over to where they stood and looked eye to eye with Will.

"So's day gots you. Dot ees goot. Ve vill make example of yoos boyce." He smiled at Will, but it was anything but friendly.

He was grabbed from behind and forced to walk thirty yards to a series of posts placed in a row about five feet apart. The rope was yanked from around his neck, his wrists were tied to the two of the posts at about waist level. Will could just touch the poles with the tips of his fingers. Two boards, with a half round cut out, were placed around his neck and secured at the posts. The height of the boards prohibited Will from straightening out his legs. He was too low to stand, but too high to sit down.

"Ve see hous you Yanks like dis." Turning, the Captain looked at the guard. "Giv dem two days!" He gave the two a glare and marched off. They had just met Capt. Wirz and they were not favorably impressed.

By noon, their legs were on fire. The bleeding from the dog bites had stopped but thigh and calf muscles were cramping up. The only relief was moving their feet back to allow their knees to straighten but that put the pressure from the board right against their throats. Will could see Jimmy out of the corner of his eye and knew that they were both in the same predicament. He finely found some relief by spreading his feet to the sides as far as possible even though it brought his chin down tight onto the board. It was going to be one hell of a long two days.

It started to rain. All that water and no way to git it into his mouth. He tried to extend his tongue out far enough to catch it, but the few drops he managed to catch did not make up for the pain in his tongue. He reluctantly gave up the effort.

Darkness settled over the area. One forth of the sentence was over. No damn way could he take another day and a half of this. He jumped, as hands touched his leg.

"Sarg?" Whispered a small voice.

"Yes. Who are you?" He whispered back.

"Donny Simon. They let me out. Said prison was no place for children. Damn Rebs calling me a child! Gotcha a box to sit on, Sarg. Got one for Cpl. Compton too."

Will felt the box under him and sat down. Another hour or two, and he would have strangled on the board. He felt a cup touch his lips. He drank.

"Gotta help the Corporal. I'll be back before sunup."

Will sagged against the cross boards, no longer stretching his neck like a chicken for slaughter. He was asleep within minutes.

He awoke to a tugging at his shoulders and the feel of the box being removed. He assumed the spread eagle position again. He drank from the cup until he had his fill. It was going to be a long day, but without the little bugler's help, he doubted that he would have made it this long.

"You still with me?" he asked, as he tried to see Jimmy.

"Oh yeah," Jimmy replied with a croak. "Had nothin' to do so I thought I might as well hang around and enjoy your company. I think we owe little Donny."

"You got that straight," Will replied with some effort. "Hope we can pay him back." He regretted not spending more time with the little bugler, but Spence, the camp cook, had pretty much taken him under his wing, and during slow time, they stuck together like glue. Still, Will felt like he should have done more.

Around noon, Will was surprised when they untied him and gave him water. He heard Jimmy moan when he was untied. The strain on his own arms brought a gasp of pain when he lowered them. The gash was ugly, but not as deep as he had thought. When he tried to take a step a moan escaped his lips as well. He resented the fact that the guards heard him. He looked down at his bloody, swollen legs, and doubted that he would be able to walk. His neck was rubbed raw from the planks. All in all, he felt like hell. In all of his twenty-seven years, he had never been in such bad condition. He turned and watched them release Jimmy and his heart went out to his friend.

They were taken to a small slit trench behind one of the buildings and allowed to take a piss. "Not many things can beat a long piss after sixteen hours holden' it," Will sighed.

"You sure got that right Will," Jimmy groaned, supporting himself with his head against the side of the building to keep from falling in. "Don't know if I'm up to another twelve hours of this shit. I'd be dead if it weren't for Donny."

"Hey! You sombitches com'long now. Ain't got all day." They were herded back to the stocks hanging on to each other for support. Thankfully, the guards did not hurry them but they made up for it with snide remarks.

Late in the day, the routine was repeated. As darkness settled over the prison, Will felt the box again being positioned. Again he felt the cup, and drank and slept. He was awakened by the touch of hands as they removed the box. "They gonna let ya out in a couple of hours, Sergeant," Donny whispered.

"Thanks Son. You did real good," Will whispered back. At sunup they were released and escorted back into the prison. Will was almost relieved to be back within the safety of the walls.

As they struggled up the slope towards their she-bang, one of the prisoners came up from behind and stepped in between them. Slipping his arms under theirs, he half lifted them up. "Looks as though you boys could use some help. Just point the way and I'll get you there."

Will pointed towards the corner and with the stranger's help they made good time.

"Let me help you boys with those wounds. Seen a few dog bites in my time but I must admit, these are real beauts. Good thing that they bled plenty. Less chance of getting infected." He deposited them outside the sleep hole and said that he would be right back. They were glad that they had taken the time to build it on the chance that their escape would fail. Jimmy wanted to crawl in and rest, wounds or no wounds, but he knew the fellow was right.

Within minutes he was back with a torn shirt. Ripping it into strips and soaking them in some of the vinegar from his ration, he carefully bound their bloody legs and Will's arm. Working quickly, but gently, he soon had them fixed up as best he could with only a shirt to work with.

"You want to tell me how you ended up with these dog bites?"

Jimmy looked at Will. He didn't want to horn in if Will wanted to tell the story. Will nodded his head and sank back, wrapping his good arm under his head and closing his eyes.

"Well it all started out with my friend here convincing me that we could break out of this place. I was agin' it but he outranks me." He looked over at Will who was peering at him from under his hat brim.

Jimmy laughed. "Let me start over."

He proceeded to tell the story, with an occasional prompting when he began to wander from fact.

At the conclusion, the stranger commented, "You boys showed some spunk, trying to get out of here. My name is Del Trenton. Danged proud to know you."

"I'm Jimmy Compton and this is my friend, Will Morgan. If you don't have a place to set up house-keeping, I'm sure Will won't object, and I'd be mighty pleased if you stayed on with us."

Del looked at Will for confirmation. Will nodded, then adjusted his hat brim and slept.

He left Jimmy settling down with Will and walked down the hill to his tent. He was pleased to see that no one had stolen anything. When he saw the two struggling up the hill it had never occurred to him to hide his kit. He took down his tent placing the pegs and two short poles, his few extra cloths, blanket, poncho and mess kit inside. He rolled them up and headed up the hill.

"Where, the hell, you goin',Del?," Fletcher yelled.

"On up the hill. This is too close to the stream." He answered shortly. He was glad to be getting away from this bunch. He had been shoved in with them on the way here and their constant gambling and course talk about women was more than he could stomach any longer.

Jimmy and Will were still asleep. He dropped his bundle and, using it as a pillow lay down to contemplate his good fortune at joining up with these two.

The following morning the gates opened and a group of guards and slaves entered. The commander started walking along the stockade wall ordering every one away from it. To their disgust they were ordered to move out twenty feet after all their hard work. The three dismantled their she-bang and dragged what remained of the reeds to the new location. Loud curses could be heard from all those who were forced to move. The wall had been some protection from the weather. Taking the skillet, Will scraped out a pattern for the next hole, and Del began the task. Fortunately, the top three feet of soil contained a lot of sand, so the digging went pretty fast. Those reeds that survived the moving were spread in the bottom of the hole. Then Del's tent was set up to cover it. They stood back and admired their work and were pleased. It wasn't as picturesque as the old one but a darn sight more waterproof!

Guards paced out the twenty feet and slaves drove in short posts at the marked distance nailing thin poles along the top of the posts. By the end of the morning, the prison had lost three valuable acres.

Del explained what the twenty men Wirz had been berating had done. "I reckon that's to keep any more from a goin' over the wall. They gave the rat duty outside in payment. Bastard! Why would one of us do a stinkin' thing like that?"

"I propose that we dig ourselves a well," Will exclaimed one morning shortly thereafter. "And, I suggest we dig it right here." He kicked a small boot heel mark in the dirt. "Clean water is something that we have to have and I don't see any other way of a gittin' it. If nothing else, it will give us something to do and maybe something to hope for. I damn sure believe in hope." So little information was available, one could only guess what was happening outside. He figured that as long as he didn't know, he might just as well think positive. This upbeat attitude became harder on a day shortly after they began the well.

That day, Gen. Winder, the commander of the prison, came in to inspect the rationing process. He decided that everything needed to be changed, which caused mass confusion among the lackadaisical Confederates. No one knew what he was trying to accomplish. The prisoners were marched around, lined up, counted, separated into groups, then recounted. They doubted that Winder knew himself what was going on. After what seemed like hours of wrangling, he summarily ordered the loaded ration wagon out and left. This departure was followed by curses from hundreds of men. Some of the prisoners were in desperate condition and the failure to secure rations was a death sentence.

The following morning twelve men were laid out for transport to the cemetery that had been started outside the palisades. Later, when the rations arrived, the same nonsense was repeated, and again, the ration wagon was ordered out.

On the third day twenty eight bodies were carried out. Finally, when the food wagon arrived some order was restored to the process and rations were distributed, by the regulation method they had been using all along. The new ration consisted of only one half a loaf of corn bread. The rations lost the previous days were never made up.

During this time the well was underway, much to the delight of the guards on the wall who had many a scathing comment on the process. It was decided that Will and Jimmy would do the digging, while Del pulled up the dirt filled boot that they were using as a bucket. With only one of the smaller men digging at a time, they could keep the diameter to about three feet. After awhile, the guards ignored the goings on, seeing as the trio didn't rise to the bait.

Will felt the work on the well was a good distraction from hunger, even if it was unsuccessful. If they did find water it would certainly add to their chance of surviving. He guessed that he was down ten or fifteen pounds from his capture. Jimmy was in the same shape. His skin was becoming thin, or so it looked. His veins were more apparent and he had lost a lot of strength in his arms and legs. He worried about Del, because he was taller than average, and appeared to be in good health. As strange as that sounded, the majority of those that had died, other than the aged, seemed to be those in good health and large build. He thought of Little Joe, a giant of a man who had died on the third day. Everyone supposed that he would be the last to go. One thing he had decided was that their best chance was to stay active and not give in to the temptation to sleep the time away. For all these reasons, the three decided to walk the perimeter every day, once in the morning and once before turning in. They avoided the tainted stream water unless they could boil it, opting for collected rain and even dew. They worked on the well that they had started on a regular schedule, as much as they felt able. Uppermost was to blend in some humor, even if was forced, and to think positive.

On these walks, Will made it a habit to visit the troops from his battalion. It bothered him not to be able to do anything for them except give them pep talks. Some were deteriorating faster than others and within weeks, the weaker started dying. He was their sergeant and it was his duty to keep them alive, but he was no better off than most of them and worse than a few. He forced himself to make the daily effort to pass a few minutes with as many as he could locate, and shake each hand.

"Hey Sarg, you hear about that rat that turned in them fellows goin' over the wall?" One of the prisoners asked, peeking out of his tent covered sleep hole as they passed. "Well they put him back in here and several of the boys identified him. This morning they found him with his throat slit. It's a mighty fine day. Yessir, mighty fine."

One morning, when Will put a boot on, it fell apart. He held the pieces in his hand and grunted. The idea of walking bare foot through the filth that was accumulating on the ground, sent a shiver down his back. He walked with one boot, but then it too, fell apart. Three days later, Jimmy was barefoot, as well. For a week, they tried to step around the grossest filth, but in time their aversion to walking in shit, piss, and vomit lessened to the point where they could ignore it.

4

RAIDERS

With the winter months winding down, the war picked up steam. The small trickle of prisoners that had puzzled Will at Libby now turned into a flood at Andersonville. In the middle of March the gates opened and seven hundred cavalrymen entered, fresh from the Battle of Olustee in Florida. Everyone went to meet the new arrivals. After talking to several of them, Will realized that one thing had not changed, which was incompetent leadership. Under the command of Seymore, they had marched across Florida, strung out along cane breaks and swamps, and miles from support of any kind. They were picked off like wooden ducks at a carnival. The survivors guessed that they lost over two thousand men. They were a forlorn group.

Later came another four hundred and fifty from the 7th Connecticut, 7th New Hampshire, the 47th, 48th and 115th New York, plus a group from Sherman's Regular Battery. Also in this group were two hundred black troopers. Losses from these regiments caused by Banks, Sturgis and Butler were bad, and the morale among them was dismal.

There were exceptions among the members of the 7th New Hampshire. The ranks of this unit were filled with hoodlum substitutes for well-to-do draftees who had paid them to take their own place in the military. These men had not intended to be real soldiers, much less prisoners of war. Out to serve themselves, they soon banded together into predatory groups called Raiders by the other prisoners. At their peak number, nearly five hundred would be interned at Andersonville.

This group did not mingle, but took over a large piece of ground on the south side of the creek, pushing out those who had already built shelters in that spot. The boldest began by stealing the clothes off the backs of those that had gone to greet them. Over the next few weeks, Will, Jimmy and Del kept a wary eye on them as they erected a large tent made from stolen tents, ponchos blankets and such. Their accumulation of other stolen items was piled against the tent for all to see, but people attempting to retrieve their belongings were severely beaten.

One of the men living near their she-bang had a watch that he was very fond of. His father had given it to him as a graduation present. Regrettably, he took great pride in showing it to everyone. He was visiting the trench when one of the Raiders asked to see it. Perhaps out of fear, he obliged, only to have the man grab his treasure and run into the crowd. He was terribly upset when he returned to his camp.

"I think we should do something, Will." Jimmy growled through his teeth. "We gotta take care of our own."

"I'm game, let's have at 'em." Del added.

"I'm going to look up Limber Jim and Keys. Heard they were trying to organize a group to take them on," Will remarked. "We better have a good force before we head over there."

Within the hour word was being spread that an attack was planned. As they made their way towards the Raider tent, it became clear that they were undermanned. Looking behind him, Will could see thousands watching, who were not willing to risk getting involved. This was not going to be a pretty thing, but it was too late to turn back. Just hope we make it through in one piece, he thought. His first inclination was to pick out a small target, but he forced himself to engage a larger opponent. He had a reputation to maintain, after all.

As the two forces engaged, Will realized that he did not know friend from foe. The Raiders knew each other well, whereas most of Will's group were strangers to one another. Five minutes into the fight, he knew that the best they could do was to try to get out of there in one piece. He regretted taking on the larger man. His foe was a real brawler. Aching from several well placed punches to his face, Will gave as good as he got but he was ready to call it quits when he lost sight of his opponent altogether. It was a mass of confusion and men who could, began to flee towards the creek. They tried to set up a defensive line, but the Raiders over-ran it. Struggling back up the hill, they were amazed that they were still on their feet and not being chased and finished off. The Raiders apparently didn't think much of them as a threat. They examined each other's bruises, and decided that they would live. Several had received minor knife cuts. One of the men later died from infection.

"I must say that was a mistake if I ever saw one," Del exclaimed. He looked at the bruises that were turning purple on Will's face.

Will looked at Del's bloody nose and grinned.

"Tell me, gentlemen, did I hear someone say we went into this for a watch?" Jimmy inquired. "Aside from trading it, I can't think why a person would be interested in what time of day it is."

The encounter did bring out some interesting facts that explained their failure. The Western Armies, under Grant and Sherman, were chiefly made up of men from the same social and economic backgrounds. Many were volunteers with a moral stake in their military service. It was natural for them to band together for the common good. The Army of the Potomac was made up of many varied groups and backgrounds. Everything from city folks to farmers, sailors to store keepers. Many who were foreign born did not speak the same languages as one another, nor did they speak English well. They had been drafted or had enlisted for the army pay. Finally, most had been in Andersonville too short a time to have developed any new loyalties. They were more apt to establish small groups that kept to themselves. They would all have to work together to beat the Raiders. It was a puzzle what catalyst could be found to bring that about.

In the weeks after the brawl, the Raiders were more brazen and ruthless than before. Beatings and murders became common-place. Broad daylight found groups of ten to twenty raiding parties roaming at will. Loot from these raids was used to curry favor with the guards. While hundreds died of starvation and disease the Raiders got fat on fresh meat, flour, potatoes, vinegar and anything else that the guards could get for them. There was no scurvy in the Raider ranks. They were well organized, well fed and spoiling for a fight.

Rumors began making the rounds about another possible retaliation against the Raiders. Ned Carrigan, a Cpl. from Chicago, put out the word. It was rumored that he had been a prize fighter and had killed a man in the ring, with one blow. It was a fact that no Raider would stand up to him in a fair fight.

He and Will talked at some length about just how they were going to turn the odds to their favor. Small groups had been working to bring the various factions together. Many who had been on the receiving end of the Raiders' brutality showed interest in joining in if needed. But could they be trusted to fight or to run?

About a week later, as a fairly large group of prisoners was herded in, it happened that the threesome were near the gates. One of the Raiders waiting nearby volunteered to "…help you boys git squared away." Before they could be warned, they were led straight into an ambush by the Raider mob.

"Let's git 'm!" Jimmy shouted, as he launched himself into the mass of struggling men.

Behind him, Will picked out a Raider that was one of the worst and grabbed him from behind. As the man turned his head to see who had him Will gripped the man's ear in his teeth and bit down hard. He could feel the ear detach from the man's head and heard him scream. He spit it out, let go and charged towards another man. On seeing the blood streaming down his partner's neck the new target escaped before Will could reach him. He caught sight of Jimmy riding the back of one of the Raiders, a man called Rooster. Jimmy had attacked the worst of the worst. He started for the pair in hopes of protecting Jimmy's back. One of the newcomers hit the big man square in the face with a punch that must have come from knee level. The huge head snapped back and Will was able to jerk Jimmy free. They beat a hasty retreat up the hill hoping that Del would meet them there.

The newcomer caught up with them halfway up the hill and thanked them for their help. Both Will and Jimmy liked him from the moment he stuck out his hand to grip theirs in an enthusiastic shake. "What the hell was that all about?" He had a confused look on his smiling face.

"Well Partner, you just had the pleasure of meeting our welcoming committee and I must say that you came out of it better than most," Jimmy replied with an answering grin.

"Yup, those fellows like to make everyone feel right at home," Will added. "They're called Raiders, or New Yaarkers. Long on the Yaaaarkers. They're street toughs that make a living at other folk's expense. They make the Rebels seem right benevolent. Ya gotta' watch your back. Find yourself a partner or two and stick together."

"Well, my name is Jack Turner and if you boys are available, how about me sticking to you? I know you can fight in a pinch and I don't back down from a fight neither. What do you say?"

"Done." Will extended his hand. He took in Jack's stocky build and thick wrists. He would definitely be an asset. Jack had a square face, with brown, deep set eyes. His nose had a definite bend from an old break. His mouth was wide, and his cheeks dimpled.

"Jesus, Will where did you get all that blood on your chin? You alright?" Jimmy asked with concern. In all the excitement, he hadn't paid much attention until that moment.

"Took a feller's ear off." Will answered.

Jimmy and Jack stared at each other. "Did ya bring it back so we could cook it?" Jimmy asked. "Shore could use some meat in the skillet." Inwardly, he was remembering the fellow at Libby, and what Will had threatened to do to him. By God, he had actually meant it. Up to this minute, Jimmy had taken it as bluff.

"Nothin' but gristle," Will exclaimed with a shrug. He wiped most of the gore off his beard with his sleeve.

For the first time, Jack took a good look at the other longtime prisoners around them. Within a twenty foot circle at least thirty men sat or lay on the ground. He was shocked to count five that were near death. Thick tongues turned black as they protruded through cracked, swollen, toothless gums. Two, he thought dead, until he caught a slight movement of hand or a blink of the eye. Few had much in the way of clothes of any kind. All were extremely thin, much like Will and Jimmy. The only difference was the swollen legs and feet of those that were in the last stages of dying. All had skin darkened to the point of blackness by the small pitch fires they hunkered over for warmth. Beards and head hair were gnarled and twisted into bizarre forms. Some sticking straight up, others off to the sides, some spiraling upwards.

Jack could feel sickness coming on. Cold perspiration beaded his forehead, and his stomach started to roll. He tried to force himself to look away, but the horror of these men held him transfixed. He felt a slight tug on his sleeve and turned to see Will watching him. It was not a look of condemnation, but one of understanding. Clearly he knew what Jack was thinking. The newcomer looked down, embarrassed.

Will slapped him on the shoulder, and the three made their way to the she-bang where they could now see Del waiting.

"Del, this is Jack. Jack, this is Del. Looks like we'll be enlarging the sleep hole."

Jack lay out his kit, which consisted of a tent, blanket, coat, shirt, socks, mess gear and poncho. "I figure we can all share this stuff. Say what's that hole over there?"

"We're digging ourselves a well. Clean water is damn hard to come by." Jimmy answered.

Jack walked over to the rim and looked down. "Good grief, I can't see the bottom. How far down does it go?"

"We're right at twenty four feet, but it looks a lot deeper from the bottom up." Jimmy looked proud. "We try to put in a hour or so a day. Del's too big so he empties the boot, and helps us get out. Only one can work down there at a time 'cause of the space."

Amazed that they would start such a project in the shape they were in Jack was at a loss for words. Also, he was just a little daunted at the unpleasant idea of climbing down into it's depths. He was glad he was too large. He looked away, with a slight chill. He sure didn't like such close quarters, at all! They all sat or squatted down, and he took some time to size up his new friends. Will and Jimmy were like two peas in a pod, as far as size and shape. Neither stood more than five foot six or seven, and he would have been surprised if either weighed over a hundred pounds. The only thing that separated them was their coloring and their eyes. Will was dark, his eyes almost black and deep set, or perhaps just sunken from starvation. Piercing, was the word that came to Jack's mind. They appeared to look right through him. So far he had not seen the man smile. Jimmy, on the other hand was fair, his hair bleached almost white by the sun. He had hazel eyes that sparkled with merriment. Even when serious, his eyes gave the impression of silent laughter. He liked Jimmy from the start. Will would require a little more study. Regrettably, they were both on the verge of death, or so it seemed to Jack.

He shifted his attention to Del, who was quite tall. He had a hangdog look about his large soulful eyes that drooped slightly at the outer corner that made Jack want to laugh. His face was long, with a long slender nose. A chipped front tooth that gave his smile a little character. His reddish colored hair was matted and weirdly shaped, and like everyone else, his lower face was covered in a scraggly beard. He stood erect with a relaxed and comfortable demeanor that made him easy to like.

He'd noticed that both Jimmy and Del looked to Will for leadership. The faded sergeant stripes on his tattered coat ranked Will above the others, but it was more than rank that made him the leader. Nor was it size and physical strength. My God, he was hardly more than a skeleton. His black hair curled up in grotesque tangles from the pitch pine fires. Matted beard covered his lower face almost completely. His nose had a decided eagle beak prominence that on most might look comical, but didn't on Will, not with those chilling eyes. It went through his mind that what Will was, was dangerous. It wouldn't do to provoke him and he looked away before Will caught his eye. Jack was sure he'd earned his position. It would be smart to follow their lead. He had witnessed the ear biting, and the eagerness that Will showed in joining the attack, spoke volumes.

All three looked at the fine condition of Jack's contributions. These things just might save their lives.

That evening after their last walk around the compound as they sat before the she-bang, Will spoke seriously to him. "Jack, let me fill you in on a few rules of thumb that just might keep you alive." Sittin' here in this spot for near three months, a person learns a lot about how to stay alive. It's mostly in the head. If you give up, you're a gonner. Take the men that came in with Jimmy and me. Most are still alive, whereas many of those that came in later passed on within a month or so. The reason, I figure, is that our condition got worse and worse sort of gradual. We all got skinny over a period of time, as the living conditions worsened. For them, comin' in with a full belly and fine shape, the shock of all this was just too much, and their minds couldn't adjust to it. You know first hand how that feels. You felt it as you looked at those men on the way up the hill. I've seen that look a thousand times. Point is, they gave up and that was the beginning of their end. You listen to me Jack, you start letting yourself give up, you let one of us know. It's bound to happen, Partner, and you can't fight it alone. One more thing, don't drink the creek water. Use your tent or poncho to collect dew, or rainwater. Get a stick and stick it in the ground. At night drape a piece of cloth as clean as you can find over it. Suck out what moisture you can, each morning. As other pearls of wisdom come to me, I'll pass them along. For now that should give you plenty to think about. Tell us about yourself, Jack. What's goin' on out there in the real world?"

"It's just my opinion, mind you I'm just a lowly private, but I think the war is goin' pretty good. Seems like we win more battles than we did a while back. Now that we got Grant and Sherman we seem to keep on their tails pretty good. I figure if we'd had them boys to lead us from the first, we'd a had this here fight won a long time ago. I was under Grant when them Rebs got me. We was one damn good army, for sure. We had them Rebs on the run most of the time. Can't believe they caught me. We was a runnin' them down, when the next thing I knowed, they was a runnin' us down, and I'm lookin' down the muzzle of half a dozen guns. No, on second thought, it was a full dozen." He grinned.

"Hope we live long enough to meet them boys someday with a gun in our hands and no wall between."   Del said with his hang-dog look. "I've seen about all I want of this place."

"So what did you do before you got in the army?" Jimmy asked.

"Mostly followed cows around Missouri. Not what you would call a real excitin' life but lookin' back, danged if I wouldn't trade this place for a mouth full of trail dust."

"Wouldn't we all," Jimmy added. "I left the purtiest, sweetest little gal in the whole world to save the nation, and here I sit with you ugly varmints. Don't seem fair."

"Here we all sit," Will said with resignation. "Young uns have no respect for age or rank. What is the world commin' to? Ugly varmint." He shook his head.

"What is the story on rations? I'm as hungry as a horse." He regretted his remark as soon as it left his lips. Obviously, the three weren't eating regularly.

Will smiled sadly. "When we first got here, the ration was one quart of meal; one sweet potato; a piece of meat the size of two fingers and from time to time a spoon of salt. The first thing to disappear was the salt, followed by the sweet potato. The meat shrunk in size to one finger, and then, just like magic, it plumb disappeared too. At the present, we are eating cowpeas."

"What the heck are cowpeas?" Jack asked, a look of bewilderment on his face.

Will had to grin and Jack was amazed at the transformation in his face. "Don't rightly know for sure. Heard that it's the seeds of some plant. I think they feed it to livestock. We get two thirds of a pint."

"Well that ain't so bad, if'n it tastes alright." Jack mused.

"That's for each of four messes which consist of ninety men. They count them out. On a good day you might get six or seven."

"Jesus! What do you get on a bad day?" Jack asked, incredulously.

"Not a damn thing. And there are more bad days than good. Most of the boys gamble for them. They call it *bluff and draw*. We don't seem to have much luck with that, so we eat what we get. On a real good day, we might get a half brick of the roughest damn corn meal you will ever eat. Feels like it's a rippin' yer throat out. We try not to think about what it is doin' the rest of the way down."

There was no call to rations that day.

Will took out the harmonica from the pouch and rolled up the new poncho, placing his head on it. Looking at his friends he swooped the harmonica in a circle, placed it to his lips and started to play.

As the plaintive melody swelled around him, Jack thought over everything that Will had just told him. He looked out over the prison and a feeling of dread filled his heart. He would remember this night as long as he lived.

Will descended into the hole. Some days he didn't much mind it' but today he was so weak that after fifteen minutes, he was unable to continue. He had filled up only three boots of dirt. Hardly worth the effort. He struggled as Del pulled him up.

That night they took turns on the harmonica. Both Will and Jimmy had progressed far beyond the days when their neighbors would groan and move away. As a matter of fact, now people would move in closer to hear the music. Looking around, most could be seen swaying or rocking back and forth, eyes closed, remembering better days, and hoping to see them again. Over the next six weeks prisoners came in in steady numbers. Some days several dozen were added, while other days a hundred or more. Then something stirred the armies to life and as a result, the gates opened to hundreds of new arrivals. Dozens took up residence along the upper deadline. Will waited a day for them to get settled in before going over to inquire on the progress of the war effort. There were several sergeants in the group but they seemed to be taking orders from a private. He was by far the oldest in the group. Will guessed his age to be in the fifties. The man was tall, with a black chopped beard streaked with gray and deep set gray eyes. A long, slender nose made him, in Will's opinion, a very striking figure.

He was giving Will the once over as well, and smiled a greeting as he approached. "Mornin' neighbor, names True, Cyrus True." He extended his hand.

Will noticed the pieces of thread that outlined a pattern of stripes on the man's sleeve. At least at one time he had outranked Will. "Will Morgan, Where you boys from?" Will asked, shaking the hand.

"We're out of Pennsylvania but spent some time in Danville prison 'till they closed it. I hear they emptied the prisons at Richmond, as well. How many you figure are here?"

Will looked out over the prison and guessed between five and seven thousand. He had no way of knowing that within the next two weeks, that number would swell to thirty five thousand.

"Sounds about right. It's a shame these boys of mine ended up here. Damn fool generals. All go to the same school and learn the same mistakes. I predict that in all the wars to come, good common sense will never be learned by the, so called, military leaders. The idea of marching a formation into cannon fire is beyond comprehension, and why they can't see it rankles me no end. This is the result!" He swept his hand over the prison. "That's what happened to us. Damn fools making decisions without even knowing where the enemy was or how large his forces." He shook his head. His chin jutted out and he patted the thread pattern on his sleeve. "Wasn't the first time I gave them some advice they didn't appreciate." He grinned down at Will. "They don't take criticism very well. Fact is I been up and down the ranks like a man on a ladder pickin' apples."

"Had a few run-ins with Indians down in Texas. Those boys knew how to wage war against great odds," Will replied, with a grin. "They were good. Spend hours blasting away at them and never get a good shot. A blur here, a rustle of grass, a shadow, maybe a flash of color. The only thing I actually saw was arrows a comin' our way." Will shook his head with a look of disgust. "You have family?"

Cyrus smiled with pride shadowed by a hint of sadness. "Oh yes, a wife and three daughters. Two married and three grandbabies." He paused, tears coming to his eyes. "My two boys are gone."

"Hope you don't mind my askin', but why are you in this mess? You sure weren't drafted."

"I love my country. My folks came from over the sea with only what they had on their backs. Got free land and worked hard at making it pay. Pappy took off. Don't know where, or why he didn't come back. We made a good farm, and never went hungry or without a roof over our heads. My daughters' families are working that land and adding to it. We did it all with our own hands, and I have no truck with slavery. No sir, don't believe in it. John Brown was a good man. His heart was in the right place. Would have been honored to have known him." He ran his hands through his thinning hair, and glanced over his men, with a look of pride. "What brought you to this sorry mess, Will?"

"'Fraid to say, my reasons were not as noble. Mostly it was boredom at cooking for a ranch crew, and chasing cows. I wanted excitement. I must say that I saw my share during the fighting. But," he swept his arm over the view of the prison "it just can't get any more exciting than this."

Over the next few weeks, Will often sought Cyrus out. He was a man of great insight, and seemed to enjoy Will's company. Being a good listener, Will learned much in regards to life. Hours were spent on a wide range of topics. He learned more about raising animals then he knew existed. It was like being back with his Dad except they had more in common being both outdoors men.

5

THE NEW ARRIVAL

It was a hot, muggy day sometime in July. It had started like all the others, but it was one that Will would always remember. He had no idea of the date and didn't care. It was worthless information like the time of day. All their days blended together like some endless nightmare. He wasn't going any place soon. The humidity was oppressive and moving was more like swimming than walking. They had gone down to the slit trench, as they did every day though there wasn't much to do there, what liquid they did take in just ran out of their skin. They had slowly made the rounds of his men and their condition was gnawing at him. Several had died the previous day. It was a battle to keep from succumbing to the temptation to just throw up his hands and quit.

Around noon, the mess wagon pulled in and it was heaped with something. Their spirits were lifted by the shear bulk of the load. They hurried down the path, ignoring the sweat running down their bodies and the throbbing heat. As they neared the wagon, they were disappointed to see the mound of dirty roots piled in the back.

"Take all ya want, Yankee bastards." The driver ignored their looks of disappointment.

Will bit into one of the roots and, although on the sour side, it wasn't all that bad. The others followed suit and then filled their arms with as many as they could carry. They chewed thoughtfully on the tough roots as they made their way up the path. Dampness, either from sweat or the humidity, covered their faces and saturated their clothes. The small movement of air through their wet clothes somewhat counterbalanced the heat of their exertion. Exhausted from the effort when they got back to the she-bang they slumped down, careful to allow air to circulate around them.

They scraped off some of the excess dirt, and slowly continued to munch the roots. It wasn't something they would intentionally eat, given a choice of just about anything, but it did fill their stomachs without making them sick.

When they had eaten their fill and hidden the rest in the she-bang, Will sat with his back to the dead-line. He closed his eyes and pulled his knees up to his chest, wrapping his arms around them. Clasping his fingers, he lowered his head and dozed. It seemed only moments later, when he was roused from his stupor.

"Company's a comin'," Jimmy announced with a touch of enthusiasm. They didn't get many visitors, and Limber Jim was always a welcome sight. "Must be damned important to walk up here in all this heat."

Will peered from under his hat at the three approaching guests. He didn't recognize the man with Jim or the third person who was smaller, perhaps a youngster. The kid's face and head were covered by an old blanket hanging to his knees. Damn, Will thought. Why would anyone wear a blanket on a day like this? He shifted his attention back to Jim. He was surprised to see the concern on Jim's face. One thing that Jim never showed was worry but he was showing it now.

Jim had stopped twenty feet away and turning, spoke to the two strangers. The taller of the two helped the other sit down, then sat down and put his arm around the slight frame to keep him from falling over. The smaller man was definitely tired from the walk up. The stranger glanced at the four men, then devoted his attention to his comrade.

Jim came on ahead. "Don't bother a gettin' up." He sat down, with crossed legs, facing Will. His obvious agitation brought a tense feeling to the pit of Will's stomach. Something bad, Will thought. Real bad.

"I need to talk to Will alone, boys. Nothin' personal."

Jimmy, Del and Jack nodded and moved out of ear range.

"Will, we have ourselves a problem and I need your help."

"Sure, Jim. Anything I can do, I will. You know that."

"That's why I'm a talkin' to you. What I'm about to tell you must not go beyond us and as few as have to be told to do this job. Only those you trust completely with your very life.

"I'll need Jimmy, Del and Jack in on anything that I have to do."

"Fair enough. Call them over."

Will motioned for the three to join them. As they sat down, Will leaned toward Jim. "What kind of job?" Will whispered, feeling sure he was about to get involved in something he wasn't going to like.

Jim scanned the people in the immediate area. Could the four keep this secret? He felt sick to his stomach letting it go beyond his own people, but he needed Will and his location. "What I am about to tell you must not get out. It could mean life or death to these folks," he reiterated for the others.

Will nodded, still wondering what he was getting them into. "I'll vouch for my men. Every last one of them." He peered again at the two huddled figures in the distance.

"The fewer the better, Will. I'll let you be the judge of that."

"What in Sam Hill are you talking about Jim?"

"What I have to tell you is that we have a woman in here, a lady. Will, she is going to have a baby!" He felt relief that he had spoken the words. Now the responsibility rested with Will.

They all looked in appalled astonishment at the small blanket covered figure. Their minds trying to accept what they had been told, but recoiling at the realization that a women was stuck in this hell hole.

"Maybe nothin' would happen if the word got out, then again, all hell could break loose. I'll be damned if I want to take the chance. I'm trustin' you and your boys. I figure your location and sleep hole is the best we can ask for. You don't git people just wanderin' through. Air is a lot better up here too." He looked up at the guard, shaded by his umbrella, twenty feet above them. "Maybe he could be of help, if things go awry."

None of the four had spoken a word. They were too stunned to come up with anything to say. A woman in this place! It was too horrible to believe.

"I guess we go ahead. I'll introduce you. Don't you boys go a gittin' up and bowin' and all that stuff. A hand shake will do just fine." He looked at the four dumb struck men to be sure they got the message. "Remember, anyone a watchin' has to think that she's a man."

Jim walked over to the two and squatted beside them, letting them know that the men had agreed to the plan. He helped the woman up and the three made their way to the she-bang. The tall man looked at them with a mixture of hope and fear. He was placing his wife and unborn child in the hands of these strangers, and they looked terrifying.

Will motioned for the woman to sit near the dead-line, with her back to the compound. She opened the blanket and looked at her new protectors. She gave them a timid smile, but fear was in her eyes. She extended her hand and they each gave it a gentle shake. Tears were running down their cheeks. My God, they thought. A woman in here.

"Wish we could'a had some warning, we could'a cleaned this place up some." Del was obviously embarrassed.

"It'll be just fine. Call me Janie." Her voice was as soft as a gentle breeze.

"Name's Harry Hunt." The tall man said as he shook hands all around. He had a strong grip and a voice to match.

"Glad to meet you, Harry. I'm Del, this is Jimmy, Jack and Will. Will is the top dog in this area. I imagine he'll be making the decisions."

"No, it's too much for me. I'm bringing Cyrus into this. He is a lot smarter than I am. He's a damn good man. Oh, sorry Ma'am, He's a good man."

"Janie, Will." She gave a small laugh.

Will blushed. "Right." He rose and hurried to Cyrus's tent. Cyrus was sleeping. Will gently shook his foot until the man awoke. "Sorry to wake you Cyrus, but I have a problem that maybe you can give me a hand with."

Cyrus came wide awake. "Just catchin' up on my rest, Will. Tell me about it."

"Come with me. You'll have to see for yourself." Cyrus frowned, then smiled. Anything to break the boredom was welcome. He extended his hand and Will pulled him to his feet.

Together, they returned to the others as Harry came crawling out of the she-bang alone. "Cyrus, I'd like you to meet Harry Hunt. Harry, this is Cyrus True." They shook hands. "Cyrus, Harry is new to Andersonville. He's here with his wife Janie and their expected child."

Cyrus's head jerked up. "She's not in here? Inside the stockade?" Their expressions told him it was true. His knees buckled. Del and Jack grabbed him just in time to keep him from falling. His voice was tense. "In here?"

"She's going to have a baby, Cyrus. Hoped you could help us out."

"Of course. Of course. Is she in there?" He pointed to the shelter. Harry nodded.

"I'll need to talk to her." Harry gave him a nod of consent and Cyrus lowered himself to the ground and crawled into the shelter. She was laying on her side, watching him. She tried to smile.

"My name's Cyrus." He took her hand and held it gently. "Birthed my own babies, all five of them. Don't you worry. Between you, me and the Lord, we are going to deliver you a fine baby. Terrible place to bring a young'in into the world, and that's a fact. Terrible. You have any idea of when it's due?" He looked into her soft brown eyes and was reminded of a fawn. She was a pretty little thing, and to end up in a place like this and with child coming to boot, it just wasn't right. He blinked tears from his eyes.

"I think pretty soon. Maybe a couple of weeks. I don't really know for sure."

"Good, that will give us time to get ready. Maybe we can get you out of here before then." He petted her hand. He wanted to hold her close, shield her from this place, but knew that he couldn't.

"I don't think so. The man is charge here just laughed when Harry pleaded with him to keep me some place else."

"Wirz?"

"No, I think he was there, but a General Winder made the decision."

"Damned fool! Sorry, that just slipped out." Cyrus stammered. "It's this place, Ma'am."

"I understand. Don't you fret. Please call me Janie. I'm so glad you're going to be helping me. I don't think my husband has any idea what to do."

"To be honest, I didn't know too much about it with the first one.

Delivered lots of calves, colts and some puppies, but a human is a lot more stressful. By the fifth one, I felt like I had the hang of it. I'll need to talk to your husband and Will now. Janie, don't you worry." He raised the back of her hand to his lips.

He crawled out and joined the others sitting in the area in front of the shelter. "First thing to do is to get this place cleaned up as best we can. Food might be a problem, but if we can get some of the boys to kick in some of their rations, from time to time, we should be able to keep her weight up. At this point, she seems to be in fair health. We have to try to keep her that way. Hopefully we'll get some rain. We need to save as much fresh water as we possibly can if we do." He paused, thinking. "We'll need ten or fifteen men who like to sing." He looked at their bewildered expressions and grinned.

"Sing?" Jack asked. "Why?"

"When the baby comes, there's a lot of pain. During that time, we'll need singing. Singing loud and long. We can't have all the men around here hearing her, if we intend on keeping this a secret. We'll need five or more songs for them to rehearse to set the stage. I figure those boys will have to know why they are doing this so let's be careful to get boys we can depend on to keep quiet."

Will was relieved that Cyrus was prepared to take over. He felt the panic leave him, to be replaced by simple fear. That, he was used to.

"How on earth did you and Janie end up in this place?" Del gave a voice to the principal question in all their minds.

"Actually, it started the day we were married. I own, or used to own, a sailing ship that worked along the coast hauling cargo from New York to Florida. After the ceremony I had arranged with the Captain and crew to take everyone on a short cruise. The guests were all looking forward to the experience as we headed out of the harbor toward the open sea. An hour into the cruise, we were stopped and boarded by a Union Revenue Cutter. My vessel was commandeered and ordered to Charleston, South Carolina to pick up some freight. Everyone was amenable and we all set out on what we thought was a lark. We were stopped again and boarded outside the port and informed that the well armed boarding party represented the Confederate States of America. They told us that Fort Sumpter was under attack and they were formally at war with the United States. We were to be arrested for sedition. After much haggling, I convinced the authorities to allow the wedding party to return home. I wasn't able to include myself. Janie insisted on staying with me. We had done nothing against them and I was sure that in a week or two they would see reason and we would be released. If I'd had any idea what we were in for I'd have sent Janie home if it had to be in a trunk. We have been shuffled around for over a year now, with no end in sight. The previous prisons were not that bad, nothing like this, I can assure you. Though they were far from the hotels and town houses my wife is accustomed to. My impression is that the war is not going well for the South and they are shutting down some of the smaller prisons and transferring prisoners to larger more isolated facilities, such as this."

At the end of Harry's story, the men just sat quietly, pondering the hardships the two had endured and were yet to experience.

Janie spent the daylight hours in the shelter. It was enlarged and deepened to four feet. A blanket was suspended across the new addition to give Harry and Janie some privacy. As she lay in the shelter, she thought back through the pampered life she had enjoyed.

Oh! How she had taken things for granted! If she ever returned home, she would never again fail to appreciate every little comfort. Clean clothes, a bath, food. The list could go on for pages. Harry often came in to sit with her, and hold her hand. During the day, he was usually the only one to enter the shelter. Occasionally, Cyrus would stop by and spend time with her, and he never failed to cheer her up. Such a gentle man. She wondered why a man of his age was in the army, and how he happened to end up in this place. Maybe she would ask him if the time was right. However, that time never came.

She was proud of Harry. He was raised in wealth and luxury, but he never flinched when they were arrested, or for that matter, anytime since. He had fought for her release throughout this whole episode and even with the added stress of the baby, his courage never faltered. He never once thought of himself or treated anyone with less than respect.

She spent many hours thinking of the men who were guarding her. The idea of being the only woman in a prison of thirty thousand men was terrifying. Of course, the vast majority were probably upstanding men but that still left many who were not. She was sure that her protectors realized the danger to all of them, still they seemed so serenely confident in keeping her safe she could not help but be comforted.

Del and Jack were easy going men. Jimmy was the clown, and he made her smile just about every time he opened his mouth. She enjoyed listening to the banter among them and caught herself laughing at their droll conversations. She wondered about Will. He was much more reserved then the others. There was a melancholy in him that she wondered about. He would act as the perfect foil for Jimmy's humor, his face sober, his eyes fathomless. It was hard to tell if he was part of the joke or not. She listened to them talk about the fight in which Will had bitten off the Raider's ear. Jimmy mentioned the confrontation between Will and the man in Libby prison.

"I thought it was a bluff, but figure that fella was lucky Will didn't jump him. Found him dead some time later. No great loss to the world, and that's for sure. Will is the best friend I ever had, but in my opinion he's probably the most dangerous man a person could choose to get on the bad side of." She thought about the remark for some time. It was reassuring to know that she and Harry were on his good side.

Cyrus had been checking on Janie every day for two weeks. He had explained the birth process to her and Harry. She had felt some chagrin at having this discussion with Cyrus. She knew nothing, or practically nothing, about having a baby and resented the fact that her mother had refused to discuss any of this with her before she married. She heard Cyrus going over the procedure with Will too, when they thought she was asleep. She didn't know why.

Cyrus knew that the time was short and he hoped that he would live long enough to see it through. He wanted the chance to hold this new life before he was gone, but things just didn't feel right in his chest. Breathing was getting harder, and he was having spells of faintness. There were small stabbing sensations from time to time in his arm and legs. These were becoming more noticeable the last week or so. He hadn't mentioned this to anyone but had gone over the delivery process in as much detail as he could with both Harry and Will. If he died, it would be up to the two of them. Harry was a good man, but Cyrus wasn't sure he could stay calm enough to do it alone. Knowing Will would be there to keep things on track gave Cyrus some ease.

Only twenty-three people were aware of what was going on in their midst. Most of them had occasion to catch a glimpse of Janie, usually in the evening hours. None made any attempt to see her up close, though all would have charged the gates of Hell with a milk bucket for the honor of her company. Daily they practiced their singing. Enjoying the diversion, many others joined in with much gusto. The spontaneous air of the activity as well as the extra volume added to their cover. Janie listened to the singing and felt humbled that men she did not, nor ever would know, were doing this for her.

The birth day arrived and Janie was tense with panic. Cyrus was summoned and he took his place at her side, holding her hand and whispering encouragement. Her fears subsided with his calm assurance. He gave her a drink of water which had been saved by over twenty men when a light rain had fallen three days earlier. He wiped here face with a small piece of shirt material. "Time to take a little look see." He moved down gently messaging her stomach, trying to feel the position of the baby. "Just a little longer now. You bite down on this rag, if it gets to hurting. Will has alerted the choir, and they're standing by."

Will had positioned himself where he could see Janie's face and get them started when the time was right. He was relieved beyond words, that Cyrus was here.

The choir had gone through their repertoire and were starting again when Will heard the baby's first cry. He jumped up and began singing loudly. Heads began nodding, and smiles broke out. Jimmy, who was playing the harmonica to accompany the singers, could hardly go on for the laughter that wanted to bubble out of him. Some were slapping each other on the back. Those who were not aware of what had just happened, thought the choir were certainly having an exceptionally good time. The joyful singing continued into the night.

Private Conner had been shocked the first time he had climbed the ladder to his guard station and had looked down into the thousands of milling prisoners. The smell had caused him to throw up. He didn't think then that he would be able to do this but as time went by he had hardened himself to the sights, the sounds, and the smells. He watched patiently as the singers eventually quit and drifted off to their own shelters. It was dark down there, but a sliver of moon allowed him to see movement. He knew the prisoners that lived in his corner, not personally, but he knew many of their names and could guess what they were like as men. He knew they were real soldiers, not like some of the rabble down there. Not like some of the rabble in his own army. As he thought of those miserable souls, he wondered about the singing. It seemed rather odd that the men he understood them to be would suddenly take up song. Some of the singers came from a distance to join in. That was unusual too. Well, maybe it was just a way of putting their suffering out of their minds. He could just see this group starting it for the effect it had on morale. Tonight had been different though, almost joyful, with laughing and back slapping that seemed to go on for hours. Now it was still except for the normal sounds of suffering and death. He missed the singing that drowned out the dying, it helped his morale too.

Over the next two nights the singing would break out again from time to time. Never quite like before. After a few minutes or an hour it would just dwindle away. There didn't seem to be any rhyme or reason to it. He could feel something in the air he couldn't quite put his finger on and it made him a little uneasy. On the third night, his questions were answered.

He had taken his usual position sitting on the stool, heels hooked on the rung. His gun was leaning against the wall beside him. His knees were against the logs and his arms were folded on a level place on top were he could rest his head on them from time to time. It was going to be a long night. Maybe Curt would relieve him early, but he doubted it. He hadn't slept much and he was tired. He let his head go down and started to doze off. He was jolted awake by a sound like a baby crying. The men started singing. His ears must be playing tricks on him. It must have been some sound made by the men below. No way was there a baby around these parts. Still, he'd probably better not let himself sleep again, after all, he could get himself shot for it. The singing tapered off, and he listened carefully. Nothing. He'd just about decided he was imagining things when there it was again! It was suddenly choked off as if someone had placed a hand or something else over the tiny mouth. He had a little sister, and he damn well knew the sound a baby makes.

He had to tell someone and right now, but who? He ruled out the officers, as he didn't like or trust any of them. He remembered the kicks and cuffs he received from time to time for not moving fast enough, no, they wouldn't understand a thing like this. Hell, he didn't understand it himself. Then he thought of Dr. Kerr. He was new at the post. The Doc had recently treated a black eye and numerous bruises he had received at the hands of several of his drunken fellow soldiers. It had been a real knock down, drag out fight and he had done pretty well against them. Him being the only sober one there, helped. Anyway, Doc Kerr had treated him decent. He quietly climbed down the ladder, and headed away from the command post and toward the small house that served as the doctor's quarters.

He knocked on the door of the dark building, feeling guilty about getting him up, but unless this was a total wild goose chase it could be really important. Damned important!

Moments later, a light came on and the door opened. Dr. Kerr stood holding a small oil lamp. He was wearing only pants. No shirt and no shoes. His hair was messed but he smiled when he saw who had knocked. "So Private Conner, have you been in another fight?"

"No Sir. I found a baby!" Mathew stammered. "I found a baby!"

"A baby what?" The doctor smiled at the fidgeting boy.

"A baby person." Mathew was having a hard time talking, he was so excited. "I know what I heared. It was a baby, for sure. Honest."

"Where did you hear this baby, Mathew?" The doctor figured it must have been someone visiting their camp from the town.

"From my post, Sir." Mathews eyes were as big as saucers. "It was comin' from down there, amongst the prisoners. They got themselves a baby in there somehow."

The doctor pulled on his boots over bare feet and threw on a shirt. "Show me where you heard it?" It was ridiculous of course but, then again, the young soldier was really upset and it shouldn't take long to solve the mystery and be back in bed.

He followed the boy up the ladder and together they stood listening in the darkness. The sounds and smells of death and dying below tore at his heart. He had complained to Wirz, who had taken over the prison when Winder had been given command over the entire southern prison system. It had done no good but he hadn't given up. They continued to listen for some time. He had decided the boy had only heard an owl or something when he caught the start of a tiny quavering wail. Immediately, the men below began to sing and the sound was lost. It was impossible! A baby inside the stockade? How could it be?

"You're right, Private Conner. That was surely a baby. You did real good, son. Now you'd best leave this to me." He patted the boy on the shoulder and climbed down the ladder. Returning to his quarters, he tried to decided how best to handle this amazing problem. He thought about waiting until morning, but ruled it out. If they suspected that Conner had heard it cry they could move the child and it would be impossible to find. He put on the rest of his uniform and walked to the main gate.

There were a number of guards at the entry station. Picking two he ordered, "You two men, fetch a stretcher and report back here on the double. This is an emergency."

The two men hurried off and returned shortly with the stretcher. "We got it from the hospital, Sir. They want it back."

"They'll get it back." Looking at the gate guards, he ordered them to open up.

"Y'all want it opened now?"

"Yes, now. We're going in. Keep an eye out, we'll be back shortly."

The two prospective stretcher bearers looked at one another with shock then turned and ran into the night. There was no way in hell they were going to go into that place at night without a whole platoon of armed guards.

Picking up the stretcher, the Doctor again ordered the gates opened.

His voice had taken a hard edge that was not lost on the remaining guards. After a few moments of clanking chain, the two sets of gates were opened and Dr. Kerr pushed his way inside. Holding the stretcher under one arm and the oil lamp in the other, he entered the main stockade and headed in what he hoped to be the right direction.

He had never been inside and had a hard time navigating the maze of trails. The stench of death assailed his nostrils. That he, in his Confederate uniform, was in here alone with no weapon definitely made him uneasy. This might qualify as the dumbest thing he had ever done. He fought his fear and trudged up the hill.

Del was out keeping watch when he saw the bobbing light and the man in gray holding it. They had been discovered, that was a given. Well this was no place for a child to grow up and maybe it was all for the good. Anyplace would be better than here. He bent down and shook Will's foot. "We got company." Will crawled out and took in the situation.

"I'll git Harry up. Why don't you meet him and show him the way. The guy has guts that's for damn sure."

Del nodded and headed in the direction of the light.

When Dr. Kerr reached the shelter, they were all waiting. The baby was asleep in Janie's arms.

Dr. Kerr looked at the mother and baby in amazement. He knew he was there for a baby, but was still shocked to actually see it and a woman too, for God's sake. He reached out and touched the back of the little boy's neck. He bowed from the waist to Janie. "My name is Dr. Kerr and I am here to escort you out of here. Is the father present?"

"Yessir. My name is Harold Hunt and this is my wife Jane and little Harry Junior. We would deeply appreciate any help you can give us."

"I'll need help with the stretcher, gentlemen. Would you be kind enough to let us carry you down Mrs. Hunt?"

Moments later, all was ready. Del was in front, Jack in back and Harry holding the baby. Before she climbed onto the stretcher she held out her hand to Will, who was staying behind, with Jimmy. As he took her hand, she put her arm around his neck and kissed him on the cheek. He couldn't feel it through the beard, but he would cherish it always. "Thank you Will."

"My pleasure. You have a great life." Tears stung his eyes.

"Would you tell Cyrus goodbye, and that he will always be in my thoughts and prayers."

"I'm sure he will like that, very much." Will was choking up. He gave a two finger salute to Harry as he watched them leave. He was relieved that they were getting out of here, but the loss of their presence brought an emptiness that surprised him.

"Damn Will, I'm goin' to miss them somethin' awful."

"Yeah, me too, Jimmy, me too."

The next morning, Will visited Cyrus. He knew that Cyrus would regret not being able to say good-bye. He would miss Janie and the baby as much as they all would. Cyrus was curled up in his shelter. He looked like he had aged years since yesterday. "The Hunts were taken out last night, Cyrus. She told me to tell you thank you for all you did for her and the baby and that you will always be in her thoughts and prayers."

Cyrus looked sad, but quickly smiled. "She is a fine lady, Will. We are all the better for having had her with us. Before she came I knew there was a reason for my lingering on but had given up on what it could be. I was ready to die three weeks ago but I knew I needed to stay around when she entered my life. The Lord needed me to help bring that child into the world. Now my job is done, I can go in peace." He lifted his hands up to his face and looked at them. They were trembling. "Should have been a doctor, don't you think Will?" He smiled and lowered his hands to his chest. "I've got this great coat. It's in darned good shape, I want you to take it. It might help you make it out of this place. Hang in there and take care of yourself. You're a good man. Glad I got to know you." He closed his eyes.

Will looked down at the old man, knowing that his time was short. He wanted to refuse the coat but he couldn't kid himself that Cyrus would be needing it. "I'm proud to call you friend Cyrus True. I will honor your memory and your wisdom."

He didn't open his eyes, but a fleeting smile crossed his face.

As he lay dying, Cyrus thought of his troopers who fussed over him, keeping him company and sharing what they had. He knew that he was loved. They were his family, now. He regretted the pain that his passing would cause them but the strength to continue was gone. He was thankful that he had met Will. It had been a comfort and a joy to be able to express his thoughts on life to such a receptive friend. He hoped that the advice he shared with Will would serve him well.

That evening, Will stopped to check on Cyrus who was stretched out on the ground, and he could see the fire of life in his eyes was fading. The older man was unable to speak, but seemed content to listen to Will talk about Jimmy, Del, Jack and his years of chasing cows in

Texas. Will felt that he was losing a father. Cyrus smiled, from time to time, but became increasingly withdrawn. Will finally took out his harmonica and began to play.

Cyrus closed his eyes and smiled as the sound of music drifted through the evening air. It sounded almost like his fiddle. He always enjoyed music and hoped the men would keep up their singing. He longed to sit in front of the old stove with his fiddle and his Olivia, and to hear her sweet, clear voice singing a familiar hymn. His daughters had grown to women to make a father proud. They were the gift he had given the world. Oh, and to hold his little grandbabies once more. To hold them close and listen to their laughter. He silently mourned his two boys, shot down at the very start of their lives in a charge against the Rebs. Maybe on the other side they are waiting for me now, he thought. Just reach out my hands and they will touch me. He tried to raise his arms, but they were heavy. He hoped that God would look favorably on him. He had tried to live by the Good Book. Yes, he would be with Olivia and the little ones once more. Would they know he was there? Would they feel his nearness as they remembered him? He hoped so with all his heart. He tried to hum the melody he heard but no sound came out. He could feel himself dozing off as if in sleep, but he knew that he would not be awakening to another day. Clasping his hands over his chest he relaxed his body drifting with the melody and waited for the end. He opened his eyes for one last look at the fading sky and saw the twinkling of the first star. His breathing slowed, hesitated, then stopped.

Will was to remember the Hunts, from time to time throughout his life, wondering if they had indeed survived the war. It wasn't until after nineteen hundred that he would read about a reunion of

Andersonville veterans in the newspaper. It seemed Dr. Kerr was there to verify the birth, which had been rumored for years. Harry and his family had indeed survived and returned to New York in safety.

6

PROMISE MADE

During the next three weeks, the four accomplished very little beyond staying alive. Will and Jimmy didn't seem to change much to look at. Each day they checked their teeth for signs of scurvy. They were free of it so far. They figured it must have to do with those brown roots. If you could chew them to start with they did some real good. Jack had lost weight, but he had been husky when he came in. Del had also lost some pounds but because of his height and bone structure, it wasn't too obvious.

The Raiders posed an ever increasing threat, even to those who had nothing left. A number of trustworthy men had moved into their immediate area for protection, all thin and worn but tough where it counted. They kept continually alert to the activities in the camp, moved around only in groups and always posted a guard at night. Their evening and morning circuits were now as much reconnaissance as exercise. Tension was building up, and in each small community within the walls there were heated discussions of retaliation. Something had to break soon. These enclaves, divided by military loyalties, ethnic or social background and sometimes even religion tended not to mingle. The black prisoners, especially, seldom strayed away from their comrades. The sheer number of prisoners was also against them in any attempt to organize.

It was late morning of another steaming day, when most of the others were off on various errands, when Jimmy announced his urgent need to visit the trench. Will had had a bad night, with wrenching stomach pain, and begged off.

"Give me a little time, Jimmy, I can make it," Will had told him, from inside the she-bang.

"Can't do it, I've put it off as long as I dare. I was hoping that Jack or Del could go with me but they're out trying to find some wood. I'll probably see them on my way down. Don't worry, I'll be back in an hour at most."

Will fumed as time went by and there was no sign of Jimmy. He should have forced himself to go. Maybe he had met up with Del and Jack. He kept watching the trail but after a time he decided he had to go look for them. He was half way down the slope, pressing his hand against the pain in his stomach, when he spotted Jack and Del coming toward him carrying Jimmy slumped between them, head hanging down, toes dragging in the dirt.

"Oh, no! No!" Will hurried forward, his stomach pain forgotten. "What happened? My God, what happened?"

"Got stomped by Rooster," answered Jack through clenched teeth. "Snuck up on him from behind, knocked him down and stomped on him. By the time some of the boys heard him holler, Rooster had run off. He's hurt bad, Will, real bad."

The three of them carried Jimmy to their camp. Jack threw out his blanket and they laid him down. He was unconscious and his arm was broken. Two bones protruded from the skin. Bruises covered his face and chest and his breathing was shallow and labored.

"We got to straighten that arm and git it splinted before he wakes up, 'cause there's no way we're take'en him to the hospital. He'll come back with a stump for sure, if he comes back at all. Most that do, don't make it a week," Will said as he took off what was left of Jimmy's shirt sleeve, exposing the wound. "You boys hold him steady while I pull on his arm. Do we have splints?" Will was thinking clearer now and took the two tent pegs thrust out from the crowd that had gathered. He knelt beside Jimmy, gripped his arm and hand firmly. He pulled until the arm was straight. Quickly the sticks were placed and wrapped with cloth. Jimmy moaned but did not awaken. Someone arrived with water so they could clean him up some and access the damage. There was no way of knowing what problems might be lurking under the bruises. Will knew that the broken arm would never heal right. The bone ends were shattered.

That evening Will started to work on the skillet handle. Rage and worry kept him awake most of the night. Having inquired around for some sort of tool to work the handle, Pvt. Stemberg who either had, or could find just about anything, came up with a three inch piece of file. It would take time, but Will figured neither he, nor Rooster were going anywhere soon. Holding the skillet on edge between his knees, he slowly stroked the handle with the shard of file.

Sometime that night, Jimmy started to moan, then drift off again. He continued this for hours. At times, Will thought that he was trying to talk, but was unable to understand him. It was a long night and frustrating, knowing that medical supplies were just outside the walls if they could bring themselves to take the chance.

Surprisingly, Jimmy awoke the next morning and, aside from severe pain in his arm and stomach, seemed to be on the mend. "What happened to me? One minute I'm pullin' up my pants, and the next thing I'm here feelin' like I've been kicked by a mule."

"You aren't far wrong, and that's about the long and the short of it. Seems Rooster got you from behind and damn near killed you."

"Should'a killed him that day he jumped Jack. Should'a gouged his eyes out and bit off his nose, like you was gonna do to that guy in Libby. Had my chance and didn't take it." He gripped his arm and tried to look at it, but the bindings had it well covered. "That sure hurts." He gritted his teeth. "Don't think I can help on the well for awhile."

Will knew that Jimmy's work on the well was over. "Don't you worry about it, we'll leave some for you when you git ta feelin' better."

Jimmy's condition worsened and by the third day they knew a decision would soon have to be made. In all that time, neither Will nor Jimmy had gotten more than a few hours sleep. As long as Jimmy was suffering, Will was attending to him as best he could. Anxiety ate at him constantly. He knew that Jimmy would probably die, but he wouldn't let his heart accept it. Somehow, some way he hoped for a miracle.

"Will, we have to talk some serious talk, here. We both know that I might not make it through this. Outside, maybe, but in here, I don't like the odds."

"How you feel about going to the hospital?"

"You know they'll take my arm. Only as a last resort, Will. You'll have to be the judge of that if I'm out of it. If gangrene sets in we'll have no choice. Right now it appears to be lookin' that way." A tear ran down his cheek.

By morning, the wound was seriously infected. Thousands of flies were swarming around the arm. They were finding ways around the bandages, and laying their eggs in the wound. Now, there was no other choice.

The three of them carried him down to the gate and called to the guard. The gate opened and two orderlies came in with a stretcher and carried him off. Outside they laid him down at the end of a line of prospective amputees. Desperate need was about the only thing that would drive the men to seek help here. In the filth of the stockade the least scratch was capable of creating that need. The moans and screams from the hospital were horrible and it smelled worse than it had inside. "Ya got yerself a hour wait." It was obvious by his expression that the orderly enjoyed his work.

On entering the tent, the first thing Jimmy saw was a doctor in a smock splattered with overlapping layers of blood, from old and dry, to fresh. It looked ghastly. He groaned with pain and dread.

"Set him up here." The doctor ordered, pointing to a long wooden table. It had turned black by countless bloody saturations. Swarms of flies took off as he was placed on the table. The doctor looked him straight in the eyes. Jimmy thought he saw compassion there, behind the dogged resolve to complete his ugly task. "Hold his legs boys. We need assistants over here." He yelled. Two other men came over. One held his good arm and chest down while the other gripped the bad arm. They had done this many times before. Jimmy gasped from the fiery pain that raced up his arm. "Here we go. Hold him still."

Jimmy turned his head away, but not before seeing the glint of the bloody, curved knife in the doctor's hand and the small saw next to a pan of bloody water. The knife came down. Jimmy screamed and passed into blessed oblivion. One quick cut around half the arm, then switching his grip the Doctor cut the other half. Dropping the knife in the pan of water, he picked up the saw. Ten quick strokes and the arm was off. He shoved it off the table, into a bloody box with the rest of its grisly assortment. Thousands of flies flew from the box, but were back within seconds.

Later, Jimmy was brought back to where his three friends waited. He was moaning gently as he started to wake. They carried him up the hill, leaving a faint trail of blood drops the entire way. The doctor had left a string tourniquet around his upper arm, but it didn't seem to be doing much good nor were the stitches that held the skin over the end of his severed arm.

:Put me down, boys, put me down. Lordy, that hurts." They set him down beside the she-bang. The others stepped away murmuring among themselves and shaking their heads. Will dropped down beside him.

Through clenched teeth the boy gasped, "If'n it goes bad you have to help me. Damn this hurts. Least they could'a done was give me a shot of whiskey." He was pulling his legs up, then stretching them out. Over and over.

Will wanted to still the boy's thrashing as it might do more harm to his arm and was ghastly to watch. He could almost feel the boy's pain himself. "You know that I'll do my best for you. You know that."

"I mean more than your best. If this don't get better I want you to help me end it. Promise me that you'll do it. I need a promise. I can't go back there. I just can't."

Letting the words sink in, Will gripped the boy's hand and said, "I promise." Those were the hardest words Will had ever spoken. "You'll pull out of this. You can beat it." He tried to think of something else to say but couldn't. Jimmy quieted down at that, and exhausted and appalled, they both remained silent.

Will knew he would probably have to keep that promise. Deep down, he wondered how on earth he could do it. His whole soul revolted against the idea. He loved Jimmy like a brother, like a son! He couldn't!

As if he could read Will's mind Jimmy repeated. "Will, you have to keep your promise. Bein' dead is one thing, but dying is different. I don't want to go out like some of these men, crying and screamin'. No Sir! I want to go quick."

Will didn't say anything. He knew he was trapped. Like it or not. "Jimmy, you have my word." Will spoke quietly and sincerely. "You have to tell me when you're ready. But for now, let's think about you gitt'n better. We've been through a lot and we'll get through this. Want me to play some songs for you?"

"Can't Will. Rooster has it and he has my Twyla." Jimmy began to cry. "He took her." His chest heaved as he sobbed. He'd realized that the pouch was gone when he woke up that first day, but didn't say anything to Will. He didn't want him to fret about it. At least, until after.

Jack and Del, nearby, had heard enough to get the gist of what Jimmy was asking. This was between the two old friends and they were not part of it, but they felt it deeply. They were grateful that they were not being called upon to do what was being asked of Will.

Will looked around and they nodded their heads. Jimmy was right. Will remembered seeing the pouch around his neck as he headed down the trail. Jimmy had insisted he should carry it because of Twyla. Will had understood.

Will knew that the loss of the picture was a devastating blow to Jimmy. Hell, he was feeling pretty bad about it as well. He tried to sort out his feelings. It was just a picture after all. No, it was more. It was hope. Hope for a future that seemed way beyond their reach. The harmonica was a reminder of the beauty that still lived somewhere in the world. Besides, it was his! He picked up the file and skillet and grimly went to work.

Two days. Two days of endless pain. Will stretched his cramped legs, and the movement awakened Jimmy from his semi-conscious state. The pain from the blackening stump brought a groan from his cracked lips. His eyes were stuck shut. As he feebly groped at them with his left hand Will wiped them clean with a damp cloth. He could see a layer of thin clouds and from the weakness of the sunlight that shown on them he figured it to be toward evening. He'd made it through another day. Damn, he thought, it would have been better for everyone if I had died in my sleep. He peered up at Will. Their eyes met, and he was embarrassed to see the empathy there. He tried to lick his cracked lips but his tongue was too dried and swollen. Will wiped his lips with the damp cloth. It felt better. The pain from his arm brought a groan. His jaw was clenched so tight that he could taste blood.

Time to cash in my chips, he thought. Tired of living, tired of thinking about death and tired of the pain. He cleared his throat and gripped Will's hand. "It's time. Can't take another day of this. Please tell Twyla that I loved her to the end, and I'll always be with her." He paused to get his breath. "I figure it's time to go sit on the rock and cool my feet in the creek. I want to go home now." His grip hardened. "You're a good friend. Best I ever had. You'll take care of Twyla for me? Make sure she's doin' fine? Please?"

"Sure, Jimmy, don't you fret about her. I'll make sure she's fine. Good-bye, dear friend." Bending over he touched his lips to Jimmy's forehead. Tears were burning his eyes.

Jimmy shifted his gaze to the empty sky. He would have liked to have seen even just one bird flying free before he left.

Nearby Jack and Del looked sadly at one another. Del reached over and gave Will a squeeze on the shoulder, then briefly took Jimmy's hand. Setting it down, he stood up and motioned to Jack who did the same. After one last look at Jimmy, they walked over to join a small group of friends who were keeping vigil. Jimmy was liked by all, and would be missed.

"It's up to you, old friend." Just do it quick, he thought. He managed to croak a feeble "Let's do it partner."

Will lifted Jimmy onto his lap with the crook of his elbow around the boy's throat. He paused while they both looked toward heaven for strength. A lone heron glided across the yellowing twilight sky. A last look showed Will a peaceful smile on the sweet familiar face. He closed his eyes and took a deep breath. As he tightened his hold he could feel the boy struggle briefly his good hand reaching up to claw at his arm. His brain, in frantic turmoil, was screaming that this could not be happening. He kept telling himself that it was not real, that someone else was responsible, that he only watched from the sidelines. He continued to hold the boy tightly after his resistance had ceased. He had to be sure. There was no way he would ever find the strength to do this again. No way in hell. Even after he was sure he continued to hold on as if by doing so he could keep things as they'd been. His face showed none of this struggle. After all, who else would he have do it? Who else could Jimmy have asked to live with it? Live with it he would, night and day for as long as he had breath in his body. He had just murdered his best friend.

After a time Jack and Del returned to the silent pair. Seeing that Jimmy was gone and realizing Will was not ready to let go they nodded their understanding and squatted down. Nothing had to be said. They had all been together through too much to need words. Will forced himself to look again into the face of his friend and tried to remember what he had looked like when they first met. It was hard to see the once handsome, smiling young man in the skeletal face covered with filthy matted hair. Back then, he had been so full of life, with a quick laugh and a ready smile. Will had liked him from the first time they met, and through this time of deprivation a bond as strong as that of brothers had grown.

Will let his mind drift back to their meeting. Both were still in the infantry at that time. He had relived that day often in the last few days.

Down one of those nameless roads, after mile upon mile of marching, guns had opened up to the right, across a wide field of flowers. Turning and advancing into the musket and cannon fire, Will could see the faces of the Rebs peering over a waist high rock wall. He would have given anything to have a rock wall to crouch behind. He remembered the hair tickling the back of his neck and the tightening of his stomach muscle as if to deflect the oncoming bullets. There was smoke along the firing line ahead and bullets screamed past. There was also the dull thud of lead hitting men. He had forced himself to move forward. Screams, God, he would never forget the screams. Shedding his heavy backpack, he lifted his gun and aimed. Movement! Fire! Crouch down, reload, stand, aim and fire, crouch, reload, up again, march forward, aim, fire, reload. It went on for an eternity, an unholy staggering dance to the screams of the wounded. Back and forth. Advance, fall back, regroup, advance. His legs and arms were getting heavier than he could bear but it still went on. There was so much gun-smoke it burned his lungs, his eyes were half blinded. Aim! Fire! Reload! Then, all at once, silence, except for a bugle sounding retreat.

Will remembered looking around, dazed, to realize that the Rebs had broken off the main engagement. He sank down on the ground, too tired to retreat. He could see fallen soldiers near him. There was Jeff, lying way over against the wall, with a gaping hole in his chest. His eyes seemed fixed on the wound, a look of bewilderment on his pale face. Over there Frederick, lying on his stomach, with his face pressed into the crook of his arm as if in sleep, except the back of his head was shot away. Will stopped looking. Forcing himself to all fours, he crawled toward the safety of the trees, dragging his gun behind him. Sporadic firing continued, bits of dirt were being kicked up by the lead. Will flattened out snaking along, trying to merge his body with the soil, finally finding a small ridge of rock he slid over it to relative safety. It was so low he hadn't noticed it going in.

The sun was down and the war was mostly over for another day. All was still, except for occasional sniping and the moans and cries of the wounded stranded in no-man's land between the two lines.

"Water, please, water. I'm shot, help me. Oh please help me, help me." Pitiful voices, so near, yet he couldn't take the chance with the snipers still active.

Will slumped exhausted behind the stones, thankful for the scant protection they provided. He wondered why they were ordered out into the open field when they could have fired from the safety of the rocks. True, it was less than a foot high in places, but it would have given them some cover. Damn poor judgment on someone's part. Sons of bitches!

Though he was safe at last from the gunfire, he was not from the voices. He could still hear them, maybe he always would. Peering over the wall he could see bodies in the fading light. They were everywhere. Hundreds of dead, beyond help. The cries, moans, and mutterings rose up from those among them that still clung to life. He had to do something to stop the sounds. He put his hands over his ears, but it did no good. Wearily he shoved his gun in along the base of the ridge and, shuddering, pulled himself over the top. He could see movement ahead and crawled toward it. Within seconds, he was dragging a wounded soldier toward the higher wall. Helping hands reached over and lifted the man to safety. He returned for another, and another. He had to stop the voices. An occasional shot was aimed in his direction, but he ignored them all. He knew that the wounded enemy would be shot in the morning if their comrades didn't come for them and their cares would be over. He never participated in the killing of wounded. He realized that there was not enough medical supplies to take care of their own, let alone hundreds of the enemy but he couldn't stomach it. If they had lost the fight today, then the Rebs would be killing the Union wounded. It was the way war was.

It was late when he found Jimmy. He was about done in. As he had reached the fallen soldier he first asked him how bad off he was. Jimmy replied, between clenched teeth. "I do believe that I'm a mite under the weather. Yes sir, just a mite." Will remembered grinning, as he dragged the boy towards the wall. He hadn't smiled for so long that he thought he just might have forgotten how. Jimmy always had a way of bringing a smile out of the worst possible situation.

The Rebs finally broke off the engagement completely and disappeared into the night. Scouts reported the area clear the following morning. The Colonel declared a time to rest and clean equipment. The execution squad was out in the field, looking for those enemy that had made it through the night. The sporadic gunfire seemed to go on for over an hour.

A soldier, with a bandaged head and a bad limp, came down the line asking, "Who's the feller that saved my butt?" As he approached Will, one of the nearby men pointed him out. "That'll be Sergeant Morgan. That's him right there. Spent most of the night out there. Damn fool!"

"I wouldn't call him that, partner, he saved my skin." He looked down at Will, who was bent over his gun, too tired to look up.

"Sergeant Morgan. You the one that pulled me in last night? If so, I do believe I owe you one."

"Probably. I didn't see many others out there." Will replied, looking up at him through squinted eyes.

"Put 'er there, Sergeant. My name is Jimmy Compton and I'm damned pleased to make your acquaintance. Those boys put a nice crease in the side of my head and took off the top of my damn ear. Then, to add insult, I twisted the heck out of my leg when I fell.

Those Rebs were still shootin' at me way after the fightin' stopped. Why did you take the risk of coming out to help us?"

"Danged if I know. Maybe you folks was disturbing my rest." Will replied. "Glad to see you're up and around this mornin'. Hell of a mess out there. Times like this I wish we had someone upstairs that knew what the hell they was doin'. Don't look like we learned anything from fightin' Indians. Ran into a few of those while pushing cattle in Texas. They have it down pat. Sure don't stand up and march into gunfire. Shucks, most of the time we never even saw 'em. When I become General, I'm damn sure goin' to consult with the Indians."

"You sound like someone I wouldn't mind goin' into battle with. I just joined the regiment last week. Hope I get to know you better, Sergeant."

He remembered the following year of shared good times and bad. A time of terrifying engagements and long periods of boredom. Then the cavalry came looking for horsemen and both volunteered. They both were ready to put an end to all the marching, and were both at home on a horse.

He looked down at the still face. So damn unnecessary. If only he had been with Jimmy that morning. That damned Rooster and his crowd. Damn them all.

Will shifted Jimmy's body on his lap attempting to close his open eyes and mouth to thwart the invading lice. Could he have made a difference in the shape he was in? Maybe yes, maybe no. If only he had kept the pouch with him there mightn't have been any temptation for Jimmy's attacker, still, the man had a grudge as well. It was a useless circle of doubt and guilt. He would trudge around it many times in the future. No more now. He was too drained, too broken.

Will shifted Jimmy's body again and dug a small hole in the dirt. Lifting the stump of Jimmy's arm he gently stuck it in the hole and covered the end with dirt. He tried not to notice the maggots spilling out. Burying the stump reduced the smell and it gave Will some relief to not have to see the maggots gorging themselves on Jimmy's rotting flesh. It was going to be a long night. Will adjusted his position again, still stubbornly holding Jimmy's body. His muscles would protest his sitting in the same position all night but Will could not bring himself to move the boy aside so that he could lie down. He stretched his arms and straightened his back as best he could. He felt an ache in his chest, and tears in his eyes.

He didn't know if he had done the right thing. If the circumstances had been reversed, it would be what he wanted, but was it right? Will wiped the tears from his face. Strange, he thought he was beyond that. Was he crying over Jimmy or his own sense of loss and vulnerability? He felt an emptiness in the pit of his stomach along with the ache in his chest. Jimmy had just about made life worth living in this pit. His eyes felt the sting of more tears. He did not bother to wipe them away. The night passed slowly.

The camp was beginning to stir. The ground appeared to come alive as the thousands of men wakened. Within minutes they were milling around, talking, coughing, checking to see who had died in the night. Another day at Andersonville had begun. What horrors would this day bring?

Del wakened and sat up with a groan. He stretched his long arms and tried to rub some circulation into his long skinny legs. He looked over at Will, sadly, as he remembered the previous evening.

"Mornin', Will."

"Mornin', Del." Will was glad he had Del and Jack. There was comfort in Del's long face and hound-dog eyes. One had to feel some better just looking at him.

"Damn, Will, I'm sure gonna miss him. He was too good a man to end up like this." He squatted down and took Jimmy's hand in his. He looked into the dead eyes and shook his head. Del's eyes were filling with tears, and he looked away, embarrassed.

"We need to get him down to the road. Let me give you a hand."

"No thanks, I can manage." For some reason Will felt that this was something he needed to do alone.

Jack, who had been listening to the conversation, muttered under his breath something about Rooster's family background, adding something about his mother, but neither Will nor Del caught it. They were all of the same opinion, however.

Will struggled to get out from under the body but was too weak and his leg joints felt as though they'd never work again. "On second thought I do believe I will need some help." He shrugged his shoulders, and forced a weak grin.

"Sure thing." Del stood up, stomped his feet a few times, and bent down to gently lift the stiffening body off of Will's legs. Del appeared to be frail, but his willowy height still retained an impressive degree of strength. He picked up the body with little effort and looked down at Will. "You need help?" Will rolled to a kneeling position, then to a squat and finally stood up. It went through his mind that the labor of just getting off the ground was taking longer as the weeks dragged by. Del slid his arms under Jimmy's, locking his fingers over his chest. Will took his feet. As the stump was pulled from the hole in the dirt, Will mashed the area with his foot. The stump was horrible to look at so both diverted their eyes, concentrating on the ground.

With Jack opening a trail for them through the maze of rotting tents, sleep holes, and hundreds of milling men, they made their way down to the road. Out of respect, the men generally made an effort to clear a path for those bearing the dead. However, as they passed, thousands of eyes took in the condition of the corpse, hoping the body had something of value, like usable clothing. In this instance, they were disappointed.

Upon reaching the road, they saw other bodies being laid out, side by side. Gently lowering the body, Will was handed a piece of string, a scrap of paper and a pencil stub. After printing Jimmy's name and unit on the paper he tied Jimmy's big toes together with the paper in between. Del muttered something under his breath and Will noticed his look of anguish.

Will needed to say something but managed only. "Bye Partner." There was anger in his voice, an anger that had been building from the time Jimmy was attacked.

Will was glad to get back to their sleep-hole. The smell of the camp was much worse down by the gates near the stream. Out of habit, he scanned the plot of trees over the top of the stockade. As bleak as it was, it afforded him a small sense of freedom. Squatting on his haunches he picked up the skillet and checked the sharpness of the handle while he let his mind drift back to the day he and Jimmy had arrived at Andersonville.

"I'll tell you one thing, Will." Jimmy had commented, "That pot, you stole, sure comes in handy. Don't imagine we'll be cookin' much in it, but it's a fine diggin' tool. I wonder how long it was before Johnny Reb found out it wasn't hangin' on his pack. Danged if I would have had the guts to just reach out and pick it off, like that. Say, did I tell you about Twyla?"

"Only twenty or thirty times," Will laughed. "But tell me again. I do believe that I am falling in love with her myself. In all honesty, is she as perfect as you make her out to be?"

"Damned right she is and I even like my future mother-in-law. Look at her picture again. Finest lookin' lady I ever met." He handed the small metal case, which he had opened, to Will.

"I must admit that she is that, but what the heck does she see in you?" Will had responded.

"Well, if you can't see my good looks and fine character, she can." Jimmy retorted. "Might come as a surprise to you, but I am considered a fine catch by the ladies of Willow Creek. You can take my word on that!"

"I guess, I'll have to 'cause I sure can't see it." Will smiled at the memory.

7

REVENGE AND JUSTICE

Will brought his mind back to the present. He tried to imagine what a fight with Rooster would be like. He couldn't see that it would be much of a fight at all. It was suicide, plain and simple. Why take him on? Bitterness firmed his resolve. Because he had to. He couldn't just let it ride.

He would take a minute to think of his home and family then get on with it. He pictured the farm. An ache was in his chest that had nothing to do with his physical condition. To sit at the kitchen table with them again, what he would give, to be there just one more time. He closed his eyes and remembered the last time, years ago. There had been steak, eggs, bread and milk, all you could hold. There was laughter too and later music. All the family and neighbors came in and Dad played the violin, Mom kept time thumping on a pan, and his younger brother Cole clapped his hands, stomped his feet and sang joyfully. He would probably never see them again. Maybe, after Rooster killed him, they would all see each other in heaven. He wished he was sure about that, but he had serious doubts. Where was God? How could He look down on this and not do something?

Will dug up the skillet and file he'd buried when leaving the she-bang. It would be a prize for someone, and there was no sense in putting temptation in the path of the weak. He ran his finger along the edge of the six-inch handle and then tested the end, which had been honed to a fairly sharp point. Ever since Rooster's attack on Jimmy, Will had been fashioning the skillet into a weapon. How effective it would be, he wasn't sure, but it was better than nothing. To get the pouch back would require more than just fists or talk. It would require a weapon, the deadlier the better. With luck, it might be enough. A lot of luck!

He thought about the pouch and its contents. The idea of the picture of Jimmy's girl, not to mention the harmonica, being in Rooster's possession, brought on a smoldering rage. He wished that he actually knew Twyla in the flesh and blood. He knew more about her then any woman he had ever met. He had so often listened to Jimmy talk about her, her family, his family, his hometown, and country. It was as if he had lived two lives. He had developed images of these people and places to the point that he felt that he was part of them. But it wasn't the same as looking into those green eyes that Jimmy told him about, with them looking back. Not the same as the touch of her hand, the sound of her voice or the smell of her hair. He had a need to talk to her, to explain what had happened. On the surface he knew he had done right by Jimmy but, deep down he had an abiding sense of guilt that would not go away. What would she think of him? Would she hate him for what he had done?

He was galled almost beyond endurance. Damn Rooster to hell! He gripped the borrowed file and started working on the handle with renewed fury. As he worked, those that shared the corner stopped by to pay their respects. It was clear they had thought a great deal of Jimmy. The loss of the harmonica was also a blow to them all. He thought of Cyrus. John Jay and Luke who's recent passing he mourned as well. Wiley and Curtis would probably not make it through another night. Good men, all. If they could die with dignity, so could he.

Rooster stretched, yawned and wiped the grit from his teeth with the back of his filthy hand. He gazed around the Raiders' tent at the piles of plunder. A smug smile crossed his face. It was like being a pirate, except on land. It was a good life. Well, it wasn't as good as being free, but it was a lot better to be a Raider then one of the other poor bastards. He picked up the boots he had "acquired" two days ago, brushed off some of the dirt with his sleeve and slipped them on. He was slightly irritated that they were a little large. The bum had not been as tall as Rooster's six foot three inches, nor did he have the weight, but one thing he did have was huge feet. "What the hell," Rooster exclaimed to no one in particular. "If anyone new comes in I'll look for socks today." Sitting on a small pile of loot, he fumbled around for his badge of authority, his hat. The hat itself wasn't much. The large orange feather stuck in the band made up for that and then some. He had no idea what kind of feather it was and didn't care. It made him *Rooster* and Rooster was boss. Although there were a few others that he grudgingly took orders from, in his own mind he was number one.

Before the hat he'd been called *Stick* from childhood, because he always carried a club on his belt. He hated his given name. Ian was a sissy name, and by God he was no sissy. After taking the hat away from the guy who was stupid enough to put up a fight for it, he decided it fit his style. Someone said he looked like a rooster and the name stuck. He ran the edges of the feather between his fingers to smooth it out and set the hat aside.

He'd worked on his image like an actor. Perfecting his hunched shoulders, charging walk and the menacing facial expressions aimed at telling everyone to get the hell out of his way. He was well satisfied.

He took out the leather pouch he'd taken off that little punk who had jumped him during that big brawl a while ago. It took a spell to catch him alone but getting even was worth the wait. Loosening the thong he dumped the contents into his hand. The shiny harmonica, he set aside, and concentrated on the small metal case. He opened it and squinted at the smiling face. It was as if she was smiling at him. Damn fine lookin' bitch, he thought, with a leer. He continued gazing at the face wondering what the rest of her looked like. Couldn't tell by the frilly stuff and the high neck of her dress. He had a soft spot for the long hair that flowed down almost to her lap. He pictured her body as flawless. Well maybe with a heart shaped beauty mark on her ass. He rubbed the picture on his crotch, thinking what she would feel like. He laughed out loud and closed the case. He slid it into the pouch and picked up the harmonica, running it back and forth a few times past his lips. He knew nothing of music and didn't care a hoot. It was having it that mattered. He placed it in the pouch and tightened the thong, then tied it around his neck. Placing the hat on his head at a jaunty angle, he stood and stretched again.

Mole came scurrying into the tent, slowing down to let his eyes adjust to the dim light. Spotting Rooster, he made his way through the piles of plunder to stop in front of him.

"Rooster, you got big trouble." Said Mole, grinning from ear to ear. "Some jasper's lookin' fer a fight with ya."

He was somewhat surprised. Nobody looked for trouble with the Rooster. However, Mole was one of his best scouts so it must be true. "Aye?" A grin broke out on his face, exposing the yellow-brown teeth. "Tell me about this bum, me Lad."

Mole puffed himself up. He liked feeling important and he always enjoyed bringing news that meant trouble. "Well, let's see, I'd say he's been here a long while, 'bout my height and skinny as a snake. I'd go so far as to say you could blow him over with a small sneeze." He finished with a wheezing cackle.

Rooster felt a little disappointed. He could use a good fight to get his blood pumping, but this didn't sound like anything that he could work up a sweat over. "Anythin' else?"

"Yup, you better be careful, 'cause he's packin' a pot." he added, his laughter ending with a spate of coughing. He wiped the spittle from his mouth with the back of his hand.

"You wouldn't be a lie'n to me, would ya now, cause if ya are I'll bust yur damn fool head." Rooster looked down with a glowering look. He enjoyed seeing the little man flinch.

"Honest! A damn pot! Really, Rooster, I wouldn't lie to you, honest." Sudden fear clutched at his stomach. To lie to Rooster would bring consequences he didn't want to think about. "Honest." he repeated hoarsely, "He's down by the crick." Mole took in the hooded eyes with the bushy eyebrow that ran clear across the bridge of the large nose. Rooster's hair was a filthy mat mashed down over his forehead by the ever present hat. Briar-like beard covered the lower part of his face. The feral quality of the man sent a shiver up Mole's back. He felt a little sorry for what was going to happen to the dumb fool that was calling him out.

"By damn, this I gotta see." Rooster roared. He picked up his club, checked the knife in his scabbard and started toward the opening in the tent. He hunched his head down and bulled his way forward in spite of the crowd outside. People either got out of his way or were trampled, clubbed, stabbed or all three.

As Rooster exited the tent he paused to let his eyes adjust to the light. This was good, he thought rising to the occasion. It would set an example. Scare the hell out of them. It was a good idea to put the fear in them, from time to time, to let them know how things were around here.

The word had spread like wildfire and he plowed his way through a gathering crowd.

Raiders were moving in to give a hand. They had heard rumors that a new bunch, calling themselves Regulators, were planning a fight, and this might be it. Some of the Raider big fish had come to watch the fun. Rooster, who was considered number three, thought that this might be just what he needed to raise himself in the ranks. Maybe all the way to number one. Course, he guessed this wouldn't be much of a test.

Will had been sitting cross-legged, looking out over the prison. Any other time, any other place, it would have been a mighty fine day. A brilliant blue sky, a few white clouds passing with a slight breeze and low humidity, for a change, made it a day to be enjoyed to its fullest. His eyes took in the full length of the prison. From his position at one upper end of its rectangle his view was uninterrupted down the slope to the so called stream. He had heard the original name was Sweet Water Creek. Poisoned by the filth of thirty-five thousand men it no longer deserved the name. His gaze moved on up to the farther palisade. "How many men to the acre?" He mused. Taking into account the land lost to the dead line and the expanding muck of the stream he figured it had to be two thousand or more. Many of them were too far gone to ever get up on their feet again. In the brilliant sky a bird approaching the prison veered away at the wall as if the very sky above it was tainted. He took in the small plot of ground that had been his home with Jimmy, Jack and Del. Would he be coming back? He had to get everything in order just in case. He hadn't been sure about it when Jimmy had died but he knew now that he wanted to live, whatever that life had in store for him. He had to do this thing in the smartest way he could come up with. There would be no charging straight into this cannon fire. No, sir!

Somewhere out there was Rooster. Will's mood darkened as he contemplated the "New Yaarkers" and the extra misery they had brought to this place. If only they weren't so well organized or, on the other hand, if the rest of the prisoners were, something could be done. He had heard about the Regulators but had been too involved with his own problems to pay attention. They were planning something but he did not know what, or when. The safe thing to do would be to wait for them, but waiting was something he was no good at. Not while Rooster had that picture. God, that was too much. Damn that son of a bitch. He can't be let to get away with it. I've got to either pay him back or die trying. Will checked the sharpness of the skillet handle and although he would have preferred a better edge, he was pleased with the point. Turning to Del and Jack he told them of his intentions. He was not surprised to find that they were a little less than optimistic about the whole idea. He realized that he had committed himself by telling them his plan and there could be no changing his mind now.

Del exclaimed, "That's just plain suicide, Will. Don't you do it."

Jack didn't say anything, but his mind was racing. He had lost one of his best friends, and now he was looking at losing a second. The idea that Will would stand a chance against Rooster was beyond his imagination. He looked at Will's skinny legs and arms. He could almost see through the man's skin! But looking into his face he suddenly wasn't so sure. He could see determination in the set of his mouth and something fearful burned deep in his eyes.

Del went on quietly. "This is damn serious. You are in no shape to go up against that jackass. I talked to a guy who has seen him fight and he is one ornery cuss, in good shape and big as a barn. He likes to maim and murder." Temporarily running out of words he hoped Will would say something, but he remained silent. "Stop and think Will. I've seen you a workin' on that skillet handle, but I was hopin' that you would get some sense. I guess you haven't."

"Wait it out, Will. The Regulators are up to something." Jack implored.

"I can't, Jack. It'll just end up like before and I'll be in worse shape than I am now. In that last little fracas, we got our butts kicked and hardly anyone lifted a finger to help. Besides, this is personal, between him and me."

"If you're set on doing this, I sure hope you have come up with some sort of plan. Just how do you intend to tackle the impossible?" asked Jack.

"Well, I don't see much chance either, all else being even. The only thing I've come up with is that, if I can get him into the mud, it might give me a tiny edge."

"That's a thought." Del paused mulling it over. "It has possibilities. Just how do you intend to make it happen?"

"Now that you bring it up, I figure to get him so damn mad that he goes right in all by himself. He's not exactly a thinking man. If I can lure him to a place away from the boardwalks, then get him really riled, I bet he'll just come straight across at me.

"Somehow, the thought of that fella a chargin' right at anyone makes me want to wet my pants, and by God, I ain't ashamed to tell it." Jack exclaimed. A chill went through his body. "I did hear one thing sort of queer. Seems Rooster has a habit of standin' on his tiptoes just before he charges in. Just a quirk but, anyway, it may be helpful." he added.

"Thanks, Jack. I'll keep that in mind. Maybe I should try it, I could use some height." Will replied, with a sardonic wink.

"We should get what help we can. When you plan on doing this?" Del asked. He was amazed that Will could joke, at such a time. There was a shadow of Jimmy in his tone.

"I figure I'm in as good a shape as I'm going to be so no reason to put it off. If you boys want to keep me company let's get it over with. Send Samuel down to the creek. Have him yell that I'm on my way to stomp Rooster like a damn bug."

Del nodded, smiling. Shaking his head, he immediately rose and headed for a nearby group of men to their right. What the hell are we getting ourselves into? he thought.

"As much as I dread this, I wouldn't miss it for the world. Just maybe we'll get a chance to help out. I sure wish I was packin' a gun though." Jack responded.

"As long as you're wishin,' make it a big gun." Will replied. "In fact, we could use a passel of um."

"Hell, with our luck, they'd be empty, and we'd have to use them like clubs." Added Jack with a wry smile. "What we need is a lot of good luck, at this point. Let's hope we get it. I'll help Del pick up some help on the way down. Jimmy was known by a lot of the men and well liked. I bet we can get a good number of fellows to back up your play. Lots of them have been hurt by Raiders since that last set-to."

They got to their feet. Jack angled quickly off to the left to spread the word while Will began deliberately making his way down the main path. He barely noticed the growing number of grim men heading down the hill after him. Intent on performing the task at hand, he felt very little for a man headed to what well might be his own end. He had seen hundreds die, some quick and some hard. Jimmy was right. The main thing was to go quick, and he would go quick if Rooster got a hold of him and that was a fact.

Samuel met him part way down. "I give them the word, Will. Jesus. I'll be there if'n I can be of help. I see some of the boys are a comin."

By the time he reached the quagmire, several thousand of his fellows had joined him. Many who didn't get the word followed out of curiosity. Most had good reason to hate the Raiders and, as the word spread like wildfire, they were now more than willing to get involved.

As Del and Jack came up behind him, Will said, "Last thing, if it goes bad and I don't make it, get word to my folks and explain to Twyla somehow." Both nodded.

Out of the corner of his eye, he spotted Mole threading his way quickly toward him across the creek. His eyes shifted to the man behind him pushing straight through the crowd, sending men scrambling to get out of his way. He had seen Rooster many times at a distance and when the brute hadn't known he was there. This was some different. He had to be the ugliest, meanest looking hombre Will had ever seen and swinging the nastiest club. He probably had a knife somewhere too. He forced himself to stand a little straighter and his stomach muscles tensed in anticipation. Too late to change his mind now. Gotta keep calm, look for the openings. Try not to wet your pants, he told himself with a grim smile, and take him with you if you go.

The Regulators within the milling crowd quickly assessed the situation. They had planned on a showdown within a few days, but this might work to their advantage. Clubs, knives and any other improvised weapon they had been able to garner were hastily produced and several hundred of them pushed toward the lone figure near the center of the prison.

Mole pointed out Will, across the quagmire, and then moved off to the side. No way in hell did he want to get involved in any fight. Just a good spot to watch from. Rooster would sure clean this gent's plow. Mole giggled.

As Will watched Rooster's approach, he heard Del warning him. "Watch Rooster's feet and don't panic if Rooster attacks screaming. Don't git rattled, Will."

Don't get rattled. That was a good one. He could feel the weakness in his legs. It took an effort to keep them from shaking. He nodded to let Del know that he had heard.

Stopping with legs spread, clutching his club, Rooster knew how he looked and it brought a sinister smile to his face. He glared across at Will and was sorely disappointed. Mole was right, a sneeze would blow him away. He also noticed, with some surprise, that this fellow didn't seem exactly overwhelmed either. No emotion showed on his stern features and he stood poised and relaxed as if he was at some tea party. "You lookin' to get your ass kicked?" Rooster yelled.

In the following stillness Will answered with a laugh. "Hell, I thought you'd be bigger, from what I've been told. You don't look like much you sorry sack o' shit!" He was thankful that his voice sounded normal. Get him mad. Watch for an opening. "Looks like you brought your friends to back up your play. You'll need them."

Rooster was so taken aback he couldn't think of anything to say. He finally turned and sputtered, "You Laddies back off. Rooster don't need nobody!" He advanced several paces closer to the spreading mud. "Now what the hell's got you so riled up, you little piss ant?"

"I came to get that pouch you have around your neck. I figure you can save both of us a lot of trouble by throwing it over to me." Will yelled back, with a smile.

"You ain't the one I took it off." Rooster sneered.

"No, he passed on this morning and I'm here to claim it for him." Will's mouth was smiling, but his eyes were bleak as death. "He asked me to send your sorry ass to hell if you won't give it back."

"Tough." yelled Rooster. "What makes you think I'll jist be a givin' it to ya?" Rooster felt himself getting irritated. Damn little runt talking back like that. Nobody talks that way to me.

"Because, you stupid ass, if I have to come over there, I'm goin' to kick your fat butt from one end of this here place to the other. I plan on gougin' out yer eyes and bitin' off yer nose as well. Make it easy on yourself. Toss it over," Will retorted with calm assurance. People on both sides started to laugh. He noticed that Rooster had advanced another three steps. He was almost far enough to start sinking in. It had to be soon or he was bound to catch on.

People laughing. Laughing at me, Rooster! Nobody gets away with that, no way. Without thinking, he stood on tip toes, the telltale habit deliberately acquired to make himself appear even taller.

Will laughed to see it. "You gonna do one of those toe dances for us?"

The runt laughing at him rattled Rooster further. He was either very brave or an idiot. He took four more steps toward his antagonist before more laughter from behind caused him to swing around, silencing the mob with his vicious glare. Amazingly the ground held as he pivoted back, rose on his toes again and lunged forward screaming, arms out, fist and club swinging. He plowed towards Will with giant strides through the mud. It looked as though sheer momentum would carry him across the ooze.

When Will saw Rooster raising up on his toes again, he shifted the skillet, holding the rim with the handle pointing straight ahead. Not a good grip but the best he could do. He too moved into the mud a ways but then stopped, stepping back to firmer ground. Let's see how far he's going to get, he thought, as he watched the man plowing through the mud. He had passed the narrow stream, and was again in the deep morass now less then ten feet away.

Rooster charging forward, eyes locked on Will, was oblivious to the treacherous ground. Seeing him hesitate, it went through his mind that the little runt was turning chicken. He tried to move faster. Gotta git' em he thought. Without warning he was caught fast, his left boot stuck out of sight in the mud. At last aware of his peril, he was unwilling to put his right foot in jeopardy as well. It was stomping air in a wild fury, trying to keep him from falling. His arms were out, flailing for balance. Finally in desperation his right foot went down and with a sucking sound, his left came flying out of the imprisoned boot. He was propelled forward by his own impetus completely off balance. His mind ordered his arms in to protect his body, but they were still swinging wildly, out of control. Too late, the repositioning of the skillet registered in his mind and the runt was moving toward him. He was falling forward, unable to protect himself, eyes locked on the point of the handle as it streaked forward and became lost in his midsection. He pitched forward into the mud. Will was so taken by surprise he lost his grip and moved a step backward to keep from being caught under Rooster's falling body.

Rooster's disbelieving mind was trying to make sense of the pain in his stomach. He was the Rooster, this couldn't be happening to him. He managed to push himself up onto his knees and looked down at the source of the pain. That damn skillet, what was it doing there? His fingers feebly plucked at the rim but it was stuck deep between his ribs. He realized the handle was inside him. No! no! he thought wildly. He looked up into Will's smiling face and felt the pouch jerked from his neck. The last thing he heard on earth was Will's easy voice thanking him for bringing the pouch and wishing him an eternity in hell. He fell sideways into the muck. Gripping the pouch with his teeth, Will pushed him onto his back and, placing a bare foot on his chest he reached down with both hands and pulled out his skillet.

At that moment Jack grabbed Will from behind, yelling in his ear. "We got to get out of here, the war is on. Come on." He half dragged Will, who was suddenly aware of dozens of fighting figures around him. Hundreds more were moving in to do battle. For a brief moment Will looked back at the body. Already it had been stripped bare and two men were fighting over a boot. Another, was on his knees, digging for the other lodged in the mud. The hat was disappearing into the crowd. The new owner, holding it on his head to prevent it from being snatched off by reaching hands.

"Damn, Will, ya done it. Ya done it good!" shouted Jack, half pushing, half carrying Will, from the fight. "No time to get yourself killed at this point, the Regulators have taken 'em on." Will tried to look back but Jack was having none of it. "Get back to camp, then look."

Del was bringing up the rear, moving up the hill backwards, to protect the other two from attack.

They had really rattled a wasp's nest. Overcoming their surprise, some of the Raiders were trying to get to Will. They were headed off by Regulators in numbers never faced before and were driven off. Those coming closest to Will and Jack were struck down by Del, who was weaving from side to side with both fists up and ready. He was grinning like a kid at the circus and crowing at the Raiders to "Come and get some." Not too many took him up on his offer and those that did were beaten back with well placed fists. Thousands of prisoners, seeing the shifting tide, joined the Regulators in the rout.

Once in their camp, all three stood looking back. It seemed like everyone able to fight was involved. Panic had set in among the Rebs and the cannons were aimed at the seething mass of prisoners.

Thankfully, cooler heads prevailed. Realizing the threat was not directed at them, they "stood down." Those that had seen the activity around the cannons retreated from the melee, but charged in again after the threat passed. In minutes the Raiders were either beaten or running, the triumphant Regulators in hot pursuit.

Will sank down to a sitting position, still clutching the pouch and skillet. Del carefully took the weapon from him and wiped the handle in the dirt to rid it of blood.

"I'd say, partner, that you did real good. Damnedest fight I ever saw! I wouldn't have given a plug nickel for your chances but, by damn, you sure pulled it off!" Del was beside himself with excitement. He looked down at the skillet, shaking his head with amazement.

"I must admit, I'm a mite surprised myself." Will replied tiredly. "Rooster was most obliging." He looked down to make sure he hadn't wet his pants and wasn't surprised to see his hands shaking. He carefully opened the pouch. He was almost afraid to look at the contents. Would the picture still be there and, if so, would it be undamaged? His fingers felt the familiar shape of the case and he took it from the pouch. Fingering the clasp, the case opened, and the smiling face was looking back into his. A feeling of relief spread over him when he realized he had saved her from Rooster. Del peered over his shoulder and murmured "Ah yes, she's still there. You know, Will, she is one fine looking lady. Of course my girl Betsy is too. Sure wish I had a picture of her to look at from time to time. Do you have a lady waiting for you?"

Will thought about that for a moment, taking in the glorious brawl going on before him. He debated whether to mention Rosella. He decided against it. She belonged to him in a quiet peaceful spot in his memory, not out in the open in this awful place. "No, not actually waiting for me, but I do have a lady. Some day, maybe, I'll tell you about her, or not." It brought a smile to his face. The strain of the last days and all the unaccustomed activity was catching up with him. The adrenaline that had carried him through against all odds had left him exhausted and faint. Put this out of your mind, he thought.

He lay back against the she-bang and his thoughts turned to the images Del's question had stirred. He drifted back to that day. Musta' been five years or so ago. Seemed like a lifetime. It had been a hot day and they had been riding for hours. Will was riding point, perhaps ten minutes ahead of the main body of riders, eyes scanning the bleak surroundings for the Mexican bandits who had run off a bunch of cattle from the Circle R. It had been a damn long day and they had found nothing but the trail. Off to the left was a narrow band of trees, suggesting water, so he reined in that direction. Mud shanties lined the base of a hill in the valley beyond. A few minutes later he entered the cool shade. His horse smelled the water and moved down to the edge of the stream. He was surprised at its size, perhaps twenty feet across and a foot deep. A good size piece of water for this area of Texas. His horse lowered its head and began drinking. He was in the process of swinging his leg over the saddle when he caught movement up stream.

She was bathing, facing away from him. Her long black hair shimmering in the dappled sun. She was unaware of his presence as he resettled in the saddle. Water droplets cascaded from her hair, down the curves of her back, over the round cheeks below and down her legs. Will was mesmerized. He sat watching her as minutes passed. As if she could feel his eyes on her, she turned and looked at him. He had already taken in her breasts before her hands hid them from sight. He saw the black triangle below her waist before she turned and moved further up stream where the water narrowed and she could lower herself waist deep. There was no fear in her eyes as she looked back at him, but caution, as she sized him up. He had noticed a yellow flower in her hair behind her right ear. She was beautiful. As a matter of fact, she was the prettiest thing he had ever seen. Remembering the other riders, who would be coming through the trees any time now, he moved his horse toward her, trying to signal that others would be coming. Evidently she understood. She nodded her head and with a faint smile, faced him briefly. Then turning, she swiftly entered an overhang of branches and debris and was soon out of sight. Noticing her clothes on a rock across the stream, he rode over and reaching down, gathered them up. Riding to the point where she had disappeared, he held them down. A small brown arm reached out and took them. He was looking into her face, not three feet away. God, what a face. He could have stared into those brown eyes for hours.

"Gracias, Senor," she murmured. The small smile sent a small chill of excitement through him.

"My pleasure, Ma'am," he replied, tipping his wide brimmed hat in a sweeping gesture. He realized that he was grinning from ear to ear, and then her face was gone.

He straightened in his saddle and moved away from her. His eyes caught a yellow flash and he saw the flower drifting down the stream. He reached down, picking it out of the water and removing his hat, placed it carefully in the band. The other riders entered the shade by the stream to cool off and water their horses. Will waved to them and then rode out of the trees to resume the hunt.

As he rode away he wished he knew her name. Removing his hat he looked at the small yellow flower. Rose. That's a good name. No, it should be more than just Rose. Roseanne? Rosily? Rosella? Yes, he liked the sound of that. Rosella. He placed the hat back on his head. Her face and naked body were etched in his mind. All these years later, he could still see her as if it were yesterday.

While Will dozed, Del had stretched out on his back, looking up at the late afternoon sky. He thought of Betsy, of his family and the life he had left behind. It had been over a year since he had been home and at times he was so homesick that he almost cried. It was damn hard to keep a brave face through all of this mess and he resented the fact that he couldn't keep his mind off food. He was starving, damn it! He looked over at Will and shuddered to think that he would look like that within a few months. He'd given up a good life to impress his father by going to war. Well, this wasn't doing anything along that line, and that was for sure. He'd pictured himself as the gallant hero returning from the war. Tales to tell, medals to show off, and maybe a very small war wound. Betsy would be impressed. So might his father, a big man in the railroad, driven to be successful at everything he tried. Del had never felt he measured up to his taciturn and undemonstrative father's expectations. His mother had tried to make it up to him with extra love and affection, but he had longed for love and respect from his father, as well. Being a war hero may have turned it all around, but not starving to death in this miserable cesspool.

When Will awoke and joined his friends, both Del and Jack couldn't avoid smiling at his revelation and at the lengthy preoccupation that had followed. In all their talk he had never mentioned a woman.

Finally Jack asked. "Is that all you're going to tell us? Ain't ya going to tell us anything about her?"

"That's it," replied Will with a lasting grin. Both seemed disappointed but let the subject drop. It was nice to see Will smile again.

Most of the prison seemed back to normal as evening fell, there were a few still heading back to their she-bangs and some goin's on over by the Raider tent, too far away to make out.

To everyone's disappointment, the next day Wirz decided the prison was too dangerous for the wagon to enter, so he withheld rations for the day.

One thing the morning did bring was a visitor. Limber Jim, from the Regulators, stopped by to see how Will was doing. Under his arm he carried a blanket and some pieces of clothing, including a nearly new Great Coat. "Will Morgan," he exclaimed, as he sat down by the trio. "You put on one great show yesterday."

"Thanks, glad you liked it," Will replied smiling. "However, if the S.O.B. hadn't thrown himself onto my skillet handle, I doubt if we would be having this conversation. As I recall you're hooked up with the Regulators. Wish they'd been around for that last try we had when we got our butts soundly kicked."

"Well, I think you facing up to Rooster lit a fire under some of those boys who might just have sat this one out too. A lot of people thought that bunch was unbeatable. You proved them wrong! Actually, one of the reasons I came to see you is to see how you feel about getting involved in what we do next. The Rebs have what's left of the Raiders in a stockade on the outside. The thought is to have a trial and arrive at some sort of justice. Right now, we have men looking up those that have a claim against them or have witnessed their crimes. The main idea being that we don't want any of them not held accountable. Are you interested in helping out?"

"Sure, I don't seem to have much on my calendar these days. We were planning on digging our sleep hole a little larger and kind of sprucing up the looks of our digs but aside from that, nothing comes to mind," Will said, smiling.

"You boys in too?" Jim asked.

"Sure thing," Jack answered. "We'd be right pleased."

"Great," replied Jim, rising to his feet, "We'll be in touch. "Oh, by the way, this blanket is for you, sort of a token of appreciation for the show. The clothes too. I figure your attire needs some upgrading. A man of your importance should look the part."

"What importance are you talking about?" Will asked, puzzled.

"You have to be kidding. You're the talk of the camp. Which reminds me, keep an eye on your back. I'm not sure we have all the Raiders identified at this point."

"We'll watch his back," Del replied.

"See ya boys." Jim turned and slowly made his way along the narrow path leading down the hill.

"Jim, thanks a lot," Will called after him. Jim waved his arm in reply.

"That's a damn fine blanket and coat. When cold weather comes on they may just save our skins," Jack observed, running his hand back and forth over the nap. "What say you don your new duds, and we stow our stuff and take a mosey around to show you off. Wouldn't mind seeing what's doin' down at that there big tent neither."

Will dressed in the new cloths looking kind of sheepish. He had to hitch them up with an old strip of cloth. The other two rolled up their belongings in the new blanket in their sleep pit. Then, together, they headed down the hill.

As Jack followed Will and Del down the slope he couldn't get over the fact that Will was still alive. He had felt the hair stand out on the back of his neck when Will confronted Rooster. He tried to imagine what was going through Will's mind then, and couldn't. Bravest damn thing he had ever seen. He looked at Will's skinny little form in the baggy clothes ahead of him and the temptation to run forward and give him a bear hug almost overwhelmed him. Whatever happened, these men would always be his family. He had never had a home life. No father, that he remembered, and his Mama passin' on when he was young. Living on the streets doing odd jobs to keep himself together he'd had little schooling. The army was the first time he had felt like he belonged anywhere. The only close friends he'd ever had were the two in front of him now, and Jimmy of course. Somehow, he still felt blessed.

A week passed with no word as to the fate of the captured Raiders. Several thousand new-comers arrived in that time, most from the army of the Potomac. The remaining Raiders inside the prison were busy recruiting large numbers of fellow "New Yaarkers" from this group. The Regulators were preparing to take steps before they were right back where they started. This volatile situation could explode at any moment given the right circumstances.

The following morning, six of the worst offenders were marched into the prison by a contingent of Rebel soldiers. Thousands of prisoners gathered around amid a chorus of curses. They forced the prospective Raiders to the back.

In the middle of this Limber Jim stepped up and took charge, raising his hands for quiet. A silence fell over the camp. "It is proposed we put these men on trial. I want twelve men who have arrived within the last day or two to serve as a jury."

Several hands went up nearby and twelve men were soon selected.

"Now any man who has witnessed crimes committed by these prisoners, come forward for testimony.

Over the next twenty minutes, those wishing to give witness against the Raiders were assembled and assigned a number. A Yank, who had been a lawyer before the war, was assigned to be Judge. Another, was assigned to defend them. He wasn't overly enthusiastic about the job, but said he would do the best he could. Over the following three hours, witnesses were brought forward to speak of the atrocities these men had carried out. As each story came out, the current of anger throughout the prison increased. Limber Jim spent most of his time quieting them down. Any attempt by the Defender brought jeers and raised fists. As the last man finished, Limber Jim asked if anyone wanted to speak in their defense. It almost caused a riot. Needless to say no one stepped forward. The Jury members huddled and after several minutes of talk, faced the throng. "We find the defendants guilty and that they should be hanged!"

A roar of approval resounded off the walls of the prison. The six were hustled out the gates. Most of the day was spent in celebration. The prospective Raiders kept a low profile.

Just where and when the hanging was to take place had not yet been decided. Most were in favor of hanging them inside the prison. It was felt that this would give those that had been abused the opportunity to see their assailants *get what's comin' to 'em.* It would set an example for those still inclined toward mayhem as well.

Finally, the next morning a messenger came from outside, where Limber Jim and the head of the Regulators, Sgt. Keys were consulting with the Reb command. He carried an order to assemble a group including Will's original company, about seventy, of whom remained of the original hundred, or so. They were to stand guard over the carpenters that were to build the scaffold inside the compound. The prisoners were to be hanged that very day. Those that were able were hastily organized and marched down the hill. At the end of the road leading from the South Gate was a large open space used for the distribution of rations. This was the place designated for the erection of the scaffold. Thousands were already taking up positions around the square. Will's group, which was protecting the east side, was hard pressed to keep the line. Roughly ten thousand were directly around the site, with the remaining twenty thousand taking up positions on the north and south slopes. The best views from the inside were at the upper ends of the stockade in the middle. These areas were in the direct line of fire, should the confederate guns open up, but excitement overcame caution and they filled up quickly.

The carpenters arrived with materials to build the scaffold and set to work. If it had not been for the men guarding the square, the materials would have been stolen before they hit the ground. The need for building materials and fuel for fires was acute throughout the prison. They were down to digging up roots far below the ground for their fires.

Scores of Raiders gathered around in sullen groups, cursing and threatening those assisting in the execution of their comrades. If most of his company had not carried clubs, and been more than willing to use them, Will knew that this job would turn ugly real quick. To make matters worse, he was recognized, so received additional verbal abuse. It was reassuring to have Del on his left and Jack on his right. Both were in better shape than he and would put up a good fight, if called upon. From their positions they could look out upon the vast mosaic of faces on the slopes. They were so tightly grouped that no soil could be seen.

The carpenters worked swiftly and finished up their project around noon. It was a rather simple, but effective, scaffold. It consisted of two posts about fifteen feet tall with a large beam across the top. Braces at ground level supported the posts. One end of two wide boards rested on cleats approximately seven feet up on the inside of each post. The boards extended to the center of the scaffold where they were propped from beneath. The two props had holes through the bottom ends with a short length of rope running through the holes. When the ropes were pulled these two support boards fell away allowing the wide floor boards to drop. A crude ladder was attached and the scaffold was ready.

As the construction neared completion the excitement grew intense. Outside, the Confederates were taking no chances on a general uprising. The rebel artillery was in place outside both ends of the stockade, loaded with grapeshot and ready at a moment's notice. The number four men held the lanyard cords, ready to fire. A contingent of rebel infantry with bayonets fixed was ready behind a small cavalry squad outside the gate. All the hangers-on from the rebel camp, clerks, cooks, teamsters and slaves were in attendance. They were packed into the pigeon roosts, where the guards stood, shoulder to shoulder, peering over the top of the wall and crowded around the cannons.

It was a terribly hot day and with so many people packed together, particularly around the square, Will was afraid he would pass out. His swollen joints were not used to standing so long in one place and the pain was a constant reminder of his poor health.

Sgt. Keys took up his position in the square along with Limber Jim, Dick McCullough and two others that Will did not recognize. The crowd parted and Ned Johnson, Tom Larkin, and Sgt. Goodie entered, carrying white sacks that the rebels used for bringing in rations. Will could feel the crowd ease forward and he dug in his heels and leaned into them. The South Gate opened and Gen. Wirz rode in, dressed in a once white uniform and riding a white horse. Will wondered why Wirz bothered to get dressed up for the occasion. His clothes were rumpled and dirty and he rode his horse like a sack of potatoes. Will felt sorry for the poor animal, having to carry a vermin like Wirz.

In his guttural German accent, Wirz addressed the crowd: "Brizners, I return to you dese men so goot as I got dem. You have tried dem yourselves and found dem guilty. I haf notting to do wid it. I vash my hands of effreting connected wit dem. Do wit dem as you like, and may Gott haf mercy on you and on dem. Garts, about face! Vorwarts, march." He then turned and rode toward the gate.

How could a person, so inept, be given the power to cause so much misery and death? Too bad he wasn't joining the Raiders. He surely deserved it.

The six men were marched in by the guards and turned over to Sgt.

Keys. They appeared to be in a state of shock as they looked up at the towering scaffold. For the first time the realization of their impending death sank into their minds. Until that moment they obviously had thought the threat of hanging was a bluff and maintained a facade of bravado. It didn't last long now.

"Oh my God, no. Please, no," moaned one. Their legs became weak and they slumped down. "You Lads don't really mean to be a hangin' us up there!" cried another.

"Just watch us," Keys answered grimly. After several minutes of sobbing and pleading for mercy, one spoke up. "Quiet down boys, let the preacher do the talk' for us."

The preacher had followed the men into the square but had remained in the background with his face lowered, reading the Good Book. Stepping forward he closed the book and looked out upon the multitude. In a firm voice he began to plead for the lives of the condemned, who looked out at the crowd to see if the preacher's words were having the desired effect. The assembled mass of prisoners had been very quiet since the departure of Wirz, and they strained to hear the words of the preacher. When those nearest comprehended what the preacher was saying, a swelling wave of voices rose to yell. "No, no, hang em! Hang em! Hang em!"

One of the Raiders, a short stocky man by the name of Curtis, ripped off his hat and threw it on the ground screaming, "I'll die this way first!" He lowered his head and charged the line. Those to Will's right moved to head him off but they were too late. Several trying to hold the line attempted to stop him with clubs, but in the confusion, only managed to knock him to his knees. With great effort he got to his feet and plunged into the mass of onlookers. Several Regulators followed him into the chanting crowd.

Fearing the situation was about to explode Will linked arms with Del and Jack and they held their positions. Within seconds the line was re-established. Limber Jim was able to stop another charge.

From the top of the stockade where Wirz had gone to get a better view, the vast movement of men struck fear in his mind. Assuming this was the long dreaded attack on the stockade, he started screaming at the gun crews, "Fire, fire." His captain, realizing the movement was away from the walls and not a threat, did not carry out the order. However, those prisoners in a direct line with the canisters swept to the sides. Wirz was in a panic but after consulting with several officers, calmed down and returned to his viewing position. Will had never seen so much confusion, but just as fast as it had started, it ended. Curtis, who had fled toward the muddy creek had temporarily managed to elude pursuit. Soon, he was met by a determined group that dragged him back to the square, kicking and screaming curses.

Realizing, at last, that there was no way out, the six mounted the scaffold without further resistance. Sgt. Keys announced that they had five minutes to make any last statement. All six began shouting at once, calling out to friends in the crowd, as to the disposition of their ill-gotten possessions. The preacher made a feeble attempt to guide the conversations to their salvation, but he was ignored. In despair, he put the Good Book under his arm and left the square.

"Times up," Keys barked.

Sacks were placed over their heads, and then the ropes. Several cringed at the feel of the rope, and again, legs sagged. At Keys' command two men stepped forward and jerked the short ropes and the walkway dropped. The six plummeted to the ends of their ropes. DeLaney, however, only stopped momentarily, as the rope broke he hit the ground unconscious. Keys rushed forward, knelt down and proclaimed that "DeLaney is still alive!" The sack was removed, the rope cut and water was thrown in his face until consciousness returned.

"Where am I? Am I in the other world?" he asked, bewildered.

Limber Jim muttered. "No, but you will be soon." He reset the props. As realization set in, DeLaney began to beg. "Oh my God, don't put me up there again. God has spared my life. He wants you to be merciful to me."

Limber Jim bent over, picked the man up and handed him up to Tom Larkin, who had replaced the rope. Taking the sack from Jim, he pulled it down over DeLaney's head, adjusted the knot and jumped to the ground. The supports were not set with the finesse of the first time and Jim had to wrench the support boards free with his shoulder. The platform fell and the last of the six was on his way. Just where they were going, no one knew for sure, but the vast majority had one place in mind.

As soon as the bodies were cut down, a race was on for the wood. Del managed to grab the two support boards, as dozens of hands had the scaffold gone in a matter of minutes.

Soon, the rest of the captured Raiders, were ushered in. Neither Will, nor his friends knew what was planned for this group. Two lines were quickly formed and it became evident that they would run the gauntlet. Men in the lines were waving clubs, of various sizes and shapes, and screams of anger rose in an almost animal-like frenzy. Will looked at Del and Jack, but they shook their heads. They wanted no part of it and neither did Will. He felt that what punishment they received, they had probably earned, however he was not of a mind to administer it. Keeping an eye out for anyone sneaking up on them they started back. As they neared their shebang a howl went up as the first of the Raiders ran through the shower of clubs. How many died from their injuries, Will didn't know, but he had no feeling of compassion. The misery they had inflicted on hundreds of poor souls, unable to protect themselves, overshadowed anything they were receiving now.

"I do believe that now would be a good time to kill us some lice." Del exclaimed. "I hate them as much as I do the Raiders, and we have the wood to build ourselves a little fire with enough to last a month."

Within minutes, they were naked, and Del had a small fire started. Carefully, so as not to damage the thin material, they took turns passing the clothes over the small flame, delighting in the death of thousands of lice. As there were thousands still lurking in their beards and hair, it would be only a matter of days before they were covered again, but if felt good to reduce the numbers, if only for a time.

Over the next several days, remnants of the Raider group were rounded up and suitable punishment administered. This usually consisted of a swat, or two, with a large paddle. The number of swats varied, depending on the crimes they had committed. Some of the Raiders who had curried favor with the guards, bribing them with their stolen loot took the opportunity to denounce their allegiance to the Union and signed papers of loyalty to the Confederacy. It brought some satisfaction to Will to see many returned to prison with their new clothes and blankets, only to be robbed of these possessions. He would have preferred to have never seen them again for they continued to be a problem. The Rebs, evidently, had found them worthless also.

8

PROVIDENCE SPRING

Will stood looking down into the depths of the hole, his eyes adjusting to the darkness of the bottom, hoping to see the reflection off of water. Nothing. Dread pressed down on him as it always did when he realized that he would have to go down again. What a person would do for a drink of clean water! Their only containers for collecting water were the one small ill used frying pan and some scraps of poncho that leaked too much to hold rain water long. With strict rationing a filled pan would be enough for a day and a half or so, for the three of them. They could only use the pan to dig when it was empty.

Will picked up the empty pan and threw it into the hole. Gripping the rope he lowered himself down, his bare feet searching for the familiar foot holes. Carefully he descended. It was cool at the bottom and the sounds of the prison were gone, along with the smell. He liked the smell of the dirt. It always took him back to the farm and working the soil. He took the pan and started scraping at the bottom of the hole while his mind rambled.

As a youngster, he had ridden on the back of Old Ben as the mule pulled and his Dad guided the plow through the soil. He would look back to watch his father, with his hands firmly on the plow handles, the reins draped around the back of his neck and sweat dripping off his face, and his heart had swelled with pride. At the end of the day, he and his dad would inspect the work, and it was always a thrill to see the rows of straight furrows.

When he was a little older and his Dad, injured in a fall off the barn roof, went to work in the store, it became his task to walk the plow on their small farm. It was no longer fun. At the time he resented the hours spent following Ben along the rows when he would rather be fishing. Old Ben was a good mule that never gave any trouble. Still, as he struggled through a rough patch, he would glumly tell himself that once he got a horse he'd never willingly touch a mule again. At other times, in all fairness, he realized that the elderly animal would probably have rather been standing in the barn munching hay, while Will fished. That old mule could sure run a straight furrow. The smile left his face as he remembered the day the mule died. Just dropped in his tracks. By the time Will had fetched his father, the mule was dead. Together they pulled him over to the nearest edge of the field in the shade of a cottonwood, and began digging a hole. It was the only time he had seen his father cry. Will and his brother picked some wild flowers and put them on the grave. The new mule had been the devil incarnate and had settled Will's opinion of mules and farming for a long time to come.

His memories were pushed aside by the thought of food. No matter what was on his mind sooner or later the thought of food was bound to intervene. "Up," he yelled and the bucket they had patched together from pieces of old boot shot upwards to the circle of light above. A second later, he watched it descend. Too bad it wasn't water tight he mused. An hour later, his arms gave out and he could do no more. "I'm comin' up," he shouted.

He lay gasping from the effort of his ascent. He doubted his ability to continue but with Jimmy gone, it was up to him. He had visions of dying down there because he hadn't the strength to get out. He didn't fancy his name living on as the only man buried inside the prison walls. He knew that Jack and Del would go down if they could fit but he also knew they were glad of the fact that they didn't.

"Anything yet?" Del asked hopefully.

"Nothin' yet, not even a sign of dampness. Maybe tomorrow."

"How deep, you figure?" Jack inquired.

"I'd say close to thirty feet, give or take a few." He could see Del flinch as he looked down into the black hole.

Since Jimmy died, Will had spent considerable time sizing up these friends. Their lives depended on one another. Each had to be counted on for his own strengths. Jack was definitely made of harder stuff then Del. For all his size, Del had a softness about him that would work to his advantage in a civilized environment. His tact was invaluable in their dealings with other prisoners, but he would need help physically and mentally to survive in here. He figured that the good life that Del enjoyed before the war might be the problem, but that wasn't his fault. He was a good friend. Jack was tough. His hard life on his own in the streets had tempered him. He was more content with whatever was thrown his way and was inventive at making do, but taciturn with strangers. All the same he was fiercely loyal to the two of them. Will felt that simple survival wouldn't be a problem for him. With Del to handle procurement and diplomacy, together they could make it if he cashed out.

He wondered what use they saw in him. He had changed with the loss of Jimmy. He had enjoyed using his customary deadpan expression against Jimmy's jokes. He could see by the reaction it made them even funnier. The two of them, made a joke of everything, regardless of the dire circumstances. Will could not remember laughing since that day. Everything had changed. He had withdrawn into a dark hole, and try as he might, he just couldn't get out. He must be pretty hard to live with. He must try to do better for all their sakes. He remembered when he smiled last. It was when he looked into Rooster's eyes as he shoved in the handle.

Will would have been surprised to know that Del feared him. Not fear for his own safety, because he knew that they were fast friends. What Del couldn't fathom was the power and intensity that drove Will so far beyond the limits of ordinary men. What had driven him to attack a foe like Rooster, to bite off the ear of the biggest Raider he could find, and most of all to take the life of his best friend, a man who he obviously loved as he might his own son. It made Del feel inadequate. He knew deep down, that he couldn't have done any of those things. Jack didn't want to watch when Will killed Jimmy but he had. He didn't want to but he had and he regretted it. He could see Jimmy struggle as Will ended his life, and he saw Will die inside as well in those few seconds. He was not the same person.

The days that followed showed a marked improvement in the living conditions. Organization was established by the Regulators, which ensured the equal distribution of rations. Regrettably, this did not have any effect on the quantity or quality of their food supply. It was not uncommon to see those that had starved to death during the night, using their loaf of cornbread as a pillow. Will was reduced to eating his small pellets over time as his stomach rejected any other method. The corn was so coarse that it felt like ground up glass. He was beginning to have sore gums as well, a first sign of scurvy. Aside from his preoccupation with food, this new affliction was weighing on his mind. The results of scurvy were everywhere and after watching those poor wretches suffer, he had made up his mind to cross the dead line and be shot before it became intolerable.

Will contemplated the small post barricade. He ran his tongue over his sore gums, and studied the no man's land beyond. It seemed so benign. Just a pole nailed to posts and a grassy space. Just a simple step and he wouldn't have to go through the drawn out hassle of dying. He studied the pole, picturing himself stepping over it. He shaded his eyes and looked up at the guard. The man was watching, smiling in anticipation. Will guessed that every prisoner would, at one time or another, contemplate this way out. The one thing holding him back was that he didn't want to let them beat him. No way was he going to give them the satisfaction. Not yet anyhow. The guard made a show of placing his gun on top of the stockade and thumbed back the hammer. He licked his finger and stroked the front sight. Will smiled up at him and yelled, "Go to Hell , you son of a bitch."

The guard laughed and lowered his weapon. "I'll git ya one o' these days, Yank."

Several days later, Pvt. Hogan reinforced Will's mind about not stepping across the dead line. Hogan had slipped away into a world of his own. He would spend hours talking to his family. Most of these conversations taking place around an imaginary dinner table where he ate his fill. Attempts by his friends to bring him back to reality, failed.

Then one morning he announced that he was going out to tend the stock, and turning, stepped over the wooden barrier.

The young guard yelled down. "Ya'all git yer ass back over that thar stick." Hogan, lost in his own world, proceeded toward the wall.

"Shoot that damn Yank, ya hear me? Shoot him." another guard yelled, before climbing down from his post ladder. After a moments hesitation the boy realigned his sights and pulled the trigger. The gun roared, and the bullet hit Hogan in the jaw, ripping it off.

Will was horrified to see the man's tongue still wagging in conversation as he slumped to the ground. To his relief another bullet from the second guard, who had joined the first in his pigeon roost, struck Hogan's chest, ending his misery. Will looked up to see the first guard burst into tears as his gun clattered on the cat-walk. The second guard helped him to the steps and handed him off to those down below taking his place at the wall. It was one of the few time he saw a Reb show any compassion and Will knew he would probably never see him again.

He decided that he would dive head first into the well before he crossed the dead line.

Both Jack and Del, concerned about Will's condition, spent hours each day roaming the stockade hoping to glean anything of value to trade with the guards. One rainy day this quest led Del to a young man stretched out in the mud, obviously dead or not far from it. Several of his friends were with him talking softly and holding his hand. What caught Del's eye was the buttons on the lad's coat. The guards liked shiny buttons and they would definitely like one of these. Jack waited until he was sure the young man had passed on, then kneeling beside the body, started negotiations with his friends.

He talked at some length about prison conditions and ended with a description of Will's situation. The need for something to barter with, had reached a critical point. Stopping the scurvy was imperative and one button from them might save Will's life. At first they were unsympathetic, as they had problems of their own.

Grasping for straws, Del exclaimed, "Well boys, I can see your point of view but you might hold the life of one fine man in your hands. He has been in here since day one and managed to put down that damn Rooster. I'm sure he wouldn't want me beggin' for him so I won't. Thanks for your time."

"Whoa up a mite. This the fella that actually killed that son of a bitch?"

"He's the one," Jack replied.

Without a word the man drew a small knife from his pocket, cut off a button, and handed it to Jack. "We had some trouble with that damn rat," he muttered.

"Much obliged friend. Good luck to you boys. We're up in that corner." Jack said, pointing in the general direction. "Look me up if I can be of any help to you." He stood and made his way toward the gate.

When he returned to Will, Del was grinning from ear to ear. He was carrying a small sack tucked under his shirt, which, upon sitting down by Will's side, he opened with a great flourish. Out poured seven potatoes and a quart jar of a brown substance. Will could only stare at the potatoes. He had not seen one in over six months, and here in his lap, were seven. He couldn't believe his eyes.

"That ain't all of it Will. Take a swig of what's in this jar."

Will carefully removed the lid and the aroma of molasses filled his nose. It was as if it was lifting him off the ground. The sweet smell was almost overpowering. Slowly, he raised it to his lips and let a few drops enter his mouth. It was glorious. He handed it back to Del.

"Nope, this is my treat. Now try one of those potatoes." Del could not keep the grin off his face as he saw the look in his friend's eyes. Damn, he felt good. Will spent the next half-hour eating one potato. It was wonderful.

Jack returned with a long face. He had come up empty again, and felt guilty about returning with nothing. He hated seeing Will like this. His continued failure weighed heavily upon him. He was surprised to see both his friends smiling and what was Will holding up in his hand? "My God, it's a potato," he exclaimed.

"Not just any potato," Will said. "The prettiest, best tasting potato in the whole world." Looking at Del, he said, "I want you boys to have a couple of these. We're all in this together, and I don't feel right about eating all of them. Besides, I don't want to get too fat and lazy."

"Well, you eat one a day until you have two left. Then we'll decide." Del replied.

"I insist on each of you having some of the molasses, though. So let's each take a swallow or two a day 'til its gone." Will proposed, with a smile. "That way we will all stay in good shape."

As Del and Jack took their sips of the molasses, Will watched his two friends, humbled by their generosity. There was no adequate way to thank them. They sat there content in the depth of their camaraderie.

Will wished Jimmy was here to enjoy it. He hoped that his friend was really back in Wyoming, sittin' on his rock, cooling his feet in that stream. He could picture it clearly in his mind.

The fall was Hell. The prison population was over thirty thousand. The relief achieved by the ten acre expansion northward behind the she-bang earlier in the year, had been brief. Thousands more had flooded through the gates since then. The death rate was staggering. Everywhere they looked they saw suffering and death. Will no longer made the rounds of his dwindling number of troops. The heat was still stifling.

Work on the well stopped. Will was the only one small enough to work in its confines, and he was too weak. Against all their resolve they found the safest thing was to just curl up and sleep. Don't talk, don't move, just stay still and try not to think about any of it. Days drifted by with no noticeable movement throughout the stockade for hours at a time. When rations were distributed, the strongest walked, or crawled to the wagons, but most just remained where they were depending on their more able comrades. It was hard to tell the living from the dead.

Del was sinking into defeat. He just wasn't made of strong enough stuff to live through this, he told himself. He should have stayed at home. His stomach growled with hunger. He had never been hungry a day in his life before joining the army. Hell, before he joined the army, he had never wanted for anything. Actually, army life had been hard at first. Aside from his father, no one had ever yelled at him, let alone physically abuse him. He could have let his father pay to keep him home, that was what his friends had done. He hated himself for thinking it, and tried to push the thought out of his mind. They, and others like them, were the reason the Raiders existed. Others like himself! He glanced over at Will and envied his fortitude. Even in wretched shape, he was defiant. Christ, he had killed Rooster! He felt overwhelmed by his own shortcomings. How could he face any more of this place?

He looked at the small pole marking the dead zone. He was fascinated. He knew, deep down, that he would end up in the burying field with Jimmy anyway so just do it. Just step over it and all this will be over. He was weary of living in constant fear. Tears were gathering in his eyes. He tried to wipe them away without Will or Jack seeing him. He felt helpless. He looked at the pole. He was so close that he could reach out and touch it. For months he had lived in this spot without thinking about it. This morning, it seemed to be his salvation. It was a door to God and eternity.

He looked out across the tens of thousands of prisoners. They didn't even resemble human beings. Looking down at his shrunken stomach and spindly legs, he knew that he didn't look any better. His mind shrank when he looked at Will. My God, he was more dead than alive. What kept him from giving up?

Watching Del, Will knew that something was different this morning. He caught the movement of Del wiping away the tears. He could see desperation in his face as he looked out at the stockade. What was he planning?

In a fog Del stood up. If it hadn't been for the pain in his joints, he wouldn't have noticed that he was standing. He looked down at the pole, then up at the guard, he hoped that he was a good shot. He remembered the man who had his jaw shot off. He wondered what death would bring. He had thought about it a lot since being here. The church told him that he would go to heaven. Would God forgive him for stepping over the pole? He lifted his foot up and started to lean forward. Suddenly he was yanked backward into Will's arms. He felt relief as they both fell to the ground. He had been two seconds away from death and he was still alive.

"Looks like you were about to go on a long trip, Del. Problem is, you can't change your mind if you don't like it." Will's eyes were sad, but he had a lop sided grin on his face. "We need you here, Del. Our chances are better with you. Don't let us down."

"I know. I'm not really a coward." Del murmured. Embarrassed that Will had to save him. "Just got to me this morning, for some reason." He rolled off Will and sat up.

"Guess everyone in here has had the same thoughts, Del."

"You?"

"Sure, but I have a way of getting past it."

"How?"

"Death is all around and even more so with Jimmy gone. I plan my death again and again but I plan it for tomorrow. Tomorrow I will end it. Then tomorrow becomes today and I put the plan together for tomorrow. First thing you know a week has gone by, then a month, pretty soon a year. Before you know it will all be over and we'll be home again, sitting around the table with our folks, with more food than we can eat. We'll be clean and feelin' good. Everyone tellin' us how much they love us. After dinner, we'll be a sittin' in the parlor with our whole life ahead of us. I plan that too. By ending it here, you'll never git to enjoy that life I just told you about. Just one more day, old friend, just one more day. Let's put it off 'til tomorrow."

Del was surprised when Will let go of his hand. He was so taken by the words that he hadn't noticed Will's grip. "Thanks Will."

"When times git tough, you just remember that meal with your folks. It will come, just take my word for it . Be patient just another day," he said with a grin.

After Will curled up and closed his eyes, Del thought long and hard. As bad as it was, by God he could do it for one more day. Damn right.

Will peeked through slitted eyes at Del. Take more than Andersonville to beat me and mine. No way will I give these varmints the pleasure of seeing any of us dead. Closing his eyes, he drifted off to sleep.

One night, shortly after that they had a real rainstorm, with the rumble of thunder and flashes of lightning, lighting up the stockade. They hunkered down in their sleep pit and stretched the great coat as far as it would go. At least it was cooler. The rain continued for hours with no let up. In the morning they woke to almost total destruction. Hundreds of she-bangs had been swept down the hillside along with their owners. Deep mud was everywhere. How many had been buried, Will couldn't guess. Most of the men they could see were just trying to dry out what they could salvage.

However, there was a disturbance way off toward the gates that caught Del's eye. "What do you think that's all about?" he asked.

"Let's go find out." Jack replied, with more enthusiasm than he'd shown for some time. Reaching down he grabbed Will's hand and pulled him up. The three worked their way down the muddy hillside toward the commotion.

"Water, by God, we have water," exclaimed someone in the crowd. "God has blessed us with water."

Having witnessed the deluge of the night before, Will was bemused by this show of enthusiasm. On closer examination, however, he was surprised to see a small stream of fresh water running out of a slippage in the ground. It was not just a run-off from the rain, but a real spring. Del headed back to fetch the skillet, emptied of its precious fill of rainwater already that morning. It took some time, but he managed to work his way up the line and dip the skillet into the spring. Returning to Jack and Will, he handed it to Will, who took a few swallows and handed it to Jack. They drank their fill and filled the skillet one more time before heading back up the hill. By the time they were back to their she-bang, most had spilled, so they finished off the rest.

To everyone's amazement, the spring continued to gush cool, clean water. It became known as Providence Spring, as many believed it was a gift from God. Untold hundreds, perhaps thousands, managed to survive because of it.

Within an hour, the presiding chaplain decided to hold a meeting to give thanks for the blessing of the water. Del and Jack decided to attend, Will did not. He watched his friends head down toward the large semi-circle of sitting men in front of the preacher and take a seat. Will shook his head and lay back on the ground to look at the clouds. He had plenty of time to ponder the idea of a god and was not convinced, anyway not by the god that the churches preached. If he did exist, he was obviously not concerned about the suffering of mankind. He couldn't see all this and do nothing. If he had the power of life and death, he sure didn't know how to use it. If he'd struck down a couple of dozen Raiders, it would have saved hundreds from suffering. As long as he was calling thousands to heaven, why not a couple dozen for hell? Will noticed that all the church goers that attended the weekly service seemed to die just as fast as those that didn't. Most of them died in fear of retribution as if they hadn't paid already.

That night, Will stood on the edge of the well that they had spent so many hours digging.

"What are you doing?" Jack inquired.

"I'm pissin' in this damn worthless pit." Will replied. Del and Jack climbed out of the sleep hole to join him.

9

GOODBYE TO ANDERSONVILLE

It continued to rain. The temperature remained stifling. As they huddled under it, each day the tents ability to shed water lessened. Whatever wasn't damp was wet. The two ponchos were of little help because of rips and wear. Using the skillet, they dug a trench to the well, which allowed most of the water to escape. Not even they could imagine the abject misery suffered by the thousands that had no shelter. Newcomers with tents shared their belongings with the less fortunate, but no matter the number of new faces, there were never enough supplies to meet the demand.

Will tried to ignore his guilt at having a tent over his head. That areas of the tent had long ago lost the ability to shed water was a minor irritant compared to the hardships of many.

Occasionally the rain would let up and everywhere men would be out rearranging their coverings, but there was never enough time or materials to finish the job right. A few used the breaks to wring out clothes and bedding. Nearby, one prisoner stood, looking up into the sky, shaking his fists and cursing. Eventually, the ceaseless downpour stopped, much to the relief of everyone although there were still showers with thunder and lightning almost every day. It was as if the heat of the afternoon air was boiling the rain out of the clouds.

"Hey, Yank!" The gruff whisper came from the darkness above the palisade.

Will, who had come out to stretch his legs and get some air, peered up toward the guard post. "What you want, Johnny Reb?" he answered carefully.

"Here. Figured ya'all could use these." Will heard a number of thumps on the ground nearby and covered his head with his arms. "Just got told we got to go fight. We ain't doin' too good if'n they need this bunch. Hoped I'd never have to shoot at no man, but we'll be gone tomorrow. That Mrs. Hunt is a stayin with some folks in town. Baby is a doin, fine. Heard he's workin' in the infirmary."

"Sorry to hear you're leavin', Reb. You're a good man. Don't you go tryin' to be no hero, now, keep your head down when the shootin' starts!"

Covering the ground where he had heard the thumps Will picked up almost a dozen potatoes and yams. They would have full stomachs tonight and have some left over.

The next day a new guard was in the pigeon roost. He was young, perhaps ten or twelve, and was glaring down into the compound. He quickly sighted his carbine at Will's head. Ducking back under the tent he alerted the others to the danger.

"That's just what we need. Go through all this grief and end up gittin' kilt by some damn fool youngster." Jack growled. "Let's try to keep out of sight. Maybe he'll tire of us and leave us alone."

It seemed to work. By the end of the week, the boy had lost interest and spent most of his duty asleep. No guards were posted at night. They talked of a tunnel, but were in no condition to dig it.

During the rest of August the steady stream of new prisoners did not abate. Perhaps as important as the equipment they brought, was their store of information. News! No longer did they bring stories of defeat and poor leadership. Their chagrin at being captured was lessened by their assurance that it was just a matter of time before the South was beaten. Will had made it a point to take this news with a mite of caution because too many times he had let himself be coaxed into getting his hopes up only to feel even worse when the bad news followed.

By September, however, even he was becoming convinced. He had been reclining in deep thought when he became aware of a stir in the camp. There was a tumult of raised voices. Closer he heard someone yell in a loud voice. "Atlanta's gone to hell."

Del, who had been lying on his back contemplating the clouds, sat bolt upright. "What did he say? What did he say? Does that mean it's ours? Oh yes! Let it be, Sweet Jesus! Let it be!"

Cheers broke out as the news spread. People were gathering to discuss the ramifications of such a defeat, and wondering what effect it might have on the prison. Would Sherman be coming this way? Would they be freed within days? Joy and hope, two things that had been missing, were suddenly rekindled. The Star Spangled Banner could be heard, and more and more took up the singing. The three joined hands and would have danced around in a circle like crazy men, if they were up to it. They settled for grinning and slapping each other on the back.

"We're going to make it out of here! We're going to live!" Del crowed.

The guards scrambled to arms afraid of loosing control. But, it quickly became apparent that the enthusiasm did not constitute a threat and calm returned. However, the news that Atlanta had fallen did not set well with the Rebs, and the foolish guard that announced it to the prisoners was catching his share of grief. For the first time, in over a year, Will didn't want to sleep. He was so excited that sleep was impossible, and besides, he didn't want to miss the Union troops, should they come marching in to set them free.

Over the next two days, prisoners from Sherman's army began to appear in the camp. They reported great progress in the war effort. Sherman's troops were meeting little resistance on their march to the sea and it was just a matter of time. "Just hold out a little longer. Just a matter of days."

Days passed and still no sign of Sherman. Hope was fading when the rebel Sergeant that took morning muster announced that twenty thousand prisoners would be exchanged over the next few weeks. Detachments One through Ten, a designation assigned by their captors, were chosen to be exchanged. The detachments were to be divided into smaller groups which were to be called as transportation became available.

Incredulous elation galvanized the camp. Everyone debated whether it was a fact or a trick. Hope was strong. It made sense. Sill they feared another letdown. Sherman was a threat and giving him the prisoners would slow the advance. Shooting them all and running would solve their problem too. What good were they to the Rebs now? None! It had to be true! The first group left the camp the next morning.

Should they give up their blanket and skillet to those left behind? Or should they play it safe and hang on to everything they could? They decided to play it safe. They finally curled up in their pit, pressing close to hold their body heat, and tried to sleep. It had been a long wait. They were one of the last groups to be called and were fearful of a change in plans that would keep them behind. None of them felt able to stand such a letdown.

They were awakened around six in the morning by the yelling of the guards. It had rained in the night and the air was noticeably cooler. A damp breeze swept through the stockade. Members of their group gathered up their pitiful possessions from their camp sites and straggled down to the gate in the pitch dark. The gloom was punctuated by yells and curses as they trod on others or fell into sleep holes losing their gear in the mud. It didn't take long for the three to gather up their few belongings. They paused a moment before starting out, squinting into the darkness hoping to see anything to guide them.

"Enough of this shit," Will exclaimed, "let's chance it!" They hurried down to where the others were gathering. Will gripped the skillet, pressed in between Jack and Del so the great coat could shield them all.

They were herded out the gate and walked to the town and the train tracks. Once there, they waited, in what was now a steady drizzle. By the time the train arrived, hours later, dozens had patiently waited, some supported by others for a time, until the dampness seeped into their bones and stole their life away. Will tried not to look. He was too miserable to enjoy the fact that he was out of the stockade. The three clung together under the great coat. Del draped the poncho over their heads, then stretched the one blanket as far as it would go. They were so depleted that they were unable to appreciate the cooler weather. Teeth chattering, they scanned the empty tracks, hoping for boxcars.

To everyone's disappointment, the train had only flat cars. It was going to be a cold ride. They climbed aboard and sought space near the rear of the car. Maybe they could find shelter from the wind, among the other prisoners. They were packed so tight that there was no room for anyone to stretch out. They sat with their arms around their knees, heads down. After much hissing and chugging, the worn out engine started its slow crawl in a northeastern direction. The three huddled together, backs against the wind and rain. The blanket stretched to cover all three, with the great coat, and poncho, giving some protection to their legs. No one spoke. Trying to talk above the noise would use up energy, and they had none to spare.

The hours slowly passed with no let up in the rain. The train and tracks had certainly had no attention while they were imprisoned. The noise of dry wheel bearings, the thumping of the shifted rails was even worse than before. The pain of the bone-crushing jolts up through the wooden bed, to the skinny buttocks of every man sitting on the cold, wet, boards was indescribable. There was no relief.

Looking at the dripping landscape, Will was taken back to that last train ride. The land and the dreary little groups of poorly-clad, rain washed hill folk that had collected along the right away had the same effect on him. Hopelessness. This couldn't be representative of the whole South. Who would fight for such a place?

He had to admit that he had not seen any Reb fighting men since his imprisonment. The prison guards were generally those not suited for fighting. Even the Johnny Reb that had helped them, though a good man, was an unenthusiastic soldier. The officers were no better and some downright sadistic. Those he had faced on the battlefield were damn good soldiers, and the latest prisoners held the Reb troops in complete awe. The fighting army obviously had better officers than those running the prison system.

A shot rang out from the watchers and a prisoner groaned and rolled off the car. Most were too miserable to take notice.

Eventually they passed through Macon. Will was surprised at what little was there. As he recalled, they had passed through at night, on the way down. It was hardly a town at all, some old buildings about to fall down, a smattering of shacks strewn haphazardly around. Neglect. Yes, that summed it up. They chugged on past and continued their journey.

10

SAVANNAH

On the second day the rain stopped. Along with the more tolerable weather, they had changed to a better track during the night, which reduced the jolting. The passing country was much more verdant. Gaps in the vegetation showed dark, rich soil. The train slowed as it crossed a long bridge and gasped its way into Savannah.

Will was surprised to see the city nearly abandoned. Aside from some troops and a couple of furtive citizens, there was no one. He had expected to see throngs of people. The buildings were covered with vines and ferns. The trees along the streets and in the many parks they passed covered with hanging moss. It reminded him of a lost civilization being taken over by the jungle. There were no signs anywhere that there would be an exchange. Disappointment consumed his hopes, as he met the gaze of his friends. There he could see despair that mirrored his own.

Jack spoke brokenly, "Say Will, do you remember the first day we met? You mentioned there would come a time that I would feel like giving up. Remember?"

"Yup, I sure do. Are you having one of those moments?"

"I do believe I am." Jack replied sadly. He sat with arms clasped around his legs. His forehead pressed against his knees.

"That's just great!" Will exclaimed with feigned disgust. "I git you out of Andersonville, give you a fine train ride, show off the beauties of the South, and this is how you repay me. Some folks are just damn hard to please. Go cheer yourself up." He shook his head.

"Thanks Will, I feel better already," Jack murmured "I'm definitely feeling better. You sure have a way with words that inspires hope and cheer."

At the outskirts of the city the train stopped, and Will could see two long lines of guards standing along the tracks. It was not a good sign. As the prisoners were ordered off the train, Will noticed dozens still curled up on the flatcar's wet boards. They had ridden their last train. The men were herded off the cars, and marched down the street between the two lines of guards, too demoralized to care where they were going.

They entered a newly built stockade lined with tall boards. To Will's surprise, the boards stopped at ground level. His burrowing instincts were awakened. No dead line, just nice, moist, soft soil. They were as good as gone. Looking around he spotted a number of leftover planks leaning against the wall at the far end. Others had also noticed and several dozen made a dash for them. A shot rang out and one of the men fell, writhing on the ground. The others beat a hasty retreat back to the main group in the center of the prison. A guard, perched above the stockade, was still sighting his weapon, moving it back and forth in a menacing manner. It was empty, but everyone got the idea. The moans of the man grew fainter and after twenty or thirty minutes, died away. Later two slaves came in and carried him out.

Once the guard relaxed, having made his point, the prisoners began to spread out and get themselves situated. "Let's git us some of those planks." Jack whispered. "We only have to worry about that one guard and he don't seem to be watchin' too sharp now. He don't think anyone will try it agin, after that other gent. He thinks we're scared."

"Who's going to walk over there and pick one up? You?" Will asked.

"Hell yes! You just distract him for a minute and I'll do the thieve'en."

"Don't you take too long." Will commented, as he strolled down the fence a piece and acted like he was planning some sort of escape by kicking the boards. He looked up to see the guard swing toward him then ducked back into the mass of prisoners. Meanwhile, two boards disappeared from the other end of the stack. They repeated this until they had five good sized planks, which they used to place over their sleep hole. They covered the boards with dirt to prevent the guards from spotting them.

As soon as darkness settled over the camp they began to make out signs of activity around the perimeter fence, and not to be outdone, the trio set to work. Within an hour, the majority of prisoners who were strong enough were out of the enclosure, heading to freedom.

Will, Del and Jack were soon under the fence. They cleared the town as quickly as they could and headed back along the railroad tracks. Not knowing the layout of the place, this seemed a sensible choice. They walked until they could see the bridge. Once over that, they could figure out where to go next. To their dismay, it was guarded by several sentries, huddled around a small fire. Skirting the town in hopes of finding another way out they ran into other escapees who'd had no better luck. The town was a virtual island. A river on three sides and a string of lagoons on the other. Without a boat, they faced recapture in the morning.

"I say we find something to eat." Jack suggested. "Once they round us up, I doubt these Rebs will set any better table than Andersonville, and I'm damn tired of short rations. Besides that, I'm so hungry I could eat a shoe. Either of you two have a shoe?"

Will and Del smiled weakly. They had been hungry so long they wouldn't recognize any other condition. "Let's check out some of those buildings we passed back there." Del suggested.

They retraced their steps and started checking the buildings. They were disappointed to find them either locked tight, or empty. Del found some boards about four feet long leaning against one of them. He took three. "We can use these," he said. "I'll leave them behind that big tree. We can pick them up on our way back."

When they heard the sound of troops passing down a side street, Jack whispered, "Where there's troops, there's food." He took off in hot pursuit, with Will and Del close behind. The troops they were following stopped off at a small building just outside the perimeter of their camp, then moved off to be lost among the tents. Maybe that was the building they had been hoping for. They settled down for a brief reconnoiter. When they were sure the coast was clear they crept up to the building and crouched in the shadows by the door. Needless to say, it was locked.

Del headed around the side with his friends following. He found a small window about head high and less than two by two feet square. The frame had rotted away to almost nothing, and canvass covered the area where glass had once been. Within a minute, they had boosted Del inside, and presently, a sack was handed out the opening. Jack grabbed it and set it aside. Another sack appeared and then another. Del's head popped out, "How we doin'?" he asked.

"Great, let's git while the gittin's good." Jack answered. "We have all we can carry."

Will bent to pick up a sack, but he was too weak. All the unaccustomed activity had just about done him in. It was times like this that his weakness shocked him. Jack shouldered his own bag and wordlessly gripped Will's by one corner. The two quietly faded into the darkness. Del caught up with them at the big tree where he had left the boards. Shifting his load, he grabbed the boards under his arm and they headed back to the stockade.

Del muttered. "If this don't beat all. I wonder what the hell we have, hope it's something we can use." After a few seconds of reflective silence, he whispered. "Can you think of anything we can't use?" Neither could think of a thing.

Reentering the stockade, they returned to their sleep hole. They opened the first sack and, much to their delight, found sweet yams. The smaller sack contained dry hard biscuits called hardtack and the third, potatoes. They were hard pressed to keep from yelling with delight. For the first time in months they ate their fill. Regrettably, their stomachs were so shriveled up, they could only eat one potato, and a shared yam. Then they dug a second hole inside the shelter as a cache for the food. As it would not last long in the wetness it was decided to distribute what they could not eat before it spoiled to those most in need. It would have to be done in secret to prevent a riot. Will doubted that many others would have had the same opportunity to bring food back with them much less be willing to share.

They curled up in their new sleep hole, pulled the blanket over themselves and slept. They were too tired to appreciate the fact that the ground was not teeming with lice, and the night breeze was sweet and fresh.

The following morning they gorged on as much of the hardtack as they could hold. It would be ruined in the wet before the root vegetables. The food provided for them later in the day was more generous then they had even hoped, and the quality was much better. Their ration consisted of one dry hard biscuit, a small piece of meat, a spoon of salt, two spoons of molasses and a quart of vinegar. They would never grow fat on it but with their stolen fair it gave them a real chance. For those that cared there would occasionally be a plug of tobacco issued for each one hundred men.

As they'd guessed, a continual flood of escapees were being returned to the stockade. To everyone's surprise there was no punishment. Obviously, they weren't dealing with another Wirz. They spent the day gathering fire fuel and arranging their boards to protect themselves from the rain. The next night another exodus took place. They decided to use this time to distribute some of their surplus. Most, who could, would be gone. The most needy would be left. Will, remembering the potatoes that Jack had brought him, relished the chance to pass on the favor, as he slipped a potato or some hardtack into eager hands.

Capt. Davis, the Commandant, must have been new to the job as it was obvious to the men inside that this was no escape-proof prison. It was also obvious that it would be only a matter of time before he figured that out, and took measures to make it so. Sure enough a twenty foot deadline was erected the next day. This was only a minor setback, as the ground was perfect for tunneling. They immediately joined a group that was starting a tunnel nearby. The guard was directly above their effort which they thought might be an advantage, as who would be stupid enough to dig a tunnel so close. With skillet in hand, Will joined the digging inside the shelter where the tunnel began. Jack and Del joined the dirt removal team. They carried it out in what was left of Del's boot, in pockets, pant legs, and hats. No one ever left the shelter without both hands full. It made their blood run cold to turn their backs on the guard and walk casually away to disperse the dirt away from the tunnel. They could feel the gun lining up on their backs and hear the sound of the shot in their minds. With great relief, a night finally came when they broke through five feet beyond the fence.

Once they were out and had raided the shed, liberating several unmarked sacks from the Rebs, Del suggested that they stay outside.

"Why not?" he asked. "We can eat whenever we want to and don't have to worry about the tunnel caving in."

"Sounds like a good plan to me, where do you suggest we hide out?" Will asked, with a broad smile.

"I saw a place last time, that I wouldn't mind seeing better. Follow me."

A few minutes later they were standing in the shrubbery outside a huge Palladian home, with tall pillars and wide steps leading to a pair of doors with elaborate leaded glass. "How's this?" he asked.

Will and Jack could just stare. Del gave the other a chance to get used to the idea then headed around to the back and they hastily followed. After checking several locked doors and windows, Del found a shoot into the basement for storing wood. It wasn't locked. "Looks kind'a small. You want to go first, Jack?"

The larger man straightened and took a deep breath. "Stand aside, boys, I'm goin' in." Working his head and shoulders through the opening he wiggled forward until only his legs were visible, he paused, then they too disappeared. This was followed by a resounding crash and curses. "Damn. Almost broke by neck. Must be a six foot drop. You boys circle 'round to those low windows, I'll see if I can get one open."

Minutes later, they were all inside, inspecting the wide, curved staircase and the arched ceiling twenty feet above in the faint moonlight.

"This is some place," Jack whispered.

"Why are you whispering?" Del laughed.

"Don't know, it just seems like the thing to do. Let's look around."

Del seemed quite at home, and lead the group through the many downstairs rooms ending in the back. "Just what I thought," he said, with a wide grin. "The pantry." He began opening cabinet doors and within minutes found several jars of jam pushed to the back of a shelf. "Let's see if this place has an attic."

The attic was crowded, but the small window in the front gave them a grand view of the stockade, several blocks away. They had brought blankets up from the bedrooms below and felt the luxury of curling up with a thick, clean dry blanket, for the first time in close to two years.

Just before dawn Jack said he was going to the outhouse, out back.

"Go in the chamber pot downstairs." Del suggested.

"Nope, don't want to put a smell in a house like this."

When he returned he sat on his blanket and with a scowl on his face began to pick lice off it's surface. It was a lost cause. He dropped the blanket and spoke with the same worried scowl. "I know this place belongs to some rich Reb slave owner. Still, I just can't see us fouling it up. It just don't seem right. Maybe we shouldn't stay here."

"Well," Del answered with a glance at Will, "I guess I see what you mean. Someone is going to have to clean up after us and I'll bet it won't be that rich slave owner. What say we clean ourselves up! How would that feel boys?"

This brought a sunny smile to Jack's face and they all quickly became enthusiastic.

Downstairs they found a cistern on a closed-in back porch where they could get water. It was pretty exposed but by keeping a lookout and ducking down below the level of the screens they were able to bring in enough to fill a copper bathtub they found in a small room behind the kitchen. There was also some lye soap, an old rusty razor, a partially toothless comb, some scissors and a few towels. There was a mirror too. As they looked at themselves for the first time in years they felt a real shock. They each knew how bad the others had grown to look but had not really applied that change to themselves.

Over the next few hours they worked diligently snipping and

scrubbing. The razor was hopeless but the scissors worked after a fashion. They cut each other's hair and beards down as close as they could before washing in the cold water with liberal amounts of the harsh soap. Afterward, wrapped in the blankets from the attic, they combed what was left on their heads and faces and trimmed it as even as they could. Then they piled their old clothes and the hair onto the largest piece of clothing they had and hauled it to the basement. After another look at themselves in the mirror, where they noted the improvement, they retired to the attic to rest and eat something.

Most of the owner's personal belongings were gone but after their rest they were able to assemble enough apparel from trunks in the attic and the backs of closets to cover themselves more than adequately. They all had shirts and pants gathered in around their skinny waists with lengths of rope they found in the basement and, wonder of wonders, long underwear. Will and Jack had light jackets and Del an extra thick wool shirt. All these items were obviously well worn but certainly not as worn as what they had abandoned to the basement. In a cupboard downstairs they found a couple of ragged old coats to go with the somewhat nicer one they had found in the basement. The only thing they were unable to find was shoes. They put on some holey socks they found to keep their feet warmer and the coats. It was chilly inside the house and as thin as they were they were always cold, except when they had been so damned hot. It was also hard to shake the habit of keeping all their belongings on them as well.

Three more days were spent, steadily eating at the food they had brought in and the jars of jam. During that time they could see a lot of activity around the stockade from their vantage point. Finally they realized that what they had been doing down there was digging a moat.

"Well, we have a problem if we want to get back in. Looks like they're fillin' her with water," Will said, with a sigh. "The shelter will belong to someone else, along with the rest of our stuff. Hate to loose the skillet."

As well as Will could guess, the moat was about five feet deep and perhaps ten feet across. Davis must have had his brain working overtime to come up with this idea. Will was impressed. Up to now he had not seen much in the way of imagination when it came to those associated with the rebel prison system. Later they found that after their escape the dead line had been extended to forty feet for a couple of days but this created such a problem with overcrowding, it was reset to the twenty foot mark whereupon every day a heavily loaded wagon was pulled around the inside of the stockade wall. Either the heavy wheels, or the hooves of the mules, caved in any tunnels. There would be no more escapes.

The following evening, as Will was returning from the outhouse, he heard a dog bark nearby. Before he knew it, he was surrounded by five Rebs. Finding the open window they soon collected the other two and marched them all back to the stockade.

Two other men, in pathetic condition, had appropriated their shelter and belongings so unless they wanted to physically evict them, which they couldn't bring themselves to do after their five days in the lap of luxury, and the procurement of their fine new duds, they were out in the cold, literally. The temperature had dropped considerably with the clearing skies. Will managed to locate the skillet that he had buried against the outside of the dug out, which was a relief to him. For two frigid nights they clung together and hoped that they would not freeze to death. To their great relief, on the morning of the third day, the two in their shelter died. Del dragged the cold stiff corpses out, and the three moved back in reclaiming the space and belongings.

In those early days Savannah was an improvement over Andersonville in other ways beside the better rations. The guards were made up almost entirely of seamen, whose attitude toward the prisoners was much more tolerant. Therefore they were spared the daily shootings they had grown used to. A small contingent of regular army was present, and if given half a chance, would probably have opened fire, but everyone was on their best behavior when they were on duty.

They celebrated their first night back in their digs with a small fire.

"Well, boys, if I do say so myself, the old bones are feeling a little better. My teeth are better and I do believe my joints are not as swollen as they were awhile back," Will said with a smile. Maybe it was all in his head, but just having something for his stomach to do made him sure he was on the mend.

Jack wrapped his arm around Will's shoulder and gave him a squeeze. "If you feel that good, how about a tune or two?"

"Why the hell not?" Will replied, reaching for the pouch.

Will's medical condition continued to improve, starting with the first trip to the Reb storehouse. The five days in the attic with the food they managed to steal had worked real wonders. Will thought that he may even have managed to put on a little weight. The rations for the prisoners and the guards were the same. Regrettably, this oversight did not last.

Gen. Winder made a flying visit to the camp and, when he witnessed the distribution of rations, he flew into a rage. Will saw him stomping around, cursing, while Captain Davis hung his head, nodding occasionally to the reprimand.

The distress Winder, who was in charge of all Southern prisons, must have gone through when he realized how the rations were being wasted was the talk of the prison. Davis had undone what had taken him months to accomplish; the mass starvation of thousands of the enemy. The first to go was the molasses, vinegar and tobacco. Then the much enjoyed biscuits, were replaced by cornbread. However, the quality of the cornbread was very good, and the salt ration was not cut, so grumbling stayed at a minimum.

One morning, everyone was awakened to the sounds of dull thumps in the distance. The Rebel bugler sounded *reveille*. A minute or so later, came *assemble*, and then *boots and saddle*. It was obvious to everyone that the thumping was heavy artillery coming from the blockade ships, some thirty miles away.

"Be a damn shame to be killed by one of our own shells," Jack said, with a hint of sarcasm. "Come all this way…"

"Could be a real invasion." Del suggested. "I could live with that."

They sat quietly, listening to the distant sound of the bugler directing the troops somewhere out in the field. The shelling continued on into the day, then ceased. They later learned that one of the blockade ships had shelled two of the Rebel installations, Forts Jackson and Bledsoe, protecting the passage to Savannah harbor. However, even with the subsequent capture of the two forts, the Union came no closer to the city.

Throughout this time additional prisoners continued to arrive. These included a percentage of Raiders, who were again becoming a problem. They hadn't forgotten their grudge against Will. They were continually trying to catch him alone. However, these attempts were well handled by Del and Jack, who never left his side, aided by a small group of admirers who took it upon themselves to act as additional bodyguards.

One day, their curiosity was aroused when a group of carpenters entered the prison and proceeded to build a platform, of sorts, in the middle of the camp. As they gathered around, Peter Bradley, one of the Raiders from Andersonville, surrounded by several officers and guards, climbed up on the platform and proceeded to give a speech regarding the abandonment of the prisoners by their Federal Government. He maintained that Secretary Stanton and General Halleck had refused to enter into discussions regarding an exchange, and that they had referred to the prisoners as, "blackberry pickers and coffee boilers." These were terms used to describe those slackers and skulkers who disgraced their uniform by giving themselves up rather than fighting. The idea that these men would refer to them in such terms was ludicrous to Will.

He went on to say that the government would hire foreigners to take their place and they would be forgotten. As Bradley, himself, was one of these hirelings, it infuriated Will to listen to this garbage. Apparently he wasn't the only one as a chorus of screamed epitaphs soon drowned out the speaker. The men dispersed in disgust. No further attempts were made to persuade them to switch sides. The fancy platform was torn down for fuel.

A few days later a small group of new prisoners arrived and the three headed over to catch up on any news from the front. As they approached, a young private was holding court.

"Well boys, let me tell you how we took Atlanta."

Will could feel a glimmer of hope in his gut. He moved closer, so as not to miss anything of what was being said.

"Yessir, we done took her. Damn right. We belong to the old 14th Ohio, which you might just know was right in the midst of the battle at Chickamauga. That's right, they're callin' the General, "Chickamauga Jim." We done took the fight right to Longstreet that day. Made him wish he a stayed in his tent. Anyways, we could see the steeples and tall buildings from our position and we could a heard them church bells if'n the breeze was right. We heard Uncle Billy was off to our right somewhere but we never caught sight of him."

"Tell us about Atlanta!"

"I'm a gittin' to it. Well, we could feel the excitement in the air. We knowed somethin' was about to happen and we was right. We was in a skirmish line, wait'n for the command then we was ordered to leave and take up a new position off a ways. Gerard moved his men into them works and hunkered down. We was told to make a lot of noise a movin' out, which we done with some enthusiasm. Them Rebs, a thinkin' we was in retreat comes over them works and commenced to fight. Damn, boys, they was a cuttin' Gerard's men down like wheat and kilt several officers. Riled us up a plenty but Pap Thomas had us doing all kind of maneuverin' and danged if I could figure it out, but I trust Pap to do right. When we found ourselves on the tracks between Atlanta and Macon we commenced a tearin' 'em up. Them folks in Atlanta thought we was in retreat and hustled out to catch us. We could hear a big gun a goin' off and bells a ringin'. Celebratin' our demise, so to speak. That all stopped when they figured it out. Hood brought his army back out and some of Hardy's and Cleburne's men settled in to our front. We didn't do nothin' until Stanley could git around them and trap 'em. A course, Stanley bein' Stanley, he don't show up in time and they git away. Next morning, we see 'em comin' at us and we fix bayonets and charge 'em. Dead by the hundreds, them and us. Don't know who was more riled, but it was some fight. We lost Major Wilson, Lieutenant Kirk, Capt. Stopfard, Lieutenants Cobb and Mitchell all cut to pieces and dead. Bodies a piled up shoulder high, but we kept a goin'. Them Rebs fought like crazy men. We finally got the best of 'em and won the fight, but had to take them one by one. Summin' up the losses, out of fifteen officers, nine was dead or wounded. Most a third of the brigade was lost. We ended up takin' ten guns, seven battle flags and over two thousand prisoners. Them officers that hadn't been kilt showed off the prizes and bragged about our victory. Next day we heard explosions and figured they was blowin' up their munitions. We sent out a reconnaissance and met the mayor who said the Reb troops was long gone."

"How did you end up here?" some one hollered.

"Well that there is one sad story. The two of us, he pointed to another prisoner, we was out stealin' some food. Found us a smoke house and was a fillin' our pockets with ham when all of a sudden, we was surrounded by Rebs, who also spotted the smokehouse. But I got to tell ya, we ain't a goin' to be here long. We just about got this war won. Ain't no way we a goin' to lose her now."

The three returned to their shelter. Their minds filled with the thought of being free.

On the 11th of October, an order came to assemble one thousand prisoners at the gate. Exchange, was the first thought to enter their minds. What other reason was there to move that number of people? It was going to happen sooner or later, why not meet it halfway? The guards were spreading rumors that ships could not get in to Savannah, so any exchange would have to take place in Charleston. It seemed so logical to the prisoners that there was little doubt to its being true.

It was agreed upon that the three of them would go with this first group. They hastily grabbed their possessions and joined the crowd at the gate. Others were so convinced of their impending release that they were giving away their personal belongings to those left behind. Neither Will, Del or Jack had any such illusions by this time. The damn Rebs were not to be trusted. They would believe the exchange was real when they saw Union blue and Old Glory.

They boarded the boxcars, grateful for the protection from the cold. They were packed in so tight that there was no room to lie down but it would keep them warmer. They managed to get into a corner and squat down for the long ride. To freedom? No one knew.

11

MILLEN

As the sun came up they realized they were traveling in a northwest direction and the countryside was taking on a familiar look. As a matter of fact, it looked like the same ground they had traveled when they left Andersonville. Apprehension spread through the cars. Surely they weren't going back.

Del looked at Will with panic in his eyes. "I can't go back in there, no way. I'd rather die than to go back there."

Will saw that both his friends were about to loose control. There was a restless stirring among the others in the car as well. Down deep he felt the same way, but it was his job to take care of his men and, come hell or high water, he would do his duty. He slapped them both on the back and, forcing a tight grin, he spoke out in his carrying Sergeant's voice. "What's the worry, we beat her once and we'll beat her again. We're probably closer to Sherman here then on the coast." The tension in the car eased as the men strove to get a grip on their rising panic, to face it like Sergeant Morgan, to face it like men.

Around noon as they approached a "Y" in the track the train ground to a halt. There was activity among the guards and train crew but no one could tell what was going on. A dispatch rider was spotted coming up to the train and leaving a short time later. A left turn would take them back and a right into the unknown. They almost wished they were back on an open flatcar so they could see what happening. The unknown was vastly preferable and it was with great relief that the train finally got up steam and turned to the right. Perhaps they were going to Charleston or Richmond to be exchanged. Relief and hope again lifted their spirits. They had traveled a half a mile before Del realized he had been fiercely gripping Will's knee. He released his grip, a feeling of embarrassment bringing a flash of pink to his cheeks. Will pretended not to notice.

After a run of no more than five miles the train stopped and they were ordered off. A short march through the stunted trees brought them to another raw, new, stockade. As it loomed up before them their hearts sank.

They entered the stockade and found the interior covered with slash left from the building of the walls, and in no time had fires going. The green pitch pine left on the ground made for an abundance of fire wood and for the first time, in who knows how long, they were all able to properly warm and dry themselves. Jack headed out to find water, skillet in hand. On his return, they took the daily ration of cornmeal and made a stiff dough, spreading it out in the skillet. Propping it above the flames they browned one side and then the other. Dividing it they ate in silence, so low down they couldn't bring themselves to talk. That they wouldn't be having this first meal in Andersonville was all they had thought about. They hadn't realized how demoralized they might be by still being nowhere once the train had stopped.

As the early darkness began to fall, Will fumbled for the thong on the pouch. It had been a long time since he had turned to the harmonica.

The loss of Jimmy had taken the enjoyment out of music, bringing back only sad memories. He had played it the one time in Savannah for the sake of Del and Jack. This time he once more sought it out for his own solace. Sitting by the fire, eyes fixed on the flickering flames, Will began. Heads raised at the sound, and although Will was lost in his own world he was aware of a general movement in his direction.

Del and Jack stretched out near the fire to lose themselves in the poignant wail of the tiny instrument. As he played, Will's mind wandered through the years he and Jimmy had been together. Much of that time had been spent as prisoners, all as soldiers at war. He knew that hard times forged the strongest bonds, but this time, his thoughts passed over the pain and reached for the laughter and comradeship that had made all the misery of fighting and imprisonment bearable. He didn't dwell long on the last few days of Jimmy's life and the still open wound of his passing.

"Take care of her, Will." was what he'd asked, and Will remembered his reply. "I promise." The guilt that the girl's picture now hung in the leather bag over his own heart, and that his assurance was not entirely for Jimmy's own sake had shifted in its prospective. It was a fact. It couldn't be erased but he was truly sure it was not why Jimmy had to die. His attachment to the girl in the picture was a part of the future to be dealt with then, if there was a future for him. With infinite relief he could now separate it from their past without feeling a traitor to the boy's memory.

Requests for songs were made. Happy, homey songs. He played whatever he knew and didn't quit until he was exhausted. A murmur of appreciation came from dozens of lips as well as a few pats on the shoulder. Will was not really aware of the full effect his impromptu concert had on so many that night. He would have been surprised and gratified. Curling up next to Jack, he pulled the corner of the blanket up over his shoulder and went to sleep.

The Millen stockade, as this one was called, resembled Andersonville in size and shape. However, the banks along the stream were firm and covered with a tough grass, and above all, the water supply was clean and plentiful. The winter weather and the lack of built up filth discouraged the flies and their maggots. Lice were still a problem. There was no way to completely eliminate them, but at least they were at a more bearable level for the time being.

Prisoners were divided into groups of one hundred, each commanded by a Union sergeant who assigned them an area. While Will worked with the other sergeants to establish the areas, the other two busied themselves with constructing a shelter. For the first time they had ample materials at hand. They soon had rigged a shelter that was a palace compared to anything they'd had before.

More prisoners arrived, including many of those left behind at Savannah. In a very short time, between six and seven thousand called Millen home. These later arrivals did not fare as well, the slash had, long since, been used up.

Captain Bowes, the commandant at Millen, seemed head and shoulders above the likes of Wirz, and later, Barret of Florence. Even Capt. Davis who had been a fair man in all respects and had possessed the imagination to finally cope with the escape problem without wholesale slaughter was nothing compared to the experienced and efficient soldier placed in charge here. Will's opinion was that, obviously, it was some mistake.

Prisoners were put in charge inside the prison, and rules regarding hygiene and personal conduct, were vigorously enforced. During their six week stay at Millen not one prisoner was shot. Captain Bowes introduced his sixteen-year-old son to the prisoners and announced that he would take the daily roll. The youngster always treated the men with respect and they did likewise, obeying every command without hesitation.

That the Raider element was present was inescapable and they were still seeking retaliation against those involved in the hangings at Andersonville. One day they cornered Cpl. Payne, who had been one of the two that pulled the supports out from under the gallows walkway. Pete Donnely, of the Raiders, forced a fight. Will, Del and Jack, along with remnants of the Regulators, rushed to Payne's defense to ensure a fair fight. When the fight began to go against Donnely, his supporters rushed in. Will and his friends clubbed them back. Will had never clubbed a man before, but in this instance, it was rather satisfying.

A few days later, Sgt. Goody and Cpl. Carrigan, who were high on the Raider list as the ones who placed the sacks and ropes over the heads of the six, arrived. When the word reached the Raiders, they decided on an immediate attack.

Cpl. Carrigan was a giant of a man, and it was generally agreed upon that he had been the toughest man in the entire prison population of thirty five thousand. As far as Will could tell, he was still the toughest man around. For this reason the Raiders decided to deal with Goody first. He was on his hands and knees, working on a shelter when they came up behind him.

"We want to talk to you," one of the Raiders said.

Goody, thinking it was friends, started backing out of his shelter, whereupon they attacked with clubs. To their surprise, he withstood their blows and managed to escape, with them in hot pursuit. Carrigan burst out of the crowd and delivered a well aimed blow with his club to the skull of the closest pursuer. He dropped like a rock, whereupon his companions prudently abandoned the chase.

Will reported the incident to the Sergeant In Charge, who passed the word on to Capt. Bowes' command. To everyone's delight, guards came in and arrested the Raiders, Donnely and Allen, and marched them out to the stocks, where they remained for two days. They subsequently pledged allegiance to the Confederacy and were attached as runners for the crew manning the big guns that covered the prisoners. With their removal from the prison population the serious problems with the Raiders ended.

As the 1864 elections neared, the turncoat Raiders, always currying favor, convinced Capt. Bowes that the prisoners should have a chance to vote. If they rejected Lincoln for McClellan, wouldn't that send a message to the North that their troops no longer supported the war effort? He was persuaded that the vast majority were in favor of McClellan. After discussing it with several officers, it was agreed upon that it would be the right thing to do. Ballots were printed up and with great fanfare, the Captain and fellow officers rode into the prison and proceeded to distribute them. To their chagrin, it readily became apparent that very few votes were going for McClellan, who was perceived to favor cessation and compromise. The prisoners knew that Lincoln would fight it out to the very end and were behind him almost to a man. The Rebels wheeled their mounts and departed to hoots and laughter.

The next entertainment was furnished by orders that came to submit a roll of all foreigners whose term of enlistment had expired. For some strange reason, almost everyone in Will's command was a foreigner. The other rolls were similar. Will was from Turkey. Del was Norwegian, and Jack from Canada.

The following morning, this huge contingent of *foreigners* was taken out of the stockade and marched to a large stump, upon which a Rebel officer stood. With hands on his hips, feet spread, he began to address the crowd. He began by explaining "Due to the lack of compassion of the Union in not exchanging you poor wretches and because of this obvious abandonment, perhaps you should look to other means to end your plight." It soon appeared that the Confederacy was offering them release from prison, food and clothing. To obtain this, all they had to do was renounce the Union and join the Rebel cause. At this point, Will called his group to attention and promptly marched them back into the stockade. The others did the same. The infuriated Rebel guards stormed the gate and proceeded to destroy or steal everything they could reach before they could be stopped by their unprepared officers. This action directly resulted in the death of several hundred prisoners, who perished from the cold.

Shortly after the first of November an announcement was made that one thousand of the sickest prisoners were to be exchanged. Shortly thereafter, rumor spread that Bowes, the rebel commander, was accepting bribes to be included in the exchange. The rumor had it that the range of payment started at two hundred and fifty dollars, an unheard of amount, and dropped all the way down to five dollars. If all three of them could have gotten out for five cents they would have been out of luck. Will hoped the rumor was unfounded. In the privacy of their shelter all three attempted to simulate various diseases they had observed, but found themselves to be unconvincing if not ridiculous. The vast majority of those chosen were, in fact, in wretched condition. Many, first picked, died before the exchange took place. Doubtlessly others never made it to safety.

On an early morning near the end of the month, the prisoners were awakened by the alarm bells. Ten of the sergeants were ordered to assemble their groups at the gate. Will's was among them. Shortly they were marched to the empty tracks and left standing in ranks. There they huddled against the freezing cold with teeth chattering and arms wrapped over their chests, trying to hold the heat in their bodies. Will thought back over time trying to count the times he'd experienced this same sensation, not only as a prisoner. The number was more than he cared to cope with.

The three stood with their patched together blankets and great coat pieces around their shoulders, trying to block out the frozen reality. They were too tired and weak to even think of the possibility of an exchange. The train finally arrived and they were loaded onto open flat cars. Looking back to where they had stood, Will saw several score, curled up in death. It was all so damned familiar. Were they the lucky ones or was it those curled up beside the track? Will couldn't say. Focusing his eyes to the front, he watched the train take the left turn. They were heading back to Savannah, a fitful rain had started.

By the time they neared Savannah, the rain had petered out and the temperature was almost bearable. When the train stopped and they climbed down, Will forced himself to ignore those that remained forlornly on the flatcars. He pushed them from his mind and moved off. A squad of soldiers unloaded the dead and placed them in a central area where negro laborers began to gather them up and loaded them on a cart which would carry them off to be buried. No names, rank or regiment. They just ceased to exist.

Finally they were given a short ration of a few crackers, and marched over to another train where they were loaded aboard. Will was relieved that they would be in boxcars this time. He gladly gave up the view for protection against the cold. The condition of the train, however, was pitiful. The racket it made eliminated the possibility of sleep or conversation. Periodically, it would trail to a stop and Will could hear them banging and cursing over the engine. The rebel officers tried to enlist help from among the prisoners but none could or anyway none did. To even think of asking help from the wretched cargo of this dismal excuse for transportation bound, heaven knew where, Will found damned impertinent. His indignation kept him warmer for quit a few miles.

From time to time the train stopped and a crew of Negroes headed out with axes. The doors were opened and everyone was ordered out. When the crew returned with enough wood to get the engine going again it was back on the car. It felt good to get out and stretch their legs at each of these stops and rest from the constant vibration and eternal noise. Will had no complaint. It was an improvement over some of the other train trips, especially since they could relieve themselves outside. Hunger was always there but it was more in the mind than the pain of an empty stomach.

At one point they were encouraged to get out and push when the train was having a hard time climbing a grade. Will just had to laugh at them for their foolishness and himself for taking their earlier request seriously.

The many holes in the siding allowed snatched glimpses of the passing landscape. If possible, it was even more bleak than the area around Andersonville. Farms were scarce and those he did see appeared neglected or abandoned. Will wondered if around here one judged the wealth of the owner by how much useless junk he had piled up around his house. Still, it was something to look at and Will had to admit that he was enjoying the chance to criticize the passing landscape. As uninviting as it was, it was better than starring at a stockade wall.

Well after dark when the train stopped in the middle of nowhere for wood, instead of waiting to be put back on the train they were marched under guard to a nearby stream and told to make camp. Rations were issued and they settled in for the night. After a time they could hear the train start backing up. The sound lingered in the still night air for what seemed a very long time. They were hardly aware of the exact moment when it was no longer heard. Will figured it was going back for more prisoners. Over the next several days this was proved true. More and more prisoners arrived until the rolls were up to the seven thousand mark. There was nothing to make a shelter or a fire as there was no stockade, only a heavy guard. They had absolutely no idea where they were and most of them were more interested in just staying alive than escape. The name of this new camp was Blackshear.

In no more than a week, the original one thousand were ordered to assemble for immediate transport to Savannah for exchange. Again, it all seemed plausible and hopes soared. Even Will was half convinced. They were encouraged to sign a "parole" paper which, in effect, prohibited them from taking up arms against the Confederacy "until properly paroled." After a lengthy discussion, it was agreed upon to sign the papers. They were suspicious of this new tactic but couldn't see how they could be prevented from getting back to the fight if they were "properly paroled," whatever that was. Stacks of parole papers were placed throughout the area and within an hour, all had signed.

Reassembled, they were given an oath to abide by their agreement and two day's rations were distributed. They were marched down to a waiting train in disbelieving jubilation where they climbed aboard. The Rebels assigned just a few guards to the train, some taking up quarters in the caboose. They paid no attention to the prisoners.

Escape would have been easy during the trip, they could tell they were near the ocean where they might be picked up by one of the blockade ships, but the surety of exchange eliminated any desire to try. Why bother when exchange was just around the corner? This time excitement, as well as noise and discomfort, eliminated any chance for sleep. People talked constantly throughout the stops, exchanging addresses, promising to get together in the future. Just listening to the talk cheered Will up and calmed his doubts. He took out the harmonica and played until his lips were sore.

As the train neared Savannah it slowed down, stopped, then reversed. After a short jaunt down the track it stopped and ran forward again. This was repeated several times leaving the prisoners shaken and doubtful. Finally it pulled into the town and the reason became apparent. It had been killing time so that the troops could get organized to prevent a last minute riot or escape attempt. Two heavy lines of troops, with bayonets fixed, lined the sides of the track. The parole was a trick to allow the transfer of a large number of prisoners with very few guards. They were allowed off the train to stretch their legs, then reloaded to continue the laborious journey toward Charleston.

As they crossed over the Savannah River into South Carolina the long span groaned and creaked with the weight of the train. The river appeared deep, as well as wide, and Will wondered if the whole damn thing would fold up, like a deck of cards and collapse into the water below. He really didn't care one way or the other, at this point. He pictured himself falling into the rushing water as the bridge collapsed. Should he try to hold his breath, as he went under, or just breathe deep? He was amazed when the train reached the other side and maybe just a little disappointed.

12

CHARLESTON

Sarah looked at herself in the large mirror. She made a few adjustments to her long auburn hair. She rearranged her necklace and decided that she was ready. Her best friend Bonnie had learned that a large number of Yankee prisoners were arriving by train, and she and some of her friends were going down to the station to look them over. She didn't like the Yankees for what they had done to the South. Most of the Yankees she'd met seemed rather arrogant and glum. Not at all like the gentlemen she knew. Oh well, it was something to do and might be rather fun to see them humiliated. She heard the train whistle and hurried in the direction of the depot. Several of her girlfriends met her at the clothing store and together they arrived as the train stopped.

"Oh I just can't wait to see those Yankees. I surely enjoy watching them taken down a peg. They are so sure of themselves," her friend Lacy said with a giggle. "Oh! I'm so horrid." She made a pretense of silencing herself by placing her fingers over her mouth.

They all laughed and peered down the tracks to where guards were unlocking the doors to see the prisoners emerge.

As the prisoners climbed down from the cars, Sarah was shocked to see how wretched they looked. As they filed past, she was aware of them sneaking glances at her and her friends. What started out to be a lark, suddenly became very uncomfortable. She tried to look away but before she could, her eyes made contact with the dark brooding eyes of one of the prisoners. Her first thought was that he looked like a rag bag. He straightened his shoulders, attempting to disguise his deplorable condition. Then, to her amazement, he gave her a broad grin and a not-to-subtle wink. She was shocked, and could feel her cheeks turn pink. How impertinent, she thought. Suddenly, she felt like crying. Probably close to death, he still had the inclination to make a pass at her. She decided that she could not look at these poor creatures any longer. As she turned to leave, she noticed that some of her friends had already left. There were no feelings of triumph.

The next day, she asked her Aunt Agnes if she and her lady friends were going to distribute food to the prisoners. She'd had a hard time sleeping and had spent much of that time thinking about the cheeky prisoner. He was starving, but almost all of them were. Maybe it was his attempt to show pride in himself, that set him apart. She felt that he had wanted to look as good as he could for her. Maybe he thought her special. After all, he did smile and wink at her, not any of her friends. Maybe she would go with her aunt. She told herself that it was a nice thing to do, but down deep, she just wanted to see him again.

It was late evening when they entered Charleston. The streets were well lit. The smell from the burning whale oil hung in the air. People were walking to and fro, apparently, without a care in the world. The stores seemed to be well stocked. Will was amazed. It was hard to believe that the horrible places he had been were part of the same world. They were ordered off the train and formed into two lines then marched down the street. It was hard to tell which group was more interested in the other; the pathetic prisoners or the curious towns people. Will was captivated by the sight of so many people dressed in fine clothes, talking, laughing, going about their business. He suddenly felt embarrassed at his own appearance, at least his wild hair and beard were mostly gone. He tried to see his reflection in the store windows, but could not pick himself out from the crowd. He just blended in with everyone else. He thought of waving, but decided against it. No sense making a fool of himself. At that moment, he caught sight of the group of girls. How long since he had been this close to a girl? He stood straighter and tried to look serious but when his eyes made contact with one of the young ladies it was as if Jimmy was there, prodding him to do something outrageous. Before he had time to think about it he grinned at her and winked. He was past before he could witness her reaction. He thought he smelled perfume, but it may have been wishful thinking. The episode made him feel rather giddy.

Within a few blocks, they made a right turn and immediately entered an area of complete devastation. There were no more lights, piles of rubble filled the streets and gutted buildings looked down on them like ghosts of death. It gave Will a strange feeling, to go from the one extreme to the other in a matter of seconds. It suddenly occurred to him that this must be the maximum range of the naval guns. The idea that Union ships were within gun range was exhilarating, the idea they might be killed by one of those shells, however, tended to dampen his enthusiasm.

They were led to a large vacant lot and told to sit down. No one had to be told twice. It had been a very long and trying day. Within seconds someone yelled, "Here comes one of em'!" It was a shell from the blockade ships. Looking seaward, a narrow ribbon of light was rapidly approaching. It sailed over their heads with a long "wish-ish-ish" then a thump as it hit the ground. A second's silence, then a loud roar and crash of buildings being torn apart. They could feel the vibration of the blast through the ground. Ten minutes later, the show repeated itself. As terrifying as the first shell was, it readily became just an irritant to the weary men.

Eventually, the Rebel battery awakened and returned fire, for about an hour. The Union fire kept up throughout the night. Each time there was the same prolonged warning, then the thunderous crash. The word was that this had been the routine for over a year and would probably continue until the city was captured. The maximum range of the shells was so predictable that beyond that distance the life of the city went on uninterrupted.

The early morning rations were minimal, but rumor was to expect them to be augmented by quantities of food brought in by the town's people. Will remembered hearing about the generosity of the Charlestonians from other prisoners who had been here earlier. Many citizens were not sympathetic to the cause of secession, others were simply compassionate Christians who were concerned about the horrible condition of the prisoners.

Sure enough, soon several wagons loaded with produce and a group of townsfolk bearing baskets of food arrived. A great rush of men descended on the small group, and Will, Jack and Del rose and moved in that direction at a more dignified pace. Will worked his way through the crowd until he was within ten feet of one of the food wagons. It was a shock to see that many vegetables in one place. He could smell them, and it was delightful. As his turn came, a matronly looking lady handed him a potato and a handful of carrots. She smiled sweetly and said, "I hope that this will help."

Will smiled and nodded his thanks. Across the tongue of the wagon, he saw the girl from yesterday. He looked at himself, and realized that he did not want her to see him closer. The clothes, though better than most, were so filthy he knew his smell would turn her stomach. He worked his way around the wagon and eased his way up behind her. Leaning forward, he breathed in her scent of soap and a whisper of perfume. With great regret, he backed away and hurried to where his friends were waiting.

To every one's disappointment, the time spent in Charleston was brief. Fresh rumors were circulating daily about the progress of the war. To hear of the Union's success brought a new onrush of hope that could hardly be repressed. Not included in the rumors was the fact that Sherman had cut loose on his march to the sea and it was possible that he would turn in their direction. The news had reached the guards however, and near panic accompanied their preparations for the hasty abandonment of the city.

With reluctance, the prisoners climbed aboard the train. After one final look at the beautiful city Will glanced down the tracks to what might lie ahead. It told him nothing. To their relief, the engine was pulling boxcars. The hissing of escaping steam from the worn out engine ensured them a slow ride. When the cars were loaded, sullen guards were posted on top of them. The idea of leaving a warm fire and being exposed to the chill rain on the boxcars did not sit well with them and Will heard muttered curses that brought a smile to his lips.

Morning found them crawling northward. Some of the prisoners in the other cars fashioned crude saws from hoop iron they found inside and proceeded to cut holes in the floor. With great caution, they dropped down between the tracks and waited for the train to pass over them. Fortunately, the guards topside were too intent on their own misery to be watching for escapees. Will did not know how many actually made it to freedom, as several were brought back the next day. As no one in their car had a saw, there was no way they could join the fugitives.

13

FLORENCE

After a two day run to the north west, they arrived in Florence, still in South Carolina. Actually it was more of a rail junction than a town. That night they slept in an open field, surrounded by guards. Early in the morning they were marched to the stockade. As they arrived they were forced to wait for the death wagon blocking the gate to complete its grizzly task. Apathetically, Will wonder if the slaves loading the wagon understood the sacrifice these men had made for their freedom. It might have consoled him to know of the thousands of black freemen that had joined the Union army to fight and die for the same cause.

The wagon lumbered off and was replaced by a group of Rebel officers led by the prison commander Lt. Barrett. Puffing out his chest, Barrett screamed, "By companies, right wheel march." As there was no division into companies, it was complete bedlam as the prisoners tried to comply. Several of the Reb officers began to laugh, whether at the Lieutenant's mistake, or the prisoners complete disarray was hard to tell but it goaded him beyond reason. His face red, eyes popping, he screamed the most vile language imaginable, drawing his revolver and emptying it over their heads. This had no immediate effect on the confusion so he took the gun from the holster of the officer next to him and emptied that as well shrieking all the while. Most of the prisoners had given up trying to deal with this tirade and just stood waiting dejectedly. As he sputtered to a breathless halt he was led away before he passed out from his ranting. Obviously the man was a chip off the same block as Wirz and Winder.

The stockade and the fifteen acres of ground it surrounded was almost a duplicate of that at Andersonville. Five acres were consumed by the stream and swamp and another two or three were lost to the dead line, reducing the usable acres to seven or eight. Instead of the pole and stake marker for the dead line this one consisted of a shallow ditch which completely faded out in places. The guards did not hesitate to shoot a prisoner who mistook the line. If in doubt, shoot first, ask questions later, was their creed. With additional arrivals, their numbers soon swelled to fifteen thousand. This was relieved by the rapid death rate, and an exchange of several thousand of those in the worst condition. The number leveled off to around eleven thousand.

Unlike Andersonville cleanliness was encouraged. Streets were lined out, which made movement easier, and best of all, the rations included molasses and rice, as well as a few spoonfuls of vinegar augmented by what food local citizens could contribute.

The need for fuel was critical. All loose fuel within the stockade was used up before their arrival and the stumps were soon hacked, chipped, and sawed away. Then the roots were followed to a depth of as much as twelve feet. Mud huts sprouted up and afforded some protection, but a heavy rain would bring them down on the occupant. In desperation some had their friends bury them at night. Their faces, covered with a cloth if possible to reduce the sting of the icy rain was all that was left exposed. In the morning they would be dug up until their last morning.

Before long Winder arrived. The men agreed that he and Barrett were a pair to draw to. Both were cruelly sadistic inflicting pain and misery for no other reason than their own entertainment. Barret, being smarter than Wirz, used his cunning to make their every waking moment a living Hell. The rations were immediately cut and punishments increased.

Shortly after Winder's departure, Barret, suspecting an escape tunnel was being dug, proclaimed, "No rations will be distributed until the location of the tunnel is exposed, and those responsible for it, turned over to me." No tunnel was being dug. Many assumed that he was looking for an excuse and a tunnel was plausible.

The rations were already minimal, so any interruption was death for many. The first day without food took quite a number, the second took many more. It was evident that unless a tunnel was "found" and someone turned in, the entire camp could perish. A tunnel was hastily dug to show the Rebs, and volunteers entered a draw, Jack and Del among them, to see who would be sacrificed. Will was physically discouraged from entering by the other two. They reasoned that he would not stand a chance of living through any punishment. Luckily for them, four others "won" and were marched over to the gate to be delivered to Barrett. The bravery of the four men to be subjected to Barrett's brutality was not lost on the rest of the population. By the time rations were distributed, the men were so starved that most did not take the time to cook anything. Unable to digest the raw food in their condition, many died within a few days.

The following morning, after Barrett finished his hardy breakfast, the four men were led out of their cell and their thumbs tied behind their backs. A rope was thrown over the ridge board of the guard house, and each man took his turn being suspended off the ground by his bound hands. All four had vowed to take their punishment bravely, but the pain was too excruciating and the afternoon was filled with their screams. All were unconscious when cut down and after weeks in the hospital were left more or less crippled for life. After that incident, life settled down to a cold dreary routine inside the stockade.

"Will, look at all these fellows, will you? What is different?" Jack asked.

Will scanned the men grouped around the ration wagon. "Damned if I know what you're talking about. They all look the same to me," he replied.

"That's just it. They are all the same. Everywhere else there were always newly taken prisoners coming in. Here, we're all on our last pins and our own rags are about the best around. What do ya suppose it means?"

Will thought about it awhile but came up cold.

"Another thing, have you noticed these guys with their hands and feet rotting off? What in thunder is causing that?"

"I can fill you in there," replied a passer-by. "It's dry gangrene. It happens after frost bite. The flesh just dies and rots off."

"Christ !" exclaimed Jack, with a shudder. "Does it hurt as bad as it looks?"

"They claim it don't, and if it dries out and turns black it stops progressing. Had to take my carvin' knife to some of my friends that got like that. They said it made 'em feel better not to have to look at it. Not so good if it keeps on though. Hurts like sin when just the bone and tendons are left. Don't worry, you'll get used to it."

"You're wrong, friend, I'll never get used to that," Jack answered emphatically.

"We'll see," he said. "I thought the same thing."

Regrettably, his prophecy proved true as the sight of men with dead appendages became commonplace. It was a slow process, taking weeks to reach the sloughing off stage. As there was no pain involved the victim's mind tended to disconnect with the affected part by the time it was ready to drop off. It was just a blessing to have the damned thing gone. It even ceased to disconcert the ones who stumbled over the withered body part on his way across the camp.

Guided by the weather the dreary days turned into dreary weeks. On dark, damp days, all but the most necessary activity stopped while everyone curled up together to keep as warm as possible. When the sun shone those not sunk in the numbing lethargy of near death went about locating the dead and conducting their ongoing war with body lice. It was routine to scoop out hands full of the tormentors from one's sleeping area after a week of inactivity. They hated to use what little fuel they had to rid themselves of the creatures but in the end it was the only way to preserve their sanity. Every tiny fire was circled with men burning the lice out of their clothing. After that entertainment was over there was nothing more to do. There was not enough conversation left to waste energy in talk. Their numb minds could find little hope of ever living through this.

Death came with less violence than at Andersonville. No shooting of prisoners or fights between men. No circle of friends to witness the passing. Here it was a quiet, unobtrusive shadow passing among them, choosing this one or that. They were all so close packed, it was sometimes hard to tell who it had visited. One morning they answered when gently shaken, the next morning they didn't. It was common to have a companion die in his sleep, curled up snug against his friends unnoticed, until they tried to turn over and found him stiffening.

Will spent most of his time curled up between Del and Jack. Silently each fought to maintain his own identity. Will tried to focus on the events of his life. He remembered his childhood, his days in Texas punching cows, and his encounter with Rosella. He recited a litany of names over and over in fear that they might be lost to him forever. His family, friends, men he had worked or fought with, and places he'd been. Tracing his life like beads on a rosary until the names were more like a chant than a history.

Christmas came on a cold, sodden day like so many others. It brought them no respite. Indeed, it sent many even deeper into a despair from which there was no return. The number of dead, by the end of the day, was nearly sixty. For sheer hopelessness Will would remember it as the lowest point of his entire life.

The new year, however, started out on a high note. They learned that General Winder had died in his sleep. If not able to jump for joy, at least the men could smile, as they huddled in the cold. It was brought out, after the war was over, that Winder had bragged that he was, "Killing more Yankees than twenty regiments in the field." This was certainly a fact. Through deliberate neglect, he had personally been responsible for the deaths of thirteen thousand prisoners at

Andersonville alone, and as many as twenty five thousand throughout the system.

Will had to wonder, what kind of God would allow scum like Winder to die peacefully in his sleep with a full stomach? Well, at least he was gone. It then passed through his mind that with his last breath Winder had probably gasped. "Cut the damn rations for those Yankee sons-a-bitches." It was the only thing he smiled about, all day.

As January slowly dragged into February rumors of huge successes by Sherman's army, brought in by the slaves that came to remove bodies, began circulating. These were substantiated by the increased vigilance of the guards. Word was that Sherman had marched through Georgia with almost no resistance. Within days, word spread of Sherman's imminent attack on Savannah. The knowledge that they would never see Savannah again warmed the hearts of everyone. But where was Sherman now? Would he proceed into South Carolina? The rumors didn't include the destruction of Hood's Rebel forces at Franklin and Nashville.

As they followed the daily flow of information it was hard to imagine Sherman being able to move so fast against the likes of Hardee, Dick Taylor, and Beauregard, who should be putting up a stiff resistance. That these units were destroyed, or in retreat, was more than they could imagine.

It wasn't long after the rumors started that they were awakened to the rumble of trains going by, heading north on what they had learned was the Charleston and Cheraw Railroad. This continued all day long at half hour intervals. The word was spread that Sherman had taken Branchville and was swinging around toward Columbia, and points to the north. Charleston was being evacuated and the garrison, munitions, and stores, were being moved to Cheraw.

Orders came for one thousand prisoners to be ready to move out. Will, Del and Jack looked at one another. Would it be better to wait and see if Sherman arrived, or flank into the group leaving. It was a difficult choice to make.

"Hell with it," exclaimed Jack. "I say we chance it and stay here this time. Sherman can't be too far off and I see no sense in running away from him."

They watched the thousand march off, then the second thousand the next day, and so on, until the population was down to around eleven hundred. By burning everything of little value left behind, such as old clothing and tent material, they managed to have the first fires of any size since they had left Millen. The activity renewed circulation to their bodies as well as their minds.

Five new prisoners were brought in. The first they had seen in a long time. They were well fed, healthy and exhibited open disdain for the Rebs. One of the rebel officers invited them all. "Come up to Headquarters, and we'll parole ya."

"Oh go to hell! Old Uncle Billy (Sherman) will get us out of here by Saturday," said one with contempt. "I suggest you boys pack up and get the hell out of here a'for he shows up. He ain't gonna look kindly on how you been treatin' these boys."

Will, taking in the exchange, was amazed to see the look that passed over the faces of the Rebs. Turning to Will and the others, the new man said, "Don't you boys be a worried now. Everything is goin' just as planned. Shucks, we haven't been called to a battle line since, I don't know when. Uncle Billy would just love to have them skunks stand and fight, but it seems all they want to do is run. Just, you keep your spirits up."

Listening to the man talk, Will could feel a glow of hope spread through him. Turning to the others he knew that they were feeling the same excitement. Everyone was grinning from ear to ear.

14

FREEDOM!!!

The following day, all those able to walk were marched out to the waiting train. Those unable to walk were carried over on wagons. Those too weak and near death were left in the mud to die. The train started off in an easterly direction. As they passed near small towns along the way they could smell smoke and catch a glimpse of flames from burning buildings. Will didn't know if it was Sherman or if the Rebs were destroying anything that might be of value to him. At this point, he didn't care, just as long as it was going up in smoke. They were near the front of the car and one of the men nearby had opened a hole in the rotten boards in the front wall. The forward car was filled with Rebel officers, and an old black servant was sitting on the rear platform.

The prisoner called the elderly man closer. "Well, Uncle, where are they takin' us?" he asked, with deference.

"Well, suh, I s'pose if'n ya'all was to think on it, ya jus might could guess." Turning his head, to be sure no officer was listening, he continued. "Dey's a goin' to take ya'all to Wilmington ifn' they can git you there."

"What do you mean, if they can get us there? What's to prevent it? There aren't any Yankees between here and Wilmington, are there?"

The old man's eyes shown with a light of glee. "Dem Yankees took Wilmington yisterdee." Hearing something from the car ahead the old man slipped back across the coupling and into the back door.

As the miles slipped by they were all tense with growing excitement. Other men had succeeded in picking larger holes in the sides of the car and they had shouted the news to the car behind. They were fairly prepared when the train came to a sudden, jolting halt. They could see Rebel battle lines strung across the tracks, the first many had seen in years. Will was shocked at the wretched condition of the Confederate troops. Uniforms tattered, most were barefoot, and nearly as thin as the prisoners on the train. Obviously, they were preparing to engage in battle. The question was, when it broke out, would the helpless prisoners be right in the middle? They were all off balance, craning around to try to see out the holes when the answer came. The train jerked backward sending the occupants sprawling. As it gathered speed it lurched from side to side preventing them from regaining their former positions. As they bounced around inside, it felt as if the whole train was going to run off the tracks. After what seemed an eternity it stopped and they were allowed to get off and stretch.

Will stood at the edge of the crowd of prisoners watching a group of officers in heated conversation. They were drawing in the dirt with sticks, then rubbing the drawings out with their boots. Will would have given a dollar, if he had one, to know what they were going on about. He could see that a large white flag had been stuck on the front of the engine and pointed it out to the others. In his mind it could mean only one thing, they were contemplating a possible encounter with the Union Army and had no intention of fighting. Finally they all re-boarded the train.

They slowly proceeded forward, stopping every once in a while. At each stop several officers would disembark and trudge up the tracks to reconnoiter. When they returned the train would cautiously move forward. Late in the afternoon they came to a last grinding halt and Will could see rifle pits dug in along the track but no sign of the Rebel troops.

The officers got off and stood in a gloomy knot near the engine, facing away from Will, as he strained to see what they were looking at. He could make out men dug in up ahead, but was unable to distinguish the color of their uniforms. A captain, Will recognized from Florence, came walking back along side of the prisoners' cars. Will could see his pale face clearly. His teeth were clenched. His eyes held grim defeat. He yelled orders to the guards on top of the cars. "Git down offen thar and form a line." They complied, though they looked as if they would rather run for the hills. They were in no immediate danger because of the white flag but perhaps, in their apprehension, they had forgotten it was there.

The prisoners began to taunt them and this abuse continued until the train started inching its way forward when they subsided into an uneasy silence. The Rebs, holding their weapons pointed down with arms extended out from their sides, followed alongside the boxcars. Before long Will could make out the grand royal blue of the troops awaiting them. So superb looking in dress and manner. So unlike the deplorable condition of the Rebels. As a soldier he felt a tinge of pity for the departed southern fighting troops. Most of the riff-raff that had looked down on them from their pigeon roosts were another story.

As soon as the train stopped and the guards opened the doors, everyone jumped to the ground in excitement. The young Captain in charge made an effort to get them in order but most ignored him. Some did take the opportunity to tell him what they thought of him, his army and his cause. He blustered impotently as he returned to his fellows in defeat. Some prisoners started directly off toward the waiting troops while others veered off to a small stream. Will, Del and Jack were among this latter group. They were thirsty and they wanted to wash off as much of the southern filth as they could, cold as the water was. They shook out their clothes and rinsed off in the stream. Redressed and with teeth chattering, they followed the others through a make-shift gate manned by a Rebel and a Union clerk who checked them off. They were officially free!

Helping hands reached out to them, some guiding some carrying, as they proceeded along the tracks away from the battle lines. They were kind and respectful of the rag tag band. Everything about them made Will proud. They asked many questions and Will and the others answered as best they could. Their own questions were forgotten in the wonder of the moment. Presently they arrived at the bivouac area where there were wagons laden with provisions. A doctor was there to put restrictions on what food to administer to those too weak to stand. They would be spoon fed over time until they were in better shape. He advised the rest of them not to overdo. They could hold only so much in their shrunken stomachs but they vowed to do the food justice as lines were formed. It was amazing. Boxes of hardtack were opened and the contents handed out with abandon. If a man looked wistful, he was handed more, if he still lingered, he was told, "There's plenty, you can come back. You just take as much as you can carry."

And so it went, with pickled pork, coffee and sugar. Will had never been a heavy coffee drinker but he found himself drinking cup after cup. He couldn't seem to get enough. The tray of pork almost melted in his mouth, giving him a heady feeling of euphoria. The smells, those glorious smells of cooking food. He thought he might faint from the aroma that hung in the air.

Will could hardly comprehend the fact that it was all over. He felt he should eat frugally and hide food away as if they were still in prison. There would be no returning to a stockade, no more starving, it had even warmed up a little, it was all too much to take in. He stretched out on the bare ground and went to sleep. When he awakened, several hours later, he was amazed to realize that he was covered with a clean new blanket. He had to run the reality through his mind again and again to test its truth. He assured himself that Jack and Del were nearby then drifted off to sleep again.

The smell of meat cooking drove them out first thing in the morning. The fact that there was no frost during the night made it even easier. The sight of unlimited food stacked up on makeshift tables, stunned their senses. It was hard to tell who was enjoying it more, the men receiving the food or those who were handing it out. Will found himself sneaking an extra biscuit under his shirt and was embarrassed when he realized he was seen by one of the soldiers.

"Hey, you can't take an extra biscuit 'cause there's a new law. You have to take at least two extras," he said with a broad grin.

As they ate they conducted an animated conversation with the troopers left to aid them. God! It was so good to talk and laugh again!

"Well, aside from food, which you have already eaten, what else strikes your fancy?" asked a clean shaven, handsome young man. "You name it and we'll try to get it for you."

In less than a heart beat, everyone nearby exclaimed with one voice, "Soap!"

"That's an easy one." he laughed, "Don't you boys wander off. We'll be right back."

"Wander off? No way in hell I'm goin' anywhere. Not with soap comin'," Jack said with a smile.

Shortly, the men returned with chunks of soap and some towels and began counting off those who wished to bathe. The three of them managed to get in the first group and made a bee line for the stream. Stripping off their filthy clothes, they waded into the cold stream and sat down to lather up. When they had scrubbed all over and rinsed off, they dragged the remnants of their clothing into the water and had at them with the soap. The satisfaction of watching the lice float down the stream with the dirty suds was almost as enjoyable as being clean. They were glad they had been able to wash their hair and beards. The hair and whiskers of most of the other men were hopeless mats that would have to wait until another day. Relinquishing the soap and towels and, wrapped in their new blankets, they hung their clothes on bushes in the weak sunlight to dry. By midday most of their clothes were dry enough to put back on. They were all dressed and ready to enjoy the noon meal prepared especially for them. They found a place in the sun to eat and dropped off to sleep afterwards, only waking when the main body of troops returned for the evening meal.

After breakfast the next morning those that couldn't walk were loaded on wagons. With the rest following, the wagons started up the road. Before long they crossed over a pontoon bridge then over a rise into Wilmington. Will was amazed at the size and apparent wealth of the city. With strong forts for protection, it had flourished throughout the war. Wealth provided by the daring blockade runners had given it a gloss that rivaled San Francisco, for charm and elegance. On the river behind it much of the mighty Union fleet was anchored.

Down the hill they marched, heads up, walking tall. The sun was shining in a cloudless sky and Will was absorbed in the sights. The blue of the water rivaled that of the Union troops in full battle gear. The tangled masts of the ships were highlighted with colored flags. After the drabness of the stockades, his eyes could not get enough of the life and color before him. A nudge from behind brought him out of his reverie. Then he was pushed violently as one of the men behind fell into him. Losing his balance, he tumbled forward, striking his head on a large rock. Del and Jack were at his side in a rush.

"You hurt?" Del asked, as they gently lifted Will to his feet.

Will was dizzy and bleeding from the head wound. "Hell no, I feel great. Take more than that to keep me down," he retorted. As they proceeded, however, his gait was unsteady. Blood ran from gashes in the palms of his hands, where he had tried to break the fall. He gently rubbed them on what was left of his shirt. Damn, he thought, come all this way and danged near kill myself falling down a hill.

As they neared the docks a small steamer slowly moved up, and sailors jumped off securing it to pilings. The Captain came out on deck and, with the aid of a bull horn, announced that, "This vessel is the Thorn. She will be taking on those of you in the worst condition.

The General Lyon, coming into view, will take on those in better shape."

All three queued up to gain access to the General Lyon. It was clear that Del and Jack were still in fair condition. Will on the other hand was painfully thin, and with the bad cut on his head he was directed aboard the Thorn. He attempted to follow the other two along the dock but was gently guided to the Thorn's gangplank. They turned and waved at the slight figure. "We'll see you in Annapolis in a few days, Will. You take care of yourself and don't go fallin' off the damn boat."

"Oh don't worry about that, I'll hold on real tight. See ya." He walked up the narrow plank. Finding a place at the rail and toward the stern, he settled down and watched as the rest were loaded aboard. On down the dock he could see his friends boarding the General Lyon. He wished that he were with them and fought down the urge to weep. He was surprised at himself and guessed the fall had shaken him more that he'd thought. After all, in a couple of days they would all be back together again. He gripped the rail and dangled his feet over the side, looking down into the churning water. He had made it.

As soon as the boat was full, the lines were cast off. They moved out into the river and headed toward the open ocean. As they made their way down river a number of smaller boats were moving back and forth, looking for Rebel mines. Will, who had never been on a sea voyage in his life, was so engaged in sightseeing, he didn't pay much attention.

Presently, the General Lyon pulled into view and slowly came closer until Will could see the faces of the men at the rail. He searched for

Del and Jack, but was disappointed. Then, in a burst of speed, the Lyon moved up alongside and then pulled ahead. As they passed everyone waved, and again Will searched for his friends. They all looked so much alike, it was impossible to pick out Del and Jack, but he knew they would be waving. He waved back and resumed his sightseeing. Pretty soon he stood up to see if the General Lyon was still in sight. To his disappointment it was just rounding a bend. From the bow area he heard raised voices. Then there was a rush of people toward the stern. The boat heaved beneath his feet and he felt himself lifted upward, then nothing.

15

FRIENDS DIVIDED

Jack and Del had been sitting on the stern, perched on several large metal ship parts that they didn't recognize, making small talk. Del had been talking about his plan to go to work for the railroad. His father was a man of influence and would help him get a good position. He also talked of marrying Betsy, if she would still have him in his present condition. Jack suggested that he get another suit of clothes first. They were laughing at this exchange when a huge explosion erupted around the bend behind them.

"My God, what was that!" Jack exclaimed He knew, but didn't want to believe it.

"That can't be the Thorn. It can't be." Del muttered. They were on their feet, their eyes glued to the river behind them.

They waited for the Thorn to come into sight but saw nothing. A pall of smoke billowed up beyond the tree covered ridge that obstructed their view. They continued to scan the river for a sign. No boat came around the bend as long as it was in sight.

Jack looked into Del's shocked face, tears streaming down his cheeks. They were unable to speak.

The next day they were tossed by ocean waves. The food they had eaten came up to torment them. The smell from below deck prevented them from going down to help out the sick. They stayed on the stern, trying to ignore the occasional stench that wafted back to them from time to time. By the next day, most had gotten over the sickness but the area below deck remained a place to avoid at all costs. Rations were distributed, but there were few takers. Some that took their rations got sick all over again, causing a chain reaction among many of the others. All had a new appreciation of the navy.

Three days later they pulled into the harbor at Annapolis in Maryland. During the entire trip they had not said fifty words to each other. They had seen it, but could not, or would not accept the fact that Will might have been killed in that explosion.

They were marched off the boat and up to the hospital. It was a beautiful place and the cleanliness of everything dazzled them both. As they entered, men were standing on either side and without a word removed all of their tattered clothing, wrapping them with towels. They were ushered into another room with a row of chairs. Men stood behind each chair with scissors and razors. Within seconds, it seemed, they were shorn of their filthy hair and beards. Others led them to the next room which contained large tubs of hot soapy water, with two men with sponges at each tub. As they stepped in they were set upon with a flurry of splashing water and sponges. They were then surrounded by men with towels, who proceeded to dry them off in seconds. Finally, they were led into a room with long tables where clothing was neatly stacked. As they passed along the stacks, men judged their size and handed them a full set of clothing. It had happened so fast and without a word being spoken that they had a hard time adjusting to the sudden change in their condition.

Once dressed, they were ushered out onto the lawn where tables and benches were set up. Orderlies carried platters of food out and placed them on the tables.

"By God, Del, you sure look different. I think I liked you better before they cleaned you up. I don't think Will will recognize us when he gets here. He damn well better show up."

"He'll show up. Takes more than a mine blowin' up to git the best of him." Del repeated over and over to himself, Show up Will, show up.

They took up a position overlooking the dock and waited. But as the hours went by there was no sign of the Thorn. Disheartened, they reported to the hospital bed number they had been given with their clothes. The rooms were immaculate and the beds were covered with white sheets and blankets. They climbed in, exhausted with the days activities, and went to sleep.

The next morning, at breakfast, they spotted a boat pulling into the dock with ex-prisoners. They pushed their plates of food away and rushed down to see if Will was aboard. Questioning those men they knew had been on the Thorn, who knew Will, they were disappointed as one after the other knew nothing of what had happened to him. At last, one of the men being carried down on a stretcher, gave them the bad news.

"He didn't make it, boys, I seen his body layin' on the bank with the other dead."

Del was stunned. "You sure it was Will?" his voice breaking.

"Well I couldn't tell by the face, cause it was in bad shape but I seen the pouch around his neck. And I knowed that pouch when I seen it. Damned sorry to have to tell ya." The man was carried on up the hill and into the hospital.

They returned to their bench and sat in silence. Remembering.

Andy and his dad had been out in their skiff fishing all day but their luck had been poor. They saw the big boat churn on past them and were swinging around to go home when the second boat appeared. Waiting for it to pass, they were suddenly engulfed in spray as an explosion lifted the large boat out of the water. Debris fell around them, steam covered the water. Their skiff was tossed around like a match stick and they clung to the sides to keep from being thrown out. They heard men screaming but were unable to see them. They rowed in the direction of the screams and came upon men in the water. Reaching into the water, Andy's father pulled in one, two then three of them.

"Head to shore Andy, head to shore!" As Andy strained on the oars he saw other boats reach the scene to join the rescue effort. These were manned by the sailors that had been searching for mines. Working swiftly, with a minimum of wasted effort, they were in the water, pushing the wounded towards their boats, where others reached down and lifted them up to the decks. Andy continued to row, straining against the oars. Within minutes they felt ground and Andy jumped out and secured the rope to a stump. Helping his father, they lifted the three men out of the boat and placed them on the ground. Already, people were arriving to give aid. Andy and his father made five trips out to where the boat had gone down before giving up. They had brought fifteen men to land in their small craft. The navy boats had finished off-loading their dead and wounded as well. They continued to cross and re-cross the area where the boat had gone down. The dead were left by the shore and the wounded taken up the beach into the trees. Word was sent for a boat large enough to carry the wounded back to Wilmington.

"Andy, I think they have the worst under control, but they need some medical help, and the closest I can think of is Doc Morrison. You get on your horse and see if you can fetch him down here. Tell him he's needed real bad."

Andy scrambled up the bank to his horse and leaping on, headed in the direction of Doc's place.

Doc had just loaded his pipe and was settling into his favorite chair when old Scruff heard the sound of approaching hoof-beats and gave the alarm, a few loud barks, then trotted to the window to see who was coming. Doc's wife, Mary, glanced out, dropped her towel on the table and headed in the direction of the door. "Looks like Andy, Doc. I wonder what brings him over here in such a rush?"

"Could be just about anything, I suppose. I imagine we'll know shortly." He stood up and placed his pipe in the saucer by his chair. He followed Mary out to the stoop.

Andy galloped into the yard and swung off the horse. Seeing Doc in the doorway, he yelled, "Doc! We need you down at the river. One of those boats full of war prisoners hit a mine and there're dead and wounded piled up everywhere. Dad says to come quick!"

"Andy, you start hitchin' Biscuit to my buggy while I fetch my bag." Doc retreated into the house to grab his medical bag and a coat. He supposed it had to do with that explosion he'd heard awhile back.

He had been retired from practice for the last few years and enjoyed being a man of some leisure. A younger doctor had pretty much taken over. Doc hadn't minded, but as he gathered his things, the excitement was still there. It sounded like a real bad accident. Was he still up to it? He figured that he would know, one way or the other in a very short while. As he opened the door to leave, old Scruff squeezed out between his legs and loped toward the barn.

When Doc got to the barn he helped Andy finish with the harnessing. Old Scruff jumped up into the buggy. Before starting out, Doc scratched the dog's ears briefly. Then they were off at a brisk trot. They had put on a lot of miles going out on calls through the years and that went for Biscuit too. Biscuit was getting pretty old for doing much running but at a good trot he could still eat up the miles. That would have to be good enough. Andy galloped on by him and through a break in the trees leading to the throng of people gathered on the bank. Horses and buggies were everywhere and Doc had to weave his way through them, but at last they were able to stop within a few yards of the injured men.

The confusion that had marked Andy's departure now looked more like an organized effort. Several people recognized Doc and explained what they were doing and what was needed. The dead were lined along the bank, as the sailors would be picking the bodies up later. The wounded were divided into groups according to the severity of their injuries. Doc headed toward the group that held the most seriously wounded men. There was definitely enough work to do and he was wishing that he were thirty years younger. As he worked, he was pleased at how fast it was coming back to him. Although he was seeing conditions that he had only heard about, he didn't panic, didn't waste time on unnecessary medication. This must be something like a battlefield, he thought. He had wondered how he would measure up under those conditions and here he was, treating a score or more men with terrible injuries and he knew he was doing a good job. Dozens more were injured, but there was nothing more he could do.

Naval doctors arrived in several wagons loaded with medical supplies, and Doc took a well deserved break. He realized that his old bones were acting up a bit and his back was aching. He soon went back to work and helped finish the job. Wagons arrived and loaded the injured for transport to the nearest hospital. Ships were not readily available, so wagons were hastily dispatched which meant a longer and rougher trip for the wounded.

Doc watched them depart. Mentally crushed to see so many wounded men, obviously in wretched condition. He still felt pride in the good he had done for them. Glancing around, he wondered where Scruff had taken off to. He was a little irritated to see the dog digging around the bodies. Not just digging but whining. Strange behavior, Doc thought, as he called Scruff to his side. The dog ignored him and continued to dig at the bodies. Usually, the dog obeyed instantly. Doc gave up the calling and walked down to see what he was up to. He could see the body that had attracted Scruff's attention, and by the looks of the fellow he was better off dead. There was a pouch, of sorts, around his neck but that was not Scruff's concern. It had something to do with the man himself. Squatting down, he placed his hand on the chest and was startled to feel a faint heartbeat.

"I need some help down here, quick!" he called. Several men who had been standing around discussing the explosion, hurried down the bank. "Get this fellow up to my buggy there, and be gentle. He's breathing but I don't think it would take much to kill him."

Following up behind them, he wondered what to do with this man. Everyone else had left for the hospital way off across the river. "Damnation!" he said, to no one in particular. The men glanced back. They had known Doc for years and had never heard him cuss.

Moving around them, he rolled out the lap blanket he always kept in the boot and spread it out in the back of the buggy. "Put him in there. Easy does it. Thanks a lot. If anyone asks, tell them I'm taking him to my place."

"Sure thing, Doc. Good luck with him! From the looks of him, you're going to need it."

Andy had remained with Doc while his father had gone on with one of the wagons. "Anything I can do to help?" he asked.

"You sure can! Ride up ahead of me and tell the wife that I'm bringing home a wounded man. I need her to set up the spare room. Tell her that I need the scissors and the supplies out of the middle drawer. You got that? And Andy, no reason to run your horse because I'll be going slow."

Andy nodded and gathering up the reins, mounted his horse and disappeared into the trees.

"Get up here, Scruff! You did a good job. Gid'ap! Biscuit, let's go home." Slapping the reins, he followed Andy up through the trees.

As Doc pulled up in front of his house, Mary came out to meet him. Andy stepped down from the porch and took the reins. He wrapped them around the post and went to the back of the buggy to look at Will. He quickly looked away and busied himself with wrapping the blanket around Will's legs. Mary had come down the steps to join Doc and Andy at the back of the buggy.

"Let's get him moved inside, Andy. Honey, did you find the scissors? This boy is going to have to be sheared so that I can see where to start."

Mary produced the scissors from her apron pocket and handed them to Doc. "Good, let's cut off the majority of it right here so's we don't end up with all that filth in the house. Andy, help me turn him around." As light as Will was, they had no trouble shifting him around so that his head was toward the end of the buggy. "Hold his head Andy. Try to support his neck. Hold it right there."

Andy tried not to look down, as he cradled the man's head in his arms. The left eyeball was hanging out of the eye socket, and was crushed. A bright red gash laid his cheek open, exposing teeth. Andy had the feeling that he was going to faint. He shifted his eyes to Biscuit and kept them there.

Five minutes later, the filthy hair was piled on the ground and Doc was relieved to see that the damage was no worse than he had expected. He could feel Mary at his side as she slipped her arm around his waist. "Oh Doc, such a young man. Do you think he'll make it?" she whispered.

"I'll do my best. You two get his legs and I'll get him under the arms and we'll take him inside. Go real slow up the stairs."

Once they had him in bed, Doc brought a lamp over and hung it on a hook in the ceiling over head. He took a critical look at the face and determined that the left eye was gone for sure. As bad as that looked it was not life threatening, as long as it didn't get infected. Moving closer, he examined the rip in one cheek that stretched from his mouth to his left ear. Damned ugly tear but he was confident that he could handle it. Cuts, and scratches covered much of the left chest, but stitches would take care of the cuts. Scratches would mend on their own. Actually, the man's starved state worried him more. He had never seen starvation before, but this was just about as bad as a man could get and still be living, he guessed. Reaching down for his medical bag, he took out his tools and went to work.

Take your time. Don't make any mistakes. One step at a time and you'll be safe. He told himself. As the time slipped by, he was unaware of Andy heading home, but did feel Mary busying herself with cleaning the mud off of the young man's body.

"That's all that I can do for him now," Doc announced, bending backward and rubbing his sore back muscles. "Let's get him bundled up and then get some sleep ourselves."

"You go ahead, Doc, you've put in a long day. I'll sit with him in case he wakes up in the night." Doc leaned over and gave her a peck on the cheek. Dimming the light, he started out of the room. Stopping in the doorway he looked back at his wife fussing with the blankets. He felt himself to be one lucky man.

Will could hear his folks talking in the kitchen. Not clear enough to pick up the words, just the tone. He heard them laugh, along with the sound of wood being put in the stove. Out in the yard he could hear the occasional crow of the rooster and the clucking of the hens. Once, he thought he felt his dog's tongue on his hand. He dozed off. Later, he felt the cool soft hand of his mother wiping his arms and chest with a damp cloth. He made an effort to open his eyes but couldn't manage it. He dozed again.

A rooster awakened him. Again he could hear the voices. This time he was also aware of the severe pain in his face. He realized his entire body felt as if he had been kicked repeatedly by a horse as well. He still could not open his eyes, but he was too tired to care. Moving his hands, he felt the clean, crisp sheets and felt the nap of the blanket around his neck. I'm home, he thought. What a strange dream. He slept.

He awakened, some time later, to the soft hands and the damp cloth on his mouth. He moved his head, trying to see her face. Still couldn't open his eyes. His face hurt something awful. He tried to reach up to feel his face but his arms were pinned under the sheet. It didn't matter, he was home. It had all been a dream. He slept some more.

Later that afternoon Mary noticed his hand movement and called Doc, who was having his morning pipe on the stoop. "I think our visitor is awake, Doc. You better come in and have a look."

"I'm on my way. It's time we had a look at that face."

Doc carefully removed the bandages covering his eyes, then rewrapped it so the good eye was exposed. Will found himself looking into the face of a stranger. Kind eyes, he thought, and a nice smile. He had half expected to see his father's face. He realized that he was not in a dream. The stockades had been real. In that case, where was he? And what was that glorious smell?

"Don't you fret young man, you had a bad accident, but I think you are on the mend. Could I interest you in some of my wife's famous beef broth?"

Will managed a nod and he was lifted up and pillows placed behind his head and back. His chest hurt as well as his face. Breathing was an effort. Mary came in with a bowl in her hand and sat down beside him. She was the sweetest looking lady he had ever seen. In her seventies, as was the man, they carried an aura of lifelong good people. Will attempted a smile.

He felt the spoon touch his lips and tasted the warm broth. He had never tasted anything so good in his life. He finished the bowl and settled back in the bed. Mary wiped his mouth with the cloth and left the room. He savored the warmth in his stomach and tried to remember what had happened to him. He could remember being on the boat, and seeing Del and Jack pass by. Then nothing until the sound of voices in the kitchen. He slept.

Doc followed Mary into the kitchen where she started washing the dishes. Doc picked up the towel and started drying. "Well, Honey, I think that young man is going to make it just fine. Did you see the look on his face when he tasted your broth? I doubt he's tasted anything that good in some time."

"I must admit, I almost cried, Doc. He is just so terribly thin and weak. I can't help but wonder what he must have gone through to get to this condition, but I don't think I want to know. What kind of people could do this to him?"

"I don't reckon I know, but from the looks of those fellows with him, they all suffered the same punishment. Never saw anything like it in all my life and hope I never see it again. I'm just glad that I left you here so you didn't have to see them." Doc shook his head, remembering the pile of dead bodies laid out near the bank and realizing that if it weren't for old Scruff, this young man would probably be dead as well. "I wonder how he is going to react to his new face? That worries me."

"Well, we'll just have to help him through it. There's more to life than a handsome face, and it will look a lot different when the swelling goes down and he gets his color back," replied Mary , with a faint smile.

"What are you smiling about? I've not seen that look in your eyes for a while."

"I'm really not sure but for the first time in ages, I feel needed. I feel that I can make a difference in someone's life, and it's a good feeling. This may sound foolish, Doc, but I am thrilled that he is here and that I can take care of him."

Doc hung the towel over the chair back and put his arm around her shoulder. "I must admit that I've had the same feelings. When I was tendin' to those boys at the river, I felt like a new man. I was doin' good deeds again. It feels good knowing that some of those boys are alive today because of what I was able to do for them. The old man hasn't lost his touch. Maybe I should start my practice again," he said with a grin.

"I think one patient at a time is enough. Besides, you didn't look too spry when you got home, as I recall. Sort of looked like a muddy swamp rat that's been pulled through a knothole backwards," she grinned.

"Well, my dear, now that I think about it, I was feelin' a might run down." he nodded. "The spirit is willin' but the old bones just aren't what they used to be, and that's for sure. I'm goin' out to the barn to see if I can scare up some eggs."

He glanced in at Will first, and it gave him a good feeling to see the young man sleeping peacefully. Damn shame about his face, he thought. As Scruff got up from his blanket and followed, Doc looked down and scratched his ears. "Good dog, Scruff." Encouraged by the attention Scruff flopped on his side and rolled over on his back. Doc scratched the upturned stomach. He loved the old dog. He'd found him, as a puppy, hiding in the barn. Must have been ten or twelve years ago. No finer dog walked the earth, as far as Doc was concerned. Inside the barn, chickens ran in all directions, and Doc saw a few eggs in the hay. He placed these in his hat and searching around, found a few more. Setting the hat on the ground, he picked up the curry comb and ran it over Biscuit's back. Doc was a man at peace with the world. A loving wife, a nice home, a good horse and a faithful dog. No one could ask for anything more. Oh, and some mighty fine hens that provided him with eggs.

Again, the sounds of voices awakened Will. The pain, around his face, was intense. He moved his hand up to see if he could feel the cause, but found it bandaged again. He could see through his right eye however, and spent some time taking in his surroundings. The room was neat as a pin. Flowered curtains on the window, a small dresser, with a variety of articles on the top. A mirror, which he was unable to look into. He noticed a side table with a pitcher and bowl, and a tin cup full of water. Carefully, he reached out and picked up the cup. Lifting his head, he managed to get most of it down. It was good water. Mary came into the room and noticed the empty cup.

"How are you feeling?" she asked with a smile. Her hands were busy rearranging the covers.

"First rate, ma'am," Will murmured. He tried to smile, but the effort hurt his cheek.

Mary took his hand, patting it gently. "Can you tell me your name?"

"Will, ma'am, Will Morgan. Where am I?"

"Well, Will Morgan, you were on a boat that ran into a mine and sank. My husband found you and brought you home. He is a doctor. You can call him Doc. Most people do, and I'm Mary. Let me get you some fresh water."

While she was gone, Will tried to remember the boat sinking, but gave up. How long had he been here? He remembered yesterday, but that was about it. Mary came in with the water. "Would you like some more?" she asked.

Will nodded. With a little help he managed to finish off the cup of water.

"Mary, if Doc is around, would you get him for me, please?"

Patting his hand, she nodded and left the room. Within a few minutes Doc came in and sat on the edge of the bed. Smiling, he gently shook Will's hand. "What can I do for you Will?"

"'I need to go to the outhouse, Doc. That water is running through me like a leaky bucket. Can you help me get on my feet?"

"You feel up to it? It's about thirty paces out there. I don't know if I can hold ya' if you fall," Doc spoke with gentle concern. A fall could do great damage if he fell forward onto his face.

"Just get me on my feet, Doc. No way I'm going to soil the bed." Gripping Doc's arm, he managed to swing his legs off the bed and with a little help, got in an upright position. Pausing, he lowered his feet onto the floor, and with an arm around Doc's shoulder, they shuffled out of the house.

Will concentrated on putting one foot in front of the other. He was acutely aware of the pains in his face, but also the various cuts and bruises on his chest. Doc turned him around and he slumped down on the wooden bench. Doc closed the door. "Don't you go a fallin' in there, Will," Doc exclaimed.

"That would just about be the last straw, Doc. If I do, just kill me with a shovel and leave me here," Will whispered through clenched teeth. Doc laughed.

On the way back, Will inquired about the bandage on his face.

Doc hesitated. "You lost an eye, and the side of your face took a lickin'. Right now, it looks real bad because of the swelling and discoloration. That will get better in time." Pausing, he added. "I did the very best I could do, Will. I wish there was more I could have done for you."

As they entered the bedroom, Will edged over to the dresser and looked in the mirror. He was startled. Not so much with the bandage but by how he had changed in the last three years. Regrettably, none to the good, he thought. "Can you take the bandage off, Doc?"

"Sure can, but are you sure you're up to it? Like I told you, it looks pretty bad right now. Be better to wait a few more days."

"No, let's get it over with, so I don't waste time wondering about it. I'll be all right."

Doc carefully removed the bandages, and Will stood starring at his reflection in the mirror. The shock was almost overwhelming. Was this really him? He didn't say anything for several minutes. At last, he turned to Doc, and with an attempt at a grin, said, "Won't have to carry a stick around to keep the ladies away, will I?"

Doc didn't know what to say, so said nothing as he rewrapped Will's face with clean bandages. He helped him into bed and started to leave the room. He was almost to the point of tears. He had done the best that he could do, under the circumstances, but the shock must have been awful for the poor young man.

"Hey Doc, thanks. I mean that, sincerely, you did good. As a matter of fact, I never did have to carry a stick." Ignoring the pain in his cheek, Will grinned. "Say Doc, before you go, did I have a pouch with me? It was on a string, around my neck."

Relieved, Doc crossed to the side table and removed the pouch from the drawer. "This what you're talking about?" he said with a smile.

"Thank God. Thought I might've lost it." Loosening the thong, he took out the metal case and opened it up. The picture was undamaged. Smiling, he handed it to Doc.

"Is this your wife?"

"No, Doc, but someone really special." During the next hour Will told Doc about Twyla, Jimmy, Del and Jack. Doc listened intently. He had heard rumors of Andersonville, but up until now had doubted that the rumors could be true. After listening to Will, he realized that the rumors were not as terrible as the reality.

As Will was talking, Mary had stood outside the doorway listening. She lifted her apron to her eyes. When the telling got too hard to bare, she went into the kitchen and put her mind on cooking. There was nothing she could do to compensate for all the grief that Will had endured but she could do something about his wasted body.

Exhausted from the talking, Will allowed himself to doze off. Doc rearranged the covers and tip-toed out of the room.

That evening Doc and Mary discussed the story Will had told. His arrival had changed their lives. It made them horrified witnesses to the atrocities that men could impose on one another. However, it had also made them witness to the grand strength men could call upon to overcome these hardships. They could not have been more proud of Will, had he been their son.

Over the next two weeks, Will gradually became stronger and the pain in his face, more manageable. The bandage was off and the fresh air seemed to soothe the wounds. He put a salve on each day to keep them from drying out. Other than that, he rested, with an occasional trip to the outhouse, or stroll to the barn. He spent a lot of time with Biscuit and old Scruff. To rub the old dog's ears, and brush the horse reminded him of his own dog and horse. The sounds and smells brought back the feeling of homesickness that he had blotted out of his mind for so long. He wondered if they were still alive. He hoped so.

Will took down the bridle from the peg and went out to where Biscuit was standing. The old horse raised his head when he saw him approaching and met him half way. Putting on the bridle, Will led him over to the fence and with some effort, stepped off the second rail onto his back. Biscuit was somewhat surprised, not having been ridden in years, but he accepted the rider. Will just sat, enjoying the feel of being on a horse again.

Doc, who was taking all this in from the corner of the barn, laughed.

"Hey Will, where you headed? Biscuit looks like he's ready to go for a ride. I'll catch the gate." Will rode out into the pasture with Scruff trailing along behind and, just allowed the horse to roam around. At the end of an hour, Will's butt was sore and he was ready to get down and turn the horse loose. Walking up to Doc, he could not keep the smile off his face. "There were times when getting on a horse was the last thing I ever wanted to do. But I must say, not knowing if I would live long enough to ride again, was hard. Sittin' on Biscuit, felt darn good."

Together, they headed toward the house. They could smell something good cooking in the kitchen.

That evening Will brought up the subject of his leaving. Doc put his pipe on the dish and thought about it for a spell. For reasons, other than medical, he didn't want Will to leave. He was sure getting used to having him around. He would miss the talks. He had learned so much from Will. About places he himself had never been, things he would never see or do. He had never been farther away than Maryland, where he went to medical school, and it was a real pleasure to listen to Will talk. He was going to miss him.

Mary was thinking similar thoughts, only from the woman's perspective. Will was so appreciative of everything. Every meal was special to him. He raved about everything she fed him, regardless of how simple. He was such a gentleman. His mother had taught him manners and he always made her feel so...how would she put it?... motherly. Yes, motherly. She and Doc had never had children and although Will was hardly a child, she enjoyed caring for him. Yes, and worrying about him also. What would his life be like? Would he overcome the wounds? She surely hoped so. He was such a nice young man.

"When were you plannin' on leaving?" Doc asked.

"I was thinking in a week or ten days. I figure five weeks is long enough," Will replied. "I have gotten a lot of my strength back and feel considerably better than I have felt in years. I can't go a livin' off you folks forever, and to tell you the truth, being around you has stirred up a homesickness in me to see my own folks again. Been near four years since I left them the last time, and it's time to get on home."

"Well, you know that you are welcome to stay as long as you want but you know best. It has been a blessing having you here with us."

"I was wonderin' Doc if the three of us could just sit awhile, this evening? It would mean a lot to me. You and Mary give me a feelin' of inner peace that I haven't had in some time." Later, as they sat in the living room, Will took out the harmonica and began to play. He was happy that the scar would not prevent his playing. He had to restrict his puffing on that side of his face, but it didn't seem to matter much.

Doc smiled and left the room for a few minutes, returning with his fiddle.

Eight days later Will was in the buggy with Doc and old Scruff, heading to town. Saying good-bye to Mary had been hard. Such a sweet old lady. He was going to miss her. He looked at himself in the mirror at the black patch covering his lost eye. It certainly improved his appearance. He had decided to let his beard grow out a little to cover the deep cheek wound. He looked at the clothes that Doc had given him and he felt humbled. Doc wanted to buy him new clothes, but Will said that he would rather have Doc's old ones. "New clothes don't mean anything to me, but wearing your old clothes is special."

The shoes, a little loose, still felt comfortable and the soft socks made his toes wiggle with delight. Doc didn't know what to say. The thought that this young man thought his clothes were special made him feel humble.

Neither talked much on the way to town, both lost in their own thoughts, not looking forward to saying goodbye. As they entered the main street, a boy jumped off the walk and ran over to the buggy. "Doc, how ya doin'?" he asked. "Is this the fellow we brung to you?" His eyes roved over Will. He tried not to stare at Will's face, while extending his hand. "Guess you wouldn't remember me but I was there when old Scruff found you."

"Looks like I owe you a thanks, partner." Will replied, as he shook the outstretched hand.

Turning to Doc, the boy said, "I gotta run now. I gotta' get on home." With a wave of his hand he jumped up on the walk and disappeared in the crowd.

Moments later they were outside the train station. It suddenly dawned on Will that he had no money to buy a ticket. Seeing the look on his face, Doc laughed and told him that there was several twenty dollar gold pieces in his watch pocket. Before Will could protest, he said, "Don't you go worrying yourself about it. You get to where you're goin. That's the main thing. Same thing for the clothes. And see that you write, every once in awhile to let us know how your doin'."

Will took the extended hand. "You can bet on it. Thanks for everything, Doc." Without thinking, he embraced the old man, who responded in kind. Stepping back, they both had tears in their eyes.

He reached down and rubbed Scruff's face. "You take good care of Doc and Mary."

After purchasing his ticket to Annapolis he took a window seat where he could see the platform. As the train departed Will caught a last sight of Doc, standing in the buggy, waving, Scruff sitting beside him on the seat. He wondered if he would ever see them again. He doubted it, and felt a tightness in his chest. He tried to think of other things. His thoughts turned to Del and Jack. Where were they?

16

THE BROTHER

The two guards stood silently as the third opened up the cell door. There was apprehension in all three, for they had tangled with Sean O'Grady more than once. When the cell door opened, they withdrew their night-sticks and peered into the darkness of the cell.

"On your feet, O'Grady." shouted the turnkey. "You have a visitor." In his left hand he carried manacles and a chain.

Sean had heard the clinking of the chain as the guards moved down the corridor towards his cell and was surprised when they stopped at his door. He seldom had visitors to break the routine, which was a twenty-four hour lockup. He remained on his mattress until the guard repeated his command. It gave him a small feeling of power and control. After the second command, he stood up and thrust his arms out in front of him. The turnkey carefully sorted out the chain, then placed the manacles on Sean's wrists and locked them. The second set went on his ankles with the chain fastened to both. As he fastened the last lock, there was a noticeable sigh of relief from the two guards. Sean heard it and smiled inwardly. As he was ushered down the narrow hall followed by the three guards, he wondered who his visitor was. It had been several months since anyone had come to see him. The break in the monotony was worthwhile, regardless of who it might be. Maybe he would find out what was going on out on the street. It had been almost a year now and he had, pretty well, lost touch with the outside world. After passing through several barred gates, he was directed into a small visitor's room. Sean was pleased to see Que sitting behind the long, narrow table.

The pathetic look on Que's face brought a grin to Sean's lips.

Que had heard Sean and his escort approaching, and he felt a small measure of relief. He did not like being in this place alone. He had had his share of run-ins with the law but so far had escaped imprisonment. To actually enter the prison gates took all the courage he could muster and he had debated coming at all. Fear was the force behind his decision because if Sean heard this story from someone else, it would look bad. One thing Que did not want was to get Sean riled up. Just thinking of it raised the hairs on his neck. He could feel the sweat pop out on his forehead and sweat started dripping from his armpits. He saw Sean smile at him and he returned it. Sean looked absolutely frightening with his light red hair long and shaggy, covering up most of his face. A beard hung almost to his chest, concealing his lower face and neck. Que tried to ignore the smell of unwashed body and bad breath. He was having a problem with his legs jumping nervously and had rubbed his sweaty hands on his thighs until his palms were raw. No way did he like being in here.

Sean let his eyes take in his little friend, and wondered what had happened to force him to come here to see him. It wasn't just to be friendly.

Que was a small, timid, man with a round bald head. He had acquired his name for the bald head and for his pastime of hanging around the pool hall. He was probably thirty years old, but looked much older. He looked up at Sean with pale watery blue eyes and smiled again, showing off yellow teeth with a noticeable gap, a little left of center.

Sean slid a chair over to the table, across from Que and sat down. The turnkey left the room and the two remaining guards took up positions against the rear wall in back of Sean. They casually tapped the palm of their hands with their night sticks.

Que focused on Sean, trying to ignore them. As their eyes met, Que was thankful that Sean was his friend. Sean was big. Hell, he was bigger than big. His shaggy head connected directly to his massive chest and although he had been in here almost a year, he still looked the same. For a moment they just sat and grinned at each other.

"Well, me boy, what brings you back out here?" Sean asked. "I'll be doubtin' if it's to see the inside of this here place agin."

Que hesitated, as he really hated to upset Sean. Just say it, he told himself. "Sean, I'm a bringin' ya some bad news. I guess the best way to tell ya is to just say it. The fact is," He paused one last time, "your brother got hisself kilt."

Sean sat up-right, the front legs of his chair hitting the floor abruptly. The guards jumped. The smile was gone and his blue eyes turned to ice. "Are ye' sure o' what you say?" his voice cracked. "Are ye' sure?"

"That's what Mike Sullivan is a sayin' and he says he was right there when it happened. He bribed some guards to get hisself out of prison, on a medical release or somethin' or they might'a got him too. He probably would'a told you hisself but he got stabbed over a bottle of beer and he's still in bed. But he claimed to have seen it all."

Sean didn't hear the last few words, as his mind was trying to cope with Stick being dead. It just didn't seem possible. It had to be a mistake. No damn way. He pounded the table with both fists. The two guards gripped their night sticks and went into a defensive crouch. When they realized there was no threat, they resumed their position, tapping their palms with the sticks. Several minutes passed with neither of the two men saying a word.

Que was relieved that it was over and more than content to just sit and wait for Sean to speak. On the other hand, having said what he came to say, he had a wild desire to jump up and run out of the room. He pressed harder on his jumpy legs.

"You have Mike come see me. I want to git it straight from him. You understand?"

"Aye. I'll look him up as soon as I git back. I'm sorry Sean."

"You done the right thing. You go on now. I gotta think on this a spell." Sean stood up, looked at Que one last time, then turned toward the door. One of the guards hastily opened it and followed him through. The door closed firmly behind them.

Que retreated out the door he had entered, forcing himself to walk. No sir, he did not like this place one damn bit.

As Sean entered his cell, he cursed himself for not getting the name of the one that killed his big brother.

17

LAP OF LUXURY

Del and Jack waited around the hospital on the off-chance that Will would suddenly show up; that somehow he was still alive. After three weeks had passed, they could wait no longer and left for Washington. The paymaster had made the rounds and had given each of them two month's wages plus twenty-five cents a day for each day in prison. With their new-found wealth they looked forward to getting to Washington and into some real civilian clothes.

Late that first evening in the capitol, as they were taking in the sights, they decided that every prisoner released must have headed for the same place. Familiar faces were everywhere and the two were up all night, roaming from one saloon to another. In one, they managed to meet two beautiful *ladies of the evening* and later they spent an hour or two in a rather grimy hotel room. As neither had had a drink in almost two years, they were hopelessly drunk in short order. Later, when they ended up on a park bench, deep in a discussion of life in general and what they were going to do next in particular, they decided that, aside from the loss of most of their money, they must have had a great time. Both admitted that they remembered little, if anything.

Attempting to focus his eyes on Jack, Del exclaimed. "Let's go see my folks in Baltimore. My Dad can get us a job with the railroad. He's a big man on the railroad. He can get us a real good job. How does that sound?"

"What does he do on the railroad?" Jack asked, trying to straighten out the newspaper that was protecting his legs from the cold.

"He's an engineer," Del replied. "He's a big man on the railroad. He'll get us a good job." Del was trying to focus his mind on his father and not having much luck. Always wanted his father's love and respect but it was a no go, he thought. No medals, no glorious wounds, no major battles to impress him. Nothin'. What the hell, he still missed the old man, and besides, he wanted to see his mother more than his dad.

"Sounds like a good idea to me," Jack exclaimed. "I sure don't have anyplace to go or people to see. Let's go!"

"Right now?"

"Where's a train heading to Baltimore? Let's go find one." Jack, clasping his newspaper and Del, his half empty bottle, headed toward the sound of trains in the distance.

The following evening found them in Baltimore. Jack was impressed with the city. Large trees shaded the streets and everything was clean. He was a little rattled by the size of the place and the number of people on the streets, so he stuck close to Del, who seemed quite at home. Of course, he thought, he is home. A small pain still lingered in his head.

Catching a cab, Del gave the driver the address and as the buggy made its way from the commercial district to the residential, Jack was definitely impressed. These homes were beautiful. Suddenly, they were stopping in front of one of the nicer of the nice homes. Del jumped down. "Home, sweet home! You comin' in or are you going to sit out here?"

Jack climbed down and started dusting off his new clothes. There was no dust but somehow it seemed the thing to do. Running his hand through his hair and rubbing his new shoes on the leg of his pants, to ensure a shine, he followed Del to the front door.

Del was suprised at how thrilled he was to be home. Would he be welcomed or snubbed? So much still depended on his father. So many times, it seemed, he had just not lived up to expectations. Reaching for the knob he opened the door and they entered the large entry room. Jack's head was rotating around trying to see everything at once. Outside of their hideout in Savannah he had never seen inside a house like this. Never with people really living in it. Within a minute, an elderly colored servant came through one of the far doors and stopped in surprise to see the two. He squinted his eyes nearsightedly as he peered at them. Del took four giant steps forward and grabbed the old man in a bear hug, swinging him around in circles. Arms and legs flaying, the poor old fellow didn't know what was going on. Standing the man up, Del looked into his face. "It's me Albert, Del!"

"Ah, Massah Del, Sur, we thought you was dade. Oh Lordy, you is back! Great God Almighty! I'll fetch your momma and daddy." Tears were streaming down the old man's face. Jack was touched.

"That's OK Albert. Is Dad in his office?" Albert nodded, smiling broadly and rubbing his hands. "Albert, you're looking great, I missed you."

"Come on Jack, we'll corner the old bear in his den." Del was leaping up the stairs three at a time and Jack followed as fast as he could. Around a turn and down a hall Del bounded, pausing for a moment at a large double door, then turning both knobs, he burst into the room with Jack at his heels.

Harvey Trenton heard the approaching footsteps in the hall and was rising to see who it was when the doors burst in. He was faced by two laughing semi-baldheaded strangers. It took him several seconds to recognize his own son. "Son, tell me it's you. Is it really you?" His throat was so tight that he could hardly get the words out. He moved toward Del, his arms outstretched.

Del was surprised, but extremely happy. His arms encircled his father and they stood embracing. His father finally pushed him away, still holding on tightly to the front of his shirt.

"Just let me look at you, Son. We thought you might be dead. I didn't want to believe it, but the stories we heard."

"No Sir, I made it. There were times I had my doubts, but here I am. Dad, I want you to meet a friend of mine. I give him credit for helping to get me through it. This here is Jack Turner. Jack, this is my father, Harvey Trenton."

Jack could see where Del got his size. Harvey Trenton was at least six foot three, with longish brown hair and a flowing beard and mustache. Not heavy set, his height and posture, as well as his air of authority made him impressive. Jack extended his hand and it was lost in the other's strong grip.

Trenton looked down at him and solemnly spoke. "I'm glad to meet you, Sir. If what Del says is true, I owe you a debt that cannot be repaid. Come, let's go down to the kitchen. You boys look like you could stand some food. My God, Del, you're all skin and bones." Putting his arms around both their shoulders he ushered them out of the room and down to the kitchen.

Albert had hurried in to tell his wife Mattie, the family's cook about Del's arrival and she had immediately started fixing food. From what Albert had said about his appearance, food was in order. When the three came into the kitchen, she was ready for them. Fortunately, she had prepared several pies that morning. Large pieces of raison pie were waiting on the table with pitchers of sweet milk and buttermilk. Del hugged the small, black lady. She was so tiny that Jack was afraid she would be crushed. She kissed Del on the cheek and tears came to her eyes. "My little boy, my little boy. Sit!"

As they began to devour their pie, Del asked "Where's Mom?"

"She'll be home any minute. She went next door to return something. As a matter of fact, I see her coming across the yard. Let's surprise her." Harvey said, with a twinkle in his eyes. " She has been so worried about you."

The front door opened and they heard Del's mother enter. "I'm in the kitchen, Dear. I have a surprise for you." He motioned for Del and Jack to step into the pantry, out of sight. She came into the kitchen and noticed the empty dishes on the table. She tried to make sense of it but before she could, two arms were encircling her and she was being lifted off the floor. Then she was looking into Del's dear ravaged face. Del thought she was going to faint. "It's me Mom, I'm home."

Everyone seemed to be crying, including Jack, who had enjoyed the reunion, almost as much as the family. He had never missed being without a family as much as he did right now. This is what family was all about.

"Mom, this is my best friend, Jack. Jack, this is my mom, Emma."

Jack stuck out his hand but she brushed it aside and gave him a long hug. "Thank you, Jack, for being my boy's friend."

"Pleasure was all mine, ma'am," he said with a grin.

"What's this ma'am stuff? You call me Mom, you hear?"

"Come, let's go in the parlor. We have a lot of catching up to do," Del suggested. As the foursome departed for the parlor, Mattie and Albert began clearing the table. Del called back, "Mattie, the pie was great. Thanks."

"Ma'am, that was the best pie I ever ate and that's a fact," Jack added.

"Oh hush," she called back. "You'll embarrass me."

"Find a place to sit, boys. Make yourself comfortable," Harvey ordered, with a smile.

Jack settled into a chair that was so soft he had the feeling he was sinking clear to the floor. He retreated into his own thoughts, watching the three as they talked. Del was a lucky man. He thought about Jimmy and Will. They should all be here enjoying this reunion. He tried to push the thoughts from his mind and concentrate on what Del was telling his folks. He watched their faces as Del described prison life. Del had worried about his relationship with his father. He shouldn't have. What Jack saw in both their eyes could only be love.

He leaned his head back and shut his eyes, listening to Del recount the demise of Rooster. A faint smile touched his lips as he remembered Will, staring across the mud at Rooster and yelling at him to "throw the pouch over to me or I'll have to come over there and kick your butt." Damnedest thing......His thoughts were interrupted by a hand being placed on his. Surprised, he opened his eyes and saw Mrs. Trenton smiling at him.

"All that talk about what you boys went through upsets me. I don't like to think of it. When I saw you over here by yourself, I thought that I would rather chat with you. Is that all right?" she asked.

"Sure thing, Mrs. Trenton, I mean Mom. What would you like to chat about?" Jack asked.

"How about you, Jack? Tell me about you. If you don't mind, I mean."

"Not too much to tell. As far as I know, I was born in Ohio, though I can't be sure. Never knew my dad and don't remember much about my mother. She died when I was about seven. Raised for a while by my uncle but his wife didn't care much for the added mouth to feed so I left when I was around ten and been bouncing around from place to place ever since. Del is about the closest thing I have to a family. He's kinda like a brother."

"Well how did you get by?" she asked in surprise.

"Oh, I had several jobs when I first left home that didn't amount to much, but kept a roof over my head. My first job was a cook's helper. Probably one of the best dish washers around, if I do say so," Jack said with a grin. He was rather amused, as no lady had ever asked him about himself and he was rather flattered. "After several years of that,

I was promoted to cook, when the old fella' died. Eventually the boss gave me a horse and I've been following cattle around ever since."

"Didn't you get to go to school, Jack?" she asked.

"Well, can't say as I've ever gone to a real school but I learned a little readin' and writin' through the years. I have hopes of improving myself. I had a lot of time to think of what I would do if, and when, I got out of prison. I would like to be a success at something." He didn't tell her that the only word he could write was his name.

"Jack, you have already done so much. You were there for Del when he needed you and from the way he talks, without you, he may not have lived through it. I want you to know that we are forever grateful and you will always be a part of our family." Tears were in her eyes. "So terribly grateful." she added.

Jack opened his mouth to say something but nothing came out. He patted her hand with his left hand. She squeezed his right hand. He finally managed, "It's been a real pleasure to know Del and, if the truth be known, I may not have made it without him, either."

Harvey Trenton looked into the eyes of his son, truly realizing for the first time the horrors Del had been subjected to. He wanted to reach over and grab his son and hug him to his chest. He had never done that. He had never allowed himself to show affection. Why? It really made no sense now, next to the thought of losing the boy altogether. Was it because of his father? He didn't know. Today he saw strength in Del that he had never seen before. Was it because he'd never looked? Why had he been such a fool all these years? It was only after Del had joined the army and headed off to war, that the realization of his failure as a father had sunk in. As Del finished his story, Harvey rose and stood before him. "Stand up, Son."

As Del stood, his father embraced him with both arms. "I love you, Son," he whispered. "Please forgive me for being a damn fool."

"I love you too, Dad. I always did, but I was never sure you felt the same," Del murmured.

"Oh yes, but I never really knew how or when to show it. There were times, but I held back and then the chance was lost and I felt a fool. It seemed a weakness on my part to let you know how I felt. Like you might be spoiled somehow by knowing how much you meant to me. I'm mighty proud of you. I want to be very sure you never doubt that again."

From across the room, Jack and Mrs. Trenton watched the exchange between the two and squeezed one another's hands, smiling.

Mrs. Trenton finally broke the spell, saying. "You boys have had a hard day, so Del take Jack upstairs and both of you freshen up a bit. I'll have Mattie fix up something for dinner. How does steak, eggs and mashed potatoes sound? With a dish of ice cream, later on? That is, if you're up to turning the crank?"

"I'm afraid to ask this, but have I died and gone to Heaven?" Jack moaned. "If not, I must be dreaming. Don't wake me up!" He followed Del up the winding staircase, his eyes taking in the paintings and the fine woodwork in the paneled walls. Train engineers must do pretty well, he thought.

Opening a door along the hall, Del said, "This'll be your room, Jack. Albert will be up with hot water in a minute. I'll borrow Dad's razor. Let's see what we look like without this stubble."

Jack gazed around the spacious room. It was amazing to realize that a month ago, he had been sleeping in the mud on the verge of starving. Now, here he was, standing in a beautiful room with a large bed, a mirrored dresser and curtains on windows that opened to a view of a well manicured back yard. He looked at the pictures on the wall and the small, framed picture, on the dresser. It was of the Trenton family. Del appeared to be about fifteen at the time.

Albert gently knocked and entered with a large bucket of hot water, which he used to fill the pitcher in the bowl. "Is there anythin' else you need, Suh?" he asked with a smile.

"Albert, I can't think of a thing. Given a week, I don't think I could come up with anything," Jack replied, with a smile. "And I'm obliged to you for going to the trouble of bringing up the water."

"Tain't no trouble, Suh, I heard what was said down stairs, and I'm mighty obliged to you for what you did for my people. Yes Suh, that was some story! I'm mighty proud to know ya. Anything you need, you jus' call on me."

He left the room, and Jack heard him stop at Del's door, and then their muted voices. Del entered, moments later, with a razor, soap mug and brush.

Arriving at the dinner table, Del and Jack grinned at each other. "Do you feel as naked as I do?" Del asked.

"Yup," replied Jack, "and somewhat disappointed, as I had hoped to be better lookin' after all this time off from an honest job." Everyone laughed. Jack looked at the table covered in a white table cloth, at dishes filled with more food than he had seen in years, not to mention silverware that dazzled his eyes. Everything was absolutely perfect. He heard that people actually lived like this but he wasn't sure it was true, until now. He tried to visualize Del living like this, but it was hard to do. He seemed so regular. Jack could not think of one time that Del had looked down on him for anything. Up until now, he thought of them as equals. What would his life have been like if he had all this?

After they were seated, the plates of food made the rounds. Both Del and Jack had a hard time holding back from overfilling their plates. It seemed to never end. At last, they got down to the serious job of eating. Suddenly, Del stopped chewing and placed his fork on his plate. He bowed his head for a few minutes and then looked around the table at his folks, and then at Jack.

"What's wrong, Dear?" his mother asked, leaning over to take his hand.

"No, no nothing is wrong. In fact, everything is right. I was just thinking of something that happened to me in Andersonville."

"Would you care to share it with us, Dear?"

"It was summer before last. I had been there about four months, as I recall. For some reason, all the horrors of the place kinda caught up with me. One of our group died, others were dying all around us. The effects of starvation were setting in, like swollen joints, sore gums and stuff like that. It just seemed so simple to end it all by stepping over the Dead Line."

"What was the Dead Line?" his father asked.

"The Dead Line was designed to keep us away from the stockade walls, so we couldn't tunnel out. Anyone crossing it was immediately shot by guards. Anyway, I found myself looking down at it and without any thought, I lifted my foot to step over it."

His mother gasped and gripped his hand.

"Before I could do it, our friend Will grabbed me and pulled me back. I'll tell you about him later. Anyway, he told me that some day I would be home again, sitting around the table with my folks, looking at more food than I could eat. It seemed impossible. He told me to plan my death for tomorrow, always tomorrow. He said he did that. He just postponed it until tomorrow. I used that advice every day. And here I am. Exactly as he said I would be." He stopped talking. He could feel his throat choke up.

"What happened to him, Son?" his father asked.

"He died, Dad. He got us all the way to freedom and was killed on the boat from Wilmington to Annapolis when it hit a mine and exploded."

"I remember reading about that last month. Such a shame." Let's finish dinner and then we can retire to the parlor and you can tell me all about it. That is if you feel up to it."

"I think I'll feel better when I can get it all out. Yes, I think talking about it will help."

Jack was surprised. Neither Del, nor Will, had ever mentioned it to him. He remembered Del telling him about the "one day at a time" thing, but not the other. Mentally, he thanked Will for saving his friend's life.

Later, when the meal was finished, Mattie brought in small bowls of ice cream.

"I thought we were going to have to man the crank," Del said, with a look of feigned disappointment.

Mattie laughed. Skinny as those arms are, I just decided I better do it myself."

When the dishes were cleared, Harvey turned to Jack and said. "Come on up to my office, I want to show you a bridge I'm working on."

After a good look at the blueprints for the new bridge Jack laughed. "Well that clears up that mystery. When I asked Del what you did for a living, he said you were an engineer for the railroad. I thought you drove the trains."

Later that evening, when Harvey got around to asking about their plans for the future, Del mentioned his desire to work on the railroad and Jack said that it sounded good to him too.

"Now that the war is winding down, the push for a transcontinental line will see things moving in a hurry. I understand they will be starting from Council Bluffs, Iowa, probably within the month. I would guess you won't have any trouble getting employment. I'll make a few inquires tomorrow. Oh, by the way, that girl you used to court, what was her name? Betty? Betsy? Anyway, she married that Clifford fellow a few months back. I think they moved to Maine. Thought you'd like to know."

Del was surprised but only a little disappointed. He had thought he was in love with her, but he didn't feel any great loss at the news. At this point he was ready to move on with his new life. She was something from a completely different existence. He wished her well.

Smiling at Jack, he said, "Looks like I'll just have to keep on looking for that special lady."

Three weeks passed, in which Del and Jack recuperated. Both had seen and done about everything Baltimore had to offer. Jack was ready to see the rest of the world, but understood Del's reluctance to leave his family again. They were sitting down for breakfast when the news reached them that the war was truly and completely over. Lee had surrendered to Grant. To make things even better, Wirz was under arrest and was to be brought to trial for war crimes. It was indeed a very good day.

The very next day Harvey received word from one of his friends in the Union Pacific Railroad Company that there was an opening for an experienced assistant surveyor. Del was qualified for this, having spent several summers on a surveying crew. There was also a job for Jack, as a crew guard.

The day before they were to leave for the rail head at Council Bluffs, Harvey ushered them out of the house. "You boys will need some gear before you go. As long as you are working for the railroad you should look the part."

After an hour, they came out of the clothing store wearing new pants, shirts, Stetson hats and the finest boots money could buy. Harvey had not had this much enjoyment in years. "One more stop, before we head home." They strolled down the street to the gun store. "I've been looking these over and figure you'll need something like this out west." He nodded to the clerk, who took down two Winchester rifles from the wall rack, and two Colt revolvers from the display case. "What do you think?" he asked.

The only new guns Jack had ever owned, where those issued to him in the army. He knew he should say something, but could not think of anything that would be adequate.

Harvey, seeing his expression, laughed. "Listen, Jack, money is no damn good unless you can use it. I figure this is a good use of it. By God, if my boys are going off to work on the railroad, they are going to go in style."

The phrase, "my boys" was not lost on Jack. It was a humbling experience.

They selected scabbards, holsters, cartridge belts and extra ammunition. Looking at the two young men, with all their fine new possessions, Harvey felt he had never spent so little money so wisely. Yes indeed, he was one happy man.

When they were alone in the bedroom, both took turns standing in front of the large mirror. Jack gazed at his reflection and had a hard time realizing that he was looking at himself. Aside from the gaunt face, he looked better than he had ever looked in his twenty-three years.

The morning of departure arrived and the family gathered in the living room. Albert shook their hands and stepped back so that Mattie could give each of them a hug. Jack had grown very fond of them. Both had gone out of their way to make him comfortable. He wondered how long it would be before he tasted anything as good as Mattie's cooking.

Standing outside the train station, Jack shook hands with Harvey, and gave Mrs. Trenton a hug and a kiss on the cheek. Del made small talk with his father, then he embraced him. Turning, he picked his mother up, with a bear hug, and swung her around in a circle. Giving her a kiss, he set her down, picked up his gear and stepped up into the train car. Jack waved, lifted his belongings to his shoulder and followed him into the car. Through the window they both gazed fondly at Del's parents, and as the train began inching forward, gave a last wave. They looked at each other and although there were a few tears, they smiled. Look out, world, here we come, Jack thought to himself.

18

HOME

Will settled into the seat, and assessed his fellow passengers. Some were in worse shape than he, with stumps instead of arms and legs. He scanned their faces, hoping to recognize someone, but they were all strangers. He looked out the window and let his mind drift to his homecoming. It would be good to see his folks again. Being around Doc and Mary made him realize just how much he missed them and Cole too. He wondered how his little brother was doing. He would be twenty-two? No, twenty-three. It seemed hard to believe. Had Cole gone to war? He hoped not. He had a limp from a broken leg, and that would probably have kept him out. He remembered the day Cole had broken that leg. They had roped a gander that had taken up residence, with his mate, in the garden. To get to the barn, they had to pass the nest which inevitably resulted in being chased and bitten fiercely. They'd hated that evil bird. One morning, Will decided to try to rope it. Just what he was going to do then, he hadn't given any thought. On the third try, the rope settled over the goose's head and the fight was on. Will soon dropped the rope and the two boys headed for the barn on the run. They could hear the gander in pursuit but didn't dare take the time to look back. Cole reached the fence first but tripped on a pile of wood on the other side, breaking his leg. Will had lured the gander away by taunting it. Then, after chasing Will down and biting him until the novelty wore off, the gander headed back to the house, the rope trailing behind him. Spending most of the day at the Doc's office had been a treat for Will, as he was given hard rock candy. Cole, on the other hand hadn't cared for it at all. The leg had never healed just right and left Cole with the slight limp. Will was invited out behind the shed, when his father got him home, and took a good paddlin'. Later that night he heard his folks laughing about the trouble his father had gone through to retrieve the rope.

Arriving at Annapolis the next day, Will was ushered into the large hospital building, and assigned a bed. Food was served, and eventually a doctor came by to check on him. He looked at the scars and seemed to approve of Doc's work. "How are you feeling?"

"First rate," Will replied. "How long will I be here, do you know?"

"I would think a day or two, at the most. You seem to be well on the mend," He replied.

The following day, the paymaster came around and counted out two hundred and eighty dollars. Will felt like a rich man. The next morning, after asking about Del and Jack to no avail, he was on the train to Iowa, by way of the Capitol. He spent most of that first leg of the journey thinking over the last four years and wondering how much had changed in the outside world.

No one took notice of Will, as there were thousands of wounded men in Washington. He decided to spend a little time in the city as he had no great desire to ever come back. The buildings and monuments were a wonderment. He spent most of a day watching the construction of the dome on the Capital and was impressed with the ingenuity of those responsible for its design and construction. Made him feel proud to be an American. On the third day he had seen enough and boarded the train for Chicago.

After he settled into the seat, he watched with pleasure a mother and her baby sitting three rows ahead of him. He wondered where Harry and Janie Hunt were and how little Harry Jr. was doing. Would he be walking yet? Hours later they left the train and he was able to enjoy their reunion with husband and father. He envied them. He tried to imagine what it would feel like to have someone he loved hug and kiss him like the man on the platform. The man held the baby high above his head, and Will could see the baby laugh.

Will enjoyed the trip to its fullest, watching the landscape pass by and listening to the various passengers. He began to realize just how much had happened while he had been a prisoner for all that time. Occasionally, he would become involved in conversation which inevitably would come around to his imprisonment. It seemed strange that what was so central to him, was something that most folks were unaware of. Most people he spoke to had never even heard of Andersonville.

At one of the stops, crowds of people rushed the train, carrying Old Glory and yelling, "The war's over! Lee surrendered! It's over!" The message was relayed throughout the other cars. Will looked out the grimy window at the mayhem. Hugging, kissing, and dancing in the street.

It was really over. The bloody battles, deaths, misery, and prisons. He could feel tears well up. Others wept in relief and happiness as well. You should be here, Jimmy, he thought.

Bottles of whiskey seemed to appear as if by magic, and although not normally a drinking man, Will felt obliged to celebrate. As each one made the rounds, he took his swig and before long was having a hard time keeping his thoughts together. At a stop, west of Cleveland, two young women boarded the car and took the seat directly behind him. The passengers were still celebrating, and it seemed that the whiskey would never end. His eyesight was somewhat hazy when they went by, but he did notice the perfume. He thought about turning around and taking a look but was distracted by an old man who asked if he had been in the army. "Well yes I was," Will replied, trying to focus. "A couple years in the cavalry and a couple years in prison camps."

"Which ones?"

"Andersonville, Millen, Savannah and Charleston. Been in all of 'em." There was a slight slur in his answer. He made up his mind that he would take no more swigs. He felt like hell.

"Heard of Andersonville. Tell me about it."

"Be glad to tell ya', old timer." For the next five minutes, he gave a description, as best he could, under the circumstances. The two women were also listening.

"Damn glad to see you made it, Son. You take care of yerself, now." He moved on down the isle.

In reply, Will belched.

"Say, Honey, if no one is sitting next to the window, can I sit there?"

Before he could think of an answer, she was moving in front of him, supporting herself on the back of his chair. She leaned forward, brushing his face with her ample breasts. The buttons were undone, revealing a deep cleavage. Although somewhat under the influence, she had his attention. She gave him a radiant smile, with a hint of lust.

He was looking at her, intending to say something, but nothing came to mind. The pressure on his other hip brought his thoughts to the other woman pressing against him.

"My name is Maggie." The one by the window, offered, "and that is my sister Emmy. We're the Love Sisters." The one on the aisle wrapped her arm around his neck. "What's your name, Honey?"

"Will. Will Morgan." The pressure of their hips on his was giving him a very pleasant feeling. He thought they must be twins. Both had long auburn hair, dimples and blue eyes. Maggie had a few pounds on Emmy, but both looked pretty classy.

"How far are you going, Willy?"

Will had always resented being called Willy, but hearing her call him that, didn't sound all that bad. "Iowa." He liked the smell of them. He jumped when Maggie put her hand on his leg.

"Got a wife waiting for you?" Maggie asked, coyly.

"Nope. Never been married. Don't know why, being such a handsome dog." He regretted his reference to being handsome. They just laughed. The hand on his leg squeezed tighter.

"We git off at Chicago. We have a nice place there and a small family business."

"What kind?" Will inquired.

"We're the Love Sisters, Willy, you figure it out." They both laughed. Emmy put her hand on his other leg and squeezed.

"There's usually a layover in Chicago. Would you be interested in a layover?" Emmy whispered in his ear.

"That's mighty generous, ladies. I must admit that this is a pleasant surprise."

"Does that mean a yes?" Maggie asked, pushing her hip into his.

"Shore does. It's been over five years so I might have forgot how." Will's heart rate had jumped.

"Don't you go a worryin' about that. We'll teach you anything you forgot."

Three hours later they stood in front of a two story row house. They ascended the stairs and Will felt Maggie pinch his rump. Emmy led the way into the foyer, and lit a small gas lamp. Will looked into the sitting room and was impressed. Large framed pictures adorned the walls, mostly of landscapes. Thick carpets covered much of the dark, wood floors. A large oak table and four matching chairs took up the middle of the room and a small piano took up a back corner. Will peered into the well-designed kitchen, and then noticed the stairway leading upstairs. The anticipation was making him feel slightly faint. Jesus, don't go a passin' out, he warned himself.

"Are you hungry, or would you like to see the upstairs first?" There was a touch of humor in Emmy's question.

Will pointed upstairs. The stairway to heaven, he thought to himself. He was grinning, and his heart was pounding. He took Emmy's hand as she led him upward.

Entering the bedroom, he could make out the four poster bed.

Maggie lit a small lamp in an alcove, giving off enough light to see one another, but dim enough to hide any small personal flaws.

The girls began to undress. Slowly, tantalizingly slow. Each garment was carefully folded, hung, or stacked.

Will was thankful for the dim light. He was ashamed of his body. Although much improved by the stay at Doc's, it was far from the body he had before Andersonville. Then it was his turn, but the girls insisted on stripping him down to the bare naked.

At last the clothes were off and he was led to the huge bed. Maggie turned down the covers, revealing smooth white sheets. Will climbed in, followed by Emmy. Maggie went around the bed and slid in beside him. Warm, soft hands caressed his body, as well as warm, damp lips. He did his best to return the pleasure. He wondered, that if by chance he did not live through all this, would the undertaker be able to remove the smile from his face? Time passed, but Will had no thought of it. He was drifting on a cloud of passion that he had never felt before.

He awoke to soft breathing nearby, and realized that his hand was on Emmy's breast. Maggie's hand was on him, her bare breasts pressing against his back. He slept.

A shorter version of the night before transpired before they went down for breakfast. Will got dressed, but the two women put on silk robes that left nothing to the imagination. Sitting at the table, looking at the plate of eggs, bacon and bread and seeing the two watching him, it came to him that it would be hard to top this with anything better.

As he stood on the stoop, he asked them if Love was their real name. They laughed.

"That reminds me of a cowboy I met years ago." Emmy replied. "I was working out of a hotel that required everyone to sign the register. He didn't like the idea of signing, but it was the rule. He cupped his hand so the clerk couldn't see and signed with an X. On further thought, he drew a circle around it. When we got up to the room I told him that signing with an X was rather common, but it was the first time I had one sign with the circle. He looked at me and smiled, "Shucks, Honey, in a situation like this you don't think I'm dumb enough to give 'em my real name, do ya?"

Will was still laughing as the horse drawn cab arrived. Not wanting to forget, he took one more long look, as they stood on the stoop, Maggie opened her robe, and waved. "Welcome home, Willy," Emmy shouted, blowing a kiss.

Will settled in on one of the wooden benches towards one end of the train station. He watched the people go by and thought of the previous night. The fact that his face was messed up didn't seem so important anymore. As he relived the experience one more time, his nose was assailed by the horrid odor of prison. He was shocked that that smell should be in this beautiful building. He sought out the source. Huddled in a corner, nearby, a wretched figure was cowering. The unwashed face, sunken eyes and filthy remnants shook Will to the core. The man's eyes were locked on Will's. He couldn't tell if he was a Yank or a Reb. He approached the figure, slowly, hoping he would not bolt. The man tensed as Will came closer. Will raised his open hands to shoulder level to show he meant no harm. Fear showed on the man's face as well as defiance.

Siler Clemmens had been hiding in the terminal for two days after his release from Douglas prison, on the edge of town. Hundreds, perhaps thousands had been set free at the end of the war. No money, no way of getting home, except walking and Siler was unable to do that. Most just spread out, lost, roaming the city and hoping for the best. He had found the station. Maybe he could sneak on board a train. So far, he had not succeeded. He had seen the man with the patch take a bench not far from him. He was too close. He noticed the worn, but clean, clothes, and envied the man's high top shoes.

As he approached, Siler knew that he was trapped. He couldn't run. The man spread his hands in a gesture of peace. He took that as a good sign. He sneered, as a warning, but the man kept coming. He finally stopped and squatted down so that their eyes were level. Siler was studied for a moment with the man's one good eye, then he stood, turned and left. Moments later, he returned with a small loaf of bread and several pastries. He handed the loaf to Siler and waited. Siler had been taught table manners, but all that was forgotten as he stuffed his mouth. He ate as fast as he could chew. He was unaware the man had left, until he returned with a cup of water and two more loaves of bread. He had devoured half the second loaf before he could stop. He looked up at Will, embarrassed.

"Been there, partner. Take your time, plenty more where that came from." He handed Siler a small pastry. It disappeared with a look of sheer joy. "Name's Will. Let's git out of here." He reached down to grip Siler's hand that had been extended out of a long forgotten habit.

"Siler. Just got out of Douglas Prison. Ain't more'n a half mile from here but I don't reckon I can go no further."

As Siler stood, Will was shocked to see his bent legs. The man could hardly walk. Together, they shuffled out of the station, onto the sidewalk. People stared, but the two ignored them.

Within two blocks, Siler gave out. The pain in his legs was too severe. Will left him sitting on a packing box and went in search of a clothing store. Two blocks away he located a small store that had a fair assortment. Will found everything he needed and returned to Siler, who still remained where he had been left, surrounded by an air of gloom caused by the horrible thought that Will was probably not real and would not return if he was.

"Found us a bath house, on the next block. Don't mean to sound rude, Siler, but you need a good bath. Hold these." He bent down and lifted the man and carried him to the bath house. An old Chinese man greeted them, took Will's money and directed them to several large wooden tubs. Steam was rising up from the hot water. Siler took off his ragged clothes and climbed slowly into one of the tubs. Will handed him the soap as he settled in.

"I think I just might be cookin', Will." Siler smelled the soap, smiled and began to remove the months of filth from his crippled body.

"You take your time. I'll be right back." Will kicked the foul clothes into a corner.

When Siler was through, he managed to climb out of the tub, dry himself, and put on the new clothes. As he stood looking down, he realized that these were the first new clothes he had ever owned. He had never had socks before. He looked at the shine on the shoes with pride. He was still looking at his shoes when Will returned.

"What happened to your legs, Siler?"

"Rode the Mule." Siler replied sadly. "Rode the Mule four hours on, two hours off for five days 'fore I passed out and they couldn't get me on agin. Legs ain't been no good since." He gazed at his bent legs with sorrow.

"What's the Mule?"

"Kinda' like a real tall saw horse." He raised his hand above his head. "Top two by four is on edge with the top cut to a point. Then, once yer up there, they tie buckets o' sand to yer feet. Don't know if'n my family will take me back. Wuthless as a teat on a boar." That damn Sweet. I'm a thinkin' it was his ideer to cripple us so's we couldn't escape. Name should'a been Asshole. He shook his head, remembering the pain.

Changing the subject, he told Will about the new clothes and shoes. "Can't thank ya'all enough, Yank. Never thought I'd ever like a Yank, but then ya'all come along." He gripped Will's hand.

"To be honest, Siler, I have felt the same about Rebs. Guess there are good and bad on both sides. Time to put it all behind us and get on with life. Your family will be glad to have you back."

"Come on out here, I have something else for you." Will supported him as he shuffled out.

A horse, with saddle, bridle and blanket roll stood at the hitch. Attached to the saddle horn with a string was a red satin pillow with gold tassels on the corners. Siler just stared. Will helped him to the horse and lifted him up. "You'll find a compass in the bedroll. Just keep a headin' south. Here, put this in your pocket. You'll need it." He handed Siler a tightly rolled $50.00 in small bills.

Siler started to cry. It was too much for Will. He untied the horse and gave it a slap on the rump. "Go home, Siler." He watched the slumped figure move down the street, then smiled as Siler forced himself to sit erect and square his shoulders.

As the train proceeded westward, Will thought back to the days that he had spent on the miserable trains that had transported him and his friends. He could hear the click, click, click of the wheels passing from one rail to the nest, but the train ride was as smooth as glass. He slouched in the comfortable seat and enjoyed the ride.

Two weeks of riding clear from Wilmington had not dampened his enthusiasm. As the landscape changed, he thought he recognized certain hills, and lakes. As a boy, he had gone on one of his father's business trips to Chicago to buy merchandise, and it had looked a lot like what he was now seeing.

Looking out of the train window, Will began to see more familiar territory. Yes, he definitely remembered being here before. Excitement began to build up until he could hardly sit still. Later on, as the train pulled into Cedar Rapids, he was surprised to see that parts of the town were completely different, while other parts seemed unchanged. The train stopped, and gathering his belongings, he stepped down onto the boardwalk. Home.

Walking down the main street, he looked into store windows, much the same as he had as a youngster. The family store, a mixture of grocery, hardware and guns, was vacant. People glanced at him as he strode by and several he recognized, but he could not remember their names. Still, it was good to see familiar faces again. None recognized him. He was of a mind to ask about the empty building, but was afraid of hearing bad news. There was a time when he knew almost every item in the store, not to mention the number on hand and the price.

Troubled, he headed in the direction of the homestead, about a mile out of town. With the town behind him, nothing seemed different. It was if he had never left. The road had the same dips and curves, as before, and the rail fence was still standing, although leaning in several places.

The road was lightly traveled, with only a few wagons and horsemen passing him by. All looked at him with curiosity, but none engaged him in conversation. A few "howdys" or tip of the head. He didn't recognize them either, which seemed strange, because there was a time when he knew just about everyone. He no longer just blended in with the rest of the wounded. Out here, his own appearance was an oddity he supposed. He had barely gotten used to the black patch and ragged scar himself. He could understand what prevented those usually sociable people passing by from giving him a lift.

Presently, he came to the rock. It was the same rock but somehow appeared to have shrunk. It had been so huge, when he was a kid. He stood, looking at its grayish-black bulk. It was an oddity, being the only boulder that size in the area. It was forty or fifty feet off the road and as Will was getting a little tired, he walked over to it and climbed up onto his favorite spot. Will, being the older, had his seat on the top spot, while Cole sat a little lower, on the side. When they were children, they always stopped for a rest on the rock, not because they were tired but because it was just the thing to do. He rested there awhile. Those traveling the road always glanced his way, but aside from an occasional salute, or short wave, no one stopped to talk.

Cole Morgan was coming home for lunch, when he noticed the

figure on the rock. He was immediately annoyed to see someone sitting in Buck's place. He peered at the person but was unable to see the face under the shade of the hat. He noticed the stranger staring insolently, back at him. As he came abreast of the rock, Will grinned and gave him a little salute, the same one they had used as kids. Cole started to go on, in a huff, when the significance of the salute hit him. Reining in, he jumped from the buggy and trotted back toward the rock in a daze. Will was on his way down.

Cole knew it must be Buck, but the scars on his face, his eye patch and beard, robbed it of all familiarity. He was fiercely embraced to the well remembered sound of Will's laughter in his ear. Drawing back they both took in the changes of the last few years.

"My God, Buck, you're alive! We thought you were dead. We got a letter from a Del somebody that you died. I can't believe that you're here." Cole exclaimed with excitement. He kept running his hands up and down Will's arms, making sure that he was actually there, his eyes starting to sting.

"Well, little brother, there were times I doubted I'd ever see you again, but here I am and I'll be danged if you aren't all grown up. Looks as if I'll have to look up to you from now on," Will exclaimed with a laugh. "How about a lift to the house?"

Will smiled. He had not been called Buck in four years and realized that to his family he would always be Buck. He remembered the county fair and the sheep riding. He had been six years old and his grandpa had entered him in the contest. He remembered the thrill as the ewe had run off when the man let go of the rope, making little jumps and zig-zags. After five or six seconds, he had fallen off but received a third place ribbon. His grandpa ran out and picked him up and swung him onto his shoulders. When they reached his proud parents, his grandpa declared that Will was one fine buck-a-roo. The name was shortened to Buck and that was what everyone called him. He missed his grandpa.

Cole stepped up into the carriage, and slid over so Will would have room to sit. Will stashed his bundle of extra shirts and socks on the floorboards and they rode on toward the house.

"How are the folks?" Will asked.

Cole paused for a minute then, with a choked voice, said, "They passed on, Buck. Mom died of a fever two years ago and Dad just gave up. Had no desire to go on without her. He tried to get over it, but got more down as time went by. We didn't hear from you, and had guessed you'd either been captured or killed. We had no way of knowing. I think Dad thought the worst."

Cole remembered that last day. He thought of it often. Dad had gotten so frail. He had starved himself to death over a period of three weeks, taking only small sips of water, from time to time. Cole had felt so helpless and he had wished that Will were there to give him support. He had never seen anyone actually die before, as Mom had died in her sleep. But he was alone. Dad's breathing became weaker and weaker and then stopped. He had held the lifeless hands that had once lifted him high in the air. They were good hands and Dad had been a good father. He could have used Buck's strength those last few days. He reached over and squeezed Buck's knee. To get the letter from Del, was almost too much to handle. If he hadn't had Candace and the baby, he really didn't know if he could have made it.

Will felt as though he had been kicked in the stomach. The folks were dead. He didn't even get to say good-bye. He was crying. Not a very manly thing to do, he thought, but the loss was so sudden and unexpected. He felt the hand squeeze his knee and regretted not being here for Cole. Would his being here have made a difference? He would never know. He wiped his face with his sleeve and they rode the rest of the way home in silence.

Looking at the house, he was pleased to see a fresh coat of paint and the porch and roof still straight and trim. A lady came out the door and stood with her hand on the porch railing, watching them enter the yard. Cole yelled with excitement, "Honey, Buck is back. He's alive!"

Candace stepped out into the yard, meeting them at the hitching post. She had a glorious smile, Will thought. A fine looking woman, to say the least. Then he recognized her. "Candace! It's nice to see you again!" He stuck out his hand.

Laughing, she brushed past his hand and gave him a quick hug. "Handshakes are for friends, Buck. Hugs are for family. Say hello to your sister-in-law." She put her arms around him and drew him to her again. The softness of her body touching him.

"Sister-in-law? What have you two been up to in my absence?" He held her at arms length, taking in her beauty. Turning to Cole, he exclaimed, "How did you ever get such a lovely lady to marry you?"

"It was my good looks and sweet talk. Not to mention a lot of good luck." They all laughed.

"Come inside, you haven't met your nephew, Sherman." Candace took his hand and lead him into the house.

Looking down into the crib at the tiny baby, Will remembered little

Harry Jr. and could hardly believe it was his own brother's boy. Candace picked the baby up and handed him to Will who promptly panicked. Carefully, he held the baby for a few seconds, then handed him back. "I'm afraid I might drop him."

"Let's go into the parlor, Buck, we have a lot of catching up to do. I'll fill you in on the folks and the store. I just can't believe you're really here. This is one of the happiest days of my life." Looking at Candace, he added, "along with the day Candace said she would marry me." He smiled as he put his arm around her.

Will listened to him without saying anything. He was having a hard time realizing that the folks were gone. There was really nothing to say. They were gone.

Cole could see that Buck was grieving the loss of their parents, so he started with the store. Cole told him of moving it to a larger location. That train travel had increased the business to the point that he had hired several employees.

"The store is doing real well. It will support both of us, with no problem. That reminds me, Candace, would you fetch that letter to Buck, from Dad?"

Retrieving the letter from a small desk drawer, she handed it to Will.

He looked at his father's familiar scrawl and his fingers trembled. Opening the letter, he read:

Dear Buck,

I am writing this, not knowing if you will ever read it. I pray, that you are still with us. When your mother died, I lost the will to live. Cole and

I have talked it over and the store is to be divided in half. You boys always got along fine. However, I have a feeling that the store is not in your blood. You are too much like your Mother. I must admit that at times I have envied you. I have also felt like riding off over the next hill, but the pull of home and security and business was stronger. If this is the case, Cole will make you a cash offer for your share of the store. I pray this letter finds you in good health. I have always been proud of you boys.

Good-bye my son,

Dad

Will placed the letter on the desk. "Cole, I don't want a share of the store. That was between you and Dad. I'd like to stay on here awhile, to get my health back. Then I have some business in Wyoming to tend to. In the meantime, I'll help out as best I can. If it's no bother, I'll fix myself a spot in the barn. Is the tack room still there? I'm traveling pretty light."

"I noticed that, Buck. Are you all right? You look so thin." Cole asked with concern.

"Thin? You should have seen me seven weeks ago. I've fattened up considerable, since then," Will said with a grimace.

"Well if you stay here, I intend to put some weight on you," Candace replied. "I have dinner on the stove. You boys go wash up and we'll talk later."

After they had eaten, between the three of them, they had the tack room cleaned out and organized in no time. Cole brought a small stove from the store and he and Will installed it, as well as a new bed and table and chair with some of his old things too. It was perfect. That evening, Will retold his experiences of the last four years, much as he had to Doc. Omitting the last few days with Jimmy. He had not mentioned it to Doc, and could not force himself to mention it now. He still felt guilty that he was here, and Jimmy dead. Cole interrupted with questions, from time to time, but mainly let Will ramble on. Candace listened to most of the story but felt obliged to tend to the baby during the worst parts. After an hour or so Will sat back. "That's about all there is to tell, Cole. This has not been a good four years." Candace came out of the back room and put her arms around him and held him tight for several seconds. As she stood back, he saw tears in her eyes. "Welcome home, Buck."

Later Will stretched out on the bed and looked around the familiar tack room. Three saddles hung from a beam. He looked at them and wondered how many miles he had sat on his. Thousands maybe. A layer of dust had settled over his and his fathers saddles. Cole's had a light coating, as he had used his up until the time he bought the buggy. The blankets and bridles hung from their pegs, as well as two ropes and a halter. He was home. He tried to put the past behind him but he knew the ghosts would always be there. With the familiar tack around him, and the smells and sounds from the barn, he went to sleep.

Early the following morning, he wrote a letter to Twyla.

Dear Miss Pinkham:

It brings me much pain and sorrow to inform

you of the passing of Jimmy Compton. Perhaps you have already been notified, but as I was his best friend for several years, he asked me to contact you. He passed away around the twelfth of October of last year. And did not suffer long. He spoke highly of you, and you were on his mind when he passed away. I promised Jimmy that I would make sure that you are fine. Please write to me, to put my mind at ease.

Your servant,

Will Morgan.

Will read the letter several times before mailing it. It didn't sound the way he wanted it to but he decided there was no good way to inform someone of a death.

He wrote a short note to Doc, enclosing the money he had borrowed. Looking through his old dresser they had brought from the house, he took out the scrap book and took out a picture of himself, which he included. He'd promised to write again, when he had more to say.

When he got to the house, he and Cole started the day with a breakfast that was more food than Will would have had in a month or more, in prison. There were times when he dreamed of the taste of eggs, bacon, pancakes, and pie, and wondered if he would ever taste them again.

Afterward the two brothers walked the fields as they had as kids, reminding each other of things they had done in their childhood. Every now and then they would stop and hug one another. When Cole left for the store, Will walked to the cemetery, located near town on a small rise. The familiar white picket fence looked as it always had. He walked along the path, reading the familiar names of folks he once knew. The family plot was located towards the back and he slowed as he tried to gather strength. He visited the graves of his grandpa and grandma. He remembered the joy they had given to his life. Beside them now were the small white headstones with the names of his parents. His mind had refused to accept the reality, until he saw the headstones. He sat on the small bench and thought of them. Hours later, he returned home. He and Candace sat on the porch with Sherman and waited for Cole to come home. He was at peace with his folks, and looking forward to tomorrow.

Will went to work in the new store. Keeping busy made the time go faster, but by the end of the first month, he had a feeling of being caged up again. That Sunday evening Cole brought him something wrapped in a rag.

"I think you'll need this." He said, as he unwrapped the pistol from the bundle. "I remember when we were growing up, that whenever you got fiddle footed, you always went out and shot the hell out of that old stump."

Will took the old pistol, eyeing the familiar lines. It was still in good condition. Cole had taken good care of it. "Thanks, Cole. I wasn't aware that it was so obvious." He remembered leaving the gun home, when he stopped there, before entering the army.

"You take as much time as you need to kill that old stump. There's no pressure here. Here are some boxes of shells," Cole said, with a smile. "What's left of it is still there waiting for you."

With the pistol on his lap, Will thought of his father who had been a fine gunsmith. When he and Cole were young, Will had often pleaded with his Dad, to no avail, to let him test fire the repaired guns. When he had reached fifteen, his father finally relented. From then on Will could usually be found after school, banging away at the stump. How many thousands of shells he had fired, he didn't know, but by the time he was eighteen he was a fine shot and extremely fast on the draw. In those days, not many were concerned about a fast draw. The gun was a tool, but to Will it was more than that. It was the one thing that he knew he was very good with. There was something magical about it. Three years later he had said good-bye to his family, and the hated store, and headed for Texas and the unknown.

As the days passed, Will spent most of the time in the store, and blasting away at the stump in the evenings. Actually, it was rather pleasant, now that a lot of the itch in his feet had been scratched. The customers, who had looked uneasy around him at first, now took no apparent notice of his scars. He had purchased another patch, when he was on the trip out, on the off chance that he might lose one. They gave him a rather roguish look and the scars were fading out some. He could live with that, as he'd darned well have to. He enjoyed the physical work in the feed room and continued to get back his strength. The swelling in his joints had diminished and arm and leg muscles were filling out the skin. It was a good feeling to be alive.

Why hadn't he heard from Twyla?

He wrote again informing her that if he didn't hear from her, he intended to come to Willow Creek. The winter months went by slowly. His room in the barn was quite comfortable and he enjoyed catching up on his reading. He was elated to read that Wirz had been found guilty and hanged. He would have liked to have seen that. He wondered if Wirz had any premonition when he watched the six Raiders die? He hoped so. He also got another view of the Confederate army. Reading how they had fought on, with so little in the way of clothes and materials, gave him a strange feeling of camaraderie. He knew what it felt like to be down-and-out. He thought of Siler and Col. Sweet, who ordered him to Ride the Mule. Bastard should have been up there with Wirz.

He was also pleased that his speed and accuracy with the pistol had returned. If the weather was not too bad, he usually spent at least an hour a day blasting away at the stump. It was getting smaller by the week. His solitude also afforded him time to play the harmonica. Taking care of the horses passed the time and he was soothed by their calm presence. His dog, Scout, had died, as well as his horse, and he felt the loss. They had spent many good hours together. He wished that he had spent more time at home. He had let his family down by not being here to help out. He found time to visit the cemetery, from time to time. It was hard to realize that he would never see them again or here their voices. Reading the names of his grandma and grandpa brought additional sorrow. He had been out in Texas when they passed on. They were good people.

Will enjoyed the evenings alone in his little room reading the newspaper, and it was a shock one evening to read, in a lengthy article on the Wirz trial, that decisions by northern politicians had played a role in the conditions at Andersonville. The article printed a letter from Wirz suggesting turning large numbers of prisoners over to the Union for humanitarian reasons. It stated that the letter went unanswered and that a train loaded with Andersonville prisoners was turned away from a Union fort in Florida. Rather than return them to Andersonville, the train was ordered to slow to a crawl. Prisoners were allowed to leave the train and seek relief. Medicines were embargoed by the North and requests for medicine for prisoners' welfare were rejected. Will read and reread the article. The hate he felt for Wirz was hard to retain. He remembered Siler's experience in Douglas. Maybe the truth was that there were good and bad on both sides. He vowed to put blame behind him. Too much of his life had been wasted already. It was insane to waste more of it in bitterness.

As winter turned to spring, Will decided that he would have to go to Willow Creek to see about Twyla. She had not written him and he was concerned. He had promised Jimmy, and that was that. Cole and Candace could see that he was becoming restless and that his stay was coming to an end.

One evening, Cole asked Will to stay with them after supper. Will held the baby, he was no longer afraid of, in his arms as they sat by the fire and discussed his plans. Briefly leaving the room, Cole came back with a long bundle. Handing it to Will, he took the baby. "These are a present from Candy and me, Buck. I hope you like them."

Out of a saddle scabbard, Will withdrew a new Henry repeating rifle. The brass shone in the light of the fire. It was one fine weapon. He was pleased to see that it had a scope. He had seen a few in the army but had never used one. Sighting through the kitchen doorway, Will lined the cross hairs up on the wall calendar. He liked the heavy, solid feel of the rifle. "It's a beauty, Cole."

As he finished examining the rifle, Cole handed him a new Colt 44 revolver. Setting the rifle aside, he palmed the revolver, rolling the cylinder, getting a feeling for the weapon. He had thought about getting a newer pistol to replace his old one, but had no idea Cole would anticipate his intentions. The rifle was a fantastic weapon. Will was overjoyed. Heading out west, a man either lived, or died, by the weapon he used and the skill he possessed. In Will's case, he didn't have much concern about the latter and now the former was handled as well.

"I don't know what to say, Cole. You didn't have to do all this."

"I know, big brother, but that's what little brothers are for. You don't know how my world was turned upside down when I thought you were dead. This is a partial payment for all the things you did for me when I was growing up. You have always been my hero. Listening to you tell about what you have been through, I knew you deserved the very best. Which reminds me, while you were at the store today, I added two more essentials. They are waiting for you in the barn." Laughing, he grabbed Will's arms, practically lifting him off the floor.

Candace picked up the baby and followed them out. "Cole has been telling me about this surprise for a month, so don't think you can leave us behind."

Cole grabbed and lit the lantern by the back door. He was practically running, by the time they reached the barn. "Come on, come on, shake a leg." Swinging the barn door open and holding up the light, he exclaimed. "What do you think?"

Will stopped dead in his tracks. Tied to the mangers, were two iron gray horses. Will moved closer, running his hands down the neck of the closer mare. She was at least sixteen hands high and the smooth muscles of her legs and the depth of her chest, hinted at her strength and staying power. She turned her head and forced her black muzzle against his chest. He stroked her and rubbed her ears. He was in love.

"That's Missy." Cole exclaimed with enthusiasm.

Will wrapped his arms around the mare's neck. Turning to Cole with a huge lump in his throat, all he could do was grin.

"Check out the other one, Buck. I figured you would need a pack-horse to lug all your gear. I think Dolly will do pretty fine. Well, what do you think?"

Will stepped around the first mare and took in the second horse. They were almost identical, except the second mare was a little heavier. They had the fine lines of quality animals. Will could have spent the entire night just running his hands over their shiny coats. He had wondered if he would ever ride a horse again, during those prison years, but he never pictured himself with animals of this caliber.

Candace had given the baby to Cole and started petting Missy. "You realize, Cole dear, that you have started something. When are you going to buy one for me?"

"Got two of them on order, Honey. When I saw these, I got the fever to put the buggy in the shed and start riding again. They will be here in a couple weeks. The only thing you need now, Will is a decent saddle. No way am I going to allow you to use that old one. Besides, the damn mice have pretty much eaten the underside out."

Reluctantly, Will followed them back to the house.

Relaxing around the pot bellied stove, Will reached over and took the baby from Candace. "What did I do to deserve all this, Cole?" Will asked humbly.

"I don't know where to start, Buck. Remember teaching me how to swim in the creek? How about the tree house? And letting me go with you to the dances, even though you had a date? Teaching me how to ride a horse, and rope? Or helping me with my school work? Buck, I could go on all night. Everything I am is a result of you doing for me. It's my turn to do for you. Besides," he said grinning, "I used the money from your half of the business."

"We need to talk about that. I don't want, or deserve, any of the store, Cole. I took off. You and Dad did all the work and you have a family to take care of. I've got my government money. I'll be just fine. I can live real cheap."

"Well, if that's how you really feel about it, I'll let the subject drop," Cole replied.

Candace started to object, but Cole shook his head. Will could see that she was not too happy with the decision. Over these last few months her estimate of Will had grown with each day. Cole had been almost suicidal when he got the letter from Del. If it hadn't been for her and the baby, she dreaded to think of what he might of done. She would miss Buck terribly.

Will looked at Candace, as he had every day since getting home. She was everything a wife should be. She and Cole were like two peas in a pod in their goals and methods. They both worked hard and were considerate of one another and of other people. The folks would have been pleased to see the house and barn. He figured the floor was clean enough to eat off. The food was first rate, and she kept herself looking nice. Yes, Cole was a lucky man. He wondered if he would ever be so lucky. Well, he would never get one if looks were important, he thought. It was one of the few times he felt sorry for himself. It only lasted a few seconds before he remembered the hundreds of friends and the thousands of strangers who had perished. He was damn lucky to be here. He thought of the Love sisters. Hell, they liked him fine.

Looking down into Sherman's small face, he smiled. I would make a good father, he thought. Sherman, had been named after General William Tecumseh Sherman. A fine name for such a little jasper.

Heading back to the barn he could feel spring in the air. Although he thoroughly enjoyed being back, he had the urge to be on the move as well. He wondered why Twyla had not written. Was she all right? Well, he would find out shortly. Settling down in his bed, he could hear the horses eating their hay. His horses. Every night he had heard the sounds of Cole's horse, but somehow, this was different. These beauties were his. He got up several times in the night, to make sure it wasn't a dream.

After working until around ten in the morning, Cole came into the warehouse, and suggested they go down to the saddler's to pick out a saddle and bridle. They also found a pack saddle, ropes, halter, and every thing else they could think of. Two hours later, they carried their purchases back to the store. It was considerable, in Will's mind.

"Something is missing. Better to have extra, than to not have what you need, and that's all I will say on the subject! Oh, I remember what's missing." Going into the store, he returned with a spy-glass. "This may come in handy. You may need it when you don't have the rifle. Besides, I think they are really fun to look through."

Two days later, Will was loaded up and ready to ride. He had decided not to load the horses on the train. He wanted to get used to the animals, and the ride to the next town was only thirty miles. He would take the train from there to Council Bluffs. He was also eager to test the new weapons. His old pistol was wrapped in oil cloth and tucked in his saddle bag.

19

WILLOW CREEK

In the community of Willow Creek, Nate Baldon emptied the small sack of mail out on his desk and began to sort through the envelopes, poking them into the small boxes with the corresponding name. As there were only thirty boxes, the remainder went into the general delivery box on the end. As he scanned the names on the envelopes, he was surprised to see a letter addressed to his wife. Miss Twyla Pinkham, General Delivery, Willow Creek, Wyoming. Return address was a W. Morgan, General Delivery, Cedar Rapids, Iowa. Who would Twyla know in Iowa, and who was W. Morgan? Looking around to make sure Twyla was still working in the restaurant, he carefully tore the end off the envelope and withdrew the letter. Checking on Twyla's whereabouts one more time, he began to read its contents.

Jimmy's parents had received word from the army that Jimmy had died. Earlier there had been that short note from the guy in Baltimore. He'd had to give that to Twyla. She'd been right there, but had managed to destroy her answer. Nate still had a lingering doubt. This letter seemed to add proof that Jimmy was, in fact, dead.

The marriage to Twyla had been a mistake from the start. He knew she was carrying Jimmy's child. It would have given him great satisfaction to possess her and the child when Jimmy came home. He had never liked Jimmy, who had bested him in so many things. His marriage to Twyla was to make up for all that. Now it was pointless.

He had to grudgingly admit that she had made an effort, but the harder she tried to please him, the more irritated he became. Hell, he just wanted out of all this. He wanted to sell off the damn ranch, sell the stores, and head to California. And then there was Sammy, a continual reminder. Every time he looked at the little boy, he could see the resemblance to Jimmy. The set of the little mouth had the same look of satisfaction Jimmy expressed when he had just beaten him at something. Sammy looked nothing like himself, and he resented the fact that everyone knew.

As he finished the letter he assessed the situation. If he gave her the letter, she would know that he had opened it. That didn't bother him exactly, but it would be better if she didn't know and better if she didn't read the letter. He liked her to be in doubt about Jimmy's death, it gave him one up on her to know something she didn't. Damn. He couldn't throw it away, because if it could be proved, later on, that the letter had been sent to Willow Creek, he would be in deep trouble. One doesn't mess with the damn government mail. If he only lost the franchise it would be bad enough, the little stipend from the post office came in handy but the idea of going to jail did not set well. He would have to come up with another plan. He would dead file it. No one ever went into the dead file, except himself, and later on, if there were no inquiry, he could burn it. Opening the bottom drawer of his desk, he pushed the letter clear to the bottom of the stack of dead file letters. He put the letter out of his mind and continued sorting.

Two months later, he was irritated to find another letter. Same name and return address. Stick the damn thing in the dead file, along with the first one. Hopefully the guy would give up, and this would be the last. He didn't bother to read the contents. If he had, he would have read that Will was on his way to Willow Creek.

Finishing with the mail for the day, Nate moved back into the store. He felt pride looking around his domain, but also a touch of resentment. He hated being tied to the place, and he hated the ranch his folks had left him, but liked the power they gave him. He was a big man in Willow Creek. It didn't matter that Willow Creek was just a little hole-in-the-wall town. He was treated with respect. He was not a man that many people were fond of but that went with the territory, he reasoned. Thankfully, the new house was finished and they were not stuck out on his ranch. He hated the smell, he hated the work, and he resented Twyla's continual push to improve the place. She wanted it back to the same condition it was when his parents were alive. It wasn't where he wanted to live, so why bother?

The new house was a vast improvement. There was nothing more that had to be done. The location, two miles from town, was an irritant. He would have preferred a lot right in town, but on the other hand, if they had built in town, it would have stifled his relationship with Dot. He allowed his mind to drift back to the last night they had spent together. He caught himself smiling. She may not be as good looking as Twyla, very few were, but she didn't nag him about a few drinks, or ask anything of him. He had gotten damn tired of being nagged. The fact that she sang at the saloon, and from time to time sold herself, didn't bother him anymore. When he wanted her, she was there.

Lately, when he came home drunk, Twyla ignored him, set out his dinner and went to bed. A damn cold bed, as far as he was concerned.

The silent treatment was more irritating than the verbal battles that had usually ended in him slapping her around a little, to shut her up. There was no way to shut up the unspoken criticism. With her coming to the restaurant each morning, wearing her bruises like so many flags of honor, the whole lousy town had known about their ruckuses. The townswomen gave him the fish eye when they came in to shop, but what the hell, they had no other place to go. Besides, he was her husband and he would damn well run his house the way he saw fit.

As the store was empty at this time of morning, he sauntered through the arched doorway into the small restaurant. The smells of breakfast drifted through the air and he realized that he was hungry. "How about some bacon and eggs?" His voice was a little too loud and the tone had a sting to it. He liked it that way. Let her know that he was on the peck. Two townsmen and a girl from one of the ranches saw him enter, but ignored his presence.

Twyla had seen Nate come into the restaurant and dreaded having to put up with his attitude. Last night had been bad. His drunkenness was almost more than she could handle. The effect his profane yelling had on Sammy was even worse. He was such a sweet little guy. How could anyone do anything to frighten him? She had never seen Nate show any affection toward the boy. He obviously regarded him as a rival for her attention. She had to admit that at times her only feeling for Nate was disgust, and his drinking was becoming far too frequent.

Jimmy had left her with a world of misery, as well as with his son. If only they had known her condition before he left. Or if they hadn't spent that afternoon out at the house. Every spare hour, they had been out there working. There was so much to do before they got married. Jimmy insisted the house had to be livable, before they "tied the knot." He had no intention of carrying her over the threshold at his folk's ranch. She had agreed. If only they had just worked on the house. But if they had, there would be no Sammy. She could not picture life without him. He was the most precious thing in her world and she would make the best of things, for him, whatever it took, and how ever many bruises she might receive.

Why Jimmy felt it so important to get himself involved in the war was still a mystery to her. No one else from Willow Creek left to fight, so why did Jimmy? Duty. That was his excuse. It was his duty, as an American, and besides it would be over in a couple months. She diverted her thoughts. No use going over it again.

She was aware of the relationship between Nate and Dot. At first, she was angry, but not anymore. The more time he spent with Dot, the less time he spent with her, and that was just fine. The whole town was aware of the little trips Nate took up the back stairs of the saloon several times a week. At first, she was embarrassed, but now she was over it. She would get by and so would Sammy.

20

RAILROADING

Arriving at the rail head near Council Bluffs, after days on the train, Del and Jack were glad to get off and stretch their legs. It had been one long trip.

"This is really something," Jack said, as he took in the swarms of men and materials around the large field. Thousands of railroad ties were being stacked, as well as hundreds, or perhaps thousands of lengths of rail as well. There was movement everywhere: men, horses, wagons, buggies. Neither had seen such activity since the first few months of the war. It appeared much the same, a mass of confusion which was, in reality, a well organized army of workers, each doing his assigned tasks.

Jack motioned to Del and they made their way to a high point from which they could get a better idea of what was taking place.

"I would imagine the office is that big building over there," Del said, pointing toward a cluster of small buildings and one large one. They carefully made their way through the confusion and arrived, safely, at their destination. A large sign over the main door read. *General Offices-Union Pacific Rail Road.*

They entered a large room filled with a wide variety of people. Some were in fine clothes, strolling around, barking orders, but more were clerks in shirt-sleeves, green visors and armbands to keep their cuffs out of the ink. The rest seemed to be laborers. A window, at one end, had a sign that read *Employment*. They made their way in that direction. The line was long and it looked like they would be in it all afternoon.

Within minutes, however, a clerk came over and asked. "Are you Del Trenton and Jack Turner?"

"I'm Del and this is Jack."

"I thought so. You boys fit the description I got from the office. I've been keeping an eye out for you. Please follow me." They stopped at a large door with the name Major General Graenville Dodge on a small metal plate. The man knocked, then they entered a spacious office. A large bearded man, sitting behind a wide desk, raised his head and scowled. "These the men we've been waiting for?"

"Yes sir," the clerk replied, and left the room, quietly shutting the door behind himself.

There was a short more roughly dressed man leaning on the corner of the desk. He had a long black whip looped at his waist.

The big man stood and offered his hand. "Glad to meet you boys. Known your father for years, Del. This is Jack Casement. He's the man in charge of the works around here." Introductions and hand shakes were made all around.

Casement began to speak. "Well sit. Take a load off. The General says you boys are going to be on the survey crew. Let me tell you how it is around here. We intend to lay a minimum of two miles of track a day. I want at least four on good terrain. That means you boys will be working, at the very least, fifty miles ahead of the crew. There will be times when you might be out there as much as three hundred miles. I want the most direct route you can give me with the smallest amount of blasting and fill. You understand that?"

"Yes sir," replied Del, standing.

"Good. You'll be working with Steven Petree. He is my lead surveyor. You do as he says, no back talk. He knows his business. Looking at Jack , he sized the man up. "I reckon you to be the guard?"

"That would be me, sir, Jack Turner." He squared his shoulders and looked the man in the eye.

"You any good with that fancy rifle? You better be, 'cause we will surely have Indian trouble, before all this is over. I damn sure don't want anyone on this crew being picked off. You're going to be out there with seven surveyors, and five other guards, and if you aren't on your toes, you won't last long and neither will the crew. You keep a sharp eye. You understand me?"

The General glared. "Two years ago I had those Redskins cleared out, but our illustrious Congress made peace with them. By God now we have them cuttin' our damn lines, and harassing the crews."

Before either could form a response, he added, "Good! Glad to have you boys on board."

Casement went on. "You'll find Petree on the main line. His car is the third one back. He's expecting you."

With that, they resumed their discussion involving the pile of papers on the desk. Del and Jack stood for a few seconds before realizing that they had been dismissed. They beat a hasty retreat.

"Not what I would call a friendly sort." Jack grumbled, as they left the car.

"That's for sure, he sounded just like my Dad when he was doing his big boss thing. With luck, we won't see too much of him."

They started for the main track. It was not hard to find as everything else seemed to be going in the same direction. Locating the car, Del knocked.

"Come on in," a voice responded.

They entered a passenger car that had been gutted out to hold a desk and several large drafting tables piled with maps. An assortment of surveying equipment took up the majority of the rest of the space. A tall, lean individual, seated at one of the drawing tables, waved them over.

"Welcome. You must be Jack and Del. My name is Steve Petree." After shaking hands he pointed to a large map and said, "This here, is where we propose to lay the track." He ran his finger along the map on the north side of the Platte, than westward through the Rocky Mountains. "We'll stick to that route as far as feasible. I haven't been out that way as yet, but I hear from our scouts that the terrain is suitable. We'll soon see how good that information is. We can expect Indian problems. Several of the hunters have been attacked so we'll have to be on our guard. When we work, we watch. When we take a breather, we watch. I have no intention of decorating some teepee with my scalp. Got it?"

They nodded.

"Which one of you is my assistant?"

Del nodded. "I'm Del Trenton. This here is Jack Turner."

"Good. You know what to do out there?"

"Yup. Worked summers surveying back east and I've a pretty good understanding of what to do and how to do it."

Turning to Jack, Petree said, "I want you roving between Del and me and the rest of the crew. Don't get too far off. From what I've heard, those Indians can sneak right up on a fellow, if he isn't watchin' like a hawk. You see any of them, you give a shot in the air, then beat it back to whoever is in danger. If in doubt as to which one that is, head toward me. I'm not what you'd call a great shot. I'll need all the help I can get," he laughed. "We'll be heading out, shortly, to end-of-track. You boys make yourself to home."

During the next few days, Del and Jack learned a lot about track laying. They also learned a few things about their bosses. The previous year, Maj. General Dodge had lead troops into the Plains and attacked Indians along the proposed route. He was so successful in removing the Indian threat that railroad promoters lobbied to have him put in command of what would later become, Colorado, Utah, Nebraska, Wyoming, Kansas and Montana. His tactics were ruthless. At one point, while clearing the Platte valley of Indians, his officers refused to continue due to sub zero weather. He had them arrested. The next morning, thirteen men were found frozen to death. Within two months he had cleared the area for a hundred miles on either side of the line. By fall, Congress forced him to withdraw for political reasons and the Indians again moved in to disrupt the railroad. It was plain to Del and Jack that they would not encounter any friendly Indians.

Casement was an ex-cavalry officer. Barely five feet tall he kept the crews running like clockwork. Snapping his big whip he veritably flew from one place to another, always there when something needed him.

Finally their train pulled out, and both Del and Jack watched the passing landscape with great interest. Excitement gripped Jack, as he thought about his future. An honest to God job, with good pay. His momma would be proud of him. Three days later when the train stopped they hadn't seen much more than they did that first day in that flat and monotonous landscape. Steve gathered up several papers he had been drawing on, and put them in a leather tube. They all gathered up their bed rolls and carried them outside.

"Fetch those bundles of stakes and grab that gear by the door. If you boys are ready, let's go earn our keep. There is food and canteens to pick up on our way out. Better bring one of those extra boxes of ammunition, just to be on the safe side. There's a crew out about a hundred miles. We make it a point to bring out supplies when we can. Most of the time we're out more like two hundred. We'll have to get cracking when we get there. The track crews are putting track down pretty fast and we need plenty of time for cut-and-fill. Bridge work takes even more time and we have to be out there far enough to not hold them up. Any bridging or trestle work has to be surveyed so that the engineers can get the plans drawn and materials cut."

Selecting horses from the company remuda, they saddled up and with six pack horses in tow, headed west, along a raw grade, with freshly laid track.

Jack was elated. He had always gotten a little thrill from setting out to a new place and the possibility of danger. Just getting out in this wide open country made his blood tingle. It felt like, looked like, smelled like, even tasted like nothing else he had ever experienced in his life. Hard to believe that he was actually participating in the *Great Adventure*, part of building a railroad!

It was amazing to see the work crews organizing the huge amount of materials. Looking down the route, Jack could see the crews doing fill, directly behind were the leveling crews, followed by the track crews. As best as he could tell, they were stretched over a ten mile run. The laborers were a mix of nationalities, mostly Irish, but also German, French, English, ex-slaves, and a smattering of others that were harder to identify.

Along with the crews, came a parade of people making money from them, several saloon tents and a half dozen, or so, brothels. As the rails moved each day, the tent city followed along.

Over the next several days, Jack gave a lot of thought to where he had been and where he wanted to go. He felt bad that he had not learned the art of reading and had made several hints to Del to that effect. Del promised that he would teach him but not until they reached their destination. He was looking forward to it but had doubts as to whether he could learn. He had looked at the printed pages, but they meant nothing to him. He thought of Jimmy and Twyla, and of Will. They had made a promise and he felt bad that they had not heard back from her. He decided that he would write. All he had to do was learn how.

How great it would be to be riding along here, all four together again. He thought of the last moments of Jimmy's life, and of Will cradling his head as they spoke of death. He pictured the plume of smoke behind that bend in the river. Looking up, he realized that he had fallen behind. Putting his mind on the present, he nudged his horse with his spurs and caught up.

A week later they arrived at the survey camp and met the five other members of the crew and six guards who welcomed Jack's arrival. Most had been in the army so they felt right at home.

Jack had heard of the Great Plains, but had never given it much thought up 'til now, and it seemed to stretch for ever. Gently rolling grassy waves, followed by more and more. Nothing on the horizons except an occasional mass of thunderclouds, and then a rain that seemed to be alive with lightning. It was a sight to see. He relished every minute of it.

During the next month their progress was rather uneventful. Jack was losing the edge of excitement he'd started with. It was hard to keep concentrating on watching for Indians when none were ever seen. However, on one particular afternoon that all changed.

Sweeping the hills to the north of the route, Jack caught a movement in a small clump of stunted brush. He focused on the spot, trying to decide if it were Indians, or just game. He did not have long to wait. From a position a hundred yards in front of where he had been concentrating, a dozen or so Indians arose, seemingly from out of the ground. He reined his horse around while pulling his rifle from the scabbard and managed to get off a warning shot. Bullets went flying, and to his amazement, several arrows passed by. Craning his neck around, he spotted several more Indians within fifty yards of where he had been standing. How had they managed to get that close without him seeing them? It made the hair stand up on the back of his neck.

He raced toward Steve whose normally tanned face was drained of color. With rifle in hand he was taking a position behind the pack-horse. The rest of the crew had taken cover in a rough circle, and were waiting to repel a possible attack. They waited in silence. Nothing else happened. Eventually, to be on the safe side, the guards rode out in ever widening circles until they were satisfied that it was safe to resume work.

The Indians had retreated, disappearing as mysteriously as they had appeared.

As weeks went by these confrontations occurred more frequently. The deceptive terrain, not at all as flat as it looked, often allowed them the cover to get within fifty yards before being seen. Another guard was added to the crew.

Tiny was a large, bearded man. He had a huge gut, that hung over his belt, like a sack of meal. He always had a plug of tobacco in his mouth and was spitting constantly. His clothes were faded buckskin and he wore moccasins, which looked as if they had seen a thousand miles of bad road. Jack was not too impressed with Tiny, until the next confrontation. While Jack was temporarily pinned down, and the other guards too far away to help, Tiny had wounded or killed at least one of the attackers with a shot of over three hundred yards. He then came galloping full tilt down toward Jack, screaming like a scalded pig, his deer skin hat flapping like a demented bird behind his head, long hair blowing wildly. Jack had to admit, Tiny was a fearsome sight. The Indians seemed to have the same impression and retreated forthwith. Jack decided he liked Tiny a lot.

The railroad proceeded in a steady pace through the early fall. As the weather started to worsen, the surveying crew stayed a little closer to the bed crew. Bad weather slowed the whole process and it was easy to get overextended. No sense in getting out there too far ahead.

Then the snow started to fall and to make matters worse, the good terrain turned to bad. The only good thing about the weather was that the Indian attacks dropped right off. It was surmised that they had gone off to their winter hunting grounds, wherever that was. The problem with this was the boredom. Jack and the other guards usually made a circle every morning out a quarter of a mile, or so, to check for intruders. The only prints they found were of game. Some of which ended up on the dinner plate. No sign of horse or man showed up on any of these rides. Jack's best entertainment was the book learnin' that he did in the evenings. He had attempted several letters, in his head, but had not gotten down to putting them on paper.

Del and Steve and the other surveyors, were having a hard time of it. All their work had to be done on foot, and that meant cold feet. They often needed to remove their gloves to handle the equipment and that meant freezing hands. Getting back to their tent, and the welcome heat from their little pot bellied stove at the end of the day gained new meaning at each drop in the temperature. The surveyors shared one large tent while the guards slept in the other. A third tent was devoted to supplies. To the disgust of the guards, company rules stipulated that two guards would be on duty during the night. Jack was starting to lose interest in working on the railroad.

Back at end-of-track, new work crews were rotated in to take the place of the worn out bed crews. The work was extremely hard, even in the best of weather, and to maintain any progress at all, required fresh men. The *Ladies* tents became fewer and fewer. They would return in the spring, when the weather was better. The work crews were saddened to see them go.

Still the survey crew worked on unrelieved. They were unaware of what was taking place a hundred miles behind them and wouldn't have cared if they knew. It looked like it was going to be a damned long winter, and it was. How many miles they covered in those five months, Jack didn't know, but it seemed like thousands. Most of the time, he enjoyed what he was doing; seeing new country and not having many cares. His reading skills were comin' right along, and he was pleased that he was not too stupid to figure it out. He thought a lot about Twyla, and the promise he had made to Will. Del seemed too busy in his job to give it much thought, but it weighed on Jack's mind. They should do what they promised.

The occasional trips back to end-of-track were something to look forward to but with the ladies gone, there wasn't much to do once they got there. Del looked forward to seeing the bridges that crossed gullies that he had surveyed. Within weeks, they would be connected by track as the crews moved forward. Jack looked forward to the threat of Indians, more out of a need for excitement, then anything else.

Activities there picked up as an early spring arrived. More men had come, a saloon and a few of the ladies had set up shop. Del and Jack had ridden back for additional supplies and to deliver the engineering drafts for several small bridges that would have to be redrawn at headquarters and sent to milling. For the next two days, they enjoyed the fresh food and socializing. Their business finished, they reluctantly prepared to head back to camp, some hundred miles west. Several miners joined them, for there was safety in numbers, and on a cold, clear morning the group headed out.

On the morning of the third day, as they were gathering their gear, Jack spotted a new tent a short way to the rear of their camp. Two gray horses were staked out beside it. He called to Del. "Have a look."

"Whoever owns those sure has himself a fine pair of horses. Look at their heads, will you. Have you ever seen anything more beautiful?" Del asked.

"Not that I recall," Jack replied, "and that includes most of the ladies in my life."

"Well, we better git this bunch a movin' or we'll never git to camp. I imagine the boys will be glad to see us, especially all this canned food were bringing 'em."

Soon the group was mounted and moving out along the trail that they had staked out over a month before. Del noticed a form curled up in the small tent by the grays. Must have come in late, whoever he is.

Damn fine pair of horses, Jack thought, I wonder who the gent is and what he's a doin' way to hell and gone out here. They had left two cans of peaches near their still burning fire for the traveler. No sense in puttin' it out, if the rider could use it.

It had been a hard ride the previous day and Will had been bushed by the time he saw the faint camp light. He decided that bedding down near the camp would be a little safer. He would be able to sleep more soundly than he had for days. He had been following the railroad stakes because they were going in the right direction.

In his haste to get some sleep he had forgotten the rifle in the saddle scabbard. He was relieved to see it safe. Some sound from the departing group of riders had wakened him but he felt so snug he had stayed in his bed roll while they left. They were already a mile or so away. They were up early, he thought. Nice of them to leave the fire. He noticed the peaches then and opened one with his knife and after drinking the juice, ate the peaches. He slipped the second can into his pack. He wiped the juice from his chin and silently thanked the strangers for their generosity. He decided against a hot breakfast, and with a few side drags with his boot, covered the dying fire with dirt.

He saddled up, loaded the pack horse and mounted, then followed the group out along the trail. Soon the tracks of the majority of the riders, headed off in a southerly direction. Perhaps they didn't work for the railroad, he thought. He had noticed some mining gear on several of the mules last night. Two of them rode on, following the staked trail.

They had disappeared around a turn and judging the lay of the land, he decided to head in a more northerly coarse. The route the train would need might be more level but it was heading quite a piece from where Will wanted to go.

Moving up the low hillside he could soon make out the two riders way out ahead of him. Watching them, he noticed they both had carbines resting on the saddle horns, and each led three heavily laden pack horses. He saw movement in the tall grass below. Taking out his spyglass he spotted at least a dozen mounted Indians making their way toward a meeting with the two men who where obviously unaware of the danger. The Indians dismounted and moved into the scrub brush that stretched from where they left their horses to within twenty yards of the survey stakes the riders were following. They were completely out of sight of the two riders and it was obvious to Will, that they would be able to get very close before being noticed.

Will took the lead rope from his saddle horn and tethered the pack horse to a clump of scrub brush. He left the knot loose, on the off-chance that he would not be able to come back for it. Moving down the slope at a fast pace he realized that he was too far off to warn the men, so proceeded toward the scrub brush that hid the Indians. When he had ridden as close to the raiding party as he dared, he dismounted, and taking the Henry, moved closer on foot. Within minutes he could see the movement of the tall grass that marked the progress of the dismounted Indians. Occasionally, a feathered head would rise to get bearings, then disappear again. They were creeping forward on their stomachs toward the unsuspecting riders. He could see the near rider. His head was moving back and forth in a searching motion but he was clearly still unaware of the danger. He used the glass to determine the location of each Indian, then, using his crossed legs as a brace, sighted down on the one at the back of the pack. Three had crawled out onto short grass, exposing their bodies to Will. He remembered his dad telling him. "Always take the rear turkey, that way it don't spook the others. By the time they figure it out, you can get two or three."

Will lined up the sights on the back of the last Indian. He paused. Hell, he thought, I have no quarrel with them. If folks were taking over my land, I might feel a might testy too. Moving the sights to the right of the Indian, he gently squeezed the trigger, the gun bucked, and the Indian flinched, looking around to see where the bullet had come from. By this time, Will had shifted to the next Indian and repeated the process, with the same result. After the third shot, they all were fearful. They heard the shots, but saw nothing. They could not be sure where the shooter was, or if the next shot would be more accurate. Will smiled, as he saw the confusion. He thought of breaking off the engagement, but his ego got the better of him. He didn't want them to think he was a bad shot, so he searched for something to shoot that would send the message. One of the shields that they carried, had a painting of a buffalo skull, and he placed a hole between the eye sockets. The message was clear.

Jack heard the three spaced gun shots, but couldn't figure out what they meant. He scanned the side of the hill where the sound originated and saw, what looked like a thin mist of gun smoke, drifting in the morning light. Seconds later he saw a puff of smoke and then heard another distant report. Looking around desperately he caught a fleeting movement from the now retreating Indians. Aiming carefully, he managed to nick one of the ambushers, missing another, as the rout began. Jack aimed and fired again and then once more. The Indians had broken from cover, but soon disappeared into the brush. Within seconds they could be seen, now mounted, high tailing it to the northwest.

"Damn, Jack, that was close. I was looking in that direction and didn't see a thing." Del exclaimed. "How did you see them?"

"Didn't see a thing until that feller up on the crest of that rise stirred 'em up for me. Let me see your spy glass." Looking toward the hillside he could make out the shape of the shooter standing up and moving over to a stubble of brush that had shielded his horse from view. He couldn't see the face of the shooter but he would never forget that horse. Putting a shot in the air, he saw the shooter return the gesture. The distant figure mounted, and with one more wave, moved over the crest of the hill and out of sight.

Jack relished telling the story when they arrived at camp two days later. "Well whoever he is, I'd like to shake his hand. I think he saved our bacon. Danged grass could hide an elephant. Can't say that I've ever seen one but I hear they're pretty big." Everyone laughed. He didn't mention the tingle of fear he felt when he realized how close those Indians could have gotten before being seen. He figured less then twenty yards. He would have been dead.

21

SHOOTOUT

Retrieving Dolly, Will moved off toward the north. If he moved fast enough he could substantially widen the distance between himself and the Indians, which seemed like a very good idea. Putting the horses into a ground covering lope, he continued he pace, on and off for the next several hours, only taking short periods at a walk, then back to the lope. The horses were in fine condition but Will didn't want to push them overly. He wanted to know that there was something left should he need speed later on. The rest of the day was uneventful. Will turned westward.

As the days passed, Will continued in the same westerly direction. From time to time he could see a river off to his left, gradually getting closer. He had heard that Fort Laramie was located on a river and would be a good crossing place. He figured that if he kept it in sight, he would find the fort. The going was slow and Will took his time. No sense in running into a war party by being in a hurry.

Several days later he was surprised to see three riders approaching his camp. His impression of the three was not good. They fanned out as they neared the camp. Will's concern increased as they shifted their rifles across their laps. Damned if they don't have trouble on their minds, he thought. He noticed that they loosened their pistols. Not good. Not by a damn sight. He loosened his pistol in the holster as well and checked the location of the Henry. He felt the muscles tense in his stomach and forced himself to stay calm. No damn way was he going to let them get in the first shot. If he could get off three shots to their none he'd be alright. The first one to break eye contact, would get his first shot. By willpower, he took a deep breath and relaxed. He could feel the fear recede and a calmness take over. He was ready.

"Hello the camp. We're comin' in."   The stranger wasn't asking, he was telling.

Will didn't say anything, as the three rode up. They reined in and sat looking down at Will. They were a rough group and Will moved away from the horses. No sense in taking the risk of getting them shot. He knew, without doubt, that there was going to be shooting. They reminded him of the trio that had caught up with him and Jimmy when they escaped from Andersonville. Lean and mean.

Perhaps it was his thoughts about Twyla, these last few months, that caused him to feel concern for his own safety. He really didn't want to die. She was too close to have him die in a stupid shoot-out with three worthless saddle-bums.

"Seen you out a ways, yesterday. Where you headed?" The man was perhaps forty years old, with a mean set of eyes and a sneer on his lips. In a way he reminded Will of Rooster.

Will didn't answer. The three took that as a sign of fear. Their horses moved around, restless, as the riders tried to gain an advantage. Noticing the eye patch, one attempted to work his way around to Will's left side.

"We been out doin' a little scalp gatherin' and I must say that the hunting's been good." The talker remarked, spitting a plug of chew in Will's direction. Uninvited, he dismounted. The one moving to Will's left remained mounted, hand gripping the rifle. Will noticed the scalps hanging from the saddles, and wondered if any were from women and children. "Those appear to include children, that right?" He was only guessing, as they all looked pretty much the same.

"You got a good eye. Them and the squaws was runnin' like rabbits, when we got 'em." He took his eyes off Will to fondle his trophies. Will's bullet struck him in the side of the face slamming him against his saddle. The horse shied away startling the second horse and rider. Before he hit the ground, Will swung around to the intruder to his left, sending his second shot into his chest. The third, grappling with the reins of his startled horse, had managed to get around behind Will and slide down on the far side of his mount for cover. Swinging the rifle over the saddle, he got off a shot, but missed. Will fell to the ground and placed a bullet under the horses stomach and through shear luck into the leg of the shooter. The man fell away from the horse, still hanging on to the reins, trying to keep it between himself and Will. The wildly dancing horse pulled away, then bolted and left the man exposed. Will placed his shot into the man's upper chest. He looked at Will with shock as he was driven backward, falling to the ground. He arched his back to look at Will. His eyes wide.

"What the hell?" he whispered, between clenched teeth. His fingers clawed at the bloody wound.

"You boys were taking too long a look at my horses. Besides, you folks that shoot women and children have pretty much worn out your welcome on this here earth." He put the second bullet in the cowboy's forehead. The man jerked, then lay still. Dumping the saddles and bridles off the two horses, he turned them loose. He'd have to ride after the other one, he couldn't leave it out here saddled. Will looked at the scalps with their long black hair, not knowing if he should bury them or just leave them. He tried not to wonder what the owners had looked like, or which were women and which were children. He decided to leave them where they were. Looking around, he removed one of the riders' scarf and placed it over the scalps to keep the flies off. Sons-a-bitches. He picked up the rifles and pistols and tied them on Dolly. Looking down on the three bodies, he felt a grim satisfaction. "You wore out your welcome," he said out loud.

Hearing the gunfire, the small band of Indians stood and looked toward the sound. It could not be too far off, and they knew that they were close to the man who had spoiled their ambush. The spacing of the shots was a mystery, not the pattern of one hunting game. They mounted, and with great caution, headed on. The first two horses, they spotted right away. The other moved into sight after a few minutes, about a quarter mile away. Bison Stands moved toward the lone horse. The others moved on, in the direction of the two together. Dismounting, they dropped down and slithered through the tall grass, until they spotted the three bodies. Cautiously, they stood and approached them. They knew who the men were when they saw the mounts as they had several skirmishes with these men before. On discovering the scalps, they quietly thanked the man on the gray horse, but who was this white man who had killed their enemies?

One of the young men gently picked up the scalps and wrapped them in a leather pouch. The others examined the bullet holes in the bodies of the three men. The man that put the bullet hole between the eyes of the buffalo, was also deadly with a pistol. Inwardly, they were glad that the three had found him first. This white man would be talked about around many campfires. Mounting, they headed north.

The following evening Will reached the river and the flat boat that served as a ferry. The town and fort were visible on the other side. It was nice to see people again. He wondered how the horses would take to the crossing but they went right on-board and took the trip as if it were an every day occurrence. Will was pleased.

The town was a flurry of activity. The large trading post was doing a booming business, as this was the only source of supplies in many miles. Will put the horses up in the stable, stowed his gear in the livery office, and looked for a place to eat. Later he found a comfortable chair on the boardwalk and spent the rest of the evening just taking in the activities. Well after dark he took his bedroll and set up camp near the edge of town. It was nice to hear the sounds of people, and their laughter.

The next morning, he rode the mile or so to Fort Laramie and was surprised to see a new steel bridge spanning an offshoot of the river. Gittin' damn fancy, Will thought. He entered the fort, which was well placed, overlooking a vast panorama in all directions. Seeing the troopers made him feel right at home. Most of the soldiers were involved in the construction of new barracks. He inspected them like a visiting dignitary. They would be great living quarters this far away from civilization. He had lunch with the troops. When they learned of his captivity, he found himself being treated as royalty. Upon inquiry, he was advised that the best way to get to Willow Creek was to ride west on the stage road about eight to ten days until he hit the town of Summit. Small stage stations were spaced every twenty miles or so, if he needed for anything. From there, he could follow the secondary stage road to Willow Creek. Will felt a surge of excitement. He was getting closer to Jimmy's hometown, and Twyla. Would she still be there?

Will thought that he just had about crossed the Great Plains but he didn't see mountains until a week into his ride and they were far in the distance. The stages passed him every other day. Some going west and others going east. The next day, four riders passed him. They were the only people he saw, except for the wranglers at the stage stations and the men on top of the stages. Will was content to proceed at a leisurely pace to rest the horses. He wouldn't admit it to himself, but he was concerned that he wouldn't find Twyla. If she were still there, why didn't she write? He found himself slowing down the horses, putting off the disappointment. She might even have died! He had a hard time sleeping at night as the possibilities swirled in his head.

The terrain began to change from the treeless waves of tall grass. There were barren escarpments with fingers of the desert to the south filling the valleys with twisted gullies and jagged mesas. Later there were grassy hills with small trees and streams in the valleys in between. Snow topped mountain ranges were visible from the hilltops perhaps, a hundred miles ahead. Will was beginning to enjoy the feel of the land. It had a wild beauty about it that he liked.

The grade began to rise and before noon of the tenth day, he entered the town of Summit. A large sign, riddled with bullet holes, proclaimed the town to be "GUN FREE. LEAVE YER WEAPONS WITH THE SHERIFF." It was a rather large town, for being so far away from anything, consisting of twenty or more businesses along the main street, and a number of houses he didn't care to count, that were scattered around the general vicinity. Will rode in looking for a livery. It was not hard to find, being the first building he came to. In the process of stabling the horses, the stableman brought him up on the latest local news.

"If in I was you, I'd carry that thar rifle, you got, as well as the hog leg. We got a couple bad fellers in town that have pretty much gotten themselves the run of the whole show."

"Don't you have some sort of law in a town this size? Sign says to leave weapons with the Sheriff," Will looked down the near deserted street, wondering where the people were.

"Shore we do, but right now, he's laid up over at Doc's place with a couple of bullets in 'im. Don't reckon he'll be up and about for some time. And with Sprigg down, that sign don't mean a damn thing."

"What happened to him?"

"Those two rannihans shot him, that's what happened. Old Sprigg never had a chance. He tried to get them to abide by the rules of the town, which don't allow no guns. They just laughed. A couple hours later, they was a shootin' up the saloon, and bustin' the place up. When he tried to talk them into givin' him their guns, peaceful like, they plugged him. Lowdown snakes."

"Seems like there would be folks around that could handle them. Don't know how two men could threaten a town this size."

"You'll know when you see these fellas. Nobody wants to be the first one dead. They're damn fast. Been shootin' up the place somethin' awful." He shook his head in disgust.

"Thanks for the warning. I'll keep my eyes open. By the way, I came by some extra guns and rifles a few days ago. I'd appreciate it if you could find a buyer. I'll go cheap."

The man looked at Will, wanting to ask how he "come by em," but held his tongue. For all he knew, Will could be more trouble. He hoped that the town had not acquired another problem to add to the two troublemakers it already had. Don't know what the world is a comin' to, with so many bad people a comin' through these parts, he thought. Must be the gold strikes in Colorado. Thank God they's a runnin' dry. He scowled as he watched Will walk down the street.

Will had contemplated selling the guns at Laramie, but thought better of it. Two of the guns had initials carved into the butts, and could have caused trouble if they were recognized.

After getting a fairly good meal, Will took up temporary residence in a chair in front of the mercantile store and watched the afternoon activities. There were far fewer people out than what he thought would be usual. He could hear the piano music from the saloon and figured that most of the men folk were probably in there. Or, maybe just the piano player and the two shooters. He kept his eye on the bat-wing doors, just in case. Several men came out, and mounting their horses, rode out of town. Two women came along the boardwalk and entered the store that he was leaning against. As he was focused on the saloon, he didn't take notice except the faint smell of soap and just a hint of roses. He looked around but they were already in the store.

The two gunmen came out of the saloon and several men who were leaving a store across the street, noticed them and ducked back inside. People peeked out through dirty windows, then seemed to disappear, until there were only the two gunmen and Will. Seeing him on the porch, they turned in his direction.

"Who the hell are you?" the larger of the two growled.

As Will didn't bother to reply, the smaller one said. "I hear you got a couple good horses over in the livery. We could sure use some better mounts. I say we take a look-see at them horses and maybe come up with a trade, straight across!" Laughing, they turned in the direction of the livery.

"Whoa up a minute. Seems you boys are looking for trouble. If that's the case, I feel obliged to give you a warning. You keep the hell away from what's mine. That clear?" He had not moved from his chair, nor had he raised his voice. In fact it was hardly more than a whisper.

Surprised, the two men turned and starred at Will. Their hands hovered over their guns. "You talkin' to us, you one -eyed jackass?" the smaller man snarled.

"You must be as dumb as you look. Who else would I be talkin' to?"

"You got a gun, I suggest that you draw it, 'cause I aim to shoot you, right here and now." warned the larger man.

Will gave a lazy smile. "If you're so set on dying today, that's fine with me. However, I think you should give it some serious thought. It's much too fine a day to die. Tell you what, I'll give you boys fifteen minutes to think it over. Go have yourselves a last beer and decide if you're really through livin'. If so, say good-bye to your friends, if you have any. Then come look me up. I'll be right here."

Undecided, the two stood there, trying to figure just what to do.

Looking completely perplexed, the smaller man mumbled something and they moved back in the direction of the saloon.

Will was irritated, rather than angry. What he really wanted was to just be left alone. What right did these two have to disrupt his day? He could feel the tingle on the back of his neck, as he debated which of the two would draw first. Probably the smaller man, he thought.

Melinda, crouching inside the hardware store window could hardly breath, she was so excited. She had seen the man seated in the chair when she entered the store with her mother, but hadn't paid any attention to him. She wished she had now. She was so close that, had the window been open, she could have reached out and touched him. He was surely the bravest man she had ever seen. She had peered out the window and watched the faces of the two bad men as they threatened to kill the man in the chair. How could anyone talk to them the way he had? They were frightening and yet he didn't seem to be afraid of them at all.

Martha Pinkham came over to where Melinda was crouching.

"Goodness, child, get away from that window! This is no place for you to be." She looked at the door and realized that they were trapped in the store with a gunfight about to take place just outside. She had already checked the back door, when she realized what was happening, but the back steps were being remade and it was a long jump to the ground. The best thing to do was to stay in the store and duck behind the heavy counter.

Melinda was too intent on what was going on outside to hear her mother. The larger man had come out of the saloon. Where was the second man? She peered through the dirty glass, searching out every doorway and alley in sight. Then she saw movement. He was sneaking up on the left. He must have circled around the block. He moved out from the alley and was on his stomach behind the water trough across the street. She was sure the man on the porch had not seen him, which was odd "Mister." she said in a low voice, "The other man is laying behind the water trough, to your left, about thirty feet on the other side of the street." The man didn't move but she heard him say, in a calm voice, "Thank you ma'am, now you get yourself away from that window."

Reluctantly, she obeyed. However she positioned herself where she could keep an eye on the big man in the street.

"Looks as if you have made your decision." Will said, pushing himself out of the chair. "No rush, if you boys want to take a last long look at life. If not, let's get it over with. I'm getting hungry." Will moved away from the window. Carefully, he stepped down onto the street, catching a glimpse of the man behind the trough. At that moment the big man made his play and his hand whipped down to his pistol. His fingers had no more than touched the grip of his pistol when his entire body was lifted off the ground and propelled backward. Melinda watched in amazement as the man was blasted out of her view. She did not see him fall. The sound of the gun made her jump. Was it one explosion, or two? Maybe a third? She wasn't sure. She waited for several seconds, then peeked out the window. The man was reloading his pistol, completely unconcerned about the second gunman. Then she saw the body sprawled halfway out from behind the trough. My God, she thought, he shot them both but she wasn't even sure he had shot twice. Well he must have, she rationalized but the sounds came so close together. She wished that she had stood up and watched. Wait 'til I tell Twyla.

Then she was looking into the face of the stranger. He was standing just outside the window peering in at her. He had a patch on one eye and a horrible scar from mouth to ear. A black beard, covered his lower face except the white scar. She didn't flinch but it was all she could do to keep from fainting.

"Thanks for your help. I didn't see that other man." He tipped his hat and smiled.

Melinda didn't know whether to be afraid or not. But decided to tough it out. "The pleasure was all mine, sir," she said with a smile.

Martha Pinkham grabbed her daughter's arm and pulled her away. Half dragging the girl, she got her away from the window. When they left, a few minutes later, the stranger was nowhere in sight. The bodies were still where they had fallen and towns people were gathering around them.

"By golly, I seen it but I don't believe it. Took them fellers with one shot! How'd he do that?" One old man inquired.

"He shot twice, you damn fool. How can he shoot two men in different directions with one bullet. Use your head," another answered.

Melinda could hardly get to sleep that night. Her mind was racing over the day's events. She had seen the two gunmen strolling around the street that morning as if they owned the place and everyone in it. They seemed invincible, and obviously just plain mean, shooting nice Sheriff Sprigg like that. She was sure the rest of the towns people felt just as intimidated as she did. Then that one-eyed man comes along and kills them both, as easily as if he were swatting flies. He was a wonderment. She spent the next morning in a fog of anticipation watching for him, while her mother shopped. She made an effort to act like a lady and pay attention but had lost all interest in shopping. Well, he was much more exciting and she wanted to know more about him. But, evidently, he was gone. Would he ever enter her life again? She sure hoped he would.

She and her mother paid their respects to Sheriff Sprigg. Her mother had once had a fancy for him, before she met Daddy, and they always spent some time with him when they came to Summit for supplies. Her mother was shocked to hear that this fellow was inquiring about Willow Creek. "What is this world coming to with gunfights and all. We don't need that kind in our town."

Melinda was thrilled! Then, she wondered if Nate had sent for him. It would be just like him to employ a gunman to back up Cap. She lost some of her enthusiasm. If, in fact, he was just a hired gun she could do without him. On the other hand, maybe he wasn't. Her enthusiasm returned.

The stage to Willow Creek arrived and she reluctantly got in. Martha climbed in and sat beside her daughter. A drummer climbed aboard and sat across from them. The stage lurched and the horses went into a slow trot. She could hardly wait to tell her big sister. She wanted to chatter on about it with her mother, but Martha kept shushing her. A lady wasn't supposed to even notice such things. It was so unseemly.

The drummer, on the other hand, was eager to share his knowledge with her and listen to her story in return. He prattled on, revealing every gem of information he had been able to glean. "Did you see the two horses that belong to the mysterious gunman? No? They were handsome gray steeds. At least seventeen hands, or maybe more! Everything on the horses was new and of excellent quality including his various weapons. He had just ridden in to town not long before it happened and left the horses and his gear at the livery. He had three extra rifles and pistols put up for sale. Didn't mention how he came by them. The sheriff offered him a job but he said he had business elsewhere. Right after breakfast, this morning, he saddled up and left."

He listened to every word Melinda said about her encounter. They chatted on endlessly, it seemed to Martha. At last they ran out of things to say and the rest of the trip they looked out their windows, lost in thought.

As the stage pulled in to Willow Creek, Melinda had the door open, ready to jump out. As soon as it came to a stop, she jumped from the doorway and ran to the restaurant. It seemed to her that Ernie had kept the horses to a slow pace on purpose. She loved him dearly, but today she wished that he had pushed the horses a little bit faster.

She burst through the door, and seeing Twyla in the kitchen, exclaimed. "I saw two men get shot! I actually talked to the man that killed them. Oh, it was awful! No, it was inspiring. Yes, inspiring." She was out of breath from her dash and excitement.

Twyla put her arm around her little sister. "Calm down, Honey, and start from the beginning."

She recounted her experience, adding details as she went. It was a glorious story. "And on the stage, I learned that he had two beautiful gray horses, I didn't see them but the fellow that did said they were the best looking horses that he ever saw. Oh, Twyla! You should have been there. Oh, and he told Sheriff Sprigg that he was coming here!"

"Well it does sound like you had an adventure, but I think I'll pass on that type of entertainment. Now help Mom and me bring in the goods." She wondered why a gunfighter would be coming here. Must be just passing through. Just what the town needs, a gunfighter. The thought of Nate bringing in a man like that crossed her mind but she didn't see the need. Cap pretty much ran things around here as far as keeping everyone cowed.

Several boxes and sacks were handed down to the up-stretched hands. The main purchase of inventory would be arriving by wagon in couple of days.

"Thanks, Ernie." Twyla smiled as he descended from the top of the coach. "Come in for dinner. I have fresh mince meat and a cream pie."

"You can count on it. Heard what Melinda told you. Got to admit that it was somethin' to see. He warn't much to look at, but I sure liked his style. Sure don't know what he wants here. Hope it ain't trouble." He wheeled the horses around and drove the coach into the wide doors of John's livery.

Twyla tried to think of a reason, but finally gave up. If he showed up, she would probably find out.

22

THE MEETING

Will could not see through the window-glass very well because of the dust, but he had the feeling that the mysterious voice on the other side had come from a very pretty young lady. He was wondering about that when the liveryman started patting him on the back.

"Come on mister, you need to talk to the Sheriff. He'll want to know what happened, straight from the horse's mouth, so to speak."

Will followed him down the street. Along the way folks came out to clap him on the back and shake his hand. By the time they reached the Doc's back door, at least a dozen people were with him.

Sheriff Wayne Sprigg had heard the gunfire and the ensuing silence had him worried. What the hell was going on out there? It had been quiet all morning, and it didn't sound like them trouble makers just shootin' up the town. They had just about shot everything up yesterday. He heard the clump of feet on the planks out in back and prepared himself for the worst. It could only mean another killin'. He clenched his fists in frustration.

The door burst open and the room was instantly filled with people. Those that couldn't get inside recounted the episode to each other excitedly out back. "By God Sheriff, you should'a seen it. This here fella' sent both those gunslingers to hell. You should'a seen it."

"Hell man, I woulda' if I warn't a layin here on my death bed," Sprigg exclaimed with irritation. Looking at Will, he asked, "You want to fill me on what happened?"

Will told the barest details. His story was backed up by a chorus of, *damn rights, that's rights,* and a few *Amens.*

"Looks like you saved me a lot of trouble. I don't rightly believe that I could take those two, even if the fight was fair. I think I'm gettin' too damn old for this type of work. You lookin' for a job?"

"No thanks, Sheriff, but I was glad to help. Am I free to go in the morning? I have business in Willow Creek."

"Of course, you are, son. I just wish I could think of a way to keep you here longer. We could sure use you around these parts, and that's for sure."

"Well, I appreciate that and if I come back through this way, I'll look you up." Will liked the old man on sight. He had a pink, bald head that had not seen the sun in ages, a scraggly beard on his jutting jaw, keen gray, squinting eyes and a bulbous nose. Together these made a face that one had to smile at. His hand shake was firm.

"What's your handle, Son?"

"Oh folks call me Buck, Sheriff. Just Buck."

"Well, Just Buck, hope to see you again some time," he said with a grin. Sprigg always prided himself in taking a man's measure right off, and aside from the one eye and scar, he liked what he saw in Buck.

Will and the stableman made their way back to the livery. "Do you mind if I sack out here in the barn?"

"I'd be most pleased to have you as a guest of the establishment. Don't see the likes of you come in every day. Sure wish I'd a seen it though. They tell me you got both of them with one bullet. That right?"

"No, I used two," Will replied with a smile.

"Sounded like one long gunshot to me, but I'll take your word on it. Either way, that was fine shootin'." Later, as he lay in the hay, he still heard whispering from the stableman's office. Two men in opposite directions killed with one bullet. He smiled, as he drifted off to sleep.

Early as he was the next morning, Will still had a few delays getting out of town. He was a celebrity among the other early risers and was showered with questions. They didn't allow him to pay for his breakfast and when he re-entered the barn the old man had both horses ready to go for him. He felt like he was leaving home again. Everyone was waving and telling him to come on back anytime. It was an uplifting send off and that was for sure.

"Fore I forgit, I got twenty dollars for them guns."

"Thanks. Keep five for the bother."

"Hell, wasn't no bother a'tall. Pleasure was all mine. If I' a kept them until after the shootin' I coulda' doubled the price," he said with a laugh.

"I appreciate it," Will said as he took the money and put it in his shirt pocket.

Will decided to detour from the stage road in order to get a better look at the country. He had ridden to the top of a rounded hill a ways from the road when he noticed the stage go by down below. Hours later he paused at a small way station back on the stage road. As he dismounted at the trough, an old man came out and stood watching him. "You got to be the feller that done in the two in Summit."

It wasn't a question, just a statement.

"News travels fast in these parts."

"Shore do and that's a fact. To tell the truth, I got the whole story from Melinda, on her way back to Willow Creek. Seems she was right in the thick of it, even warned you that one of em' was sneakin' up on you."

"Matter of fact, she probably saved my life, or at least kept me from taking a bullet."

"Stage stops here for an hour's rest and then goes on into town. She didn't stop talking the whole time. I love her like my own, but she can sure carry on," he laughed.

The afternoon ride had been slow as each mile gained in elevation. There was a golden slant to the sunlight as he entered the main street of Willow Creek. The town lived up to its name. Willow trees lined the creek that paralleled the main road. The streets had a clean windswept look and the requisite number of businesses were prosperous looking though there wasn't two of anything. It felt good to get near mountains and streams again. The air was clean and crisp up so high and even higher mountains could be seen in the distance, each ridge and gully standing out in the clear golden light. If he hadn't business to do he would ride on up into those mountains and explore their secret places and on over to the other side to see what was there. This country was more to his liking than any he had ever seen before.

Will counted more than two dozen occupied homes in the town proper, and he'd seen a smattering of small ranches along the route. It was obvious that the town had been much larger when the mines were open. An assortment of rusted mining equipment was piled here and there and he'd passed a number of buildings that were just shells. The main mine building loomed up behind him in a state of sad disrepair.

Judging by the sun, it was four or five. He still had enough time to get his business started. Fifteen or so horses lined the various hitching rails and there were a dozen or so people out on the boardwalks. Several stopped to look, probably at the horses, he thought. First thing was to find the stables. Here again, it was easy. It was, by far, the biggest building in use, in the entire town. Obvious at a glance was a small hotel and a saloon, with several of the horses in front of it, and a small restaurant attached to the mercantile. He dismounted and led the horses inside the stable. The construction was impressive, built to last. Huge hand squared beams mortise and tenoned together constituted the main framework. He was taking it all in when a small but burly black man came out of the office. Ignoring Will, he seemed transfixed by the mares. He looked past middle age, but his arms and upper body were those of a younger man. He didn't acknowledge Will until his inspection was over.

"Them's fine lookin' animals, Mista. You wanna sell 'em?"

"No," Will replied, "Doubt if I ever will."

The man sighed, "Well, don't do no harm to ask." He reluctantly pulled his eyes away from the horses, looked at Will and smiled. Will caught a look of caution in the smile. Something about the eyes. They were not smiling.

Will laughed. "I'd like to leave the pack horse here for now. I've business to take care of but I'll be back a little later. I'll probably be staying a few days. You have room for them?"

"Room is what I always got. My name is John Hamner, John Henry Hamner. I own this here place. My boss and I, we comes out here together. We built this here barn and was doin' pretty good. He got throwed, and hit his head on the fence out back. Kilt him. Then the mines went to pot. I been runnin' it alone for goin' on two years now. I'm also the town smithy, so ifn' you need yer horses shod, or metal work, you let me know."

"I'll do that. They call me Buck." Will replied, looking at the squared beams. "Well, it's, by far, the best lookin' barn I've ever seen, and that's a fact."

John grinned. A compliment was always welcome. Hell, a man with an eye for craftsmanship couldn't be so bad. He looked up at the beams, with pride.

Mounting up Will road out into the street and out of town. He was looking forward to seeing Jimmy's ranch. After all the hours of listening to Jimmy talk about his place, it was high time for him to actually see it.

A couple of miles out he took note of a fancy new place off to his left. It was surrounded by large trees that must be several hundred years old, Will thought. Another mile up the road, he passed the side road that must lead to Jimmy's folk's place. From there the way was overgrown with weeds, obviously, not used very much. He could see the house up on a rise, nestled in another stand of large old trees. The setting was similar to that of the new house, back yonder.

The gate was leaning against the fence with a broken hinge. The house was obviously abandoned. The only sign of life was a well tended patch of flowers growing in a small space under one of the windows. He thought that a little strange. Dismounting he entered the house. It appeared to have been used in the not too distant past. Trash and scattered cigarette butts littered the floor. It made Will's heart sink to remember how much this place meant to Jimmy. He checked out the barn and found it in better condition. Obviously, it was in regular use. Hay was stacked at one end and fresh manure littered the stalls. By the looks of things, they hadn't been cleaned in a long time. He spent a short while looking over the property outside but daylight was fading fast. It was a mess but it appeared livable. He would think on it and return in the morning.

John was sitting in his chair, leaning it back against the office wall.

"See ya found yer way back. Thought maybe you got lost wanderin' around." He wanted to ask where the stranger had been but decided that was a mite too nosy just yet.

I see you have a hotel, can I get dinner there? I see the café is closed."

John's expression turned dour. "Family problems." He didn't elaborate. "About ready to take some stew off the stove. There's plenty for two if you have a mind to join me.

"Sounds good John. I've got a can of peaches I've been carryin' around forever just for such an occasion."

He didn't stay long. They had eaten their fill, talking about general things and both were soon yawning. Will got a good night's sleep at the hotel and was out early in the morning. He rode out toward the ranch, this time turning toward the Compton place. As he recalled it wouldn't be too far. The road crossed a large tract of cleared land and ended at an open ranch gate. He could just make out the house which had been built into the side of a hill. His eyes took in the neat yard and fencing. As he approached he could see two figures on the porch enjoying their morning coffee. He reined up at the hitch rail but did not dismount.

"Good mornin' sir, ma'am. Do you mind if I dismount and water my horse?"

The man came out into the sunshine his rifle held loosely in his hand. Will smiled gently at the familiar features and the shock of unruly fair hair that differed from Jimmy's only in its streaks of gray.

"Help yourself. Stretch your legs awhile," the man replied, with a forced smile.

Will noticed the set jaw beneath the large handlebar mustache, and clear, penetrating hazel eyes. He knew that he was being sized up and wondered what the verdict would be.

Miles Compton was a cautious man and he knew there was no way that he would get off a shot if anything happened. He had slowed down a lot in the last few years. Losing Jimmy had almost finished him off. He had kept himself together for Verna's sake but there wasn't much left of the man he'd been. After looking into the stranger's ravaged face, Miles heartily wished he hadn't come. The man talked well, but he was one mean looking gent. Was it the man himself or the terrible damage that had been done him? Perhaps it was the total picture. The gray was led to the trough, but it didn't drink. Why did he come here? It had nothing to do with a thirsty horse.

"My name is Miles Compton. This here is my wife, Verna." As he spoke he could feel the fear in his gut. His grip tightened on the rifle stock. His finger caressed the trigger.

"Pleased to meet you folks. My name is Buck." He smiled and tipped his hat to her. He'd debated telling anyone who he was, at least until he found out what was going on with Twyla. Things just didn't feel right. The unanswered letters and the situation at Jimmy's place just didn't add up. Maybe he'd just better wait until he had a handle on the situation. He couldn't go changing his name now. Stick with Buck.

"I must say you have a nice place here. Looks as if you can see for a week." He turned his back on the couple and took in a view that a man should be able to enjoy for a lifetime, and not get tired of. Again he felt the pull to explore everything it held. Turning back he said, "I noticed a ranch to the south that appears to be abandoned. Do you know who owns it?"

"I own it, mister, why?" There was apprehension in his voice. He clenched the gun tighter. Should have made my move when he turned his back, he thought. He regretted thinking this way. Damn Nate.

"I may stay the winter in these parts and I was lookin' for a place. I could go as much as fifteen a month. I'd pay in advance for nine months." Will smiled the best smile that he could muster.

Miles was surprised at such an offer out of the blue. Fifteen dollars was a reasonable amount and they could use the money, but cash in advance was not what one expected around these parts. Was this stranger riding for Nate Baldon? That snake was not above putting his own man on the ranch to somehow get it away from them.

"Let's talk awhile," he stalled. Why had the man turned his back to him?

They mounted the steps and took chairs on the porch. Verna went inside and brought out more coffee, handing a tin cup to Will. Will caught Miles looking at his face, the older man looked away, embarrassed.

"That's all right. Got blown up in the war. Lucky to be here, eye or no eye."

"Our son was killed in the war. Died in some place called Andersonville. He was a good boy. Rode for the Union." Miles remarked. The sadness in his voice wasn't lost on Will.

"A lot of good men died in there." This time, the sadness in Will's voice wasn't lost on Miles. He looked at Will, searching for a hint of guile, but found none. The grief was genuine. "You know a man by the name of Baldon?"

"No sir," Will answered, "I just got into town. Only man I've met is the man at the stables."

"What do you think of him?" Miles asked. He leaned forward to hear the answer.

"Seems to know horses. His place is clean and well organized. Easy to talk to, looks you straight in the eye. I'd say he's a good man and tougher than he looks at first glance. Don't think I would care to be on his bad side."

No mention of John's color. Man must be a Yankee. That was good. John was a good friend and to speak badly of him would be the end to any dealings with this stranger. He found himself warming up to Buck whether he wanted to or not.

"Well, I'll let you folks talk it over and be back tomorrow to get your answer. If you give me a lease, I'll probably want to fix it up a mite but I'll pay for any fixin' I do."

"Sounds more than fair, Buck." Looking over at Verna, he caught her nod. "As a matter of fact we can save you the trip. Let's go in the house and we'll draw up a paper." A half-hour later the ranch was Will's for the next nine months. What would they think if they knew how Jimmy died? It saddened him to think that they might hate him.

He rode back to the ranch by way of a short-cut Miles had shown him. On impulse, he rode down to the creek. He remembered Jimmy's last words. "I'm goin' down to the creek to sit on the rock and cool my feet." There was the rock. Pulling off his boots and socks, he sat on the rock, and cooled his feet. He stroked the rock with his hand and stared at the water. He missed his friend and thought of him often, but at this moment his feelings rose up in a lonesome wave. He had to speak aloud to Jimmy or burst. "Well Partner, here I am a coolin' my feet in your creek. Wish to hell it was you instead of me." He glanced around to make sure that no one but Misssy had caught him a talkin' to the dead. He sat for close to an hour on the rock, just thinking about his friend. It was so unfair.

Back in Willow Springs, Will entered the stable and dismounted. John looked out at him from behind his desk.

"I'm back, John, which stall do you want her in?"

Coming out of his office, John put a short rope around the mare's neck. "You can put your gear in that room over yonder. I'll take care of your horse."

Will stripped off the saddle and bridle and John led her away. Will followed when his gear was stored. John had put her into a stall next to the other gray and given her a scoop of oats. "I'll give her some hay when she cools off a bit. Don't you worry none about them horses, I'll take good care of 'em."

"John, if you're not too busy, could we sit and talk a spell? I would like to find out a little about the town and country hereabout."

"Why sure, always got time to visit. If I don't got time, I takes it anyways," he said with a laugh. "What ya want to know?"

"I just got back from the Compton place. Had a talk with Mr. Compton and got a nine month lease on that spread about a mile to the south west of his. You know the place?"

"Oh sure. But I'm surprised that he done leased it to ya. No offense. But it's a spot real close to his heart. Has to do with his son that was killed in the war."

"He asked me if I knew a Nate Baldon. I got the impression he thought that I might have something to do with him. The possibility seemed to make him a might cautious."

"I can understand that." John replied, with a grin. "That Nate

Baldon is one shifty cuss and worthless as they come. He owns a spread out beyond the place you're rentin'. You'll be right in between 'em. Nate has been after Miles to sell him that place for years, but no one can make Miles do what he don't wantta do. I'm not right sure, how he come by it in the first place." He paused, and a grin spread across his lips. "You sure won't never have to worry about Injuns while yer there."

"Why's that?" Will asked.

"The old timer that built that place, built it to last. Put in a rock foundation, even hauled in cement for it and built a fine fireplace, as well. There won't be any fire caused by that chimney. No, Sir-ree Bob! About twelve years ago, a few of them braves decides to add Ol' Charlie's scalp to their belt and chased him into the cabin. When they got up the nerve to go in after him, he was gone. They swear he didn't come out, just up and disappeared. Bad medicine, as far as the Indians were concerned. No one ever seen hide nor hair of Ol' Charlie again. Anyhow, getting back to Baldon. He got his ranch when his folks passed on. Damn shame, they was good people. Don't know how they ended up with Nate. Sorry sack of cow pies! He and his wife Twyla lived out there till he had a new house built, a couple'a miles out of town."

Will's head came up. "Twyla?"

"Yup, that's her name. She had a little boy after they married," his voice softened. "That little Sammy is a fine young lad. I look on him and his momma as family." Leaning forward, he added. "I take offense at any man that causes them grief. I take offense at Nate Baldon, for all the good it does me."

Will got his meaning. Smiling, he looked back at John. "I think it likely that I will as well, John. Yes, so will I."

John smiled. "We have an understanding?"

Will nodded. "Tell me about Twyla and Sammy."

The smile vanished. "What you a gittin' at?" There was no way that he was going to say anything to cast dirt on her reputation with this stranger.

Will realized his mistake and said nothing more while he gathered his thoughts. Obviously, John was a good friend of Twyla's family. Will figured he needed to confide in someone if he was ever to get to the whole story. John appeared to be a made-to-order confidant.

"Maybe we can both do some good for Twyla and Sammy. Let me start at the beginning. I met Jimmy Compton on the battlefield in 1862. We had been involved in a real barn burner that day and we'd lost count of the times real estate had been traded back and forth. That night, both sides had wounded men out between the lines. The screaming was all but intolerable. I was in a pretty safe position and was able to crawl out amongst them and managed to bring a few back to our lines. Jimmy was one of them. He became my best friend. The best friend I've ever had. I was with him when he died in Andersonville Prison. His dying words were to make sure Twyla and his folks were alright." He didn't elaborate on Jimmy's death.

John was having a hard time thinking of a way to explain Twyla, Sammy and Nate, that would not put Twyla in a bad light.

Will could see he was thrashing out a problem and took a different tack. "How old is Sammy?" He asked.

Somewhat relieved, John said, "Four years last month."

A little arithmetic made it obvious to Will that Jimmy must be the child's father. He had gone to war not knowing that Twyla was carrying his baby. Oh, Jimmy, he thought, What must she have gone through when you didn't come home? He knew the answer as well as why his question got such a hot response.

"She got married," John spoke defensively. "The boy needed a father and a name. She hadn't much choice! She got the name, but the boy got no daddy. Lousy son-of- a-bitch."

"Would you care to elaborate on that?" Will asked quietly.

"He treats them both mean. I know for a fact he hits Twyla from time to time. She is like my own daughter to me, and still there's nothin' I can do about it. First time I made a ruckus, his damn crew paid me a visit. They put a few lumps on me and said they would burn me out. Threatened my friends as well. Twyla got all up in arms too. Told me to butt out. She could take care of herself. But, I tell you this, Buck, he lays a hand on that boy, I'll take a gun to him and to hell with his crew. Only decent man workin' for Baldon is Seth Pinkham. He's Twyla's little brother. He's about twenty or so."

Will could not remember Jimmy mentioning Twyla's brother.

"Seth's a good boy. Nate hired him when he was courtin' Twyla. Tryin' to impress her, I guess, by puttin the boy on his payroll. The rest of them are all trouble. You watch out for Cap, when you meet him. He's a bad hombre."

"Thanks for the information, John. Keep this conversation under your hat."

"Shore will! I must say, I feel better knowin' that there's someone else on our side. By the way, Twyla's sister, Melinda, has about talked my ear off about some gunfight over in Summit. The description she gave of the winner reminds me of you. Probably not too many one-eyed gunfighters hereabouts." He was grinning broadly.

"You're probably right," Will replied, matching his grin.

"If'n you're hungry, try the restaurant across the street. That and the store belong to Nate, but the food is good and the service is the best around. Water is around back of the place if you're inclined to clean up a bit."

They shook hands and Will headed across the street. He caught movement at the window of the restaurant, but the sun was reflecting off the glass and he wasn't sure just what he had seen. He veered to the left and proceeded to the back of the building. Taking off his hat, he hung it on a peg and removed the eye patch. He pumped some water into the pan and washed the dust off his face. Looking back at the building to be sure no one was looking, he took off his shirt and shook the dust out of it, then slipped it back on. Wetting his hair, he ran his fingers through it. Checking his reflection in a small mirror hanging on a nail, he figured he was as good as he would ever get. He replaced the patch, and took pains to make sure that his shirt tail was tucked in neat. He carefully placed his hat on his head, taking care not to mess up his hair.

From the shadows of the kitchen, Twyla and Melinda had been watching every move he'd made from the time he rode back into town. They couldn't help but notice his lithe torso, as he took off his shirt. White scars criss-crossed the smooth muscles that rippled across his chest, back and arms when he shook out the shirt.

They hurried to their stations in the kitchen before he entered the restaurant. Twyla was expecting someone a little more imposing after Melinda's description. Perhaps six foot four, and a couple of ax handles wide at the shoulders. Will, average height, slim and wiry, didn't quite meet her expectations. However, he did have a gorgeous body, or at least he used to. She felt herself blush with such thoughts. Could he really be the same person Melinda had described? He did have only one eye, so he must be the gunman, and no two people would have those horses.

When Will came in the door he saw four square tables, with red and white checkered cloths. Four wooden, straight backed chairs were placed evenly around each table. Several drawings of deer and bear hung on the side wall. A wide opening led into the store. There were shelves of stock, and a counter covered with jars of candy at the far end. A wide, un-glazed window opened between the dining room and the kitchen, as well as a door. Melinda hurried through the door, smiling sweetly.

The only patron, a young cowboy, had finished his meal. He paid and giving Will a nod, left the room. "Where would you like me to sit?" Will asked, returning her smile.

"Oh, just anywhere," Melinda answered, breathlessly, moving to a table by the window. "How's this?"

Will removed his hat and set it on the floor. "First rate."

"We met, yesterday." Melinda was so excited that she could hardly get the words out.

"We did? I must be getting old, to forget a girl as pretty as you."

"The window was dirty. I told you where that other man was hiding."

"Ah yes, the phantom voice. I thank you again."

"What can I get for you?" she asked, sweetly.

"How about four eggs, a small steak and coffee? Maybe a glass of water would help get rid of the trail dust." Then he added with a grin, "Oh, while those are cookin' could I have a piece of pie? Do I smell plum?"

"She smiled and nodded as she walked to the kitchen window and gave the order to Twyla. "Here Twyla." She said, as she handed the order through to her sister.

Will caught himself, starting to turn to look. Forcing himself to remain calm, he gazed through the wide doorway to the store, directly in front of him. He told himself that a few more minutes, more or less, didn't matter, but he could feel excitement building with the knowledge that Jimmy's Twyla was just a few feet away.

A pair of customers entered the store and began sorting through the stock of shovels sticking out of an open barrel. Melinda groaned softly, as she went to wait on them. She would have much preferred to stay in the restaurant and wait on Will. Where was that damned fool Nate, when she needed him?

Twyla brought the food out on a tray and Will watched her closely as she transferred the plates to the table. The picture, that he carried, did not do adequate credit to her beauty, he thought. When she turned her head to face him, he looked into deep green eyes that took his breath away. He also noticed a dark blue bruise on her right cheek. Remembering John's talk, he figured he knew what had caused it. He was no ladies man. He'd pretty well steered clear of them but he'd been raised right and knew how a woman should be treated. No man at all had any business hitting one, he was sure of that. This was what Jimmy had wanted him to prevent. This was why he was here. His eye squinted, and his face transformed into an expression that startled Twyla. She retreated to the kitchen.

Will glowered down at the plate of food but did not see it. He could feel the cold rage that welled up in him and fought to control it. His fists were clenched tight. She was so lovely, he wanted to protect her, to put his arms around her and tell her that she would never be hurt again. He realized the foolishness of the thought and it broke the tension in him. He was a complete stranger to her and she would be horrified, and probably scream her head off, if he did such a thing. He took several deep breaths and started to eat. He'd frightened her, he knew, he'd better get a grip on himself. He didn't come here to get himself tied down for good, if that was what he wanted he might as well have stayed in Cedar Rapids. As he was finishing, a man entered the store and put on an apron. Will studied him. Not bad looking, as far as looks went, but Will had an idea, now, what meanness the man was capable of. He had a wicked grin on his face as he allowed himself to picture putting a bullet right between the man's eyes.

Twyla, cowering in the kitchen, asked herself, had his awful anger been directed at her? Why had his expression changed so when he looked at her? Then she remembered the bruise. She'd had so many of them that at times she forgot. But why was he so concerned about her. It wasn't any of his business. Still, if she had ever seen the desire to kill, she had seen it now. She could still feel the tingle around the base of her neck. Yes, size not withstanding, he surely could be a killer. She'd had just about enough of violent men in her life. This one surely was interesting just the same, but best not get too close.

As Will was finishing up, a small boy burst through the restaurant door, caroling out, "Mom, I'm hungry."

Will looked at Sammy's curly blond hair and big hazel eyes. Closer inspection caught the familiar features and expression, and he knew this was indeed Jimmy's boy.

Sammy, not paying any attention to Will, looked at the menu, pretending to read it.

"Pie, Mom."

"Pie, what, young man?"

"Pie, PLEEESE," Sammy said, laughing.

"Come over here and take a seat, young fella," Will said, with a grin. "Hate to eat alone."

Sammy climbed up on the chair facing Will. "You got a thing on your eye, mister," he said. Concern in his voice. "How come?"

Twyla overhearing, cringed at the boy's directness.

"I do?" asked Will with a look of shock lifting the patch. "Are you sure?"

"Sure am. You got no eye." He was plainly intrigued. He leaned forward to get a closer look. "Where did it go?"

Will pretended to check his shirt pockets, then picked up the hat and checked inside and under the hat-band. "Don't know, Partner, but will you keep a look out for it?" Twyla brought out a small piece of pie, and being careful not to look at Will, placed the dish in front of Sammy and returned to the kitchen.

"Sure will. What's your name?"

"Buck," Will answered. "What's yours?"

"Sammy. You wanna see my horse?"

"Why I'd be pleased to take a look at your horse. Where is it?"

"John's," he replied. "Let's go."

"Whoa up there, Partner, you better eat first. Always better to look at horses on a full stomach."

Will watched him closely, as he ate his pie. Jimmy was right about Twyla making one damn fine pie. He smiled, as Sammy licked his fingers and picked up the plate, to lick it clean. He remembered doing the same thing when he was little. Some things just don't change. He picked up his plate and slowly licked it clean.

Sammy laughed out loud. "You do it, too!" he said, pointing at Will.

"Sure don't want to waste any of this pie," Will retorted. Twyla came out and collected the dishes. She made sure that she did not present the bruised side of her face to him again. She had watched the back of Will's head as he talked to Sammy. Rather strange, a gunman who prefers to eat with a four-year-old.

Will paid his bill, noticing the puzzled concern in Twyla's eyes. He gave her what he hoped was a reassuring smile. He didn't know if it worked or not. "That was a real fine meal and the service was first rate."

As they started to step off of the boardwalk, Will almost jumped as he felt the little grip on his finger. He looked down, and Sammy said, "I can't cross the street alone."

Will grinned.

Melinda returned from the store side of the building, and together the women watched Will and Sammy cross the street. Sammy was trying to get in step with Will, who obligingly shortened his stride, and together they entered the stable.

"Did you see that? Cutest thing I ever saw," Melinda said with a laugh. Twyla was still not sure of this man with the one eye. She had seen that flash of danger and wasn't about to forget it.

"Uncle John, let's show 'em Pete," the boy chirped as John came out of his office.

John looked at Sammy, and grinned. "Why sure, you lead the way."

They looked Sammy's horse over. Will took the time to check his teeth, as well as hooves and gazed into the small horses eyes, as if communicating with him. "He says you're a good rider."

"He does?" Sammy exclaimed. "He said that? He can run real fast, Buck."

Will nodded, with a straight face. John was trying to hold back a laugh.

"Let's see Mom's horse." He led them to the next stall. The bay mare looked up and came to the door. Will looked her over. She had good lines. He pretended to listen to the horse and exclaimed, "She told me her name is Bell. Is that right?" Will remembered Jimmy telling him of the horse he had given Twyla, a bay with two white stockings on the front legs.

"Wow," Sammy wide eyed, was almost speechless. "Let's go tell Mom."

They re-crossed the street, and Will ushered Sammy through the door. "See ya later, Partner."

He returned to the stable. He had a laugh with John as they readied the grays, then shook his hand, mounted and reined in the direction of the ranch. He was glad he'd arranged to stay there. He didn't want to be right in town and, he now knew, it would take some time to be sure that Twyla was going to be safe. The bruise on Twyla's face brought back the same feeling of cold rage. One way or another, he would put a stop to it.

As he approached the ranch buildings, he paused to get a better look. A porch covered the entire front of the house, and he remembered Jimmy talking about adding it. He had noticed the bedroom addition, on his previous visit, but hadn't taken much of a look. He had been upset with the condition of the place, and his mind hadn't gotten past the filth. He did remember a small kitchen and a dry room next to the fireplace. What was it about the dry room? Oh yeah, he remembered. He would have to look into that.

His eyes took in the steep cliffs looming up behind the house. Somewhere, up there, was a cave. He scanned the face of the cliff, but couldn't find it. In several places, he thought he could see a trail, but it was so faint, he wasn't sure. A water-fall tumbled over a low point in the cliff, and from what Jimmy had said, made a fine swimming hole at the base. He would look into that also.

Entering the fine old barn, he took in the good condition of the structure. It had been made to last. Will figured the size to be roughly thirty by sixty feet. For the time it must have been built, it was a large barn. He wondered who had gone to so much trouble.

He stripped off his gear and turned the horses loose in a small pasture in back of the barn. He watched them as they trotted around the perimeter, then stopped to roll in the grass. He was pleased that both had rolled over from side to side. He remembered his dad telling him that was the mark of a good horse. He didn't know if he was being teased or not, but their rolling over pleased him just the same. His father loved animals, and passed his philosophy on to Will and Cole. He missed his folks.

He passed back through the barn, and headed toward the house. Seeing the flowers starting to wilt, he detoured over to the well and fetching a bucket up, watered the small plot, saving the last few swallows for himself to drank. This is fine water, he thought.

As long as he had a good barn and good water, everything else would be secondary.

Going to the house he opened the sagging door, and propped it open. Get a little fresh air in, he thought. He stepped through and began a critical evaluation of what it was going to take to get the place in shape. He could see that he was not going to run out of things to do for awhile.

The main room was rectangular, with the massive stone fireplace covering most of the back wall. The stones were large and well placed. That cement had been used to fill in between them was almost unheard of, considering the age of the building and it's distance from any source. A close look at the fire box showed no loose mortar. It would easily warm the entire house, Will had no doubt. Opening the narrow door into the dry room, it all came back. A small safe hole was located behind the board with the coat pegs. Jimmy had discovered it by accident when he was testing the strength of the pegs. Will stood facing the center peg. Pulling out on the two end pegs and turning them, like a ship's wheel, allowed the board to swivel, revealing a hole behind. Reaching in, out of curiosity, Will wasn't surprised to find it empty. He replaced the board in its original position, and pushed the two outer pegs firmly in.

He then re-entered the main room and crossed to the bedroom. A rickety chair stood in the corner. He sat down as his eyes took in the room. Will let his mind relive those moments when Jimmy had shared the hopes and dreams that were bound up in this place. Damn that Rooster! Still, this is what Jimmy would have come back to. Twyla married to this bum Nate and his own boy calling Nate, Father. Jimmy had been rigid in his ideas of right and wrong. He wouldn't have wanted to interfere between a man and wife but it would have broken his heart. Maybe it was best he was here himself to take care of it. He had no such compunctions where his promise to Jimmy was concerned and nothing to gain by breaking Nate's head but satisfaction.

He got up, giving himself a mental shake, and went into the kitchen. He began the process of cleaning up and getting rid of everything he didn't want. The things Jimmy had left behind for his return were damaged and broken and there were empty cans and other piles of trash everywhere. He found a sorry excuse for a broom but it helped a little. Several hours later, he sat on the porch and looked at the junk he had piled up in the yard. It was a beginning. He found himself talking aloud to Jimmy once more, just sharing some of his thoughts about what had transpired that day. He also mentioned the bruise. He'd never felt comfortable talking to the dead before. He had some doubts about the afterlife. It did seem to raise his spirits, however, and there was definitely something about this place.

He spent that first night in the barn. He told himself that his reason was the filth, but deep down, he thought he could feel Jimmy's ghost in there. In the morning he loosened the thongs on the extra supplies he had brought clear from Iowa. Spreading them out on a fairly clean spot on the barn floor, his spare coat made a strange thump. Inside, was an oil skin package containing a money belt and a note.

> *Will, here is a thousand dollars to see you through the winter. Don't thank me, it came out of your share of the store. Take care of yourself.*
> *Love, C&C*

Well don't that beat all, he thought. It would definitely come in handy. He remembered the look Cole had given Candace when he refused money. Just like Cole, he thought. Thanks little brother. It was a sizeable amount of cash. He rolled the belt up tight, he would put it in the safe hole.

The next day, Will saddled up and rode back into town. He had a list of things he would need, and it would give him a chance to see Twyla.

Stopping at the stable, he asked John about the availability of a wagon and team to get his purchases out to the ranch.

"No problem, Buck, I got one that ain't being used today. Tell you what. You go on over to the store, and I'll have Chief bring it around."

"Who's Chief?" Will asked.

"Don't know his Injun name but everyone around here calls him Chief. He's as old as a rock and has taken up residence in my loft. Says he's too old for the Injun life. He picks up small change doin' stuff for people. You'll like him. He won't go past the gate to your place, though, because of the bad medicine, but he'll get it as far as the gate."

Will got his first close look at Nate, and he was not impressed. He was tall, maybe six feet and had a rather long, thin face that was handsome enough but weak, with a small well-trimmed, light brown mustache over thick lips that gave him a pouting, dissatisfied expression. His light hair was neatly trimmed and combed. Remembering the bruises on Twyla's face, he had the urge to grab him by the throat and slam him against the wall. Instead he just gave him his evil squint eye look. It had the desired effect. Nate took the list and practically ran to fill the order. Will strolled into the restaurant. Twyla was there, alone, and Will took a chair at the same table and placed his hat underneath.

Seeing Will enter through the arched door, Twyla found herself smiling. What had Nate thought of him she wondered. Was she actually happy to see him, or was it just the habit of smiling for the customers? She didn't think she knew for sure. She was curious, that she was sure of. She gave him a few minutes to decide what he wanted to eat, then approached his table. She noted the hat under the chair and the still damp hair. Well, he had some manners.

"Good mornin' ma'am. What a beautiful day to be alive, don't you think?" Will asked, with his best smile.

"Why yes it is, now that you mention it. And what would you like, this fine beautiful day?"

"Well now, I guess I could handle three eggs, some bacon, and milk, if you have it." Will replied.

"Coming right up." She retreated to the kitchen.

Will looked out the window but his mind was on Twyla. After a few moments, he got up and went to the door to the kitchen. He watched her as she prepared his breakfast. She had her back to him and went about her business, unaware of his presence.

Several strands of hair had pulled loose and hung down her back. It was a light brown and shone in the morning light. He couldn't see her face, but could hear her humming to herself. He tried to imagine hearing and seeing this beautiful woman every morning. He had his eye closed, in thought, when she turned and caught him standing there.

"Is there anything else I can get you?" she asked.

"Oh! Yeah, a couple of eggs and some bacon." Will stammered. Turning, he went back to his chair. He could feel his neck turning red. That was a damn fool thing to do, he thought.

Twyla placed his food on the table and smiled. She could see the color on his neck and realized he was embarrassed. She almost asked him if he liked what he saw, but bit her tongue. She could feel a slight flush on her own cheeks, too. She'd better watch herself with this man.

Where's Sammy?" Will asked.

"He's with his grandma, this morning. You made quite an impression on him. He tells me you talk to horses and they talk back. Is that right?" she asked, with a smile.

"Oh sure. I can do that. As a matter of fact, while I was talkin' with Bell, she mentioned that you prefer not to ride a side-saddle, and prefer pants. Also, that you've had her for about five years. A gift she said, as I recall." Will spoke with a look of deep concentration. "Yep, that's what she told me. And your birthday is April 16th. To top it off, your favorite color is yellow."

Twyla didn't have an immediate response. How did he know that? Maybe John mentioned it to him. Yes, that had to be it. "You have been talking to John."

"That's true, but he didn't tell me," Will smiled, smugly. "I have a way with animals."

She left him to his meal. He was a strange man. John must have told him, but why would he bring up her birthday and favorite color. She couldn't remember mentioning her favorite color to anyone.

Paying his tab, he looked into her green eyes. "Thank you kindly for the meal. You have a way with eggs and bacon. They have never tasted better." Tipping his hat, he turned and reentered the store.

Nate had assembled the items on the list, and Will paid the tab. After accepting the money he pretended to arrange the jars on the counter to avoid looking at Will while he asked, "Where do you want these delivered?"

Will noticed his tone of resentment, but let it pass.

"I'm staying over at the Compton's other place. The deserted spread.

Over toward your place, I think. You know it? But I don't need it delivered. I've a wagon coming."

Nate was stunned. He had been trying to get that spread for going on four years. If he could add it to his own holdings it would increase the value of his ranch, greatly. When he sold out, it would put him on easy street. He didn't need this aggravation. Someone living on it only muddied the water. He'd have to have Cap pay this joker a visit. He wouldn't be out there long. He didn't envy Cap the chore. The look the stranger had given him was enough to make him sick to his stomach. God, he hated fear. But it was there. Always had been and would probably be there 'til he died. It pleased him to realize that he had the same power over Twyla. A self-satisfied look passed over his face. Yes, he had the power.

23

CHIEF AND CAP

When the wagon pulled up, Will got his first look at Chief. He liked the old Indian at first glance. Just how old he was, Will could only guess, but his face was heavily wrinkled and some of his teeth were missing. He wore a tall felt hat with a feather in the band. It had once been black, now it was the color of dirt. A grimy red bandana was wrapped around his wrinkled neck. A frayed, old suit coat, and baggy pants covered his skinny body. He wore no shoes. Looking at Will, he grinned a snaggle-toothed grin. Will could not possibly fail to respond in kind. Together they loaded the wagon.

"My name is Buck, Chief. If you don't mind, I'll tie my horse to the back, and ride with you."

Chief said nothing but moved over to one side of the bench seat. Will tied the horse to the wagon back and climbed up beside him. A flick of the reins and the horse moved into the street and out of town. Nate stood on the boardwalk, hands on his hips. If looks could kill, Will would have been dead.

"John tells me you live at the stable. Says, you prefer staying in town," Will said, just making conversation.

Chief pondered the statement. "My bones like feel of straw, and warm of animals on cold night. Food from store beat food out there." He gestured in the general direction of the mountains. "Chief is smart man, you betcha."

"You have a squaw?" Will asked, with a straight face. The idea of Chief having a woman, was enough to make Will smile.

"You betcha! Good lookin', good cook, good in bed," Chief replied, with a wistful look.

"Sounds like you have a fine woman. Why don't you stay with her?" Will asked, with a straight face.

Chief pondered again. "Chief forget where teepee is." He slapped his leg, and began to cackle.

After fully appreciating the joke, Will asked, "How long you been in these parts, Chief?"

"Them trees," Chief said, pointing to the large trees in front of the new house, "they this high." Chief, raised his arm to shoulder level. He gazed off, lost in thought. "Mountains, were the hills of prairie dogs." He smiled. The one eyed man believes me, he thought.

As they approached the ranch gate, the smile on Chief's face turned to concern and then to fright. "Whoa," Chief yelled. As the horse came to a stop, Chief handed the reins to Will.

"Chief stay here. Bad medicine." He nodded toward the ranch house, and climbed down from the wagon. He settled himself against the closest fence post. "Chief stay here," he reiterated.

Will laughed, as he unloaded the wagon. Chief was quite a character. He was looking forward to spending more time with him.

When Will returned the empty wagon to the gate, the Indian seemed surprised to see him alive. He looked at the house and shook his head. "Bad medicine," he said solemnly.

Will smiled. "Think you can find your way back to town?"

"Find town. No find teepee." With those words, he slapped the reins, and headed down the road. On the way back to town, he thought about the one-eyed man and the house of bad medicine. Maybe the one eye had protected him. He remembered his cousin, Running Nose, telling him about the battle with Old Charlie many years ago.

Charlie had killed a bear. The hunting party came upon him while he was skinning the kill. They had finished off a bottle of whiskey stolen from an old miner, otherwise they might have left him alone. As it was, they decided some bear meat would suit them just fine and the claws would look good around their necks, but Charlie didn't want to share. During the ensuing argument they decided to take the old man's scalp or, at least, make him think so. Realizing they couldn't be depended upon, in their condition, not to carry out their threats, he gave up the bear and jumped on his horse, racing toward his house, several miles away, with them in hot pursuit. He managed to beat them to the door just in time to slam it in their faces, but not before he had been hit by a stray arrow. That one of them had actually hit him was a total surprise, considering the effect the whiskey was having on their accuracy. They took up positions around the house and proceeded to shoot a few arrows at it, in a desultory fashion. Charlie did not return their fire. After several hours, when they began to sober up, they entered the house to find no one there. He couldn't have gotten past them! Where then had he gone?

The Great Spirit must have taken Charlie. Perhaps he had turned into smoke and vanished with the smoke of the well banked fire. It troubled Chief no end. He'd better not dwell on the matter. He had a hard enough time sleeping as it was.

Turning his mind to different matters, Chief smiled as he rode on toward town. He enjoyed making people laugh and through the years had made a place for himself in the community. He couldn't think of a single person who disliked him. There were a few, like Nate Baldor, that ignored him, but dislike? He didn't think so.

As the wagon bounced along the road, he felt his age in all the familiar places. As close as he could guess, he was in his seventies and although he was not as spry as he used to be, he knew he could ride a horse like the wind, if he had a horse. He'd been a fine rider when he was young. He let his mind drift back to those days.

He had a hard time remembering his mother. She died early on. His father, he remembered even less well. He had not been around much, usually out hunting and fishing with the other braves. He had drowned in a rain swollen river not long after his mother had gone. He did remember Buel, however. He remembered, as if it were yesterday.

Buel had ridden into their camp on the most magnificent horse the lonely boy had ever seen. The skins of beaver were piled high on his travois. He carried a long gun in the crook of his arm and a pistol and large knife on his belt. A huge red beard covered the lower half of his face and long hair hung down his back, almost to his waist. He was wearing a buckskin shirt and pants, covered in fringe and fancy beadwork. A wide brimmed, flat crowned hat, leather leg coverings, and moccasins, finished the effect. He was magnificent. This was the first white man that the boy had ever seen and he was awestruck.

The man looked down and, thumping his chest, said, "Buel." He had responded by thumping his own chest and saying "Kneeling Elk." The stranger, having trouble with the Indian name, pointed to him and said, "Chief." And so it had been. It was the beginning of a friendship that had lasted many years and many miles. Thinking of the hunts they had shared, Chief felt a sadness in his heart. Chief had taught Buel the language of the Lakota, and in return, Chief had been taught the language of the whites. Buel had been a very wise man and excellent teacher, and Chief was a good learner.

He smiled at the broken language he used around town. It was one of the little jokes he played on those that preferred to look down on him. It made him feel good. Come to think of it, it made them feel good too. He had to chuckle to realize that at least part of the joke was on him. No sense in taking himself too seriously.

The only one he talked openly with was John Henry. John Henry and his partner, Jackson, had taken him in, not long after they had started the livery, giving him a place to sleep and enough odd jobs to keep a full stomach. He had left the tribe when his eye for the squaws had led to several knife fights. It had been only a matter of time before he would be killed, or would be forced to kill someone. Most of his early years had been spent with Buel. He had only returned to his people when his mentor had died. A man long in tooth when they had met, he had lived many more summers with Chief by his side. Ah! they had been a pair! Buel had left him the long gun, pistol and knife. These treasures he kept, wrapped in oil cloth , hidden under the tool box at the stable. He and John Henry would take them out, from time to time, to clean and oil them.

As he grew older Chief missed the teachings of his tribe. He thought more about death as it grew closer. He wanted to believe in a life after death where he would be young again, riding the prairies and mountains with Buel. Would they be going to the same place or would he be in some white man's place? He hoped they would be together. Those were good times. Would John Henry come there too? He and Jackson had been soldiers together and had fought the Indian. In the end, they had become the Indians friends. Yes, and Jackson too, they should all be together, Chief thought. Perhaps, if he were lucky, he would have a fine looking squaw that could cook. He pondered this. The squaw cooked, raised the children, gathered the wood, prepared the food, made the clothes and took care of the old ones while the men rode out to hunt and fight in glory. Was this fair? What if they changed places in the after life? Chief would be a squaw. He felt just a little bit afraid at that thought.

The fear of the ranch house was also real. His cousin's description of the encounter with Old Charlie made the hair raise on the back of Chief's neck. How had he disappeared? It had to be the spirits. If that was true perhaps the rest was too. He slapped the reins and firmly put his mind on a large piece of pie. Thinking of Twyla's pies, he cheered up.

Will attacked the job ahead with pleasure. Restoring Jimmy's ranch, annoying Nate, pleasing Twyla, whatever the reason, he was enjoying himself. Taking his new broom, he proceeded to knock down the spider webs which festooned the ceilings of every room, as well as a dozen or so mud-dobbers nests. When the floor was swept Will could see a vast improvement already. The years in the prisons had sure made him appreciate being clean. Maybe it was the ability to control his environment that was such a thrill. He brought in buckets of water and proceeded to scrub the board floors. Taking a break from cleaning, he re-hinged the door and nailed down some loose boards on the porch. It was a great day.

Nate watched the stranger help load up the wagon and tie his horse to the back. He kept on watching as he climbed up beside Chief and they moved off down the street and out of sight. He was in a simmering rage. What to do? Send Cap and a few of his crew over to run him off? Threaten Miles again? Hell, I'll do both, he thought. He stormed into the restaurant and glared at Twyla. Was she a part of this? She was alone in the place, so he felt free to do, or say, anything he wanted.

"Well, old man Compton's done it now. He's leased Charlie's place to that damn one-eyed son of a bitch. Why would he do that? If he thinks he can keep me off that place, he had better think again." He pounded his fist on the counter, for emphasis.

"Buck?" Twyla asked, in surprise.

"Whatever his name is. You on a first name basis with him?" He glared at her through squinted eyes. She had seen that look too many times and refused to be intimidated.

"I don't think he gave his last name. That was the name he used when I heard him talking to Sammy. I assumed it was his name."

"You watch the store, I have to go out to the ranch," he said, as he opened the door and stomped out.

I think you had better walk more softly around Buck, Twyla thought to herself. You may be stirring up a rattlesnake. Somehow, the thought brought a smile to her lips. Then she felt a tinge of concern for the stranger. She had seen Cap and his friends push people around and it wasn't pleasant. Why was he staying here in Willow Creek? Why did he want to stay on the ranch? It was in terrible condition. Another thing that seemed strange was that, when he arrived, he left almost immediately in that direction. It was like he knew exactly where he was going. She was anxious to talk to Dad Compton.

Another thought entered her mind. There goes the weekly rides out to the ranch to water the flowers. It was the only connection she had with her lost dreams and she was saddened, and a little resentful.

She watched as Nate rode out of the stables and kicked his horse into a hard gallop. Twyla was relieved to see him go. Anything that kept them apart for any length of time was a blessing. He did not look at her as he viciously spurred the horse.

That's right, Nate, take it out on the horse, she thought. Damned fool. She returned to the kitchen and was removing two pies from the oven when Melinda came in.

"Hi Sis." She exclaimed, with a smile and a hug. "Those smell wonderful. I saw Nate charging out of town. What put the burr under his blanket? He looked furious. Looked right past me."

"Buck was in. He had breakfast and bought some supplies. He told Nate that he had leased Old Charlie's ranch."

"The ranch?" Melinda's eyebrows rose.

"Jimmy's and mine. I must admit that I was surprised too. I assumed that he was just passing through."

"Well if I know Nate, he's on his way out to fetch Cap and the crew to run him off. I wish Seth hadn't gone to work for him. Most of that crew is a bad influence, to say the least. I miss the men his folks had."

"Me too. He does seem to be enjoying it, but I worry." She paused, thinking about Buck. "I got the impression, yesterday, that Buck isn't the type to run."

"Well he sure didn't run from those men in Summit. You should have seen it." She rubbed the goose bumps from her arms. Her eyes were bright with excitement. "Oh, speaking of Buck, Janet came in yesterday evening, after you went home, and she said she heard Buck and John Henry talking about you." A little twinkle in her eyes did not go unnoticed.

Twyla looked at her with surprise. "What were they saying?"

"She only caught a few words but John Henry seemed embarrassed at first, then spoke so low she didn't hear much. It ended with something about you and Nate. John Henry told Buck he was glad to have him on your side. She was sure of that part."

Twyla was tempted to march right over and demand an explanation from John. After all, she had been clear about him minding his own business. She didn't because she knew that if he wanted her to know what was said, he would tell her. He could be as stubborn as a mule when he set his mind to it.

"I think he likes you, Sis."

"Who?" Twyla asked distractedly, already knowing the answer.

"Why did he get so upset over your black eye? Concern might be normal, yes, but killing mad? I don't think so. You think so too! See! You're blushing."

"Oh, for Heaven's Sake! It's from the oven."

"Right," Melinda winked and laughed. "You know better. I think it was love at first sight."

"Put your apron on and mix up some more pie filling. You're being silly."

Nate rode hard to the ranch, taking out his wrath on the horse. By the time he reined in it was in a heavy lather, breathing hard, and on the verge of falling down. Seth, who had been working in the corral, saw the rider approaching and stood by the fence to see what was up. Seeing the condition of the horse, he was indignant for the animal and bitter toward Nate but he knew better than to say anything. He had a real soft spot for animals and disliked seeing the abuse Nate dealt his horse.

He knew that he had been hired because Twyla was his sister, but he tried real hard to be a good hand. He had to admit that he enjoyed being a part of the crew. Having a man like Cap to work for made him feel important, although he was afraid of him. If the truth be known, he was afraid of them all, including Peevey, the old cook. At eighteen, he had lived a rather dull life until he got this job. Being around gunmen was a thrill. However, he was getting tired of being afraid.

Nate dismounted and leaped up the stairs to the porch. Cap, had heard the horse approaching, and met him at the door.

"Got a job for you, Cap! Compton put a man on the old ranch. I want him off. Take whatever men you need and pay him a visit." He slapped his hat against his leg in frustration. His voice cracked with anger.

"You talkin' about that fella with one eye? I heard he plugged a couple gents over in Summit the other day," Cap asked softly.

"That bother you?" Nate snapped.

"No, just wonderin' if it was the same gent." He spoke in the same tone, but he thought, Watch your mouth Nate, I don't take smart talk from any man, and that includes you. The remark, "Take what men you need." rankled. I don't need any help, he thought angrily, but to prove it he said, "I'll take Seth, with me." The boy was trying real hard to punch cattle, but was no great shakes with a gun.

"Seth," Cap yelled, "Saddle our horses, we're ridin'."

Seth was surprised. Cap had never asked him to ride along with him before and on the heels of Nate's arrival, it had to be important. Within a few minutes the horses were ready and together they rode away from the ranch. It looked to Seth as though they were heading in the general direction of the old spread. "We headin' over to Charlie's place?"

"Yeah, we have a job to do. Seems we got a squatter movin' in. We're goin' to move 'im out."

"Think there might be some gun play?" Seth tried to keep the excitement out of his voice but failed.

"That will be up to him. You stay out of it. Nate wouldn't like it if I got you killed."

Seth could feel the tension building up. He felt a rush of excitement but also a small stab of fear. He was relieved to be told to stay out of any shootin'.

Will saw the two riders as they entered the gate. He strapped on his gun belt, tied the holster and stood on the porch, waiting. The larger man was obviously in charge and Will assumed him to be Cap. Not a bad looking man, with even features and a dark brown, well trimmed mustache. Hope I don't have to kill you, he thought. He didn't pay much attention to the other man as Cap would be the problem, if anything started. He did notice the smaller, younger man was not armed.

Seth took in the figure standing on the porch. He was a man of normal size maybe he could even be called small by some. His face was shaded by the brim of his hat so there was no clue there. Cap had mentioned the shootings over at Summit, so Seth was looking for something extraordinary in the shooter. He saw nothing. On second look, he did notice how casual the man seemed. He was apparently not in the least concerned about two strange riders coming into the yard. The gun on his hip had its holster tied down with a thong. His hand, though relaxed, was not far from the gun butt. Perhaps there was more here than met the eye.

"Howdy, Gents. Nice day for a ride. I seem to still have three chairs. Light a spell, if you like," Will offered, smiling.

"Thanks." Cap replied. Cap had noticed everything Seth had, and more. He was acutely aware of the one unblinking eye, the slight shift of body that would shave a fraction of a second off his draw, and how he'd stood to put the afternoon sunlight to his side. Cap felt a small trace of caution, which surprised and disconcerted him. It had taken him by surprise that the stranger had spoken first. Cap had his demands all formed in his mind but he hadn't had a chance to open his mouth. Anyway, the invitation would get him off the horse which gave him an edge if it came to gun play.

"Yeah, thanks," Seth echoed.

Together, they dismounted, climbed the steps and sat down. All three chairs were lined up against the wall, so all three were looking outward. It would be very awkward, if it came to a gun fight. Cap wondered if the man had planned it that way.

Seth got his first close look at Will. The eye-patch and scar gave him a start but they were only on the surface, the hard lines of the man's expression and the fierceness of that one eye changed his whole prospective of the man. "Looks as though you been doin' some house cleaning." It was the only thing he could think of to say. He leaned back in his chair and became absorbed in looking at the far hills. He was glad that Cap was between them.

"You would be right. I'll be staying here 'til next spring, so thought I'd clean it up some. Whoever's been using it, left a hell of a mess." He jutted out his chin towards the pile of rubbish stacked in front of them.

Seth felt uneasy. It was Nate's crew, him included, that had done this. Well he hadn't, actually, but he was part of the crew, so it was his fault too. He felt a little ashamed.

"That's the reason we rode over to talk to you. Seems as though our boss don't want anyone livin' here. I guess that means you should give some serious thought to just moving on," Cap said. There was a sharpness in his voice that was meant to provoke the stranger.

Seth caught the curtness in Cap's tone and he breathlessly awaited the one-eyed man's response.

Will leaned back in the chair, until he felt it touch the wall. He sat quietly, forming his response. Interlacing his fingers across his belt, he replied. "I've been waitin' four years and come two thousand miles to sit on this here porch. Now that I'm here, I don't figure to leave until I get good and ready. You tell your boss that your crew is welcome to use the barn in case of getting stranded out in the weather, and that the water is always available. The house is mine and no one gets inside without an invitation. Also, no smoking in the barn. I expect it to be in the same shape when you leave as it is when you enter."

Now it was Cap's turn to ponder. He was taken aback at the man's response. Obviously, the fool had no idea who he was a talkin' to. "Seems to me, you're in a bad spot. My boss wants me to get you off and I have a crew to back me up. Not that I need one, you understand." Although trying to resist it, Cap was feeling a degree of admiration for this galoot.

"Let's look at your options. You can try to run me off by force, but in that case any number of you have a real good chance of dying. This is not a brag. It's a fact. I am one damn fine shot, either with my Henry, or my pistol. I don't enjoy killing but at one time or another I've been forced to take lives." He paused. "You take my proposition to your boss. I think it's fair. If he says no, maybe you should give some thought to whether you want to take the chance of dyin' for him."

Seth was speechless. He had thought Cap was dangerous, but listening to this guy made the back of his neck tingle. He talked of death like other men would talk of the weather. He seemed oblivious to danger. Wanting to turn and stare at the man, he was afraid of what he would see there. Wait until I tell Melinda and Twyla about this, he thought. Better not tell the folks I was this close to a gunfight though.

The three stood up and Will stuck out his hand to Cap. "You must be Cap. My name is Buck."

Cap was so surprised by the gesture that he found himself shaking hands before he knew it. " Yeah, I'm Cap," he replied. The strangers grip was firm, in fact, it hurt, but Cap didn't show it in his face. The man's eye was as blank as a snake's. His smile went only as far as his mouth.

"I'm Seth," Seth added, sticking out his hand. He was startled by the strength of the man's grip.

"I've heard good things of you. Glad to make your acquaintance." He gave Seth a short nod. The one eye squinted, slightly, in a friendly crinkle.

Seth grinned. How would he know about me, Seth asked himself. He was flattered. He wanted to respond, but only mumbled something stupid and decided to keep his mouth shut.

Mounting, they swung their horses around and headed out the gate. Cap was deep in thought. He went over Buck's words. He'd be damned if they weren't reasonable. In the back of his mind, he also felt a little warning signal. Maybe this would be a good time to rethink his position. He sure wasn't likin' the way Nate ordered him around like some nobody. He'd spent his life time takin' orders but there was orders he took with a smile and there was those that rankled. Nate had a habit of issuing orders that rankled. Cap hadn't worked for Nate's father for very long before the old man died, but by God, he would have ridden into hell for him. Nate, on the other hand, inspired no respect or liking. Yup, maybe I need to give this some serious thought.

Seth attempted conversation, but Cap was lost in thought. Seth had never seen him so preoccupied. Usually you knew just what Cap was thinking, either by his expression, or his language. This was something new to Seth and he wondered what was going on in Cap's head, but he knew better than to ask.

Will watched them ride out before he resumed his chores. Seth seemed like a likable young man. Had the family's green eyes. Will noticed that Seth's horse was well kept and his saddle and bridle were in good shape. Will had mixed feelings about Cap, however. The man was surely on the peck when he rode in. Will had a feeling that they had some common ground by the time the meeting ended. He hoped so, anyway.

Picking up his hammer and a few large nails, Will entered the small dry room and started to add some nails to hang clothes on the back wall. No sense in lettin' two feet of wall space be wasted. On the second swing of the hammer, the wall swung away from Will. He tried to grab it to keep it from falling, then realized that it had swung open like a door. The hinges gave a grinding noise. It was obvious that they had not been oiled in a long time. Peering in, Will saw a space of no more than two feet by two feet, with a square hole taking up the entire floor area. He looked down into the hole but it was too dark to see anything. He stuck his arm down but felt nothing, until his fingers brushed against a ladder rung.

Taking down the new lantern that he had just filled, he returned to the hole and lowered it down into the dark space. The first thing he saw was the body of a man crumpled up on the ground about seven feet below. Will remained on his stomach as he looked at the skeletal remains. The space below was larger than the opening behind the door. He knew, at once, that this was the old man that had built the place. Will could see the arrow protruding from the man's back. He was curled up in a fetal position, one hand stretched toward a hole in the far corner. Will carefully descended the rungs. Squatting beside the body, he saw the gun and rifle by the old man's side. It was plain to Will what had happened. Under attack by the Indians, he had managed to hide down here, where he had died of his wound. Will was saddened by the discovery. This man had built this fine house and barn. He had been a real craftsman. Now, what to do with the remains? He could just leave the body here, or he could take it out and bury it. Will did not like the idea of trying to pick up the pieces of the old man but eventually decided that he would rather remove it, than to know that it was down here.

Scrounging around the barn he found a meal sack that might hold the majority of the bones. Trying to get the body into the sack might be another thing. The hole had been fairly dry and the body looked pretty firmly in-tact, however, to Will's relief, the rats had eaten it into pieces. Long hair covered the back of the skull but the body was just bones. Sifting through the clothes that held the bones together was the hardest part of the job. Will retrieved all the remains he could find and placed them in the sack. Old Chief was right. This was indeed. "bad medicine."

Will left the sack with its grizzly contents on the porch while he picked out a good resting place. He chose a small knoll, off to the right of the house, and managed a hole about four feet deep, before hitting a large tree root. Placing the bag in the hole, Will quickly covered it up. He felt obliged to say a few words. "Well, Old-Timer, I want you to know that I'll fix up the house you built and take care of it as long as I'm around. You built one great barn." He went back to the house, and didn't go down in the hole for a week.

The next few days he concentrated on the yard, burning all the trash that would burn, and hauling the rest behind some berry bushes out back. He half expected to see Nate's crew come riding in to harass him but they didn't. He was enjoying himself too much to be disrupted by them.

After a week had passed his curiosity finally drove him down into the hole under the house. He was glad the body was out and buried. The main part of the hole was a natural cave. It was small, maybe five feet long by four feet wide. A hole in the corner, about two feet wide formed a tunnel heading toward the back of the house. The only thing out that way was a small root cellar. Could they be linked? He didn't much feel like crawling into the tunnel to find out. Looking around the cave he located several pint jars of gold on a ledge behind the ladder. Evidently Charlie had struck gold somewhere. A worn leather pouch contained some papers but he didn't bother to look them over in the poor light. He tucked them under his arm. Picking up the old rifle and pistol he climbed out of the hole. Pulling the door shut, he was amazed at how it blended in. From his purchases, he took out the can of grease and carefully greased the hinges. He opened and closed the door until it moved smoothly and quietly.

That evening, with nothing else he wanted to do, he got out his gun cleaning kit and attacked the rust on the old weapons. They would never look real good, but good enough to hang over the door on the two pegs. The old flint lock fit the pegs to a tee.

He opened the fragile sheets of paper and after a time was able to decipher them. Several letters were from a bank in New Jersey pertaining to some delinquent properties. The last was a love letter from a lady named Anna. No return address. In a separate envelope, he found Charlie's will. "To the person that finds this I must be dead.

Ifn' you kilt me, rot in hell. If not you mite as well have my stuff. Don't have no one to give it to. There is my claim in Colorado. If'n nobody's found it, thar's still color there. Salted the mine. Everyone knowed it so it should be safe. Anyways, thirty paces from the entrance, behind a big rock is the glory hole. Good luck. Charles Lovelace. A rather detailed map of the mine location was on a separate paper. Will refolded the papers and placed them in the safe hole.

The following morning he inspected the root cellar out back. It didn't take him long to locate the end of the tunnel, knowing what to look for. Four shelves covered the back wall. The back of the lower shelf pushed in, revealing the shaft. With lantern and shovel, Will crawled in. A small cave-in blocked his way but with a little work, he opened it up. The smell of dirt and the cramped quarters brought back the memory of the well in Andersonville. It was not a good feeling. He backed out of the hole and rearranged the lower shelf to hide the opening.

Cap and Seth rode into town to confer with Nate. Cap knew that Nate would give them hell for not running Buck off, but Cap really didn't care. As long as he didn't get fired, he'd play the cards the way he wanted. He was right. Nate was not pleased.

"What are you telling me? That he's still there? I told you to run him off." Nate's face was red and his fists clenched.

"The way I see it," Cap explained, "is that we let him fix the place up some. He's done a lot already. That will just increase the value. No sense in you spending your money when he's willin' to do all the work for you. I don't think any of the boys would be thrilled to go over there and fix the place up."

"Yeah, you have a point. I really hadn't looked at it from that angle. We'll let it slide, for now." He disliked taking Cap's suggestion, but it did make sense.

"I'll be heading back to the ranch," Cap replied, with a grin. He knew Nate didn't like suggestions on how to do things. Turning to Seth, he asked. "You comin'?"

"No, I plan on eatin' in town. My sister cooks better than Peevey."

"I'll tell him you said that," Cap threatened, then smiled.

Seth was amazed. He'd never seen him smile before.

"Hi, big sister, how about a steak and potatoes?" Seth was grinning, as he entered the restaurant.

"Seth! What brings you to town? I saw you talking to Nate. He has been ranting all day about Buck moving into the old ranch."

"You know Buck?" Seth asked.

"Of course, silly. He ate here the first day he was in town and came in yesterday too. Sammy has really taken to him. Have you met him?"

"We just came from there. We were sent over to kick him off the place, but after talkin' to him, Cap decided it wasn't a good idea. He told Nate it was because Buck was cleaning the place up. That it would be worth more money, but I really don't think that was the reason."

"What do you mean?" Twyla asked, taking the seat across from him.

"Strange as it sounds, I think the two of them got along just fine. I mean, we all shook hands. I think Cap likes the fella. Either that or maybe he's afraid of him."

"I can't picture Cap being afraid of anyone. What else?" Twyla asked. This was interesting.

"He is sure putting in a lot of work on the place. We didn't go in, but he had all the trash out in the yard, and a bucket, broom and scrub brush were on the porch. Oh, the flowers were watered," He said, as an after thought.

Twyla was pleased. One of these days, she thought, I'll have to ride out there, and see for myself. Why not. If Nate doesn't like it, tough.

"He did say somethin' that I don't understand. He said he'd waited four years and come two thousand miles to sit on that porch and no one was going to move him off."

They discussed the statement over dinner, but when Seth headed back to the ranch, neither of them had figured out what he had meant.

24

THE FOURTH OF JULY

Jack was sitting up on his bed, finishing a newspaper article. Del had been working with him in the evenings, and to his delight, he was reading pretty well. It amazed Jack to realize that it could be so enjoyable. Writing was taking longer, but he stayed at it every night. He had decided to test his new skills by writing a letter to Twyla. Del had sent a note from his parents' house, but thought no more of it when he got no response. Jack was disappointed. After all, Will had asked them to let her know what had happened to Jimmy and make sure she was alright, should anything happen to him. The sinking of the Thorn had made Will's promise their promise. Over the past year it had crossed his mind, from time to time, but it was always when they were out in the bush. That, and the fact that he couldn't write, had held him back, so far. He didn't want to push Del about it. He was so patient about the teaching, never patronizing, and as proud as a father of how well he was doing. He never thought he would have such a fine friend. Del wrote to his parents, from time to time, but hesitated about contacting Twyla again. Maybe it was none of their business, he had told Jack. It was possible that the two were only friends and Jimmy was just making up the rest out of his loneliness.

Jack was still not convinced. He'd given his word. He'd have to take the chance of making a fool of himself to get square with his conscience. It wouldn't be the first time. So with pencil in hand he wrote:

Dear Miss Twyla Pinkham,

I am writing you in regards to Jimmy Compton. We were good friends. I was with him when he passed on. We made a promise to him to see how you was doing.

My friend Del and me is working for the Union Pacific. Del was Jimmy's friend too. We plan on taking some time off in a month or two. We will stop by Willow Creek on our way back east.

Sincerely, Jack Turner

He showed the letter to Del, who said it was a work of art. The words were spelled right, and the writing was legible. Jack wasn't sure what legible meant, but didn't want to ask. He would look it up, later, in the little dictionary Del had given him. That evening his first ever, letter went out with the company correspondence. He was proud enough to bust.

They knew they were getting time off soon because Del's father had mentioned, in his last letter, that he was arranging it. Up until that letter, Jack had lived day to day, as was his style, not giving much thought to their future. After it arrived, he became more anxious as the days went by in case something should happen to Del. The ambushes were becoming more frequent. He was no better at spotting them now than he was the first time. He didn't want to die himself but he knew he'd rather die than tell Del's folks that he'd failed to protect their boy.

He wondered why the army didn't hire Indians to teach the troops how to fight. They sure knew how to sneak up on a man. Remembering the sight of hundreds of troops being mowed down in seconds, he had to shake his head. These redskins wouldn't put up with that foolishness for a minute. What a waste of time.

Will had ridden into town for some supplies. Anyway, that's what he told himself. Actually, he hadn't seen Twyla in a week, and he wanted to check up on her, to look into her green eyes, not to mention taste her pie. That snake Nate needed an eye kept on him too. He'd pay if he continued abusing her.

On entering the restaurant, he saw her face through the kitchen window, and was pleased to see her smile at him.

Taking a chair at his usual table, he removed his hat and ran his fingers through his hair.

When she approached his table, he inquired hopefully. "Do you have any pie?"

"Sure do, what kind would you like?"

"You decide for me," he said, with a grin. "I haven't met a pie, yet, I didn't like."

She came back in less than a minute, with a large slice of apple pie. As there was no one else in the dining room, and Nate was off somewhere, Twyla asked. "May I sit down?"

"Why I'd be honored," Will replied, standing. He gazed at her, lost for a moment in her green eyes. No, the picture didn't do her justice, he thought. She would have been just the ticket for Jimmy. He couldn't imagine having her for himself. He was such a rolling stone, not even she could hold him in one place for long but if anyone could it would be her.

"How are things going at the ranch?" she asked.

"Pretty good. Got rid of all the trash, and got her cleaned up on the inside. That's a fine house. Of course, what it needs is love. I mean, it takes that to really make it a home. My mother told me that," he added, with a smile. "My mother would never lie to me."

"Tell me about yourself, Buck."

"Not much to tell, really. Born in Iowa, left home to seek my fortune. Ended up in Texas, chasing cattle. Joined the army. Spent four years in it, then got wounded. Went home to my folks, but they had died. Spent some time with my brother and his family, then came here. That about sums it up."

"But why did you come here?" she asked.

"Just liked the name of the town, I guess. Tell me, did you ever hear of a person by the name of Will Morgan?"

"No, I'm sure I haven't. Who is he?"

"Nobody of importance, just curious." Remembering the mail boxes in the store, Will smelled a rat or maybe it was a snake. "You'll have to come out and see the place."

"Why thank you, I'll take you up on that. Are you coming to the dance?" she asked. "We always have a Fourth of July dance. John has been working on cleaning out the stable for the last two days. We have it there, as it is the biggest building around."

"I'll give it some serious thought," Will replied. He paid Twyla for the pie and left. A dance sounded good. He wondered if he still knew how.

After all his chores were done on the morning of the fourth, Will took a swim in the creek in company with a bar of lye soap and donned his best duds. He took the harmonica out of the safe hole, and played a tune, just to make sure he still knew how. He was all ready when, to his delight, he caught sight of Twyla riding in the gate. He walked out into the yard and took her horse by the bridle. She dismounted before he could get around to help her off. She took off her hat and shook her long hair. He had never seen it hanging loose. It hung several inches below her shoulder blades, and the sun brought out a thousand shades of gold and brown. He forced himself to look away.

"What a pleasant surprise," she said, as her eyes took in the work, including the watered and weeded flower bed, that he had done on the house and yard. She caught him rubbing his boots on the leg of his pants, though he had shined them as best he could for the dance already. Her happy smile deepened to see the boyish gesture.

"Come on in, no sense standing out here in the sun." He rushed ahead, to cover his sudden bashfulness, and to open the door.

She entered the room and looked around. It was just like she had always wanted it to be. She caught herself before she started to cry.

Will saw the reaction, and wanted to pat her on the back, or something, but ended up just standing there. "Can I offer you a cool drink? The well here is real good."

As he spoke he hurriedly went to the fireplace and took down a small picture in a silver case from the mantel and put it in his shirt pocket. She could only tell that it was of a woman. Was he married?

"No thank you, Buck." She replied, as she dabbed at her eyes with the back of her hand.

To defuse the increasingly uncomfortable moment, Will asked, "Have you ever heard the story of the old man who disappeared from here?"

"Of course, that old story has been going around for years. I don't put any stock in it. It's just a silly story. Why?"

"I have something to show you, but you have to keep the secret. Follow me."

Entering the dry room, he opened the far wall and stood aside, so she could see the hole. She peered down into the darkness and then looked at him with amazement.

"Found the old fellow down there, with an arrow in him. He died with his hair on. Spooked the Indians, pretty good. Old Chief won't come near the place. Bad medicine. I buried him out front, on the knoll."

They returned to the front room. The revelation had eased their discomfort and Twyla accepted a drink of water and thanked Will for it. It was always a real good well. Sadness rose up in her again, so she said she would save him a dance and prepared to leave. He watched her ride away. He wanted her to stay awhile but knew that she was taking a chance just stopping by. If Nate found out about it, he was sure that Twyla would take a beating.

Some time later, he tied his horse to the rail in front of the store and walked over to the stable. More people than he had expected were milling around inside and in front of the big open doors. He heard music over the noise of their talking.

By this time, Will had met or heard about nearly everyone, and he was sure they knew all there was to know about him, so he felt quite comfortable. He found a place against the side wall and watched the activities. Benches were set up around the dance floor and a small bar was set up at one end. Perhaps a dozen couples were dancing. Twyla and Nate were one of the couples. It was obvious that Nate had started drinking early. Every few steps Twyla would have to straighten him up.

What a stupid jerk, Will thought. After three more dances, Nate staggered over to the bar, tossed down a drink, and left the stable, with another woman on his arm. Will was shocked. He looked around to see if Twyla had seen. He spotted her about the same time she spotted him. She smiled lifting her chin and walked toward him. He met her half way.

"It's time for that dance now, if you don't mind," she said. Her smile was defiant and it took his heart. Up 'til now he hadn't realized her strength, involved as he was in his duty to Jimmy and the simple beauty of her face.

"I do believe that I have been waiting for it for a lifetime," Will answered. Holding out his arms, she came into them and he felt her hand in his as the other rested gently on his shoulder. They danced.

After a second dance, Twyla asked. "Have you met my folks?"

"No, but I would be honored." She led the way across the dance floor. He was aware of people looking at them curiously, but nothing mattered, except the feel of her hand on his arm.

"Dad, Mom, this is Buck. Buck, I would like you to meet my parents, Ken and Martha Pinkham."

"Pleased to meet you sir, and you ma'am, I see where your girls got their pretty green eyes." Martha smiled at the compliment and Will went on. "Seems like we almost met over in Summit. I want to apologize for subjecting you and your daughter to that scene."

"From what I saw, and for what those ruffians did to Sheriff Sprigg, I'm sure you did what was best. Ken has to go over and play his fiddle. How about dancing with an old woman?"

"I'd be delighted. Where is she?" His smile was somewhat satanical because of the way the scar pulled at his mouth. At least, Martha hoped it was the scar.

They swirled out onto the dance floor. After a few turns, Martha looked up at him. "Buck, I don't know what your intentions are toward my daughter, but I won't have her hurt any more than she already has been. As you are aware, her husband is less than perfect, but he is her husband, and Sammy's father."

"Mrs. Pinkham, my intentions are to be a friend to your daughter. I don't reckon that a girl like Twila would see anything more in a man like me, anyway. I would do nothing to hurt her, nor do I intend to tolerate anyone else hurting her. She and the boy have become very important to me. Some day, I may tell you why." His wicked smile seemed a little sad as he looked down at her.

She felt that he was a man that could be trusted to do what he thought was right. A little fear touched her heart. What would that mean to her loved ones. With this man there would be no half measures. If he was determined to take care of Twyla, that's what he would do and the Devil take the hindmost. But why? What did she and the boy mean to him? He hardly knew them. She looked up into his face. The right side was handsome in a severe way. How had he looked before? How had this awful damage been done? What had his Mother thought to see his face so ruined? What had it done to him, inside? The music stopped before she could embarrass herself by asking any rude questions.

Others took up Twyla's time, but Melinda arrived and he danced with her twice. As she was the best looking single girl in the place, cowboys soon swarmed around her like bees to honey. Will took out his harmonica, and joined the band. Later, he asked Mrs. Compton for a dance. She graciously accepted, and they took to the floor. As he gently swung her towards the door, Will saw Cap and several of his followers, enter the building. They wore their guns and Will got the feeling that they were looking for trouble. He bent down and whispered in Verna's ear, "I hope you don't take offense at what I'm about to do, but it just might prevent a nasty scene." She looked confused but nodded willingly. He danced her across the floor toward Cap.

"Cap!" Will exclaimed with a smile. "Would you do me a big favor and dance with this lovely lady? I have to step outside for a minute."

Before Cap could respond, he was being ushered out on the floor with the lady on his arm. Verna was grinning up at Cap's confused look. "Well, I guess, ah, yeah, I, ah well....." Then he was dancing. His feet were all over the place and what he wanted to do was run.

She was chatting on about something, but he was so concerned about not stepping on her feet, he heard nothing.

When the music stopped, she smiled sweetly up at him. "Why Cap, you are so light on your feet, you surprise me. Surely you'd rather not waste your time on an old woman while all those young ladies are waiting."

"Well, ah yes, ah, I mean thank you Ma'am for the dance. I, ah, have to go now."

Before he knew what was happening he was escorting another lady to the dance floor. He didn't think he had asked her but he wasn't quite sure. Soon he was having the time of his life. His resulting benevolence spilled over and he gestured to his astonished crew to get with it! Dance! Usually, they just stood around, looking mean. Tonight, they were going to dance! He loved it. He'd worry about Nate tomorrow!

Later, as he stood by the bar catching his breath, Will walked over and joined him. "Looks like you're keeping the ladies busy."

Cap looked down at Will. He had the distinct feeling that he had been out-foxed.

"I'll admit it. I'm having the best time I've had in years. I'm sure that every one of those ladies will pay for it with sore toes in the morning. I think you had it planned that way."

"So many of these ladies are after a man of my good looks, I thought it only fair to give someone else a chance to shine." They stood, shoulder to shoulder, and watched the parade of passing dancers.

Cap tried to sort out his feelings. He'd had a hard life and it had made him hard. Maybe, in the end, being tough was not going to be enough. He had enjoyed striking fear into people, but dancing with the ladies and seeing them smile at him, was much more rewarding. He was glad that Buck had out-foxed him. Here was a man that could daunt the stoutest heart but he clearly enjoyed the friendship of the meek as well. He started to down his drink but decided against it. For some reason, he had no interest in getting sloppy drunk and upsetting the townsfolk. He looked at Will out of the corner of his eye and decided that he was starting to like him. It seemed strange, but he was beginning to like himself better, as well.

Several of his crew, swirled by with silly smiles on their faces. What the hell is my world coming to? he thought ruefully.

When the dance ended, Will crossed the street to where his horse was tied. As he was about to mount, he heard Twyla's voice from the darkness, "Good night, Buck."

The next morning, Nate was furious. By God, no wife of his would embarrass him by making a spectacle of herself with that one-eyed bastard. Seeing three of his crew across the street, he ordered them out to take possession of Charlie's ranch. By God, he'd had enough.

The three headed out to the ranch, not liking the idea of confronting Buck and wishing they could make contact with Cap to see how he would want them to handle it. The grays were quietly grazing in the pasture, but they were relieved to find no sign of the stranger.

"What the hell do we do now?" asked Virgil.

"I suppose we stay here until he comes back," Fred replied.

They waited on the porch for hours. Dark was beginning to fall when the third man, whose name was Slim, decided he'd had enough. They had been up plenty late at the dance and he was beat.

"Well it don't take no three of us to watch for him, so you two watch, I'm going to get some sleep." With that remark he entered the house.

Will was keeping an eye on them with his spyglass from the cave midway up the cliff behind the house and had decided not to confront them unless he had to. He was getting along with Cap and didn't want to ruin it. He had spent the morning looking for the trail up the cliff. After a lot of dead ends, he had located the faint path and worked his way up. The cave was far larger than he had expected from Jimmy's description. Its walls were emblazoned with layers of Indian art work. Will kept going back to study the paintings when he grew tired of watching the cowboys wait, or gazing at the valley laid out before him like another vast painting. He was disturbed and angry that one had entered his house. As evening approached, he formed a plan for the three men.

After dark, Will worked his way around and into the root cellar. He removed the shelves and crawled through the shaft to wait, listening, at the base of the ladder to the dry room. Presently, he could make out the fellow in the bedroom gently snoring and then the occasional voices of the other two waiting on the porch. Carefully, he entered the house and with the help of the moonlight, found the sleeping man's outer clothing draped over the chair. He picked up the shirt and pants and returned to the shaft. After crawling back to the root cellar, he made himself as comfortable as possible and went to sleep.

Slim awakened well after daylight, and started to get dressed. "What the hell. Which one of you bastards stole my clothes?"

Virgil and Fred came running. "What you talkin' about?" Fred asked.

"My clothes, you idiot. What did you do with them?" Slim had a temper, and the idea of one of these two takin' his belongings was starting to raise his dander.

"We don't know nothin' about your stuff. We was just a settin' in the room there, keepin' warm. That's the farthest we got from the front porch. We didn't go a messin' with nothin' a yourn. No, nor nothin' a his either," Virgil replied.

After searching the house and barn for the clothes, Slim, wearing only his long johns and boots, put on his hat and gun-belt. Draping a blanket around his shoulders, he mounted his horse and headed to the home ranch. He was in a foul mood and his head was pounding. He didn't notice Twyla coming from the other direction until there was no time to hide.

Thrusting out his chin, he straightened up and rode past her. He did not make eye contact.

"Good morning, Slim," she said sweetly.

"Mornin'," Slim grumbled. He heard the sound of her stifled laughter, but he could do nothing but ride on. Damn! Never been so humiliated in my whole life. Wait 'til I find out which one of those two stole my stuff. It was some time before the heat left his cheeks.

The two men watched Slim ride out. "Damn Fred, that was a fine joke, but I'd be careful foolin' Slim. He can be a bad hombre, if he gets mad enough."

"What the hell you a talkin' about? I didn't do nuthin'. I figured you done it."

They looked at each other, then turned to study the house. "I suggest it's time we got the hell out of here, Virgil."

"Don't have to twist my arm." They quickly headed after Slim.

Twyla finished her ride, wondering what the story was with Slim. She had seen some funny sights, in her life, but that had to be right up there with the best.

Will waited until the next morning to ride over to Nate's spread. Cap met him as he entered the main gate. "Heard one of your boys lost his shirt and pants over at my place. I'll keep an eye out for them. I came for my blanket."

Cap wanted to question Will, but said nothing. He couldn't keep the grin off his face. Slim had tried to sneak into the bunk house, but Al had spotted him. For the rest of the morning, Slim had been the target of all their jokes and bizarre speculations. The crew tried to keep their hi-jinks under control, but it was no use. Slim, in his spare clothes, finally announced that he had to ride fence and stalked out. Somehow, Will had stolen the clothes, Cap was sure, but he'd be danged if he could figure out just how he'd done it.

On returning to the ranch, Will was happy to see Miles waiting for him. He was seated in one of the chairs on the porch, smoking a pipe. "Afternoon, Mr. Compton. What brings you over?"

"Just thought I'd stop by and see if you needed anything. Seems like you've been busy. The place sure looks considerable better then it did."

Will dismounted and looped the reins around the hitch post. "Glad you came, sir. As long as you're here, I have a little something for you. Come on inside."

"What's that diggin' over on the knoll?" Miles inquired.

"That's part of what I wanted to show you. Follow me. He lead him into the dry room and showed him the hidden door.

"I'll by danged," Miles said, as he saw the door swing open.

"Come look."

He peered down into the hole, then at Will, much as Twyla had done, with much the same look of wonderment on his face. "Where does it go?" he asked.

"It's a small cave. I found Old Charlie down there, and buried him out front."

"Bye golly, those stories were right about him disappearing!"

Will removed the clothes from the pegs and rotated the board, exposing the hidden hole.

"I remember my son Jimmy finding that hidey-hole. How'd you find it?"

"Just by chance," Will replied. "Anyway, this is for you." He handed two of the jars of gold to Miles, taking the other two to carry himself as they were very heavy. I found them with Charlie. "Oh, would you please not mention this to anyone, especially Chief?"

"Why's that?"

"It's a good thing if people have certain beliefs, and Chief believes that Spirits carried Old Charlie away. It connects him to his people and gives him something he needs. I must admit, I was a little disappointed to find him. Going up with the Spirits in a trail of smoke sounds a lot better."

"Sure, you can count on me to keep it quiet, but why are you givin' the gold to me?"

"It's you're place. I'm just renting. Besides, I don't have any need for it. The way I figure, having a bunch of money might spoil me." They returned to the porch.

"Well, I don't know what to say. If that don't beat all! It'll sure come in handy for us. You have our thanks and that's enough said about it. If there's anything we can do for you, just say so. Thought I'd mention the dance and that we enjoyed your company there. When Cap and his crew came in I expected some trouble. You sure turned things around by a gittin' him to dance. Don't know if you noticed but after a time they even hung up their guns. As a matter of fact, they were the last to leave. Cap even shook my hand and thanked me for letting him dance with the wife. First time the man has ever been civil to me."

Miles put the two jars in his saddlebags and mounted his horse. Then Will handed him the other two. He sat, looking at them briefly. Then, giving a firm nod of decision, he handed them back to Will. "We'll split it. Old Charlie had no family, but I think he would be pleased if we divided it between us." Smiling, he reined his horse around and trotted out of the yard.

25

DECISIONS

That afternoon Will attacked the wood pile. There wasn't much left and it was all spread around. From what he had heard, winters here were hard, and a house without a decent wood pile was in trouble. There was ample dead wood on the property, dead limbs he could cut out, and some that had fallen from the big trees, and some smaller, but not small, downed trees near the creek. They would burn hot. With saw and axe, he put in long hours, for several weeks. His stack grew, day by day. He managed to haul several loads to the Compton's and some to the Pinkham's as well. Should they run short, he was confident that he had enough firewood to see them through 'til spring. As an extra reward for his efforts the place began to look even better with the dead wood removed. He made a stack of kindling with the small pieces and raked up the last of the mess into piles to burn after it rained some. He built a big lean-to to cover the stack. By the time he finished, a cool breeze nipped the night air.

What's this? Nate wondered. Another damn letter to Twyla, this one from some fella named Jack Turner. Ripping open the letter, he read it's contents. Oh hell, they're coming to Willow Creek. When was all this bull shit going to end? He stuffed the letter back in the envelope and dropped it in the dead file, walked to the window and looked down the street, half expecting to see them riding into town.

Winter came with a cold, cloudy day of light snow which turned heavier, as the day progressed. Twyla had gone home, closing the restaurant after lunch. The streets were deserted. Nate stood looking out the window at the falling snow, but his mind was on Dot. This would be a perfect time. He would tell Twyla that the snow was too deep to get the buggy home. He stayed at the store, on the cot in the back room, from time to time. Usually, it was when he drank himself into a stupor. Yes, perfect. It would be a slow night at the saloon, so it would be no problem to spend the entire night with her. He was filled with anticipation. Why wait, he thought. He locked the doors and headed for the back stairway of the saloon. Damn, it was cold, but Dot would take care of that!

Twyla watched the snow come down. She had no worries, as the house was well built for the cold, and she had good fires going in the fireplace and stove. As the snow accumulated, she guessed that she would be alone, this night. She smiled. Just she and little Sammy. He had also been watching the snow and wanted to go out and feel it. Tomorrow would be soon enough, she thought.

Putting Sammy to bed, she disrobed, and after a quick wash from the large pitcher and bowl, slipped into her nightgown and snuggled down for the night. She gave some thought to Buck. She hadn't seen him for a week or more, and wondered what he was doing. She looked forward to seeing him come through the restaurant door. She got up and removing her nightgown, stood naked in front of the large mirror. Was she still attractive? Her breasts were a little lower, from nursing Sammy, but her waist was still the same as before. She turned and looked at her hips and cheeks. She thought they looked unchanged with time. Slipping into the nightgown, and into bed again, she pulled up the covers and thought again of Buck.

She didn't know how long she had been asleep, before she was awakened by a thunderous crash. She leaped from her bed and rushed down the hall toward Sammy's bedroom. To her horror, she could see the night sky through a gap in the hall ceiling. A huge tree trunk lay across the hallway buckling the floorboards. Stunned, she stopped for a few seconds at this unexpected obstacle between her and her son. Grabbing limbs, she climbed over the trunk and rushed to Sammy's bed. Thank God, he was all right. He stopped crying as soon as he knew she was there. Picking him up, she fled down the stairs, only to be met by billowing smoke, belching from the fireplace. It was so thick that she had a hard time breathing. Reaching the entrance closet, she reached in, grabbed her boots, and dislodged several coats. She slipped into one and wrapped another around Sammy on the front porch, she could feel the freezing cold bite into her bare legs above the boots. She entered the barn, placed Sammy on the hay, and started saddling her horse. She couldn't stay here. The barn would only keep them from freezing, but if no help came within a few hours, it would be too late to get out. No, she had to leave. She would have to try for Jimmy's parents place as it was nearer than town, and the wind would be at their back. Sitting Sammy up on the saddle, she mounted behind him and urged the horse out of the barn, into the freezing wind.

They had not gone over a half a mile, before the drifts became a problem. She would have to head to lower ground, and that left Buck's. The horse knew the way. She had ridden this route many times when she and Jimmy would meet to work on their ranch. They turned down the shortcut, the wind was again at their back and the sheltering trees had kept the snow from drifting. The horse picked up speed. The snow was a soft powder and Bell moved quickly through the mounting fluff.

Three hundred yards from the ranch, and safety, they passed down a slope to cross a small gully that was usually dry all summer. Recent rains had produced a good-sized stream. They slowly crossed the stream and were climbing the far side when Bell lost her footing and plunged backward into the water. Twyla and Sammy were thrown clear, but Twyla hit the ground hard and a hoof struck her head. Sammy crawled over to her, crying and snuggled down by her side. The horse, limping, climbed the slope and continued on to the ranch.

Will had banked the fire and was sitting in his chair, playing the harmonica, when he heard muffled sounds in the yard. Stepping out on the porch, he was shocked to see Bell standing by the barn door. She was covered with mud and her saddle had slipped to one side.

Will rushed to the barn and opened the door. She almost trampled him as she brushed past. Lighting the barn lantern, Will grabbed his saddle and put it on Dolly. She was the stronger of the two, and Will did not know what he would find, or how much horse he would need. He sprinted back to the house, and grabbed his coat, and a blanket. Back at the barn he mounted, and with the lantern held high, rode out into the night.

The faint light picked up Bell's tracks, and he moved along at a good pace. Nearing the gully he slowed. He could see the torn up snow where Bell had fallen. He could also make out a mound near the creek, that was quickly being covered by snow, and realized that Twyla was probably under it. Where was Sammy? Fear knotted his stomach. The bank was too slippery for the horse so, looping his rope around the horn, he threw the rest of it down the slope. Sliding down with the rope to steady him, he started brushing snow from the mound. His hands touched clothing, and Will frantically scooped it away from the small bodies. Picking Sammy up, he worked his way back up the slope, using the rope. Sammy started to whimper.

"You're safe, Sammy. You're with Buck. Just sit on my horse, and hold on tight. I'm going to get your mama. Good boy." He wrapped the blanket around the small shoulders.

Returning to Twyla, he was relieved to hear her groan. At least she was alive! Lifting her was almost more than Will could muster. Although she was slim, the footing was treacherous. Using the rope once more for leverage, he managed to make his way slowly to the waiting horse. He boosted her up behind the saddle where Sammy huddled and looped the rope around them both. It would have to work he thought, grimly. He pulled the end of the blanket back to cover her, as best he could. He pointed the horse toward home. He used the reins to control Dolly's speed, and walking along at her side, held on to them to keep them from sliding off.

It was a long three hundred yards. Will opened the barn door and led the horse in. She needed little encouragement. Placing Twyla on the hay, Will lifted Sammy down and carried him into the house. Quickly he stripped off the boy's wet clothing and, pulling back the blankets on the bed, slid him in and returned for Twyla. He carried her in and placed her on top of the bed beside Sammy. As he slipped off her wet coat and boots he found her feet were like ice, to his touch. Shutting the door he took off his own dryer coat and placed it over her flipping the edge of the blankets over her feet. He quickly dug out the banked logs in the fireplace and added more. In no time he had a good blaze going. As he prepared to get Twyla under the blankets he realized she was wet clear through. He removed her nightgown and quickly maneuvered the blankets over her and turned to stoke the fire again. Sammy was making small cold noises but seemed fairly content, with Twyla at his side. He put some bricks to heat by the fire wishing he had thought of it before.

Once the room warmed up, Will pulled back the blankets and examined Sammy and then Twyla for broken bones. He tried to ignore the fact that she was naked, but was not successful. Finding no obvious broken bones, he stood looking at her naked body. He knew it was the wrong thing to do, and quickly covered her. Reaching under the blankets he gently rubbed her feet, trying to get the circulation back. He tried to think of anything else he should do for them but nothing came to mind. Soon her feet felt a little warmer and he got some flour sacks from the kitchen and wrapped two of the bricks and slipped them under the blankets at each of their feet.

He had to take care of the horses, and donning his coat, made his way out to the barn. The snow was falling so hard that the earlier tracks could hardly be seen. In the barn he striped off saddles and bridles and rubbed the two patient mares down with sacking. He inspected Bell carefully while he worked on the caked mud. Her leg seemed sore to the touch, but he couldn't detect anything broken. When they were both settled in stalls, with something to eat, he closed the barn door and made his way back to the house, exhausted.

Sammy was asleep, and Twyla was still unconscious, as far as he could tell. He studied her face. A large bruise was spreading across her forehead and the skin was scraped. All he could do was clean the wound. Then he took all the wet things and hung them up in the dry room. He was pleased at the amount of heat coming through the pipes leading into the firebox. What he would have given for heat like this in prison.

He tiredly found one more blanket and pulled his comfortable chair into the bedroom. Before he settled down, on impulse, he knelt and studied Twyla. He could see the little pulse in her throat. Her eyelashes seemed so long and perfect. Without thinking, he leaned forward and gently kissed her lips. Her eyes opened. He recoiled backward and sat down in the chair. Her eyes had closed again. What a stupid mistake! What was he thinking about? Just get some sleep you big oaf. He propped his feet on the wood box. Don't think about her. That was easier said than done. It was a long time before he drifted off. Little noises from the two on the bed woke him from time to time, and some time in the night he felt Sammy climb up on his lap and snuggle down. Will pulled the blanket up over the little guy and went back to sleep.

The snap of burning pitch awakened Twyla. She started to raise her head, but the pain was too much. What happened? Where am I? Her eyes took in the room, and she knew she was at the ranch, but how did she get here. Closing her eyes she tried to think. The storm and the tree, getting Bell, and starting out in the snow, Sammy! Where was Sammy! She opened her eyes and looked frantically around the room. There was Buck, stretched out in his chair, feet propped up on the wood box. She could see the back of Sammy's head, peeking out of the blanket that covered them. She relaxed. Buck's head was turned partly away from her so the scar was not visible. He must have been really handsome, she thought. Oh, not in a pretty way. It was a face that had character. Yes, she thought, he had character. In a way he would be as hard a man to live with as Nate. He'd never hit her, but she would never be first before his duty, and his duty usually seemed to involve violence to someone, if not herself. Was it a dream, or had he kissed her? She tried to get it clear in her head. It seemed so real, he must have. She found she enjoyed the possibility. Stretching her legs, she became aware of her nakedness. She could feel a flush on her cheeks, but again, she wasn't as shocked as she should be. She didn't seem to mind at all and she wasn't sure why. Somehow, it just seemed all right. She slept.

Will woke up and carried Sammy over to the bed and slipped him under the blankets. From his dresser he took out a pair of pants, a shirt, and some warm socks. It would have to do. He placed them on the bed, on the off chance Twyla would wake up while he was gone. He was unaware that she was watching every move he made. He put on his coat, and went out to the barn. He had purchased a dozen chickens from Miles and hoped there would be eggs for breakfast.

As soon as she heard the crunching of his steps in the snow, she got up and slipped into the clothes. She looked at herself and almost laughed. She stoked the fire and added a log. Going into the kitchen she built up the fire in the stove and started heating water for coffee.

Seth was up early and decided that he would ride into town for breakfast. It was a beautiful morning. The snow was twelve to fifteen inches deep, but was powder, so it was easy riding on the sheltered ranch road. There were drifts on the main road that made the going harder. The sun was out, and although there wasn't much warmth from its rays, it brought a brightness as it reflected off the clean snow that showed the easiest path and lifted one's spirits as well. As he passed the new house, he noticed the absence of smoke from the flues, although he could smell its acrid fumes from the road. Then he realized that he couldn't see the big chimney! What the ....! Reining into the yard, he saw the pile of stone that had been the chimney, and the huge branches of the tree laying across the upper story. He jumped down and raced into the house, calling his sister's name, but all was silent. The front room and hall were black with soot, especially the area around the fireplace but a drifting of snow had apparently put out any fire. Climbing the stairs, he was shocked to see the damage. He checked the entire house, finding no one. Out in the barn, he was relieved to see that Bell was missing as well as Nate's horse and buggy. At least they weren't pinned under the tree where he couldn't see them. He threw some hay to Sammy's horse and then headed into town. The going was rougher as he reached the more open country.

Entering the livery stable, he searched for Bell in vain though Nate's horse and rig were there. John came out of his office smiling at Seth. He looked upon the boy as one of his own. Concern replaced the smile, when he saw the look on his face.

"What's wrong, Seth?" he asked.

"Have you seen Twyla?"

"Not since she left the restaurant, yesterday. What's wrong?"

Seth told him what he had found at the house.

"Lord, oh, Lord! Let's see if Nate is around. He should know where she is. Maybe he took her out to your folk's place."

"If we can't find him, will you ride out there and see?" Seth asked, "I'll check out at Buck's and the Compton's."

John started to saddle his horse while Seth went over to the store. It was locked. Peering into the windows he could see no one. He was crossing the street, to check out the hotel, when he saw Nate heading toward the store from the saloon.

"Where's Twyla?" he shouted.

"How should I know, probably still at home," Nate answered in a belligerent tone.

"No she ain't. Dammit! She and Sammy are gone. On of those big trees fell on the house and caved in the chimney."

"She's probably with that one-eyed son of a bitch. I think he's taken a shine to her. Maybe she feels the same. I don't much care, one way or the other. How bad is the damage to my house?"

You goin' to ride out to find her?" Seth asked angrily.

"Forget it, I'm goin' to the store." Nate retorted. "I got work to do."

"You stupid, whorin' ass!" Seth screamed as he ran for his horse.

Will saw Seth coming up the road and waved. He could see the concern on the boy's face and knew he was looking for his sister. "She's here, and so is Sammy. She took a pretty good bump on the head, but I think she'll be alright. Come on in."

Both were surprised to see Twyla up and around. Seeing her dressed in his clothes, Will thought she looked first rate, and that was for sure.

"Coffee will be ready in a few minutes." While they waited, she told them about the tree falling on the house and the smoke. "Had the house burned down?" she asked Seth.

"No, but the chimney caved in so the smoke couldn't get out. Everything is black and smells of smoke, but besides that there's only the roof and a couple of walls knocked down. Oh! And a tree in the upstairs hall." They all laughed at this belittling of the damage to Nate's fine house.

"Where was Nate during all this?" Will asked.

"I assume, he was with his friend at the saloon." Twyla answered.

"I saw him coming from that direction as I was heading out here. He wouldn't even come with me to look for his family," Seth said, looking at Will.

Within the hour they had all had coffee and Sammy was up and dressed in his dried pajamas and one of Will's flannel shirts tied on with string. Will's socks reached up to his knees and he declared them just the ticket. John Henry, Ken, and Martha Pinkham arrived in John's high buggy. They were relieved to see everyone standing on the porch as they entered the yard. Will took the reins and tied the rig to the hitch post while they climbed down to hug their daughter and grandson.

"Bell fell down, but Buck got us up." Sammy informed them.

As they all went inside, Martha looked at Twyla dressed in Buck's cloths. What had gone on here last night, she wondered. She watched the two, to see if there was a hint. As she listened to the story of the rescue, she realized that it was due to this man's efforts that they were both safe, and that was all that mattered.

Later, Will watched from the porch as everyone left. The house seemed quiet and empty. The ladies had fixed breakfast while the men busied themselves checking out the scene of the fall and Bell munching hay in the barn. It had been a pleasant two hours. Now he felt as empty and alone as the house. He pressed the blankets to his face. He could still smell Twyla on them. He felt himself blush as he remembered the Love sisters. He knew he shouldn't think of Twyla that way. She was a lady. It had been quite a night. He settled down in his chair and propped his legs up. Damn leg muscles hurt like crazy, not to mention his back. What? Was he getting old or something?

As John Henry drove the buggy into the stable, Nate saw them and came out of the store. "Well, I see you had a good time last night," He exclaimed, with sarcasm. "Where the hell are your clothes? Let me guess. You shacked up with Buck and got them all mixed up."

"Where were you?" Twyla fired back. "Keeping Dot warm?"

Reaching up, he grabbed Twyla's arm and pulled her from the buggy. "Get in the store! We have some talkin' to do! The rest of you, leave us alone. She's my wife, and we have some business to attend to. This don't concern you."

Ken Pinkham wished that Seth hadn't gone back to the ranch. Alone he was no match for Nate, even with John's help. Nate was right, she was his wife and it was none of their business. It galled him to not be able to do a damn thing to help her. Why? Oh, why, had he let her marry him. Their concerns about propriety seemed shallow and stupid now.

"We're staying here in town," Ken announced firmly. "I'm goin' to talk to John. Why don't you take the boy and go visit Flora or somebody, Martha."

Nate was furious, but on another level he was thinking quite clearly. He'd had enough of this damned town, enough of an unfaithful wife, and enough of this miserable store. The stage for Summit would leave in an hour, which would be perfect. He left Twyla in the restaurant. Let her think she was getting away with it. She would find out different soon enough. Opening the safe he withdrew the packets of money. Enough to get a new start in San Francisco, he thought. The hell with the store and ranch. He could sell them from Frisco if he wanted. Meanwhile, he could manage very well with this stake. It was all they had. He'd leave Twyla the bills. He wanted out now! Not tomorrow, now! He took a valise from the back room and put the money in it. Then he added a few clothes from stock to tide him over and a bottle of whiskey. On second thought, he took out the whiskey. He could use a little nip right now. He uncorked the bottle and took several long drinks, then several more. Time to set Twyla straight he thought. Shackin' up with that one-eyed bastard. He'd show her a thing or two.

As she worked, getting things started for the day, Twyla didn't hear him come into the restaurant, or sneak up behind her. Suddenly, she was grabbed from behind, swung around and slapped across the face, then again, and again. Then he had her by the hair, and was slapping her in a frenzy. It made Nate feel powerful. He didn't want to stop. He closed his fingers into a fist and hit her four times, as hard as he could. He only quit when he could no longer hold her up. He let her slump to the floor retaining a handful of her silky hair. He scattered it over her body and looking down at her bloody face, he kicked her hard in the ribs, grabbed the valise and left. Running up the stairs in back of the saloon, he wrenched open the door, and told a startled Dot, "Pack a few things. We're gettin' out of this damn place, right now!"

While Dot was packing, Nate was watching the stagecoach. He had to time it just right. When he saw old Ernie start to get up on the box he grabbed Dot and hustled her out the door and down the steps. Climbing into the stage, Nate handed Ernie several bills. "Don't have time to buy tickets, Ernie."

Ernie was surprised to see Nate with Dot right out in public, but figured it was none of his business. "No problem," he answered. "Yeeeeyup!" he yelled, and the stage rattled out of town. He wondered if Nate was running off with Dot. He never thought much of Nate and figured Twyla and Sammy would be better off without him.

John and Ken had been watching the store, but had heard nothing nor had they seen Nate leave by the back door. The first sign of something wrong was when Nate and Dot suddenly appeared at the stage.

They ran across to the store to find the door was locked. "Stand back!" John yelled, as he hit the door with his shoulder three times in succession. The hinges tore loose from the jamb and the door fell to the floor. Stepping over it they ran to the kitchen where they found Twyla.

"Get Martha, John. I think she's with Flora, Hurry, John! Oh, God!" he sobbed as he knelt by his daughter.

Within minutes, an ashen faced Martha ran through the doorway. Seeing Ken with Twyla's head in his lap, she burst into tears but she began to wet a cloth at the sink anyway. In between sobs, she dabbed at Twyla's face and swore. She was using language that Ken had never heard her use before. He didn't even know she knew those words. She had always been so placating about Nate. He hadn't realized how much she had really hated him.

"John, you've got to do us one more favor," Ken pleaded.

"I know what to do, go get Buck. Oh, Lordy!" he said, looking at Twyla. Turning he bolted out the door.

Will heard John yelling from a quarter mile away. Something was wrong. He ran to get his guns then to the barn to saddle his horse. John road up to the barn and yelled. "Ya gotta come! That damn Nate's near killed Twyla. Beat her up real bad." He turned his horse and headed back to town.

Will caught up with him, as they entered the main street. "Where is she?"

"They's in the store," John answered as he led the way.

Twyla looked bad. Her eyes were swollen shut and her lips were split and bloody. Hell, there was blood all over the place. Will's face went dark and his eye glittered with menace. "Where's Nate?" he asked in a husky whisper.

"He's on the stage to Summit, with Dot. They left about an hour ago."

Chief was leaning against the wall. He had been looking down at Twyla. When Will entered, the old man's attention shifted to him. He took in the look on the one-eyed man's face. Oh! how he wanted to ride out with him to get the evil one but he knew that he would be more hindrance than help. "You bring him back. I will take his scalp," he said in perfect English and with deep sincerity.

Will nodded. He took one more look at Twyla and left. A few minutes later, he was on the road to Summit. He put the mare to a slow, steady gallop. He knew that the condition of the road would prohibit the stage from traveling at a regular pace. Walk awhile, trot awhile, and then the ground eating lope. After two hours he knew he couldn't be too far behind. He scanned the road ahead for the stage coach.

Nate held Dot's hand and planned his future. He mildly regretted his fight with Twyla but once started, he hadn't been able to stop himself. She asked for it. It was her fault really. He'd tried to be a good husband. Hell, he knew she was pregnant when he married her. He had assumed the responsibility of being a father as well as a husband from the start. They hadn't made love until months after Sammy was born, and then it was forced on her part. He had never felt that she really cared for him. Around town, she was all smiles, and holding hands, but when they were alone, he was no more than an unwelcome boarder. Then Dot had come to town. She did not have Twyla's beauty, but she made him feel like a man. How many times he had heard people say how lucky he was to have a wife like Twyla. What a laugh! He looked at Dot's happy face, and felt at peace. A new beginning, a better life. He took another pull on the bottle.

"Whoa, up dammit! I gotta take a leak!" Nate yelled at Ernie. Climbing back inside, he took another pull on the bottle and slumped down in the seat. He took Dot's hand again, seeking strength, as the ramifications of what he had done began to dawn on him. He tried not to think about what would happen to him if he had managed to kill Twyla. Without a doubt, when Buck found out, he would follow him to hell, if necessary. As soon as the bastard caught up with them he was a dead man. He watched the landscape slowly pass. Too damn slowly!

The horses were having trouble in the slippery mass of melting snow and mud. The coach seemed to slide back and forth across every rock and pothole in creation. They should be farther along by now, he thought, as he took another pull on the bottle. He gripped Dot's hand so hard that she pulled away. He had to take another leak. He couldn't put it off. The jolting coach was giving his bladder fits. "Whoa up. I gotta take another leak!"

This was the third stop, and Ernie was getting irritated. "If you'd put that damn bottle away we wouldn't be a makin' all these stops," Ernie muttered to himself.

The stage lurched to a halt and Nate almost fell through the door. Gripping the rear wheel, he faced the stage and began to relieve himself.

"Turn around, you damn fool. Your a pissin' on the coach," Ernie was irate. He should just go off and leave the drunken bum here, he thought to himself. Serve him right.

Nate had finished, and was in the process of buttoning his pants, when Will caught up with the stage.

He could tell that Nate was drunk. He had contemplated killing him but seeing Nate lurching around the stage he realized that his options were limited. He wanted to shoot him, but knew that he couldn't. He slowed the horse and approached, glaring at the drunk, trying to decide what to do.

Nate saw Will and stuck his hand in the pocket of his coat. He felt the pistol. He'd show that son-of-a-bitch. He gripped the smooth butt of the gun and held it tightly. He slipped his other arm through the wheel, wrapping it around the spoke. He was having a hard time maintaining his balance, and he was afraid. He could feel the fear crawling inside him like a live thing. So damned familiar. He could feel Dot looking at him from inside the stage. He had to show her. He glared at Will as he approached.

Will rode right up to Nate before he reined in, staring down at him with utter disdain. He's a worm not a snake, he thought. I'll just give him a little of what he gave Twyla. Just beat him until there is nothing left of his face. If I, and probably Twyla, had to live with a messed up face this one surely should too. I'll enjoy giving him a good whupin'.

When Will started to dismount, Nate tried frantically to pull the gun from his pocket. The sight was stuck in the lining and it refused to come out. As he jerked on it angrily, he accidentally squeezed the trigger. The gun went off and a searing pain shot down his leg. He started to fall but the loud report had startled the horses and they surged forward. It was over ten feet before Ernie got them under control. Nate had been unable to free his arm from the spokes. He had been jerked from his feet, whipped over the wheel, and then crushed under its weight.

In less than a heartbeat it was over. Will, half off his horse, had all he could do to get his own feet on the ground. He'd only half seen what had happen to Nate and that was enough. The sound of crushed bones would be with him for awhile.

"I seen it, by God. I seen it. Twern't my fault. The horses bolted. Twern't my fault." Ernie had released the brake when Nate started to button up, anxious to get started. When Buck had shown up he hadn't thought to reset it.

"It was just an accident, Ernie. If it was anyone's fault, it was Nate's. He beat up Twyla pretty bad. I was coming to get him. You just saved me the trouble."

Dot was looking out of the window at Nate's body. She was whimpering. She had a handkerchief to her eyes, and was rocking back and forth. Getting down from the coach, Ernie handed Will Nate's valise. Opening it, Will took out a packet of money and gave it to Dot. She gripped the money tightly and began to cry.

"Don't come back, ma'am. Good luck." Will felt sorry for her, but what else could he do?

"I say we load him in the boot and I'll take him on in to Summit. I know the sheriff pretty well, so I'll tell him what happened out here. They got an undertaker there and he can fix the body. I'll bring him back on my next trip."

"Would that be Sheriff Sprigg?" Will asked.

"Sure would," Ernie replied. Relieved to get the conversation off the accident.

"Tell him that Buck says hello, and wishes him well."

"He's slowed down a lot, but he has a good man helpin' him now. I figure he'll retire shortly."

Will helped Ernie stow the body on the stage, then taking the valise he turned his horse, and started his return trip to Willow Creek .

As Ernie resumed his seat and got the horses started, he wondered about Buck. Seemed like he was a good man, from what John had said. He hoped that Twyla would be alright. She would be well rid of this galoot, and that was for sure. So would Dot when it came right down to it. A man that hits women don't stop with one, by God, he thought. One minute he was a cussing Nate out and the next the man was dead. One sure don't know when the Almighty will come a callin' for you. A'course maybe it waren't the Lord in this case he chuckled wickedly to himself.

When Will reached Willow Creek, a number of folks gathered around him to find out what he'd done about Nate. If he read the looks on their faces right, it was just as well he didn't have a chance to bring him back. Nate would have been strung up before the day was out. As he told them what had happened, he saw several nodding in satisfaction.

"Twyla's over at Flora's place, follow me," an old man said. When he hesitated, John appeared at his elbow.

"I'll take care of your horse. You just go along."

Twyla was being tended by her mother. She'd been cleaned up and a cold towel covered her face from the nose up. Will was relieved to hear her mumble something. Her mother laughed. Will considered that a good sign. He motioned to Seth and Ken, standing in the background, and the three of them went outside. Will repeated the tale of Nate's passing after giving the valise to Ken.

"Can't say that it hurts my feelin's none. That man was just no damn good," Seth summed it up for all of them.

Chief shuffled out of the stables down the block, and they all had to grin. Chief had the ability to make anyone smile, like a warm sun on a cold day. He was carrying a large hunting knife. John followed and they came up the street toward the three waiting men.

"Damn! I was supposed to bring Nate back for a scalping!" Will said in consternation. He hated to disappoint the old fellow.

"They tell me Nate has gone to the happy hunting ground. I hope he goes with no weapon, that the buffalo are many, and he starves." Chief said solemnly. "Son-of-a-bitch." Looking at Will, with great

413

sorrow he continued in the same tone. "Still can't find my damn teepee." They all burst into laughter.

Cap and most of the ranch crew rode into town at that moment and stopped where they were standing. They dismounted, and tying up their horses, joined them. Concern for Twyla was written on their faces. "How is she Seth? We came as quick as we could."

"Don't know for sure, but she is talking to Mom. Guess that's a good sign." Then he told them about Nate.

"Me and the boys will stick around as long as she needs us. Tell her not to fret about the ranch," Cap assured him. "You alright with that Buck?"

"Sure," Will replied, surprised to be consulted in the matter. "You know what you're doing out there."

Cap gave them a short nod and with the cowboys drifted away toward the saloon.

26

A NEW START

He'd put off seeing her as long as he could. It had been a week since Nate's death. A week was too short to start courtin' but he'd made up his mind it was the thing to do and he needed to get started before he got cold feet and headed for the hills. He saddled up and headed for the Pinkham ranch where Twyla was staying.

Martha was at the kitchen window. She waved as Will rode into the yard. He took that as a good sign. He waved back.

She answered the door saying, "Just a minute, I'll tell her you're here." Will took the moment alone to run his hand through his hair and re-tuck his shirt tail. She came back downstairs and waved Will up.

"She's presentable, and more than ready to see you, you know." She gave Will a pat on the back, as he passed her. "She expected you days ago."

Will climbed the stairs to her room like a boy on his first date. His heart was all aflutter. Twyla smiled as he entered. Will felt a surge of compassion as he looked at her. The bruises were not as dark, and the swelling had receded but he remembered the beating she had taken and wasn't at all sure she wouldn't have some remnants to remember

Nate by. Hatred swelled in his heart but he forced it away. The bastard was dead. Time to let it go.

Even with the signs of the beating, she was the most beautiful woman Will had ever seen. He crossed the room and took her hand in both of his. He looked into her eyes, hoping that his plans for them were going to meet with her approval. "How are you?" he asked, gently.

"Much better than the last time you saw me. Fortunately I still have my teeth." She smiled. "And how are you?"

"Oh fine, I seem to wake up every morning."

"I would think that would be a good start to the day."

Will released the hand he had been holding far too long. He pulled up a chair and sat down, placing his hat on the floor. Neither said anything for a moment. He thought of the night of her accident and her naked body in his bed. He felt the heat rise in his cheeks.

"What are you thinking?" She had a mischievous look on her face. "You don't have to answer that. I think I can guess." She caught him by surprise with her next question. "Who are you Buck? What is your whole name?"

Will felt the muscles in his stomach tighten. His mind was racing. What would she say if he told her, now, how he had killed Jimmy? He couldn't jeopardize whatever feelings she might have for him. "There are some things in my past that perhaps you would find objectionable. Some day I'll probably tell you but not just now. Can't we just go along like we are for awhile?"

"If that's how you want it, but I feel that I know you pretty well. I don't think that you could have done anything that would change my feelings."

"What are your feelings, if it isn't asking too much."

She didn't say anything for what seemed like hours. She had looked away from him and out the window. "I'm not sure, to be honest. I have missed you this last week. I felt something for you from the first time you came into the café. I hadn't thought that way for years. I was in love with Sammy's father. I'm sure you have heard the story. Then I was Nate's wife. He wasn't much, but a bargain is a bargain, and I wasn't in a position to feel anything for another man."

Will didn't say anything.

"Jimmy and I knew each other most of our lives. He was a fine young man. I know that what we felt for each other was love. I think that I will always allow a part of me to love him until the day I die. Can you understand that?" She looked back at Will.

"I think I can. I have never loved any woman before, but I think I love you. Knowing you will always have a secret place in your heart for your first love makes you even more dear to me."

"Many of the qualities I loved in Jimmy, I see in you."

"Really?" Will was gratified.

"Yes, Jimmy loved animals. He would never abuse a horse, a dog, or any other animal, for that matter. He didn't enjoy hunting that much. It was what was required to put meat on the table. Like him, I think you have a soft heart for people too, Buck. He also had a powerful sense of duty and was stubborn, like you are." She paused for a moment. "If he wasn't that way we'd have been married and would have a home where you are living now. Sammy wouldn't be growing up thinking Nate was his father. Instead, we put it off so he could go away to war. That was very costly for Sammy and I'm not sure it's something I want to deal with again. I can't imagine him shooting anyone, but I know that he probably did. I don't see that in you either, although I know that you killed those men in Summit. Were you in the war?"

Will squirmed in the chair. "Yeah, but I only saw a couple years of action. Went in a Private, made it to Sergeant, and came out a wreck. Not a very impressive career. I'd rather not talk about it."

"Oh, I'm sorry, I didn't mean to pry. I was just curious. Forgive me?"

"Of course," Will replied, with relief.

"Is there anything that you'd care to tell me that isn't prying?"

"Well, there isn't much more than you already know. I wish you could meet my brother and his family. He's got a better way with words. I'm nothing special. When I left home I just bummed around. Spent several years down in Texas chasing cattle. Part of the time I was a cook."

"You were a cook?" she asked, laughing. "I can't picture you as a ranch cook. I'm sorry for laughing, really I am. It hurts!"

"Well, the regular cook kept dropping the food on the ground, then picking it up and throwing it back in the pot, but worse than that he used his fingers to squeeze his nose when he blew it and was never, ever, seen washing his hands."

"Oh that's disgusting!" She pretended to throw up.

"Well, we all thought along the same line. I complained about it one time too often. He handed me the spoon and told me that, if I thought I could do better, to have at it. He rolled up his belongings and walked off. I must say that I became a darn fine cook. I don't drop stuff and I wash with soap and water, a lot! When you get your health back, I'll invite you over for dinner."

"I'll take you up on that, Sir." she paused. "Why here? Why did you come to Willow Creek?"

"Maybe I heard about your pies and came out to steal your recipes." he said, laughing.

"You're avoiding the question, aren't you?"

"Yep, you could say that." Will was saved when Sammy burst into the room.

"Hi Buck, I was takin' my nap!"

Will stood, and reaching down lifted him up and held him high in the air. Sammy squealed with delight. "Let's you and me go check on the horses and let your mom get some rest." Will reached down and took Twyla's hand. "You take care of yourself."

"Thanks for stopping by. Come back." She looked up at Will, and for a split second, puckered her lips.

"You can count on it." Yes, he had struck the right note. Keep it light, let her get used to the idea. Let me get used to it too!

Over the next two weeks, Will visited the Pinkham spread at least ten times. The house he'd cared so much about seemed empty. The chores he'd enjoyed, were now a bother. He was aware of the improvement Twyla was making, each time he went over. Her ribs still made dressing and coming downstairs difficult but it wouldn't be long she assured him. The fact that he had a hand in Nate's death made him uncomfortable, especially when he considered his hand in Jimmy's death as well. Somehow, she seemed to sense his reticence.

"Nate wasn't always unlikable," she told him. "In fact, there were times when he could be quite charming. Dot seemed to enjoy his company. At first, that really bothered me but never as much as his drinking. When he got drunk, he turned mean. It brought out the worst in him and no matter how hard I tried, I couldn't get him to stop."

"A man has to make his own decision. Don't ever matter what other people say or think. It's up to him alone. I know, because there was a time when I drank some, but I managed to stop."

"Was it hard to do? Some folks say it's impossible for some to quit."

"It's a terrible story." Will replied, with a touch of dread in his expression. "Just terrible, and unfit to be heard by a woman."

"Oh tell me Buck." She had caught the teasing in the twist of Will's lips. "I have to know."

Will looked doubtful, as though contemplating whether she was up to hearing it. Well I've never told anyone about it, but then again, you're the first person to ask. You sure you're up to hearin' it? I'm not kidding, it is a frightful story. It may give you bad dreams for weeks. I still dream about it from time to time and I wake up in a cold sweat."

She nodded her head and gripped his hand. A look of anticipation was in her eyes.

"Well you asked for it, but don't go a blamin' me if it gits too rough."

"Just don't make me laugh. It hurts my jaw and my ribs. You promise?"

"Dang, woman, this ain't that kind of story." He looked away from her gazing out the window as if girding himself for the telling. A small faked chill went through his body.

Twyla squirmed with delight one hand against her ribs.

"When I was younger, riding for that outfit in Texas, it was customary to ride into town on payday and after a good meal, spend some time washing trail dust out of our throats with a few drinks. You sure you want me to go on?" he asked with a touch of concern.

"Go on!" Twyla said, smiling. "I can stand anything. Tell your story."

Will looked dubious, but proceeded. After a great meal, I stopped by the store and picked me out a new shirt. It was a fine shirt, blue as the sky on a summer day." He stopped as if remembering the shirt. "Anyways, I ended up at the saloon with my friends and they were duly impressed with my purchase. Anyways, we got into some serious drinking." He glanced at Twyla. "I can stop at any time."

"Buck, tell the story!"

With a shrug, Will continued. "As the evening progressed, the crew dwindled away to the point that I was the only one left. Finally I was escorted out of the place by the bartender. I looked for my horse, which I had left outside the saloon, but there were several still there and I wasn't sure which was mine. Wasn't about to be jailed for bein' a horse thief. It came to me that I should find myself a place to catch some shut eye but at that time of night, no one would open the door of either of the two hotels. I wandered around until I come up against a wooden gate. Something evil told me to go inside!" Will shuddered again. Twyla clenched his hand.

"Well, a loop of wire was holdin' the gate, so I lifted it off and went through." Another chill and a horrified look. Squaring his shoulders, he proceeded.

"The ground was wet and sticky but my legs was givin' out so I sits down. About this time my stomach turns over and my teeth start to water."

"Your teeth start to water?"

"Well that's what it feels like. Mouth starts to juice up, some. I started to swallow real fast but it wasn't no use, I could feel everything a comin' up. Came up so fast I didn't have time to turn my head. Up-chucked all over my shirt and down on my pants. Even got some on my boots." He glanced indignantly at Twyla, who had dropped his hand to grip her jaw, as her other hand was supporting her ribs. Tears of muffled laughter rolled down her cheeks.

"I fall back in what I thought was mud, but it ain't mud. It's chicken poop!" Twyla bent over, shaking her head.

"I better stop. Here I am tellin' about a near death experience and you're a laughin'. Where is your compassion woman?"

"Go on. Go on," she gasped as she took a small hanky from the table by the bed and blotted her face.

"Well if you insist. Where was I? Oh yeah. I'm on my back in chicken poop, lookin' up at the stars when, all of a sudden, I'm eye to eye with the meanest lookin' chicken I've ever seen. She commences to attack me, peckin' at the up-chuck. Within seconds she was joined by several dozen more of her insidious pack and I'm bein' pecked to death! They's a scratchin" and peckin', and makin' a terrible ruckus. I start screamin' and kickin' but it don't do no good. Just riles them up more. Suddenly I see the light. I'd heard about people that had died but come back. They mention seein' the light and feeling warm and at peace. Well I seen it, but all I felt was a thousand killer beaks tearing at my body, not to mention my new blue shirt. It was as blue as…….."

Twyla sighed in exasperation.

"Anyways, I know that I'm a goner, no doubt about it. No man big enough to whup them killers. They was a fearful bunch. Blood in their eyes, not to mention them beaks." He looked over at Twyla and rolled his eye.

She burst out laughing, holding her jaw and ribs again.

Suddenly, them chickens was gone, and I'm a looking' into the face of an old man a holdin' a lantern and wavin' a stick. For a second, I figure I've been saved, but after chasing off them chickens, he starts a whackin' me."

"'Damn good fer nothin' chicken thief!' He yells, and he whacks me some more. I manage to git on my hands and knees and make a beeline for the gate. He whacks my butt several more times before I get out."

"'Ya done upset my chickens! Probably won't lay for a week', he yelled, shakin' his stick."

"I don't argue the point. I'm on my feet a runnin' and bouncin' off walls, trees and Lord knows what."

"'Ya keep out of my chicken pen!' The old man throws a rock in my direction but missed."

"I promised myself that I would sure do that."

Twyla was nearly overcome with laughter.

I find my horse but she don't want anything as bad smellin' as me on her. No way can I git my boot in the stirrup. I spend the night in a haystack behind the stable. Next morning, I look at myself in the window glass of the store and don't much like what I see lookin' back at me. My head hurts, not to mention a thousand chicken pecks, and my mouth tastes like a buzzard's nest. I rustle my old shirt out of the garbage bin and after some help from the townsfolk, manage to git on my horse. After lookin' death in the face and survivin' I am now cold sober. Haven't had a drop of whiskey since. Well except for a few on the train at the end of the war. No more of that for me. I'm cured. Some day, when you are up to it, I'll tell you why I don't smoke."

Twyla threw a small pillow at him. "Lordy, Buck, go home! Keep this up and I'll never get better." She pulled the quilt over her face to stifle her laughter. Pulling it down to see over the top, she watched as Will paused at the door, with a look of abject sorrow in his expression.

"I almost died a horrible death at the beaks of killer chickens and you think it's funny." He put his hat on, low over his eye, so that he had to lean his head back to see her. He stuck his tongue out, then turned and left. She was still laughing as he rode out the gate and turned towards home.

He knew that he loved her and hoped fervently that it would be enough to hold him here. He meant for her to be safe as long as she lived and once the commitment was made he would have to stay to keep her that way, like it or not. He remembered how he had loved his folks too, but it had not been enough to keep him at home, even with the help of the stump.

He had to give her time to get over her losses and find the person she was meant to be. Then, before he could ask her to marry him he had to tell her everything about Jimmy. She would know him as a person by then and include that knowledge into her decision. He smiled at her reaction to his story. She would be surprised to know that it was all true.

Will did not return for a week. Her questions had made him uneasy. He shared his thoughts with John Henry, but he didn't have any answers either.

During the week Will took a ride out to the Baldon ranch. He needed to talk to Cap for Twyla.

"Welcome, Buck. Come on in." Cap waved his hand toward the ranch house. "I haven't heard from Mrs. Baldon. I've been thinking of riding over there to see if I still have a job. I hate to bother her though if she's still feelin' poorly. Maybe she'll want to sell. You hear anything?"

"That's why I'm here, Cap. She wants you boys to stay on. I've brought the pay for you and the men, and there will be a bonus for you in the spring. I have complete faith in your integrity and abilities and so does Twyla. She hasn't thought past spring, but she'll let you know as soon as she's decided. It's a beautiful ranch and she loves it and knows you'll take care of it as you always have."

Cap didn't know what to say. He couldn't remember a time he had received a compliment on his work. He didn't think he deserved one, after the fool he had been. He owed Buck a lot. Strange, how one man could make such a difference in his attitude toward life and other people. It made him feel good when he rode into town now and folks waved and smiled and took time to talk to him, even to ask for his opinion on things.

"You tell her not to worry about anything. We'll take care of the cattle. Some of the boys are braiding a new bridle for her. They are real sorry to be connected with a man that would do that to a nice woman like her. He paid us and we just followed him along like sheep and that's a damned hard thing for a cattle man to admit!"

"Sounds like a nice thing for them to do. I'm sure she'll appreciate it. That reminds me." Will added. "There is a sizeable piece of range between my ranch house and the cliff. I'd guess that the snow is much thinner in there. I reckon you have used it before, and I want you to know that it's available if you need it. Oh! I hear you lost a hand. Let me know if you need some help."

"Yep, Seth decided to give the store a try. I figure he should do alright. Be nice for him to be there with his sisters. I don't think he had much of a future punchin' cows."

Seth was up really early. He walked into the store, and looked at it from the perspective of a proprietor. He was excited. He took down the blue apron that Nate always wore and put it on. He looked at himself in the mirror that hung near the dress material. He looked good, he thought. He hadn't really been happy at the ranch and though he realized that he didn't know much about running a store, he knew Twyla and Melinda would help him get started. The folks had been helping Melinda run the store and restaurant to the detriment of their own place. So when, two weeks after Nate died, Twyla mentioned the possibilities of him taking over in the store, he jumped at the chance. They had sat up 'til two in the morning, going over plans. Seeing as how he was strong enough to handle the bigger merchandise and being as he was good with figures he would be in charge of that part of the operation and would help with any lifting or bouncing that needed doing for the restaurant. Melinda would take charge of the restaurant with her mother and Twyla to help whenever and wherever needed. Twyla would have a lot more time for Sammy, and she wanted time to get her life together.

The following afternoon, the stage arrived with a small bundle of mail, which Ernie brought over to Seth. "Guess you're the new Postmaster, now that Nate is gone."

"I suppose I am," Seth replied, with a feeling of pride. "I intend to do a good job, too." Taking the bundle into the small room that served as the post office, he dumped the mail onto the sorting table. He had some experience from helping out a few times and the store was empty. After everything was sorted into the boxes, he had one letter, to a fellow that had moved on, left over. He had no forwarding address so he decided to put it in the dead letter drawer. There were more than two dozen letters in the bottom of the drawer and as he still had no customers, he decided to alphabetize them. He was surprised to find three letters to Twyla. He read the opened letter from W. Morgan. It had the oldest postmark. Another one from Morgan was sealed. The other one from someone named Turner was opened too, so he read them and found that this man and his friend were coming to Willow Creek. That Nate! What business did he have holding out Twyla's mail. He needed some advice. He knew he should give them to Twyla, but thought he'd better talk to John first. John was a man of little education but with a wagon load of common sense. He placed the sign in the window, letting folks know that he would be back shortly and crossed the street. Entering the stables, he saw John working on a saddle. "If you have a few minutes, I need some advice."

"Advice is one thing I never run out of, Seth. What do you want to know?"

He explained the letters, and was surprised when John said that he knew W. Morgan.

"Well, I promised I would keep the secret, but maybe it's time I tol' somebody. Don't think it'll keep much longer anyhow. Buck is Will Morgan. He was Jimmy's best friend and was with him when he died. It was somethin' he didn't want to talk about, you can understand that. He promised Jimmy that he would look after Twyla. Let her know Jimmy loved her to the end, that sorta thing. Don't know why he ain't told her, but I guess he has his reasons. Maybe he's just a waitin' for the right time, I don't know."

"If that's the case, what do I do? I think he's in love with her. That may be why he hasn't told her yet. I know he has a good reason. He wouldn't hurt her for the world. So, where does that leave me?"

"The way I'm a thinkin', maybe the best thing to do is nothin'. I mean, the letters have been there for some time, and maybe just leavin' them there for a little longer won't make no difference. That third letter, from that other fellow, I'd say give her that one."

Much relieved to have shared the problem, Seth put the two letters back in the drawer, and after work, took the third letter out to Twyla.

Climbing the stairs to her bedroom, he found her just finishing brushing her hair. With it down he could see the thin places where Nate had torn some of it out but you couldn't see them when she had it put up. The swelling was gone, and her face was almost back to normal though her nose was maybe not quite as straight. Seth thought that he had the best and the best looking sisters a man could have. He walked over and kissed her on the cheek. "Found this in the dead file Sis, thought you might want it." He handed her the letter.

After reading it, she handed it to him to read. "So, Jimmy is really dead. Somehow, I always hoped that he was alive somewhere. I wanted him to see Sammy." Tears welled up in her eyes.

"Well, maybe these two men will be able to tell us something." Giving her a hug, he left the room in search of his mother and a snack.

When Melinda came home, Twyla showed her the letter as well. "I'm so sorry, Sis. I guess it's best to know for certain, but I know it isn't easy. I wonder when they'll show up?"

Their conversation turned to Will, as it almost always did. Neither could figure out why he was so secretive about his past. Every time Twyla would try to pin him down, he would politely leave. Did it have to do with the two men he killed? Maybe there were others. She couldn't imagine him doing anything against the law. Whatever it was, he was afraid of how it would affect her opinion of him. Would she think less of him if there were more killings? She had strong feelings for Will. Was it love? She really didn't know yet. He had a way of making her heart race when he came into the room. They had reached the kissing stage of their relationship, and she found that she enjoyed it immensely. He never mentioned seeing her naked, or sneaking a kiss when she was asleep. She knew he was thinking of it just the same. Could she love a gunman? She went over all of her feelings with Melinda. They had no secrets.

"Well, I think he's exciting," Melinda remarked, with conviction.

"I'm afraid I don't want excitement. I just want to settle down with someone and make a life for Sammy. Maybe even have more children. I never want to leave this valley and Nate has done one thing for me. Man or no man, I can do what I want."

"Just the same, If he was a little younger, or I was a little older, I would give you a fight for him. I like the feeling of danger. At times, I wish that I had been the one naked in that bed."

Twyla hit her with a pillow off the bed. "You are a hussy! How you talk!"

"The same as you, big Sister."

They laughed.

27

REUNION

Del and Jack had a visitor when they returned to their tent.

"Howdy, Gents. My name is Fletcher, and I do believe that I am here to replace one Del Trenton."

"That would be me," replied Del, as he took in the gangly young man holding the surveying papers he had left on his small folding table.

"Then you must be Jack." He offered his hand to each of them. "Seems you boys have earned yourself some time off. I'll be spelling you for a month. My guard is on his way, and should be here tomorrow. You're free to go anytime."

"In that case," Jack said, "goodbye. We're gone." They said their good-byes to the rest of the surveying crew and promised that they would be back at the end of a month.

Within an hour, they were packed up and headed on back towards end-of-track some hundred and twenty miles away. It'll be nice, Del thought, to sleep in a real bed again. There were times that he wished he had a regular job with a home to go to at the end of the day. He sure missed the company of a woman, and that was a fact.

It took them seven days to reach end-of-track, and to the disappointment of both, the ladies and their tents of pleasure were long gone. They took a quick look inside the three-decked sleeping cars that housed the workers and decided to tent it one more night. The idea of sleeping with so many men in such a confined space brought back too many memories. They did, however, take advantage of the chow car, which consisted of a regular boxcar with a table extending the entire length. Tin plates were nailed to the table. Workers shuffled in from one end and stood by a plate. Food was delivered on platters set down on the center of the table. The coffee came in buckets. The men filled the plate in front of them and their own cup and ate standing as quickly as possible to make room for the next shift. Upon completion of their generous meal, they departed at the other end of the car. Whereupon the swampers came in and washed out the plates where they were. Jack was impressed with how smoothly the process worked, and there was plenty of food, but he was not impressed with the quality.

They contacted the engineer and were given permission to ride the train back to a maintenance station within fifty miles of Summit. There they could unload their horses and ride into Summit where they could catch the stage that would take them on in to Willow Creek.

They had discussed their plan for weeks, and the month off was plenty of time to look up Twyla and make sure that she was alright and still catch a train back to see Del's folks. Neither was looking forward to the tears and sorrow that they brought. Jimmy's folks had probably gotten word from the Army about his death, but they had to make sure. They thought that his mom and dad would probably want to hear the circumstances surrounding his death. They hadn't decided on what to say regarding Will, if anything.

Riding into Summit, they stopped at the livery stable and made arrangements to have the horses boarded until they came back from Willow Creek.

"Seems like a real nice town," Del exclaimed, looking up and down the main street.

"Sort of quiet, though, ain't it?" Jack added. He had noticed only two saloons on the main drag and only one horse tethered outside the smaller of the two. Riders were keeping their horses to a walk and several women were strolling along the boardwalk.

"Well, we git our share of excitement, from time to time," the stable man chimed in. "Seen a few dandy shootouts, standin' right where you fellers are. Best one, was just last spring. One-eyed gent comes ridin' in. Don't recall his name. Got the most beautiful set of grays these eyes ever seen."

Del and Jack exchanged looks.

"Yessir, fine animals. Anyways, we had us a couple of no-goods, runnin' things for a spell. Shot up the sheriff and kinda' took over. Anyhow, this fella takes 'em both on and kills 'em dead. I don't think they had a chance against him for all his bein' half blind, and that's what he was with only one eye. Wasn't he? Then there was the one...Oh, I remember, feller's name was Buck."

His reminiscence was too late as Del and Jack were already heading over to the cafe. They had heard enough. Seems as though their benefactor had come this way.

Ernie was glad to see the two men climb into the stage. He never liked makin' the run alone. He was a little ahead of schedule, so it would be an easy trip. The thick horse blanket felt good on his butt and the buffalo robe kept out the cold. He pulled the brim of his old hat down to shield his face from the wind, and gripping the reins with a new pair of gloves, he kicked off the brake and with a "hee-yah" headed the team out of town. He was looking forward to a good meal and a warm bed in Willow Creek.

Del and Jack did not talk much on the way. Being together for so long, there wasn't a lot to talk about. They did discuss the stranger and the gray horses, however.

That evening, they arrived and found the town nestled in the most beautiful valley they had seen in some time. John, as usual, met the stage. Chief was with him.

Seeing the two standing there, Del asked if either knew a Twyla Pinkham.

"Sure do," replied John. "What you want with her?" His tone was guarded.

"We were good friends of Jimmy Compton. We just want to pay our respects."

"In that case, turn around and walk about forty paces. She's in the cafe, over there."

"I will lead the way," replied Chief, looking very solemn. "Follow me."

Del and Jack exchanged grins, then fell in, obediently, behind the old Indian. John watched them go into the restaurant, and thought about his promise to Will. He suspected that they just might be the two friends he had talked about. On the other hand, he didn't know for sure, and he gave his word that their talk would be just between them. He hadn't wanted to tell Seth, but their letter was an unexpected complication. Later on he had put off telling Buck because he would have to admit that he had told Seth that he was Will Morgan. He hadn't even mentioned it to Chief. Why hadn't he just told the boy to put all the letters back and forget them. He decided to just let it ride, for the time being.

Entering the cafe, the Indian announced their presence. "Twyla, two pale faces here to see you." Chief pointed to Twyla.

"Thanks Chief. What can I do for you gentlemen?" Twyla asked.

"My name is Jack Turner. I was a friend of Jimmy Compton. I wrote you a letter."

"My name is Del Trenton. I wrote you also, about a year ago. We never heard from you and decided we should make sure you were alright," Del added.

"Oh, Mr. Turner, I just received your letter a few days ago. It's a long story, but it was lost for a spell. I'm so sorry. I did get your letter Mr. Trenton and I was very grateful for your concern and I did answer it. Perhaps it was lost in the mail." Twyla hoped she didn't sound a complete fool. She thought, it's a good thing you're dead Nate Baldon or I'd kill you here and now!

Twyla indicated a table and they all sat down. "You were his friends. She gripped their hands. Tell me everything. Please."

"Are Jimmy's parents still here abouts?" Jack asked.

"Oh yes, they are about two miles away. Would you like to meet them?"

"We sure would, ma'am. After listening to Jimmy talk about you folks for so long, we feel like we already know you. I may add, ma'am, that your picture didn't do you justice," Del said with a wide smile.

"Picture?" Twyla inquired. "Oh I remember, it was in a little case. Jimmy took it with him when he left."

"That was the one." Jack replied. "If we could head over to the Compton's, we could fill you all in at once. I hope you'll understand. Going over it once is about all we're up to. Can you leave the cafe?"

"Sure, my brother is in the store, he can help out." She told Seth about the two strangers.

"Sure Sis. We'll talk when you get back." He had the feeling that Buck's secret was about to be exposed. He hoped that everything would turn out alright for him. If he could close the store, he could ride out and warn Buck, but he had several customers and they'd be sure to need him in the café over the dinner hour.

They crossed the street and, with help from Del and Jack, John soon had the buggy ready. Huddled against the cold, with Twyla in the middle, they headed out of town.

Del was going over in his mind what he would say once they reached the ranch. He really hadn't known Jimmy as well as he had known Will. He was gone from their company so soon. He remembered his youth and cheerfulness in the face of adversity and his bravery against the Raiders and against the pain he had endured. He and Will had been friends before prison and had stuck together while he and Jack had sort of done the same. He had so admired Will and gotten to know him better after Jimmy's death. Jack was shy about taking the center of attention but he might be some help. After all, Del was the one blessed with the gift of gab, and there was nothing about Jimmy that would have made his parents less than proud.

"Wouldn't mind seeing the spread that you and Jimmy were workin' on." Del bent down to speak in her ear, over the noise of the wind, and buggy wheels. "Heard a lot about it." He breathed in the smell of soap and woman.

"It's over there," she said, pointing. "A man by the name of Buck is staying there for the winter, but I'm sure he wouldn't mind visitors."

Miles was alerted to the approaching buggy by the barking dog. The three occupants were so bundled up that he didn't recognize any of them. Didn't get much company out here, particularly this time of year. He smiled as he saw Twyla push back the hood of her coat. God, he wished she were his daughter-in-law.

She stepped over the legs of the shorter man and jumped down. "Dad, these men knew Jimmy." She always called him Dad and Verna, Mom.

"Come in, come in," Miles insisted. "Go tell Mom that we need some hot coffee Twyla." Both men climbed down and shook hands.

"Can't tell you how glad we are to meet you after all this time," Del said, with a grin. Miles led the horse over to the small lean-to for protection.

Once inside the house, they took off their heavy coats and piled them on the floor in front of the stove. Miles brought in two chairs from the bedroom. The excitement at meeting these men who had been close to Jimmy brought tears to his eyes.

Seated around the dinner table with steaming cups of coffee, Del started the story. "Let me start off by telling you that he was one of the best friends we have ever had. We met him in Andersonville prison, down in Georgia and I doubt if either I, or Jack, would have made it out alive, without his help. Jimmy and his sidekick, pulled us through. They taught us how to survive. Those without friends to cheer them up in that place, didn't last long. Between those two, there was never a dull moment. I can't really put in to words how important that was to us. It would sound silly to repeat one of their jokes or stories, here in the warmth and plenty of your kitchen. But there, well, they kept us sane, that's all. He talked of you and his home here all the time, and you were all on his mind when he passed on. I think he was at peace with himself, at the end."

Miles asked, "How did it happen? I mean, how did he come to die?" He had a hard time getting the words out but he felt that he had to know the answer.

Seeing that Del was hard put to answer, Jack took over. He described the prison conditions and told them about the Raiders. He told of Jimmy getting jumped and beaten by the man named Rooster and of the theft of the picture. He could see Miles clench his fists. This was not easy, Jack thought. "Anyhow, the arm got worse and worse, and it was decided we had to let them take it off." Verna moaned, tears streaming down her cheeks. Twyla, was also in tears. Miles and Del looked at their laps to hide their emotions.

"Maybe you ought not to hear this," Jack said, softly.

"No, if my boy went through all this, we have a duty to know about it," Miles replied. His throat was getting choked up. He gripped Verna's hand, his arm around her shoulders.

"They took off the arm, but it got infected. He had less than a week to live, as best we could guess. He knew exactly what he was in for and he gave his chances a lot of thought, believe me, it was no whim. In the end he asked Will to help him along when the pain got too bad." Jack faltered to a stop.

"Will? What was his last name?" Twyla asked.

"Morgan," Del answered.

That was the name Buck had asked her about. How did he know this Will Morgan? she wondered. What was the connection?

"What do you mean by help him along?" Miles asked softly.

Del spoke again, his voice low, punctuated by a small catch now and then. "Well Sir. They had talked it all out for days before but by the time he got real bad the talk was over. Jimmy had said he wasn't afraid of dying, but wanted to go quick. I think Will helped him go quick." It was hard telling them. Harder even that he had anticipated. He wished that he had never brought up Will. How could they ever understand how brave and noble an act it was. How could they see what it had done to Will.

"You're not sure?" Miles asked. His eyes locked on Del's, waiting for an answer.

"No Sir, they were talkin' about it, so we said our good-byes and left. When we got back, Jimmy had gone. Will was holding him in his arms and crying. He held him all night, like that." Del couldn't force himself to tell them that he had witnessed the death.

Everyone was quiet, for a few minutes, thinking of the last moments of their Jimmy's life, and of his best friend holding him gently, throughout the night.

Miles looked up and asked, "Whatever happened to Will?"

It was easier for Del to go on, now the worst was over. "He passed on too. But I must tell you about his fight with Rooster. He fought him with a skillet. He sharpened the point of a damned skillet handle and called him out. Sorry, Ladies. Please excuse my language. Never saw anything like it before, or since. Skin and bones, he was, and taken' on a man the size of Rooster was crazy. We tried to talk him out of it, but he couldn't live with the idea that Rooster had killed his friend and stolen Twyla's picture. Jimmy carried it around his neck in a pouch, with Will's harmonica."

Twyla gasped. As Del was talking, her mind was going over all the little things that had made no sense to her; he knew her birthday, her favorite color, the name of her horse, and he had inquired about Will Morgan. The final thing was the harmonica. "Dad, get that picture of Jimmy and his friend."

Miles gave her a puzzled look, but got up from the table and took the picture off a small shelf. He came back and handed it to Twyla. She peered hard at the smiling face of Jimmy's friend. Could it be? There was a resemblance. "Are you sure he's dead?" she asked. Her heart was pounding. Buck was Will Morgan, and this was the secret? It just had to be. The pencil writing on the back of the picture was smudged and unreadable, but the first letter looked like a "W". She had wondered about the man with Jimmy from time to time. Serious eyes, but with a small grin. Both men were holding their pistols in a posed position.

"He was blown up on a boat on the way to the hospital at Annapolis. Several people said they saw his body."

"I think they were wrong," Twyla exclaimed, excitedly, "I think he is alive and right here. A man came here last spring, calling himself Buck. Rode straight to the ranch, and then over here. He told me that he was from Iowa and had spent four years in the war. Said he had been injured at the close of the war. He mentioned a brother. And finally, he plays a harmonica. A while back, he asked me if I had ever heard of Will Morgan. I told him no. He seemed surprised. But what if he had written me, like you did and I never got the letter? Would that be reason to change his name?" Twyla was talking rapidly, fitting all the unanswered questions into the puzzle.

Del and Jack looked stunned. Could Will still be alive?

"Can you tell us anything more about him?" Del implored. "Anything at all?"

She handed the small picture to Del. "He is about five foot seven, has dark brown hair, almost black, and dark brown eyes. He looks like the man in the picture. And he also knew the name of my horse."

"You talkin' about Bell?" Jack inquired.

"Yes, he knew her name. He wears a patch over one eye and has some scars on his face, and on his chest and back." She blushed at the implication. "I just can't tell by looking at this picture."

"Well that might be Will Morgan in the picture. I can't be sure either, 'cause he had a beard when we knew him. He wasn't in near that shape by then neither," Jack mused.

"Can you take us to the ranch, Twyla? We need to know, one way or the other, if this fellow Buck is our Will," Del asked.

"I knew there was somethin' about him," Miles exclaimed. "Knew it the first time we talked about the war. Should've come right out and told us about Jimmy, We woulda' understood." He shook has head. I knew there was somethin' about him, Miles told himself. Just knew it.

Five minutes later, the three were on their way. The Comptons were planning to follow as soon as the chores could be done and their buggy hitched up. Verna said she would bring something for them all to eat. Del was keeping the horse at a brisk trot. The impulse to gallop all the way was hard to put down. Don't get your hopes up too much. It could all be a mistake. He told himself that, but it didn't work. It just had to be Will.

Will was out in the barn when the horse and buggy entered the yard. Standing in the open door he knew the small figure in the middle was Twyla. He smiled as she swept off the hood. His eyes were only on her.

She jumped down and before he knew what was happening, she threw herself into his arms. "Thank you, Will, for being Jimmy's friend." She kissed him. Before he could realize what was going on, the taller man was down from the buggy and had grabbed him in a bear hug and swung him around like a rag doll. Del set him down and held him at arms length. He would have recognized Will anywhere. Will looked into Del's face in amazement.

By then Jack was at his side with a hug of his own. As he hung on to the two of them he gasped, "Del! Jack! Where did you come from? I didn't think I'd ever see you two again."

"We knew that we'd never see you again, 'cause we were told that you were dead. And here you are," Jack retorted, grinning.

"Let me shut the barn door, then we have a lot to talk about. Run the buggy inside, Jack."

Jack climbed into the rig and guided the horse into the barn. Glancing into the stalls, he yelled, "Del, come here. You gotta see this."

Del looked in the barn and saw the two mares. "Damnation, Will, you saved us from an Indian attack, over on the Platte. We were with the survey crew! We were within twenty yards of your tent."

"Don't that just about beat all," Will replied "So close. Let's go in, it's a might chilly out here. I saw you boys heading out to work that morning. You weren't more than a hundred and fifty yards away."

Del and Jack almost carried Will, while Twyla followed, happy to be forgotten in their happiness.

Suddenly, Will was much more to her than just Buck. It was hard to imagine him being with Jimmy, all those years. And yes, that he had helped Jimmy die. How does one end the life of a friend? The hands that had saved her and Sammy from the snow were also the hands that had ended Jimmy's life. Also the life of the man named Rooster and those two gunmen in Summit. She felt a small chill run down her back.

As there would not be enough chairs for so many people once the

Comptons arrived, Jack and Will went back out to the barn to find some more seating. While they were gone, Twyla studied Del. He towered over everyone by at least five or six inches, which would make him stand out in any crowd, but what intrigued Twyla, were his eyes. They were the kindest eyes she had ever seen. Kind eyes? They reminded her of a large, gentle dog. He had a long face, with a thick mustache, curled up on the ends, which partially covered a mouth with a smile that made her feel warm. A small chip on his front upper tooth added a little something to the overall look. She decided that he was a very handsome man. His hands were large but delicate, and he moved with a slow, yet graceful manner. He squatted in front of the fireplace, waiting for Jack and Will to return. She also noticed that he carried no gun. He was looking at her.

"Don't this just beat everything. Finding Will alive, after thinking him dead, all this time. And to meet all you folks that Jimmy told us about. It just all seems too good to be true. And Will looks so good. I mean he was almost dead from starvation the last time we saw him. I doubt he weighed more than eighty pounds. Sure sorry that he had that accident on the boat. He should have been with us." Del was clutching his hat brim, and rotating the hat excitedly. Twyla had an impulse to walk over and hug him.

The door opened and Will came in carrying two boxes. He told them that the Comptons had arrived and would be right in. Jack trailed in behind with a wide plank and a crude bench was set up against the wall. Del stood and took a place on the bench with Jack. Will sat in between them. All were grinning. "Just like old times," Jack said with a laugh. He squeezed Will's knee.

Twyla opened the door for Miles and Verna whose hands were full of baskets and pots of food. Twyla and Verna began to set them out on the table and put some to warm while Miles greeted Will who had risen from the bench. He shook his hand and then embraced him speechlessly. Will's relief was evident and when Verna joined her husband in an equally understanding embrace his fears evaporated. The couple sat on two adjoining chairs where they could hold one another's hand and enjoy the reunion.

I just can't get over you being alive, after all this time. I mean we heard that you were seen layin' with a bunch of the boys that were killed. He said that he saw the pouch." Twyla noticed the tears in Del's eyes, as he spoke. It tugged at her heart.

"That was me," Will replied, "but Old Scruff noticed that I was still breathing, and made a big fuss. Doc came over and checked me out. Took me to his place and fixed me up."

"Who is Scruff?" asked Verna.

"Doc's old dog. I must say that he was a fine dog. Sure wouldn't mind havin' a dog like him. How he figured I was still alive, I don't know, but Doc said if I had laid there until the boat came to pick up the bodies, I would have bled out."

"That explains you not showing up at the hospital. We waited for over a week, but decided that if you were alive, you would have shown up by then. We didn't think about you maybe gettin' help elsewhere," Jack replied. He squeezed Will's knee again.

"Now that you know what happened to me, what have you boys been up to since I saw you last?" Will asked.

The evening passed quickly. Twyla and Verna served dinner while the three friends talked. Miles was content to just sit and listen to them and realize that they were Jimmy's best friends. He could not have had better ones. He was sure of it. It wouldn't be a manly thing to do, but he had the desire to hold Will in his arms and to thank him for being there for his son. He was relieved when it came time to leave and Verna did it for him.

28

SEAN'S REVENGE

Sean returned to his cell and spent the next week dwelling on Stick's death. He just couldn't seem to get it through his head that his brother was dead. He wanted to get it straight from Mike Sullivan's mouth. He expected him to show up that next weekend, but he waited in vain. The next weekend passed and the next, without his expected visitor. After a month, Sean gave up anticipating his arrival. Thirteen more months dragged by.

He was awakened by the sound of the guard inserting the key in the cell door. He swung his legs off the filthy mattress and rubbed the sleep from his eyes. 'Now what?' he thought.

"Times up, O'Grady. Get your things together and step out here, and turn around."

As Sean had no things, he stepped out of the cell and turned around. He was a little surprised to feel the cuffs. Why would he try to escape, when he was being let out? Damned fools. The guard followed him at a discreet distance, directing him down the hallway, and through several doors, finely ending in a small room with a single table. A clerk was waiting and motioned Sean to the box on the table. The cuffs were removed and the guard headed toward the door.

"Give you five minutes," the guard said. He stopped to give Sean one more distasteful stare and left the room.

When the clerk left, Sean dumped the box out and recognized the clothes he had been wearing when arrested. He ripped off the offensive prison garb and put on the clothes of his previous life. They were a little large, as he had lost some weight, but they felt good. The socks and shoes brought a smile to his face. He buffed the shoes with the prison shirt, and saw a slight shine. He put his hand in the pants pocket and was surprised to find five dollars and his pocket-knife. He had assumed that the guards would have stolen them. As he was straightening up, the guard returned and ushered him out a door, into a large court yard. He remembered it from when he arrived eighteen months before.

He paused, letting his eyes adjust to the bright sunlight. Although it was still early morning, the sun made him squint. Too damn long in the dark, he thought. Another guard stood at a small gate, built into the larger wagon gate, and waved him over. The escort gave the gate guard a paper and he read it slowly, pausing to look Sean over, from time to time. Satisfied that he was the one the paper described, he unlocked the gate and stood back. Sean passed through. He heard the key lock the gate behind him. "Get a life for yourself, O'Grady. Don't come back here," the escort yelled. Sean didn't bother to answer.

An hour later, he entered the pool hall. The familiar smells and sounds were almost overpowering. As his eyes adjusted to the smoke and poor lighting, he saw several old friends, and heard a yell from Que, who scurried across the room and grabbed Sean by the arm.

"Sean, me boy. By God almighty, yer back. Hey boys, Sean! He's back!" Several came over to slap his back and make small talk but Sean soon got Que aside.

"And where the hell would Sullivan be? He never showed."

"He's dead. Got drunk, he did, and tried to muscle in on someone else's woman. Got shot dead. I wanted to come and tell ya, but I got no stomach for that place. I git bad dreams for a month a'fore I go, and two months after I git away. Honest Sean, I wanted to come."

"Well, I'll be a doubtin' ifn' you coulda added ta what ya told me, so no harm done" Sean replied. Que was almost in tears. He was clenching and unclenching his hands.

"Sean, ya gotta meet this fella over here. He knows about Stick. No way was he goin' to visit that prison, but he'll tell ya what ya want to know. Follow me." They threaded their way around the pool players to a table in the corner. "This here is Mole. Mole, this here is Stick's little brother, Sean."

Sean looked at the thin, pocked face, and the pale beady blue eyes that shifted back and forth refusing to lock onto his. The small mouth, puckered into a toothy smile, revealed gaps on each side of his front teeth. Sean would have been amazed at how many prisoners had died because of this little man. How many he had marked for death for a trinket, a button, or anything else of value. The stranger seemed to shrink as he took in Sean's size and condition.

"Who?" he asked.

Sean snarled. "You, by Gawd, better not be givin me any horse shit."

"Stick? Oh yeh, you talkin' about Rooster. He changed his name to Rooster when he got hisself a fancy hat with a feather," Mole explained. He looked at Sean, and felt the same fear that he'd felt with Rooster. They were a lot alike, with the same mean eyes. "He was a damned fine man. A good friend of mine. Everyone liked Rooster. "Barkeep," he yelled, "Beers over here." He felt he owed it to Rooster to be here, but he warn't liken' it a'tall.

"What the hell happened?" Sean demanded. His voice was almost a whisper.

"Rooster had got hisself a mouth organ and a picture of a woman from some fella. Thumped him pretty good. A couple days later, the fella up and dies. Word gits around some friend of his wants the stuff back, and he calls Rooster out. By God, I seen it all. Calls him out and calls him a bunch of bad stuff. They git into a ruckus and this here fella sticks him with a pot handle."

"A pot handle?" Sean was incredulous. "Didn't Stick have no weapon?"

"He had hisself a knife and a club, but they didn't do no good. This fella waren't real big and he just sneaks in between 'em and sticks him," Mole explained. "Nothin' we could do to help him. He was dead in a couple seconds. Damn fine man, Ol' Rooster."

"Killed with a damn pot handle." Sean was having a hard time visualizing the fight. "You catch the name of this here fella?"

"Will Morgan. Yessir, that were his name. Will Morgan. I made danged sure I wouldn't forget it. I knowed Rooster had him a brother. I figured you'd want to know. We tried to kill that skunk, a time or two, but he had too many people 'round 'im."

"What happened to 'im? Ya know?"

"Don't know. Never seen him agin after we left Andersonville. But I won't forget the name or the face of that man. Nope. Never will, and that's a fact."

"You know any way of trackin' him down?" Sean said with intensity. "I need to find him."

Mole thought for several minutes.

Sean sipped his luke-warm beer and watched him closely.

Mole finally looked at Sean with a sly smile. "Far as I know, all them that was in Andersonville come up through Annapolis, an when we got our money, they took our name and where we was from. Ifn' he come through there, well, he'd a had to a give em his home town."

"Where the hell is this here Annapolis?"

"Train people would know," Mole replied. "Yep, they'd be able to tell ya."

Sean stood and walked to the pool table in the middle of the room. Brushing aside the pool players, he dropped down on hands and knees and disappeared under the table. His hand searched for the hole, just above the middle leg, and felt the roll of green backs that he had left there. Backing out, he stood and held the wad up for all to see. "Sorry boys, but I had to visit me bank." Jamming the money in his pocket, he left the pool hall. The only thing on his mind was finding Will Morgan.

A week later, Sean entered the army hospital at Annapolis. A haircut, trimmed beard and new clothes had transformed him into what appeared to be a gentleman, all except for the cruel scowl on his face.

"Can I be of assistance?" asked a young private.

Sean turned. He disliked the spit and polished look of the young man, but hid his true feelings.

"Why I shur hope so, laddie," Sean replied, with a smile. He had been working on the *new Sean* image as he traveled down from the north. "I'll be a looking' for a very good friend a mine, from Andersonville days, lost contact after we was released. It's purty important that I find him, if he lived through them last few terrible months. I was told that all the released prisoners would a gone through here and I remember me a givin' me home town to the paymaster."

"Let me direct you to the Paymaster's office."

An hour later, Sean left the hospital. A tight smile was on his face. It was working out just like he planned it. Will Morgan, Cedar Rapids, Iowa. Next, he thought, is git a gun.

Sean was enjoying the train trip west. Although he was around twenty-five, he'd never been out of New York City. He had played it smart by laying low during the war years. He'd had no intention of gettin' shot, even if the chance was small. Stick had gone for the easy money of "standin'-in." The threat of getting shot soldiering, or getting caught deserting hadn't bothered him. True, Sean had ended up in jail anyway, but it wasn't a military jail, and there had been no threat of a firing squad. In the end, Stick was dead and he was alive.

As the train sped along through constantly new country, Sean gave his brother a lot of thought. They had been forced out on the streets when Mom died. They had no idea of who their father was, or if, in fact, they shared the same father. They took the name O'Grady, because it belonged to someone important. He couldn't remember now, just who the person was, or why he was important. Times had been hard and many a night they had spent curled up together in a packing box to keep from freezing. Most times food was hard to come by and it seemed that he was always hungry. It was like that until his brother was big enough to take what they wanted.

As his mind drifted back to those dark days, some of his memories still gave him trouble, but he told himself that they did what they had to do to stay alive.

One memory, that he wished he could forget, still left a sick feeling in the pit of his stomach. Stick had learned that it was payday at the large garment factories and it should be easy to snatch a pay envelope, or two. Sean had not given it much thought, at the time. Stick was the boss.

They had lurked in an alley next to the back door and watched the girls leaving the building. Many were laughing and chatting, while some were discussing what they intended to do with their pay. They waited until most had passed by. Stick suddenly reached out and jerked one of the girls who was walking alone into the alley. Quickly, he grabbed her money and flung her to the ground. As they sprinted down the alley, Sean could hear the girl crying, and he made the mistake of looking back at the pitiful creature. He had to really run to catch up to Stick.

"Three bucks, little brother. Not bad for a few minutes work." He waved the money in Sean's face and they ran down the next street laughing. Two days later, the building burned down and eighteen of the girls died. He wondered if the little girl in the alley was one of them. He didn't feel too proud of what they had done and he remembered not taking his cut of the heist.

As the country passed by the window, he tried to figure out his feelings about his brother. It was hard to git them straight. He guessed that he loved him, but really couldn't explain it. He remembered the times the older boy had beaten him. Stick had told him that he had to be tough, and the way to be tough was to be able to take a licking. He remembered the taste of blood in his mouth and the pain. He doubted that it had made him tough. What protected him was his size and looks. Nobody wanted to mess with him. He shut his mind to the past and dwelt on the future.

He had never missed traveling beyond the streets of New York. The farthest he had gone was to prison and that was sure no picnic. Hell, everything he needed was within a few miles of where he was born. He was a big man in his part of the city. He was somebody. Everybody respected him. He hadn't liked to fight Stick, but relished the other fights. He almost always won, and pounding in someone's face was what he lived for. He was looking forward to pounding the face of Will Morgan.

It was a surprise to realize how big the world was. Of course he knew, but he had never actually looked out at something fifty miles away. He didn't think he liked the feeling of being so small.

Twelve days later, he was pleased to hear the conductor announce that the next stop was Cedar Rapids. He could feel the thrill that was the anticipation of combat. He had run it through his mind a hundred times. He knew Stick's spirit was with him and he was determined to make his brother proud.

Sean watched as scattered farm houses gave way to a fairly large town.

It was nothing compared to New York, but was as close to a city as he had seen in a lotta miles.

With a hissing of steam and a screeching of brakes, the train slowed and then stopped. Conductors placed steps outside the coach doors and passengers lined up to get off. Sean picked up his carpet-bag and pushed his way through the line. He heard protests, but no one put a hand on him. On the platform, he looked around for the main street and headed in that direction. How was he supposed to find Morgan in a town this size?

To be on the safe side, Sean checked into a cheap hotel. He figured he might be here for a few days and he would be damned if he was gonna sleep outside in the cold. Placing his bag on the narrow metal framed bed, he walked to the window and looked down on the busy street. His eyes took in the stores across the street. On the next block, he thought he read the name Morgan on a store front. He took out the slip of paper that Que had printed the name on, and compared the two. They looked the same to him. Hurrying out into the street, he walked the short distance and there, in big red letters was *Morgan and Sons Mercantile.* Sean was not much at reading. He rechecked the slip of paper against the large painted letters and decided that it was a match.

Sean almost cheered. This was going to be easier than he thought. Check the train schedule in the morning, then look up Morgan just before the departure time. Be back on the train and gone before they could figure out who done it. His luck was with him.

The next morning he got the train schedule and walked down to the store. He'd discovered a problem as he thought through the plan. The sign had said Sons. He'd asked the hotel clerk what the rest of the sign said to be sure. There was more than one of them. He didn't know what his Morgan looked like. Still working on the problem, he entered the store and pretended to look at the merchandise. He noticed a woman behind the counter and sauntered down to the end, so he could see all of her. Damn, she was a looker. He pictured himself in bed with her. It had been a long time since he had bedded a woman, and… His thoughts were interrupted by a young man entering the store from the back room. He couldn't be Morgan. Mole had said Morgan wasn't big but he couldn't be this damned small. It would take a lot more man than this to kill Stick. Still, it was getting complicated, and he liked things simple. If he was going to pass himself off as a friend, he sure couldn't ask the guy if that's who he was. 'Hell, I need to think this over some more.'

He sat in a chair outside the door and ran the plan through his head one more time. He could eliminate the clerk as Will if he heard someone call him by a different name. He propped the chair against the wall and listened to the voices inside. He was freezing and about to try another plan when a farmer came out and yelled back. "See ya in a week or so, Cole."

His mind was racing. The clerk was not his man. He could now play Will's friend. Entering the store he walked directly to the counter. Cole looked up and, smiling, stepped across from him.

"How can I help you?" he asked.

"Well, I'm a lookin' for Will Morgan. He told me his folks had themselves a store here and as I was passing through, I thought I'd look him up. Is he around?"

"Sorry, you're out of luck. I'm his brother Cole. Will headed to

Wyoming early last spring, to a place called Willow Creek. As far as I know, he's still there. Are you a friend of Will's?"

"Aye, we was in Andersonville together. Didn't know the lad all that well, but he told me that if'n I was ever in the neighborhood, to look him up. Name's Sean." He extended his hand. They shook.

"If you don't have a place to stay tonight, you're welcome to stay with us. Any friend of Will's is a friend of mine."

"No, no, I got me a room. I'll be a headin' to Chicago in the mornin'. But thanks anyway."

His plan was re-forming as he went back to the station. Why not kill the brother? Seemed like the right thing to do. Hell, yes! He found that the train west was to leave at ten that night. I can follow 'im home, shoot 'im and be outta here 'fore he knows he's dead. Maybe I should'a took him up on spending the night. Naw, if folks saw me, they might suspect. This'll work.

An old man had gotten off a train that was soon leaving, to stretch his legs. Sean had paid him to buy his ticket west. It was a foolproof plan. At six, he left his bag at the hotel desk and sauntered down the street, looking in the store windows. When he was abreast of Morgan's he saw that the closed sign was out, and the employees were leaving. He waited in a handy chair across the street as Morgan busied himself with closing up for the day. He watched him close and lock the door and walk to the livery. In a few minutes, he came out in a new surrey, pulled by a spirited horse. Damn, how far out of town does he live? I'll just have to hoof it, he thought in disgust.

As Cole headed out of town, Sean kept up with him in the early darkness. Once out of town, however, Cole put the mare into an easy gallop. Sean was able to keep up at a dead run, but, within a hundred yards, he was walking and gasping for air. By Jesus, he thought, how much farther? His legs were cramping, and his chest hurt from the cold air. The surrey was out of sight. He kept going, walking and trotting when he could. Soon he was rewarded by house lights off to his left. He was relieved to see Morgan come out of the barn with a lantern and go into the house. His luck was holding.

Sean hunkered down by a stump and carefully lit a stinker to check the time. He had a couple of hours to wait. Might as well catch that much sleep. The long warm coat he had bought would pay for itself now. That would leave plenty of time to call Morgan out, shoot him and git back to the train by ten. He could nearly always wake up when he wanted. He was good at that. He took out the flask from his pocket and took a warming nip.

He woke with a start. His hands and feet were freezing. Had he overslept? He again checked the watch. He was cutting it a little short. He felt a little rushed as he jumped to his feet and approached the house. A dog started barking from around back. Damn!

"Morgan!" he yelled. "I need to talk to you!" He had come as close as he dared. He wanted to stay out of any lamp light.

The door opened and Cole was framed in the doorway, with the light in back of him.

Perfect. Sean aimed and fired. Cole was flung back into the house. Sean started to run. He could hear a woman screaming. He ran harder. He thought of the girl in the alley.

Cole was slumped on the floor, holding the right side of his upper chest. Blood was running through his fingers. He was having difficulty speaking. He managed to calm Candace, with a grin. "Get the rifle and fire three shots, then wait a minute and fire off three more. Keep it up until you run out of ammunition. Ben will know. Do it, Honey."

Sean heard the shots, but couldn't figure out what they meant and run at the same time. God, his legs were killing him. His chest was pounding and he couldn't seem to get enough air.

Within minutes their neighbor, Ben, arrived. "Candace, you ride ahead and get Doc up. I'll take care of Cole and Sherman." They ran to the barn where she saddled her horse and Ben began to hitch up the buggy.

Sean was almost run down by the horse as Candace raced by. It was so dark that she didn't see him crouching in the ditch. He followed her as fast as he could. He heard the train whistle and forced himself even faster. The train was pulling out as he entered the rail yard. He barely had time to grab the hand-rail on the last passenger car. He managed to get himself up on the step but was too exhausted to enter the car right away. He watched the lights of the town recede with a weary smile. He could almost feel his big brother sitting beside him. As his breathing slowly returned to normal, he entered the car and slumped into a seat. He tried to keep the sneer off his face as the black conductor hustled down the aisle, fancy duds, silly little cap. Probably thought he had jumped the train. He forced a smile as he showed his ticket. He was still having a hard time breathing.

Putting his ticket back into his pocket, he settled down and thought about the last few hours. Yes, his luck was still with him. Damn. In all the excitement, he forgot his bag at the hotel. Oh well, there warn't no time. I done good anyhow, damn good. He knew Stick had seen it all, and was proud.

Days later he asked another conductor, "This train go to Willow Creek?"

"No suh, but we can git ya pretty close. They's got a stagecoach on into Summit and Willow Creek. I"ll tell ya when it's time to git off."

The ride from Summit to Willow Creek was brutal. He was the only passenger on the run and it seemed that this Ernie fellow was going out of his way to make him suffer. They seemed to hit every chuck-hole and rock in the road. He tried to brace himself but it didn't seem to help. How the driver managed to stay on was beyond his comprehension. He'd never ridden a stagecoach before and had assumed that the ride would be smooth like the train.

"Willow Creek!" Ernie yelled as he applied the brake and brought the stage to a sliding stop. "Everybody out! End of the line!" Sean picked himself up from the floor where he'd landed when the brakes were applied. He cursed the driver, inwardly, as he opened the door.

As usual, there were a few hangers-on to greet the stage. This evening Chief was there. He approached the stage, but backed off as Sean swung the door open and stepped down. It was obvious this passenger was in a foul mood.

Looking around, Sean spotted a saloon and decided that he needed a warm-up drink. He stood at the bar, had a few quick drinks than nursed the fourth, as he took in his surroundings. There wasn't much difference in here from the same sort of place in New York. He'd soon be able to get all the information he needed and more or his name wasn't Sean O'Grady. It didn't take him long to find a fellow who'd downed just enough booze to want to talk without asking any questions. It was easy to get him going. He was more than willing, without being at all cautious and would probably forget the whole incident later.

Sean didn't have to impress the drunk with his accent, so he slipped back into his normal speech. "Say me bucko, I'm a hearin' there's a lad round here by the name o' Will Morgan. I don't guess that you'd be a knowin' where I can find him, would ya now?"

"Why, hell yes!" the drunk belched. "Hell, me and Morgan are just like this." He held up a hand with the fingers crossed. "Hell yes, him and me are good pals."

"Would ya be a knowin' where I can find 'im?" Sean asked with a smile.

"Hell yes. He's out at his place. He don't hang around town much. Don't drink neither. Nope don't drink. Just goes home."

"Where about is this here place of his located?"

"Hell, that's easy. Just turn right at the next street and go until the road stops. That's his place." The drunk pointed in the general direction.

"How far out is it?" Sean was hoping it was a walk-able distance.

"Hell, only 'bout four miles, I guess. Yup, 'bout four miles."

Hell yerself, Sean thought, I sure don't intend to walk that far. It was cold but not freezing though it would be, before morning. He left the bar and sought out the huge stables in the early winter darkness. Might just as well try me hand at horse-back ridin'.

He grinned. Wouldn't be the first time. He well remembered ridin' Elmer. Elmer was the horse old what's-his-name had for hauling his tin wares around the city. Sometimes the old geezer would let Sean sit on the big gentle dapple gray while he made his sales. Yes sir, he rode ol' Elmer good.

He entered the stable and rang the night bell, bringing John Henry down from his room.

"What can I do for you?" John asked. He was a little irritated by the stranger coming in so late and waking him from his pleasant doze in front of the stove. He didn't like his looks at all. It showed in his tone of voice.

"I'll be a needin' a horse for a few hours," Sean replied. 'Don't ya start gittin uppity with me,' he thought to himself. He had no liking for his kind and this here one was just askin' for a good drubbin'.

John looked the man over and walked to one of the stalls. He led Rosebud out. He doubted if this city dressed man knew much about riding and his size required a large horse. Rosebud fit the bill. He saddled and bridled her while Sean watched. When the horse was ready, he handed the reins to Sean. Sean just stood there.

"Here, ya put this one up on this side, and the other here. When you mount up, ya always mount on the horse's left side." John could feel the animosity in the man, and let the sarcasm in his voice speak for itself.

"I'll be a letting' ya know that I been a ridin' most of me life." Sean probably wouldn't have time to deal with the old man later but he was tempted to do it right now. No, he couldn't let it interfere with the main plan.

He had a problem getting his foot in the stirrup, so John held it steady for him. He didn't bother to thank him. He road out into the street and after much jerking on the reins managed to get going in the right direction. The way he figured it, if a plan works, don't change it. If Morgan lived in the last place, he would have plenty of time. They probably wouldn't find the body for a day or two, and he'd be long gone if his luck held. He felt lucky. Running it over in his mind, he added one little thing. It would be both necessary and satisfying to tell Morgan about his brother before he shot him.

It went through his mind to get a room at the hotel, and catch the stage out in the morning but he decided against it. Only that nigger saw him head out in this direction and who'd listen to him. Follow the plan, he told himself. Kill this Morgan fella, circle around town, hide out 'til morning near the stage road, then turn the horse loose. When the stage came by, he would just flag it down and take it on in to Summit. Stick would have been proud. He almost laughed out loud, it was so simple. It came to him that it might be a good idea to kill that uppity nigger, as well, if he had time. No sense in leavin' a witness of any kind and he would enjoy it.

It was damn dark out of town. He held up his hand and literally couldn't see it in front of his face. Hopefully the horse could see where it was going. The damn thing kept trying to turn around and go back to town so it must see somethin'. He'd passed one big fancy place with some lights but he could see by them that the road went on. After nearly half an hour Sean saw the lamp lights of another house not far off. To make sure it was the right place, he kept riding straight until he came up against a fence. That was the last place on the road all right. He smiled. It was all coming together. He rode back to the gate and dismounted. His legs and butt were already rubbed raw and he could barely walk at first. He took a single rein and tied it firmly to the gatepost. He wasn't about to get stranded out here on foot. Then he pulled the gun from his pocket and checked it one last time before creeping up the short road to the front of the house. He looked around to be sure he hadn't been seen. There was light coming through the cracks in the barn siding, but he was used to things being lit up at night, even when folks weren't there, and it didn't register in his mind.

"Will Morgan! Step out here, I have somethin' ta tell ya!" His gun was held in both hands and extended straight out in front of him. The door opened and a large man filled the doorway. Sean knew he had the right man now. God! He felt great!

"Who's there?" the man asked peering into the darkness.

"You kilt my brother, you son-of-a-bitch, so I kilt yers," he squeezed the trigger.

There was a cry from the man in the doorway, as he slumped to the floor. Sean had started toward the still form, intending to shoot him again, when the area was suddenly lit up as the barn door was thrown open. A man ran out and quickly dodged into the shadows. Sean flung a shot in his general direction and ran for the gate. He glanced back and was relieved to see the second man running toward the house. He located the horse and grabbed the rein. The damned knot was too tight. He struggled to untie it and, in final desperation, yanked on it breaking the leather. Now it was too short but he had the other rein that had been hanging loose. Swearing under his breath, Sean couldn't find the stirrup with his shoe as the horse circled nervously. He grabbed it with his hand once the animal came up against the fence and managed to get his foot in and himself up in the saddle. Rosebud had no idea what the rider wanted, unless it was to turn in circles all night. He only had one rein to pull on, and he was too desperate to get away to think what he was doing. Rosebud decided she'd had enough and it was time to go home, whatever this fool wanted. She took off down the road at a brisk trot. Sean had loosened his grip on the one rein to grab the horn with both hands to keep from bouncing off. With each step the animal took, his sore behind slapped down hard on the saddle and his teeth came together with a clap. His already wobbly legs weren't strong enough to grip the wide backed animal to keep this from happening. He cursed her and all horses with every curse he had ever heard and a few new ones as well.

He was terrified and unable to think. He'd finally realized he couldn't direct the horse with only one rein. How would he ever stop it, or get around the town? Holding the horn prevented him from trying, but he wasn't about to let go. After a half a mile without opposition, Rosebud began to slow down on her own and eventually settled into a leisurely walk. Sean still had no way to guide the horse, but at least he knew better than to pull on the one rein. He was feeling more himself now the bouncing had stopped. The horse was going in the right direction for the time being and his paralyzed brain was beginning to function though he feared he'd never be able to sit again.

Another mile passed. He could see the large house on his right that he had noticed on his ride out. Lanterns hung on the veranda, and he could see a figure standing under the light. Christ, there was a horseman riding out to the road. He jumped off the horse and led it a short distance into the darkness. He couldn't see where he was going but managed to get twenty or thirty yards off before the rider got too close. If the damned animal would just keep quiet he'd be fine.

"Who's there?" Will called out. He wasn't sure that it was a horse and rider, but he definitely heard something over in the brush. Maybe it was a deer, he thought. Suddenly he became aware of the pounding of hooves coming toward him from home.

Jack saw him at the last minute and brought his horse to a sliding stop. "It's me Will. Someone just shot Del! Don't know who or why. He was yellin' at him when he fired, but I didn't catch what he said. Del needs a Doc bad. The shooter must'a headed towards town. You see anybody?"

"Heard something off there," he said, pointing. "Too damn dark to see. You go back and do what you can for Del. I'll git Doc. I'll have John keep an eye open for anyone coming into town." He wheeled his horse and with a yell, raced toward town.

Jack turned and sped back toward the ranch.

Sean couldn't make out all that was said, but he knew now that he had shot the wrong man. The one he was after had not been more than a stones throw from where he stood, but it was too damned dark to see him. He also heard one of them say someone would be watching for his return to town. No way could he go near the place. The plan had gone to hell. He was in a panic. He still had to do the job but how?

Who would shoot Del? Will wondered as he tore along. It just didn't make sense. He'd only been here three weeks. He hadn't ruffled anyone's feathers. Maybe he had made an enemy while working on the railroad. He pushed Missy faster.

The lights of town were a blessing. It seemed like he had been riding in the cold pitch black for hours. He pulled the horse to a stop outside Doc's place and pounded on the door. "Doc, I need help. A man's been shot."

The light came on and a thin, stooped man opened the door. "Who's shot? Where is he?"

"Out at my place, Doc. I'll get your buggy while you dress."

Will ran to the stable and was groping around for a lantern when John appeared from his living quarters above the office.

"Who's that down there?" he shouted gruffly. To awaken him for the second time in the same night was asking for trouble.

"It's Will, John. Del's been shot and I need Doc's buggy."

"Hell's fire!" John growled. "I bet it was that man I rented Rosebud to. He said he would be back in an hour, or so, and it's been a lot longer than that. I didn't like his looks and I watched him head out your way."

Doc came into the livery as they finished hitching up his horse and buggy. He was not a young man by a long shot, but he leaped easily up into the buggy and, placing his bag between his feet, headed it out of town at a brisk trot. By the time Will remounted, they had faded into the night. Chief, who had been sleeping in the loft, came out and stood looking up at Will.

"If you need assistance in catching that man, I am here. I can track a flea over a flat rock, buffalo spit down a stream, or a bird's breath through the sky."

Will was, as always, surprised by Chief's command of the English language but he answered as if it was a natural thing. "He left the road somewhere between Twyla's place and mine. I doubt he'll come back into town."

"If he does, I'll take care of him for you, Will," John volunteered raising the shotgun he'd brought down with him. He would gladly kill if Will asked him to.

"Chief, I figure I'll need all the help I can get, running him down. Can you be ready to go by sunup?"

"I'll be ready. I'll need a horse, John."

"No, I'll bring Dolly," Will answered.

Chief's eyes lit up. He had wondered what it would be like to ride one of the grays. Now he was going to do it. He would be ready.

Will stopped to explain to Twyla about Del being shot and was a little surprised by her immediate reaction. She burst into tears and clung to Will a second for support. She quickly regained her composure and ran upstairs to get Sammy. Will ran to the barn to saddle Bell and was ready by the time they came out. She handed Sammy up to Will and mounted her mare. No words were spoken as they left the barn and galloped up the road.

Doc met them at the door. "He's shot bad, no mistake about that. I can't tell if he'll make it or not." Turning to Twyla, he said, "Glad you could come. Good nursing will be a help. It is going to be a very long night. You'll need to heat water, and tear some bandages from clean linen. We'll need more light, Will."

"I'll get some lanterns from the barn." He had pushed together two of the three chairs than now sat in front of the fire and settled the drowsy Sammy on them. Then he had taken a quick look in the bedroom at Jack bending concernedly over Del's still form. He needed to get out of the house. He couldn't deal with this, not now when they had finally found each other. These men were part of his family, God damn it. He brought the lanterns to Jack and said that he would spend the night outside in case the shooter came back. He circled repeatedly through the darkness with hardly a sound, checking any possible way the damned bushwhacker might use to come back. Within an hour, Melinda and Seth had shown up. His heart swelled with love for all these people who stood by him so stoutly. He knew, no matter what, he would never be alone in the world as long as they lived. That brought his mind back to Del and his heart hardened with resolve as he crept through the darkness. Seth relieved him around two in the morning. After Will showed him once around his circuit he went to the barn and stretched out in the hay and slept until five.

He awoke then and quickly saddled the two horses. Before he left, he stopped at the house. Doc, who was slumped wearily at the table with Melinda, told him that Del was still hanging on, but that it could go either way.

"I'll have to head on back to town soon, Will. Nothing I can do for a few hours. I'll be back this afternoon. If Twyla needs me, she can send someone to fetch me."

Jack got up from his bedroll by the fire and followed Will to the bedroom door. Bloody towels were everywhere. Twyla was asleep at the bedside where she had moved the third chair.

She opened her eyes and looked at Del searchingly before she looked up at Will. Her eyes looked as though she'd had very little sleep.

"I'm not doing any good here, so Chief and I are goin' huntin'. When I get to town I'll make sure someone is coming out to help you. Meanwhile, Jack can take over outside so Seth can get some rest or go back to town. I see Del's in good hands." He leaned over and gently kissed her lips.

As he followed Will to the door Jack whispered urgently. "What do you mean, Jack can take over outside? I'm goin' with you ain't I? I told his folks I'd look after him. I promised them! Now look what I've let happen. I gotta help git this guy, Will."

Will turned to his friend on the porch. He looked steadily into his eyes. "We don't know who this is, or why he shot Del, do we? Have you thought of anything that might have brought it about?"

Jack shook his head miserably. "When I came out of the barn it looked like he was headin' to the house to finish the job. He was big, that's all I could tell."

"Then he might come back, mightn't he? Seth hasn't had any sleep to speak of and someone had to keep an eye out. That has to be you. I might end up just following him back here and gettin' here too late! You see that don't you?"

Jack nodded. Yeah, Will was right. He hadn't been thinkin' it all out. "I see Will. No one will get past me this time. I hope the bastard does come back. I'll be ready for him."

Will clapped him on the back and mounted up. He looked back as he lead Dolly through the gate in the frozen dimness of first light. Jack was still standing on the porch forlorn.

It was dark. Sean had never seen dark as dark as this was. He wanted to laugh, but couldn't manage it. He had led the horse on off the road until he could no longer make out the light from the big house before he remounted. He'd also found that, if he leaned way forward over the horses neck, he could just get a grip on the short rein. The main thing was to go as far and as fast as possible. Figure out where in hell he was in the morning. The horse seemed to be able to see in the dark so he kicked it into a trot. Even though he was bent over, he was immediately knocked off by a low branch. Fortunately, the animal stopped and allowed him to get back on. He jerked the bridle viciously in his increasing frustration, causing the horse to rear backward crashing its neck into his nose that was only inches away. He almost fell off again. God damned animal, he sure as hell wasn't going to turn it loose. When he was through with it he'd shoot the damned thing. He urged it forward again, moving his hand back and forth in front of his face in case of another branch. He was poked and whipped by various unseen obstacles. His nose hurt like hell and was bleeding all over his coat. It eventually stopped, but not Sean's growing rage.

After three more close encounters with low limbs, he decided to stop until daylight. Propping himself against a tree, he sat listening to all the strange sounds out there in the dark. He could not connect any specific animal with the sounds and that seemed worse. He was afraid. What was out there looking at him? Would he be killed by being eaten? Now he was glad of the proximity of the big steady horse. At least he wasn't alone. Fear still gripped his chest. He drew his legs up under his chin and wrapped his arms around them and tried to sleep as it grew colder. It was no use. If he slept, they would get him and eat him. At first dawn, he was up and riding. Everything was crusted with ice. At least it wasn't snowing and hadn't for a while. Once the sun was clear up the ground would thaw some, even if it stayed overcast. As best as he could tell, he was heading west, and that was not the way he wanted to go. Unfortunately, if they were after him, he had no other choice, at least for a day or so.

As bad as Will felt, the sight of Chief standing in the stable doorway, brought a smile to his face, but on second glance he became aware of the dignity of the man and something feral as well, that was usually not apparent. He was wearing a headband with several large feathers in the back, and a chest piece made from bones that completely covered the thin, wool clad, chest.

He had decided to wear his regular pants in case the horse had no saddle. Besides it was too cold for bare legs and he had no leathers. He wore the moccasins he saved for important occasions. Slung over his shoulder was an old flint-lock rifle, and stuck in a sheath on his belt was a huge knife. He was applying paint to his face, as he looked up at Will.

As Chief mounted the mare, he puffed his chest out to its maximum size, and jutted out his chin. "I am ready," he announced.

"There are tracks frozen all over the road, far as I can tell. Think you can find the trail?" Will asked. No longer was Chief the town clown. The outlandish attire did not diminish the sincerity he was showing towards tracking down the shooter.

Chief gave him a look that would melt a rock. "I've cleaned Rosebuds' stall every day for ten years. I know her track. I will know it when I see it."

Will decided he'd better shut his mouth. Just beyond the road to Twyla's house, he pointed out to Chief where he had met Jack. "He probably left the road just past here. Anyway, that's where I heard something moving. I figure, if he's kept on, he's someplace to the west of here by now. I could check the other side of the road and keep out of your way. I'm sure that you're a lot better at finding tracks than I am."

"You speak with wise tongue, white man. You keep your eye on Chief, you learn a lot," Chief told Will, slipping back into the pigeon English he affected when it suited his purpose. "You are with a great tracker." His face was very stern, but Will saw a twinkle in his eyes. The old man dismounted and walked slowly up the road studying the rapidly thawing ground. Within a hundred yards he pointed down and announced that he had found the trail. "Notice, my white friend, the large size of this print. Rosebud is seventeen hands tall. Her hooves are very large. Next, the front prints turn in, and last, the shoes are new. The print is deep and sharp."

"I remember her well, Chief. Is she as strong as she looks?"

"Yes, but only for short trips. She is almost twenty-three, and has many miles behind her." He almost said moons, but was getting tired of being Indian.

"Well, if you're sure those are her tracks," Will teased, trying to look innocent.

Chief gave him a baleful look and did not bother to answer. He rode into the trees slowly with Will following. Will knew that the longer the hunt drug out, the more he would have to rely on Chief. He hoped that the old man was as good as he said he was. He sure didn't want the shooter to get away.

Twyla studied Del's shallow breathing and held his hand in a firm grip. Oh God, she loved this man. Please let him pull through this. She had never felt this deeply about anyone before and she had only known him for three weeks. She thought about Will's kisses and felt confusion, as well as guilt. She loved him too. Yes, she did, just in a different way. He had been coming over almost every day to help get the house livable and she cherished every minute they spent on the porch swing, holding hands and talking. She'd told him exactly what she wanted for herself and the boy. She needed someone permanent that she could depend on and there was no one else around here, and here was where she meant to stay. Will was willing to be that person, wanted to be that person. She had thought they would probably marry. He would be a good father for Sammy. Only at the end of the evening, when he was leaving, had he kissed her, and she'd enjoyed being kissed by Will. It was nice and proper and he was giving her the time she needed. He understood that. Not many men would.

This pull toward Del was something else entirely. It was like being swept away in the current of a river. He had never touched her but she knew she would be lost the moment he did. Of course, Del was tall and very handsome, she thought as she considered his dear face, deploring her shallowness. Were looks that important to her? 'Of course not,' she told herself. They had never been before. There just had to be more to it.

Perhaps it was the fact that death and violence seemed to follow Will around and he made no attempt to avoid them. She had witnessed first hand that steely look that preceded some decisive violent action on his part. Though it had not been directed at her, it had been frightening none the less. The two gunmen in Summit probably saw the same look just before they died and those scalp hunters. Maybe

Nate had seen it too, and that was what made him try to get the gun out of his pocket. The way he had told her that he and Chief were 'goin' huntin'' had sent a chill up her back. She compared all that to Del, gentle and soft spoken with kindness in his eyes. They were so completely different. She felt that she owed Will so much, and she knew she had led him to believe she would be his. How could she let him down now.

No, she told herself, she did love him. It wasn't in the same way she loved Del, but it was just as real. The thing was that Will loved her. She was as sure of that as she was of the sun coming up in the morning. Was it right to let it go on when she felt this way about Del? Didn't Will deserve more from a wife. Sooner or later he would have to know how she felt and then the choice would be his to make.

Chief was off and on Dolly's back a dozen times before they had covered a thousand yards. Will was truly amazed. He would look at the ground the Indian found so interesting, and see nothing to indicate anyone had been there. At times he wondered if Chief might be fooling him, but on down the line, sure enough, there would be some distinct prints that even he could see.

Chief was enjoying the hunt. It was just like the old days when he was young and wild. It all came back to him like yesterday. Obviously, the man was lost and had hurt himself as well. He caught sight of the blood with ease. He picked up the dead snag and pointed to the tree trunk where it had been broken off. "Rode his horse under the snag in the dark." Chief had a wide grin on his face. "The man is a fool and is running scared."

As the day wore on it warmed up. It was clear the shooter was still lost. The tracks seemed to have no particular pattern and zig-zagged around, occasionally doubling back on themselves. It was also evident to Chief that the man was taking his frustration out on Rosebud. She was tiring. Chief pointed out places where she had stumbled. The old man loved Rosebud as if she were his sister, and it troubled him to know that she was suffering. He worked faster.

Sean was madder than hell. Nothing had turned out the way he had planned. Everything had gone to Hell after the shooting. Shit! The damned plan was falling apart even before he pulled the trigger. He hadn't killed Morgan. He was probably on his trail right now and, to make things worse, the damned horse was slowing down and kept slipping in the thawing ground. He struck her with the snag he had broken off a tree, but it didn't do any good. She was breathing hard and her coat was covered with a lather of sweat even in the cold. He hit her again with the stick. She groaned and fell to her knees. Sean jumped clear just in time and watched the horse roll over on her side.

"God damned animal," he muttered. "Git the hell up." He kicked her viciously. She flinched, but did not attempt to stand. 'I sure as hell can't stay here until the damned thing decides to get up,' he thought. 'Gotta keep movin'. ' Taking one last exasperated look at the horse, he kicked her once more, spit on her and headed on up the trail. He was able to get a sighting on a rocky outcrop a mile or so ahead. At least the lousy beast had gotten him out of the valley. The climb had been steep and up here there were patches of snow in the sheltered places. He'd never have made it on foot. He'd have been caught out in the open. Never had he been so tired. His mind was having a problem keeping focused on his escape. He found himself thinking about sitting down for a spell, just long enough to ease the pain in his legs and chest. Maybe just a few minutes of sleep. No, better keep moving. One step at a time.

He had traveled another two miles, when he caught a glimpse of the pursuers on his trail. They were a fair piece off, but he could see the feathers. Fear gripped him. He started to run, his sore legs forgotten. He had heard of Indians and was not about to have his head scalped. Maybe they would burn him at the stake, or stake him out on an anthill, or skin him alive! Everything he had heard about Indians back home came rushing into his head pushing out reason. He realized that he was sobbing aloud. He put his hand over his mouth as he stopped and tried to think and to breath. He couldn't think of anything except to run, and run he did. All at once, his legs gave out. One second he was running and the next he was flat on his face in the mud. As soon as he could, he forced himself to his feet and staggered on, trying to take advantage of the small leafless bushes and trees to keep from being seen. Yes, he would make it to safety. He had to. Don't look back, just keep moving. He broke out into a small clearing. He fell to his knees searching for cover. There were several good-sized rocks. Not big enough to hide him from someone that was really looking, but maybe big enough for an ambush. He crawled over to the biggest and hunkered down behind it. He took the pistol from his pocket and waited, willing his breathing to quiet down. "Where are you Stick? I need you." He thought of the Indians out there and he began to cry, silently. 'Did they eat people?'

Chief reined in and jumped off his horse. "It's Rosebud, she's down!"

Will dismounted and together they squatted beside the old horse. Will cared about animals as much, if not more, than he cared about most of the people he had run into. Rosebud was no exception. He looked at the cuts to her sides, as well as to the top of her head, and wondered how a person could do a thing like that. He felt a sting in his eyes. It was time they caught this bastard. He stood and mounted

Missy, throwing down the blanket he had rolled on the back of his saddle. "You comin'?"

Chief pulled the blanket off his own saddle as well and threw the two of them over the animal on the ground. He bent and whispered something in her ear. Then he deftly swung onto Dolly's back. Without comment, he reined around Will and proceeded up the slope. Within an hour, he raised his hand and pointed, "There!"

Luckily Chief had seen the shooter fall to his knees and crawl to the rocks. They took to higher ground, riding as close as they could, then dismounted and tied their horses. Moving up quietly on foot they circled above him, trying to see behind the rocks. When they were stopped by the terrain, they knelt and discussed a plan of attack.

"Looks like you ran him to ground, Chief. Nice work. I think you may be an even better tracker than you claim."

Chief, too, was pleased. He smiled slightly but as he watched the rocks, there was a cold glint in his old eyes. Rosebud had been beaten, and there was no way the horse-beater was going to leave here alive.

"I need to work my way down to talk to him. I've got to know why he shot Del."

"He will not leave this place alive. You saw what he did. The son-of-a-bitch beat her with a limb! A man that would do that cannot be allowed to live." He was so filled with indignation that he could hardly get the words out.

"You're right. He has worn out his welcome here. But we need to be sure he's alone, that someone else isn't going to try to finish what he started. Keep me covered from up here." Will jacked a shell into the chamber of his rifle. With a nod to chief, he started making his way down toward the hidden gunman.

As he worked his way toward the rocks, he realized that Chief had lost some of his stoicism in the last hour. In his concern for Rosebud he had sounded just like a white man, and he smiled to himself.

Chief swiftly began to load the flintlock. He hadn't had the occasion to fire it in years. As a matter of fact, he wasn't sure that he remembered just how to load it. He had to trust that his hands knew what his brain had forgotten. By the time Will was within shouting distance of the gunman, he had it done, or at least he hoped he did. Watching the rock that concealed the shooter, he tried to aim from a standing position, but the piece was too heavy. Laying down wouldn't work, because the underbrush would block his view. He located a short snag on a nearby tree and he stepped to it, resting the long barrel on it. He was able to line up the sights on the rocks perfectly. Now he was ready, he only had to wait for the bastard to show himself. He was good at waiting. He could only catch the tone, not the words of the voices down below.

"You! What the hell did you shoot Del for?" Will yelled at the hidden gunman.

"I thought he be Will Morgan," Sean shouted back.

"I'm Morgan. Why do you want to kill me? I don't know you."

"You killed me brother, you son-of-a-bitch. You killed Stick."

"I never even knew anybody named Stick. You've got the wrong man."

"His name be Rooster when ye did it, when ye killed 'im dead, so I killed yer brother. How ye be a liken that?"

"You did what?" Will could hardly get the words out.

"I killed yer brother. Cole been his name, me thinks. Shot him as he be a standin' in the doorway of his house," Sean laughed. "Didn't know what hit im. How ya be a liken it, Morgan?"

Will was too stunned to speak. Could his killing Rooster have brought about his brother's death and maybe Del's? It all seemed so long ago he could hardly remember it. How could that scum have a brother that cared so much he would go to such trouble to avenge him? Well, Will felt his heart harden to the stranger. He was going to have to die too.

Will placed the Henry out in front of him as he sprawled on the cold, rocky ground. He would get one good shot, but how long would he have to wait. It could take hours, if the man chose to stay put. They needed to get back down the mountain before the early darkness and increasing cold set in. Besides, Will wanted it over, now. He picked up a fist sized rock and slung it as far beyond the hidden man as he could, while yelling, "Don't shoot 'em in the back, he's mine."

The rock smashed into the brush and Sean, thinking he was about to be attacked from behind, jumped up to protect himself. Will and Chief squeezed off their rounds simultaneously. The bullet from the Henry struck Sean in the head. A split second later, Chief's shot hit him in the chest. Sean was lifted off the ground, and landed on his back several yards away.

Will walked over to the still form. Most of the man's face was left and there was a definite resemblance between the gunman and Rooster.

He still looked mean. Usually that look died with them, but not in this case. It sent a chill through Will that there could be two of them. Was he any better himself? They were all killers when it came right down to it. His killing Rooster to avenge Jimmy had started the whole thing. This man had shot Cole and wanted him dead to avenge Rooster. Today he had died because of Cole but it wasn't going to bring any of them back. Well, it had to be done. How many times had he said that since the damned war began? Was it really true?

Cole was dead! My God! He was the last of my family. No! There was Sherman and there was Candace. What would they do without Cole? His eyes burned and he felt like throwing up. He heard Chief approaching and struggled to shake the shock and turmoil out of his head. His face regained that hard look that covered all the pain.

Chief had a look of satisfaction as he went toward the body. "Damn! That was some fine shootin', Will. You had words with him. Did he tell you what this was all about?" Chief was rubbing his shoulder.

"Yeah, he was after me. It had to do with me killin' his brother during the war. He's already shot my brother trying to get even. I got Cole killed and Del shot for what I thought was my duty. Should have waited and let the Regulators handle it."

"The who?" Chief looked confused as he continued to rub his shoulder.

"I'll tell you about it on the way back. I don't feel like buryin' this guy. How about you?"

"He'll make a good meal for the wild things." Chief went through Sean's pockets, retrieving a small roll of greenbacks and slipping the pistol into his pouch. They went to their horses in silence and mounted up.

"How come you're rubbin' your shoulder?"

Chief made a disgusted face. "The old gun knocked me on my backside. Hurts. I am too old to shoot anymore. Maybe too much powder. Yes, too much powder. Shit."

They rode along slowly as Will told Chief the story of Andersonville and his encounter with Rooster. Chief said nothing but grunted from time to time. When Will was finished, Chief thought about it for awhile. "You did what you had to, Will. Only the gods can see the future. Perhaps that is just as well."

Will gained some comfort from his words, but guilt still covered him like a blanket and he felt soiled to be a part of the ugliness.

"Whoa up, Will. We have company," Chief murmured, gazing ahead. "They are friends."

Will would have missed the six braves crouched in the brush, even if he hadn't been absorbed in his own troubles.

Chief raised his hand and Will saw one of the braves return the gesture. "Stay put, Will. They are Lakota. I will see what they want." He reined Dolly in their direction and they walked toward him. The old man dismounted when they met.

Will heard laughter, and saw much arm waving. He didn't think this was the reception he would have gotten if he'd been alone. He was real glad Chief was with him.

The Indians retreated back into the brush and then reappeared, leading their mounts. They followed Chief to where Will was waiting. He wasn't sure it was the safest thing, but he decided to dismount as well. As they looked Will over, he was doing the same, and was impressed with what he saw. They seemed rugged and extremely competent, and filled with the same feral intensity he had glimpsed in Chief. They watched him seriously, with identical dark stares.

Chief's eyes twinkled at Will. "You never told me about those three scalp hunters. Seems like every Indian in the territory knew about it except me. The grays are as famous as you are. They call you *Gray Horse Rider*. They picked up the shooter's trail this morning about the same time they caught sight of us. They've been keeping an eye on the situation, in case we needed help." Will nodded his greeting and they returned the nod. Then they mounted and melted into the brush.

They rode on and shortly they were back with Rosebud. She was still on the ground, but her breathing was normal, and she attempted to stand when they rode up. Chief slid off the gray and knelt beside the old mare. He began chanting as he rubbed her head and neck. After a few minutes he looked up at Will and said. "You go on. We will stay with Rosebud. The old girl has a few more miles in her."

"Alright, Chief but you better get her up and going before it gets too cold. Keep the blanket for her. I have to head to my brother's place. I don't know how long I'll be gone, but you take care of yourself and thanks again for the help." He paused and looked back before he was out of sight and was gratified to see that the old mare was on her feet.

It was gathering dusk and he almost road past Twyla's before he heard Jack's whistle and noticed him standing on the porch with

Twyla and Melinda. Jack came down the steps to meet him as he dismounted. Will was afraid to ask about Del's condition, fearing the worst.

Seeing the look on Will's face, Jack threw his arm around him and said. "Del is going to make it. He's lost a whole lot of blood, but Doc says that nothin' of great importance was hit and he managed to git the bullet out. If the shooter had been closer, it would a done a lot more damage. We brought him over here so Twyla and Melinda could look after him. He's inside takin' a snooze. You catch up with that galoot?"

Will answered hesitantly, "Yeah, he was Rooster's brother."

The two men exchanged a long glance. Then Jack turned to the two women on the porch and said. "I'll be damned. That's the skunk Will took care of at Andersonville."

"What happened when you caught up with him?" Twyla asked from the porch. Her arms were wrapped around herself, her hands inside her coat sleeves. Her eyes were focused on the floor in front of her.

He could tell he wasn't to be let off. "Between Chief and his old flint-lock, and my Henry, we sent him on his way to join his brother."

As Twyla listened to his answer a feeling of resentment swept over her. If he hadn't killed that damn Rooster person, Del wouldn't be in there with a bullet wound. It was as though the solution to every problem, for Will, was to kill someone.

Will walked over to the step and looked up at Twyla. It was as he'd feared, she refused to look at him keeping her eyes locked on the floor. He knew she was put off by the killing he had done. Well, he'd have to try to straighten it out later.

"Look, I have to go to Cedar Rapids to take care of some things for my brother. I don't know how long I'll be gone. I'll need to leave on the morning stage. Chief and I had a long ride and I need some rest. You tell Del I'm glad that he's going to be alright." She nodded without looking up. He stood for a moment hoping for more.

When he turned back to his horse he noticed that Melinda had come down and put her arm around Jack's waist. His hand had slipped down to warm hers. Will smiled fleetingly.

Will was asleep when Jack got back to the ranch, and he was up and out before his friend awoke. He saddled the gray and headed into town. He thought about stopping in to see Twyla, but thinking of how she had been unable to meet his eye he decided to wait 'til he got back. They had been getting along just fine. The relationship hadn't gone beyond hand holding and a goodnight kiss, but that was to be expected. He was figuring at least six months before he could ask her to marry him and a few more before there could be a wedding. He wanted to do things right, and that meant not giving the neighbors any more to talk about. He needed to try and explain how it had all come about and he needed the comfort of her understanding, now, not later. Maybe her coldness was just his imagination. He felt sick when he thought about Cole. He hadn't even been able to tell her about him. How he didn't want to face Candace and Sherman but had to. What if they turned away from him too? Was there ever going to be a time when he could do what he wanted and have what he wanted without some obligation getting in the way?

It had cleared in the night and was a lot colder. As the sun came up the frosted ground and trees sparkled cheerfully in the morning light. He was unable to enjoy the sight and was glad when he reached town. He had to get on with it, to get all this over so he could put things back together.

John Henry came out of his office and gripped his hand. "Glad to see you made it back, Will. Did you catch up with that hombre?"

This was easier. Men were always easier to deal with. "Yeah, with Chief's help. He is one fine tracker. I don't see him here but I guess he'll be back today some time. He and Dolly stayed with Rosebud. She was in bad shape, and he wanted to bring her in slow."

"That sounds like him. I think, sometimes, he likes my horses more than he likes me," John said, smiling.

I have to go back to Iowa. The shooter said he killed my brother. I've got to go see about my sister-in-law and their son. I'd appreciate it if you would ask Chief if he would exercise the grays while I'm gone."

"With how he feels about them horses, I don't think that'll be a problem. I might not be able to keep him around here long enough to help me out," John answered with a laugh.

29

ONE GONE, ONE HERE

The stage pulled up at the railroad crossing in a cloud of dust. Will was glad to have that part of the trip over. The road had not improved with age. He stepped off the coach to see that a small settlement had grown up along the tracks in the months since his arrival. A proper station had been erected and Will went inside. Ten minutes later he had his ticket. He found a chair on the platform and moving it around to the shady side of the building, he made himself comfortable. A brisk looking man entered the train station and presently he and the trainmaster came out onto the platform.

"You got any idea how long this is gonna take?"

"Nope, all they said is that it's bein' repaired. Then the line went dead again. I figure it's them Injuns a cutting' the line. All we can do now is wait. I intend to hold the train here until we get word that the rail is fixed. Hell of a way to run a railroad."

Will had gotten himself something to eat and returned to his chair when the train chugged to a stop. He took in the sleek beauty of the engine. Every square inch was clean and polished to a bright shine. He had to compare it to the old rust buckets that had hauled him and his fellow prisoners during the war. Quite a change in a short time that was sure. He gathered his belongings and climbed on board. The train seats would be better than the wooden chair, and a short nap would do him good. There were nine people in the car, and as he passed they glanced in his direction, but not recognizing him went back to whatever they had been doing before he boarded. Placing his bed-roll behind his head, he leaned back against the window and closed his eyes.

Later, he was awakened suddenly, from a light sleep, by voices from outside. It took him a few seconds to realize that the cadence of their southern drawls was probably what had jerked him awake and sent a chill down his back. He was relieved to find himself in the train and not back in a stockade. He peered through the window into the gathering darkness and saw a half dozen men sitting around a fire across the tracks from the station. They were drinking and getting a little loud. He closed his eyes and willed himself to relax. He was almost back to sleep when he heard the laugh. He sat bolt upright. That was it, not just the voices, but that laugh that had taken him back so abruptly. Could it actually be the same person? He studied the men outside, looking for the one with the laugh. He didn't have long to wait before a man across the flames turned a familiar face toward him, into the light of the fire. My God! Will thought, it is him, Lt Barret! The memory of the four men hanging awkwardly by their bound arms pulled behind their backs, came back to Will as if it were yesterday. He could hear the echo of their screams and pleading as they hung outside Barret's quarters, and of his laugh. A normal laugh but ending in a mad sounding giggle. Will would never forget it.

He looked into the face of the man across the fire and there was no doubt. He looked away and closed his eyes. How he had tried to put the war out of his mind, but here it was again. Starving men, knowing that without rations they would be dead by morning. Hundreds of men, too hungry to cook their pathetic portion of meal, choking it down raw only to have it tear their insides to shreds. Their restless eyes searching for some way to put off death, or looking to the heavens for relief, for some act of God to put an end to their suffering. His hands were clenched so tight they hurt. He fought down his first impulse which was to simply go straight out there and shoot the bastard.

Put him out of your mind. Don't jeopardize your other responsibilities. So many had died because of Barret's stupidity and brutality, and here he was, enjoying life, laughing with his friends and getting drunk. Where was justice? Why hadn't something been done? Was it always going to be up to him? Well, others had hung Wirz. No damn way was he going to convince himself to just let it go as long as the damn train just sat here. So, like it or not, it was his turn again.

Considering his options, he leisurely got off the train on the station side. He circled around the darkened building to where he remembered seeing a wheelbarrow propped against a shed. Yes, it was still there. There was a clothesline running from the shed to a shack nearby and he helped himself to that, as well. He crossed the tracks behind the train. Keeping out of the fire's light, he crouched down in the tall grass and waited.

Several of the men came his way and relieved themselves. Will was getting impatient. He was going to be in trouble if the train started to leave before he was done. The minutes slipped by. After what seemed like hours, Barret stood up, and with unsteady legs, made his way toward Will.

"Don't fall in it, you drunken fool," yelled one of his friends.

"Ya'll go to Hell! Barret yelled back. He stopped just below where Will was hidden and began fumbling with the buttons on his pants.

Will waited until he had finished, and was in the process of trying to re-button, before he made his move. With pistol in hand, he stood up behind Barret and brought the butt of the pistol down on his head. As Barret slumped forward, Will managed to grab him with his left arm and lower him to the ground. Holstering his gun, he grabbed the unconscious man's wrists and dragged him into the darkness toward the waiting wheel barrow.

Will tried to pick him up and place him in the wheel barrow three times but it kept tipping over. This was beginning to look more like a farce than retribution, and if the situation wasn't so dangerous, he might be tempted to do some mad giggling of his own. Sweat was breaking out all over his body and it was going to be hard to look like he had just been out of the train for a drink when he returned. Will continued checking the men around the fire. No one had missed Barret yet. He finally propped the limp figure into a sitting position and pushed the nose of the wheel barrow up against his back. Reaching down from between the handles he grabbed the man's shirt and pulled him back into the bucket as he levered it upright. Checking the group around the fire one more time, he headed out into the darkness. The ground was very uneven and it seemed that he managed to hit every rock and soft spot in the vicinity as he struggled along. He was developing a real respect for Ernie's expertise in driving the stage and even more for his horses. Within three hundred yards, his legs gave out. He dumped Barret on the ground under some scrawny willows by a dry wash. Taking the rope from his belt, he rolled the man over onto his stomach, and tied his hands behind his back. Squatting on the ground, he rested, and waited for his victim to come to.

The moon came out from the clouds and Will could see the dark shape of the man. It wasn't too late to back out, he thought. Just leave him here and go back to the train. He wished it were that simple. Were the men that died at Barret's hands at Florence watching to see if he avenged them? Was there a hell waiting for men like this one? Had he the right to seek vengeance against Barret and not expect the same hell to be waiting for him? The man in front of him stirred, and Will's mind focused on what he planned to do. Laws were laws, and what he had in mind was going against the law, but... Dammit! Barret just plain deserved to get a little of what he gave.

He was coming around and, befuddled by drink as he was, he first became aware of having a painful headache, then, that his arms were tied behind his back. Searching the darkness, he made out Will's dark shape.

"What the ....?" he blustered. "What ya'll up to here? Untie me, dammit! Who are ya'll?" His voice was both belligerent and fearful.

"Well, Barret, you don't know me personal like, I just happened to be in the stockade at Florence. You remember Florence, don't you?"

"That was war, dammit! I was jus doin' my duty. No hard feelins, you'da done the same." His voice cracked. "I was doin' my job. What ya'll gonna do?"

Will realized, then and there, the trap he had almost fallen into, just doing his duty. His mind flew as his plan took on a completely new shape.

I planned on givin' you a little taste of what you did to those boys you strung up and then snuff out your worthless life. Only your death would be quick cause I'm a little more short of time than you were."

Barret started moaning, and pleading. "Please don't, oh! Please. I got a wife and kids. I got little kids!"

Will stood and, taking the rope, he wrenched the man's arms up and placed his foot between his shoulder blades keeping the tension on his arms. This was nothing compared to the pain of having one's whole weight hanging from their arms for hours on end, but Barret was moaning incoherently. Not only from the pain, but from fear. The man was a cowardly, worthless waste of skin. Will had never tortured anyone before in his life and what he was doing made him sick at heart. He hardened himself, and swung the rope over a branch of the willow and tied it. He took his foot away and knew the tension was lessened but Barret continued to blubber, his eyes so filled with tears that he didn't see Will step around in front of his face and kneel down. After a moment Will gripped the man's hair and pulled his head up, so that they were eye to eye in the darkness. "I want you to think on the good men that you killed. They had wives and kids. They're widows and orphans because of you. I was going to blow your head off right here and now but I want you to think about goin' to hell for what you done. I can find you again any time. I want and send you on your way and I will. I won't let you off twice and I won't give a warning. One minute you'll be alive and the next you'll be dead. I want you to think on that too. I want you to think on what you're gonna tell your maker when you face him. Forget the duty crap and no hard feelins, for God's sake, it'll be payback time for sure. You'll never see it comin'. You understand what I'm a telling' ya? When I see you again, you're dead!"

Barret nodded his head. Tears were running down his face, and he was struggling to breath with his head held up that way.

Will let go and took out his knife to cut off a piece of Barret's shirt tail and wedged it in his mouth. He could eventually get it out but it would take awhile. At least he hoped so. He stood and took one long look at the cringing form on the ground. "You remember what I said. I'll be seein' you one of these days."

Will headed back toward the tracks, keeping his eyes open for anyone out looking for Barret. He was satisfied with what he had done. He didn't want to wake some morning and find out he had turned into another Barret. He had probably been just an ordinary man before something first pushed him to step over the line. Then it had gotten easier with each time until he became the man he was at Florence. Maybe Barret had some worse fate in store for him, at someone else's hands. Maybe the constant fear of waiting for Will to catch up with him would drive him to some kind of repentance. He smiled at the thought. Twyla would approve of that.

The train let out a long whistle, and he began to run. He couldn't take a chance on being left behind. The southerners were calling Barret, and he could see them fanning out to look for him.

He dropped down into a swale, crouching as low to the ground as he could, but still kept moving. The train whistle sounded again as he came out near the tracks and Will could see the men hesitate. All but one turned and headed back to their fire. One however, continued the search. Barret's friends were putting out the fire when Will, having circled around again, approached the train from the opposite side. He climbed aboard and took his seat. The train soon gave a loud hiss and Will could feel the wheels start to turn. The men scrambled aboard. Will was relieved that Barret wasn't with them. The last man hesitated at the door, looking back over his shoulder.

"You wait for him if you want. The crummy bastard's nothing to us!" He stepped inside and spoke to the others. "Damn fool probably passed out. He ain't one for holdin' his likker. Don't know what old Pete sees in 'im, just cause he was an officer in the war. The damn war's over an' he's not much good for nothin' now."

Well, so much for Barret's friends, Will thought. He was still a little shaky from his exertion, and thinking how close he had come to blowing the head off an unarmed man. He'd get what he deserved sooner or later without Will's further interference but it would never bring those boys back from the grave. Eventually the passengers settled down, lulled by the sway and rumble of the wheels on the rails.

Will kept his eyes open for the place that he had seen Del and Jack. They must have passed it in the night, for he never saw it. As the miles rolled by, the incident with Barret faded from his mind and Will turned his thoughts to the purpose of his trip. What would he find in Cedar Rapids? When they knew, would they blame him for Cole's death as he found he blamed himself? What would Candace and Sherman do if he didn't stay on to help them? He knew it was useless to let these questions circle endlessly through his mind, but it became harder to stop them the closer he got to home. He only succeeded when he replaced them with the good memories he had of the years of their boyhood together. The rattle of the wheels seemed to carry a voice that repeated endlessly that Cole was dead and those memories were all he was going to have.

He awoke from a light sleep when the train pulled in. It was early evening. If it weren't for Cole being killed, he would have been happy to see the familiar streets. Gathering his bag, and blanket roll, he left the train. As he walked along the boardwalk, he recognized several people he had met while working at the store with Cole, but they didn't notice him. He didn't feel like talking anyway. He looked in the windows of the store, as he passed, hoping to see Cole, but knowing that he wouldn't. He headed doggedly out of town. He felt a stab of pain as he passed the old rock. The lights of the house were just beyond and he forced himself forward. He was dreading his meeting with Candace.

He knocked softly on the door and waited. He could hear footsteps and then the door opened and he found himself face to face with his brother. He stood there open- mouthed with shock, one hand on the door frame to keep himself from falling down.

"For heaven's sake, Will!" Cole was almost as surprised as he was. "Come on in. Come in!" he stammered. "We haven't been able to reach you with all the line troubles. It's just great to see you!" He held out one arm to embrace his brother.

Will could see Cole's other arm was in a sling. As he stepped inside and dropped his things beside the door he was trying to create some kind of order from the questions jumbled in his brain. First thing was to grab Cole in a fierce hug that wrung a gasp from the injured man. He held on anyway until he could gain control of the lump in his throat. By that time Candace had come into the room with a smile of welcome and another pair of open arms. He hugged her too. Over her shoulder he could see Sherman sleepy eyed and pajama clad in the bedroom doorway.

"Do you remember your Uncle Will?" Cole asked.

Sherman didn't say anything, but stretched out his arms to be picked up.

Will reached down and swept him up high over head. "By golly, you have grown like a weed, young man. How old are you now, seventeen?"

The little boy smiled shyly and held up three fingers.

"Well, almost," Candace said, with a laugh. "Sit down, Will. Are you hungry? Don't tell what you've been up to 'til I can rustle up something for you to eat!" She bustled off into the kitchen.

Will dropped into the chair Candace had indicated with the boy, who was considerably heavier, on his lap. Cole had already taken a seat with his feet on a stool and was replacing the blanket over his legs that he had thrown aside when answering the door. Will couldn't take his eyes off him as if he would go back to being dead if he even blinked. When Cole was settled Will told him. "I was told you'd been shot by the man that did it. He told me you were dead. He was sure of it."

"You met him? I hope he told you why he did it. It was sure the biggest surprise of my life. It came all out of the blue and who or why is still a complete mystery. I almost didn't answer the door in case it was him back again."

"I guess it's all my fault. You remember me telling you about my run in with Rooster, in Andersonville? Well, he was Rooster's brother. He looked me up to settle the score and it seems he found you first. How bad is it?"

"Could've been a lot worse, and that's for sure. He wasn't much of a shot and it was a small caliber gun. It tore up my shoulder and I lost a lot of blood before the doc could fish out the slug and stitch me up. He tells me that it'll get better as time goes by, but I can't lift anything or even do much writing."

Candace had returned with coffee, bread and butter, and a warm bowl of stew in time to hear Will's admission. When Cole was finished she asked Will about his meeting with the shooter.

He looked deep into her eyes for a long moment. He saw concern there but no blame and his relief was almost overwhelming. He began to tell the story of his months in Willow Creek.

With Sherman there on his lap he gave them a running account of most of the new people in his life and the everyday happenings he'd been a part of. He glossed over the parts that would upset Candace and Sherman and emphasized the humor to be gained from the characters and situations. He didn't say too much about Twyla. He wanted to think about that some more. He soon came to the arrival of his friends.

"You remember me tellin' you about Del and Jack? Well, they showed up at Willow Creek to tell Twyla about Jimmy, thinkin' I was dead. We had a fine old reunion, I'll tell you. They'd been working for the railroad and I almost ran into them a couple of times on my way out but we just missed each other. They'd been there a couple of weeks when this shooter showed up. He came right into town, got a horse at the livery and went straight to my place. I wasn't there and Jack was in the barn when he snuck up on the house, just like he did here. He yelled something, Del came to the door and the bushwhacker shot him thinking he was me, just like he did you, and we were all just as surprised. Chief helped me track him down. When we had him cornered he told me who he was and why he was after me and then he told me he'd killed Cole." Will paused then. They didn't know about any of the killing and he didn't want them to. Let them believe that life was running the farm and the store and raising a family in a safe and friendly place. Enough of the evil of his world had touched them already. "Chief and I took care of him and I headed straight here."

"Took care of him?" Candace asked with a worried look.

"He won't be back here, ever."

Candace rose, still looking thoughtful. "Time you were in bed young man," she said as she lifted the drooping child from Will's lap.

That was the same look he'd seen on Twyla's face more than once. Yes, he needed to give her some more thought before he went back. Maybe he wasn't going to be doing her any favor by tying her to a man like himself. Maybe he hadn't the right to bring any woman into his life permanently.

Will decided to stay at least two weeks. He was anxious to get back but Cole was in a lot of pain and was unable to be much help in the store, besides he wanted some time with Sherman. It was amazing to him to see the little mind and body function. Growing and learning every day. Like Sammy he was completely honest and straight forward. It seemed a shame to teach him manners that would eventually cover that utter naturalness with which he greeted each new experience.

He set up housekeeping again in the tack room, and settled down to make himself useful. His mornings were spent splitting wood and doing farm chores and the afternoons were spent at the store. In the evenings he sat with the family talking and just being with them. He didn't know when they would be together again. He'd remembered to bring his harmonica and several evenings were spent playing tunes while Cole, Candace and Sherman sang. He'd been so certain that he'd never see Cole again he was sometimes almost overwhelmed with thankfulness. Still, somewhere inside himself, he didn't really feel a part of it. It was like looking at a pretty picture of a young family in front of the fire. A picture he could seal away in his heart to take out later to cheer himself in lonely times.

The new store was at least three times the size of the old one and it was a big job for any man to run. It took him almost a week to get into the routine. When he had last been here, Cole had always been there to handle the decisions, all he needed to do was follow orders. This time he had to decide how to handle every situation and, even worse, deal with every troublesome and picky customer. Almost as soon as he had figured out how to do the job he began to feel trapped and frustrated. How Cole looked forward to doing this for the rest of his life, he couldn't imagine. Seeing people buying supplies for their journey westward to a new country stirred up the wanderlust in his soul. He couldn't help but apply this feeling to a possible life in Willow Creek. How long before he hated it there as much as he knew he would hate it here if he had to stay forever.

He could probably handle running the ranch but Cap knew more about that then he ever would and he deserved to keep his job. Seth was as happy running the store as Cole was this one. He'd been appalled when he realized how well off Twyla was. Her ranch was huge and the big house was paid for outright as was the store and restaurant. She would have a piece of the Pinkham place in time.

With nothing but his unearned pittance from Cole and the two jars of gold he would be a kept man there. He loved her and he wanted to protect her for as long as he lived but the fact was he had done that and she didn't really need any more protection.

As he went about his redundant chores he found himself envying the adventurers loading up their wagons and heading west with their dreams. He could picture himself doing that with Twyla by his side. Maybe he could talk her into leaving Willow Creek and going adventuring. No, she had been very plain about that. He knew he loved her and thought she loved him but maybe that wouldn't be enough. At the worst times he thought that if it weren't for the horses he could just not go back to deal with it at all. No, he owed her an explanation. She had been straight with him about what she wanted and he had joined in her plans. He hated the idea of hurting her but as the days went by he came to the realization that he would have to. He knew how Jimmy had felt and he felt the same. Better a clean cut than a lingering death and that applied to a relationship as well as a life. If they went through with it, someday, their differences would drive them apart. They would no longer love one another. They would be lucky if the love didn't turn to hate.

At the end of three weeks, Will gathered up his clothes and packed his bag. Cole was doing much better and a man had been found to help with the heavy work in the store. He was anxious to see how Del was doing and to see Jack again. They didn't even know why he'd come here unless Chief had told them. Perhaps the two had returned to their jobs at the railroad. No, Del would probably still be recuperating and Jack wouldn't leave him. A wound like that would keep a man down for some time. Maybe for life. He had to be a man and deal with Twyla too. Then he would be really free again.

With hugs from Cole and Sherman and a kiss on the cheek from Candace, Will climbed aboard the train. A stab of loneliness swept through him as he waved from the window. He had no idea that it would be years before they would see each other again.

30

PROMISE KEPT

Seth busied himself organizing a shelf of canned goods. He'd been surprised and a little disappointed to find out, quite by accident, that Twyla and Del's relationship was more than just friendship. He'd assumed that Del and Jack would be heading back to the railroad. Melinda had a crush on Jack, who seemed to have taken up residence in the restaurant, but Jack was alright and he knew there was no one else around even halfway worthy of her. What bothered him was Will. He couldn't be aware of what was going on. They hadn't heard a word from him since he'd left. They wouldn't even have known why he'd gone if Chief hadn't told them. He supposed that leaving without telling his sister why had gotten under Twyla's skin. Will really should have told her himself. Still, Seth felt that she was making a mistake. Oh sure, Del was tall and good looking, and definitely had a way with fancy words and manners. He could see how that impressed Twyla, but he thought the man rather uninteresting himself. Will, on the other hand impressed Seth more than anyone he'd ever met, with the exception of his grandfather, of course. Will could get upset at the sight of an injured horse and shoot a man for attempting to steal one. He looked Cap in the face and instead of a gunfight he ended up changing him into a decent guy.

He was amazing, as far as Seth was concerned. Twyla should realize that a man like that didn't owe anybody explanations.

Mrs. Becker and Mrs. Blanchard entered the store, and Seth put his thoughts of Will aside.

"Good morning, ladies. How can I help you?"

"I must say, Seth, that it's nice to come in here and be treated with respect, for a change. Having to deal with Nate was not a pleasant experience, even when a body had money to spend. The horrible way he treated your sister just made my blood boil!"

"That's right," Mrs. Blanchard chimed in. "He was a real horse's ass!" She put her hand over her mouth when she realized what she had said. "Oh my." She glanced around the store to see if anyone else had heard.

Seth laughed. "You're not the first to call him that and I doubt you'll be the last, but I won't tell anyone you said it." With a bundle of dress material and two men's shirts, they left the store.

Twyla came in from the restaurant and gave him a hug around the waist. "How's the new proprietor doing?"

"Couldn't be better," Seth answered with a grin. "I do believe that I have everything under control. How about you?"

"I'm on my way home to check on Del, but thought I'd do the mail for you first."

"Ernie dropped it off awhile back and I have it all done." He thought for a second, then took the two letters from Will that had been in the dead letter box and handed them to her. "I've been holding onto these. Nate opened the first one and hid it in with the dead letters. He didn't open the second, just threw it in there too. I wanted to give them to you before, but with all the goings on I just put it off.

With a long look at her brother that was sharp enough to send him back to work, Twyla took the letters, recognizing the familiar scrawl. She took out the first with a snap and began to read it, trying to hide her anger. She could feel the pain in the words he had written and it brought a lump to her throat. She opened the second and read it. This reminder of his concern for her welfare brought back the guilt she felt for what she had to tell him about herself and Del. She knew that his love for her was real, and she would still marry him if he wanted but he had to know how she felt. Why did life have to be so difficult? Maybe he would stay with his family. That would be the easy solution, but she knew that he wouldn't.

She resented Nate for hiding the letters from her. Maybe if he had given them to her she could have responded and Will would not have come here. She was angry at Seth too, because he must have known about them for some time, since right after Nate died to be exact. She glared at herself in the large mirror in back of the counter and tried to picture what her life would be if Will had never come, and the picture made her feel sick. Why was she such a fool?

As she mounted Bell and rode out of town, her thoughts returned to Will. The letters had reminded her of his compassion and understanding. He had such a great heart, maybe it had to be balanced with that overpowering, stubborn sense of duty that drove her away from him. He was larger than life and any woman should be glad for his love, and she was, heaven help her, she was. Why did she have to go and fall in love with two men?

She had poured her heart out to Melinda, and was surprised to learn that she too had been in love with Will, until Jack arrived. Now, she thought Jack's shyness was cute and loveable. He looked at her with the eyes of a lovesick puppy and she thrived in the attention.

"I think I fell in love with Will before I even looked at him," Melinda had said. "Oh I saw the back of his head through that dirty window, but that's not the same. His voice was so soft, yet strong, and those gunmen were so horrible. I don't think I will ever see anyone, do anything as brave as that again, as long as I live. I just wanted to reach out and wrap my arms around him. I just knew that he was about to die. After he killed them and looked at me through the window, I saw more then the eye patch and scar, Twyla, I could see his soul. Why isn't that enough for you?"

Twyla hadn't been able to explain it. They had sat on the porch, holding hands. "Mom told me that sometimes it's hard to tell if a man is the wrong one, but our heart will tell us if he's the right one. I've heard my heart speak and it tells me Del is the one." She remembered thinking that that was easier said than acted upon. She still felt that way.

Del too, was having a hard time dealing with his conscience. He knew that women thought him attractive and he had played the flirting game many times. Twyla was a truly beautiful woman and he had been drawn to her at once. He had been knocked-for-a-loop when he realized that he was falling in love with her and that she evidently felt the same towards him. She was the woman Will intended to marry and he owed Will his very life. How could he betray him this way? He needed to tell her he was returning to the railroad and get himself up on his feet and go. They both felt the same about Will and they couldn't do this to him. He just kept putting it off, because of Jack and Melinda, because he was still feeling weak from his wound and because he wasn't sure he could live without seeing her daily. She would be here soon, he would hear her soft voice, and feel the touch of her hand and maybe share a kiss. Jack had been in to help him with his private stuff. He could tell Jack knew what was going on and was upset by it. They were letting everyone down and they had to decide what to do and how to do it before Will came back. The possibility of being separated was tearing them both apart.

Twyla came home everyday, sometimes twice, to shower attention on Del. It didn't take Jack long to see the signs. This was more than nursing a friend back to health. He could have taken care of Del just fine during the day. He was worried about Will, and felt more than a little guilty for not speaking out. Del was his best friend and had done everything for him, but this was wrong.

Because he felt uncomfortable when Twyla came home, he spent the middle of the days in town. He sat in the restaurant and watched Melinda as she bustled about. He was often joined for lunch by Chief and John. After lunch, they retired to the warmth of Johns' stove. There the three would discuss life. They were quite a trio. Between the three, they shared a lot of history. Slavery, Indians, war, cow punching, the list went on and on. Sometimes Sammy would join them for the child perspective.

Inevitably, Will would come up and Jack would tell and retell the horrors of Andersonville. He had been gone several months and they speculated whether he would nor return. Of course, it was probably the weather. It had been a hard winter.

Chief and John were listening to Sammy give them some advice on horses one evening by the stage stop. When the stage came in, they were glad to see Will at the window. It had been almost four months since he'd left. Sammy was thrilled and tried to run out in the street. Chief grabbed him just in time and held him back.

Stepping off the stage, Will was pleased to see his friends waiting. Chief had a tight grip on the back of Sammy's shirt and allowed himself to be hurried out to meet him. Sammy threw himself into Will's arms and was thrown skyward to his great satisfaction. Will set the boy back on his feet as Chief greeted him.

"I see you didn't forget how to find your way back, Will. We were thinking that you'd decided to stay and take care of your brother's place for good."

"Nope, Chief, as a matter of fact, my brother survived the shooting. I stayed around long enough for him to get back on his feet. How's Del?"

"Glad to hear about your brother. Del seems to be doing pretty good." Will had the impression Chief was going to say more but Sammy was tugging at his pant leg. He took a small bag of peppermints out of his pocket and gave them to the boy. When he looked up, Chief seemed to be absorbed in the dirt at his feet. Will wanted to press him but if there was something else wrong he'd rather hear about it in the morning. I'll need to rent a horse. Ernie managed to hit every bump and hole between here and Summit and I'm sure not up to walkin' out home, especially in the dark."

"How about Rosebud?" John asked with a smile.

"She'll do just fine. Glad to hear she made it," Will replied with a grin. "She didn't look very good the last time I saw her." At the livery, Will watched Chief lead her out proudly and put her saddle and bridle on. Chief spent as much time running his hands over her coat as he did getting her ready. When the job was done, he handed Will the reins. "I rode the grays for you. I rode like the wind. It was good." Chief was looking off in the distance. "It was good to feel young again."

Will mounted and guided the horse out onto the darkening street. Something was wrong, he thought. Chief always looked a man in the eye. Walking the horse along the deserted road, Will considered his homecoming. He was not eager to face Twyla, or to tell her what he'd decided. A few minutes, one way or the other, wasn't going to make any difference and he might as well save the old mare a hurry.

Nearing Twyla's place, he could hear laughter and voices. He recognized Del's laugh and was relieved to know that he was out and about. He saw shapes in the light from the lanterns on the porch. Jack and Melinda, were walking hand in hand toward the house. On the porch, in the swing, were Del and Twyla. They were covered by a blanket, against the chill of the evening. He reined in the horse and watched as an outsider, the way he had watched his brother's happy family in the evenings. Jack and Melinda climbed the stairs and entered the house. As soon as they disappeared into the parlor, Del and Twyla stood. As they faced one another, Del bent down and kissed her. It wasn't the short, tentative kiss that Will was used to. This was long, and lingering. He could see her arms around him, holding him to her. He felt a tightness in his chest and could feel the sting of tears in his eye. He guided Rosebud on down the road to the ranch. He had some serious thinking to do. This explained a lot. Twyla's coldness before he left, and Chief's uneasiness at the mention of Del. Of course, everyone in the damned town probably knew all about it. The question was, how did he feel about it.

As Will rode towards the ranch a feeling of rage and humiliation swept over him. Del was supposed to be his friend! She was supposed to be his girl! They should be all broke up because he wasn't going to stay, not kissin' like he didn't matter a'tall. He wasn't paying a bit of attention to where he was going and Rosebud raised her head in the moonlight and gave a derisive snort. He was startled by the noise and tickled as well. It was so appropriate, he wondered if she knew what was going through his mind. He decided to snort himself and he did, then he laughed right out loud to see how it sounded. It sounded pretty good. Here, he'd come back, intending to tell her he wasn't ready to marry and that he was riding out, expecting tears, and maybe her begging him to stay. She was way ahead of him. Kind of bruised his high opinion of himself and that was for damn sure.

Entering the ranch house, he walked over to the wall and took down the small mirror. He peered at his reflection, long and hard. 'Grow up you damn fool! Not only are you getting what you wanted but everyone is going to be happy about it. So, you love her, you know damn well you don't love her enough. Del's a good man and will be a great father for Sammy.' He hung the mirror back on the nail and walked over to the wood bin. He threw a few sticks in, watching the blaze flare up. Taking a chair, he leaned back against the wall and contemplated his future. The darkness prohibited him from seeing more of the mountain range to the west then a faint rim of light between the land and the star filled sky. A feeling of excitement brought a smile to his lips as he thought of crossing those mountains in a few days. Later he set out his gear and did some serious packing, going through the things he'd accumulated and neatly setting aside those he would leave. He paused when he came to the picture on the mantle, taking it down he looked at it one last time, and carefully replaced it.

He awakened to the familiar sound of the wind through the trees around the cabin. He noticed that neither Del nor Jack had returned. He wondered if Twyla had shared her bed. He regretted the thought, and pulling on his pants and boots, he went outside and drew a bucket of water. He took a big drink of the good water. Washed his face and combed his wet hair. He went back inside and finished getting ready. Taking his gear out to the barn, he saddled Missy. Packing Dolly, he looked around the barn and knew that he would miss this place. He would miss everyone. He was placing his hat on his head when he heard Del and Jack ride in and went out to meet them. They were happy to see him and to tell the truth, Will was glad to see them. They were damn good friends.

Looking at the bandage through the gap in Del's shirt, he said sincerely, "It's good to see you up and around, Del."

Del nodded. "Sorry about your brother. His family going to be alright?"

"My brother, managed to survive too, but he wasn't so lucky. Don't know if he'll ever get over it completely. Damn good thing that no good was using a small caliber pistol. If he'd had a forty-five, I don't think either of you would be up walking. Anything happen while I was gone?" Will noticed that Del did not look him in the eye, but he was clearing his throat to speak when Jack cut him off.

"Nope, can't think of anything off hand. Old Chief's been coming out every day to ride the grays. I'd have to put them out in the pasture when I left in the morning cause he wouldn't come on the place. Spent as much time rubbing them down as he did riding them," Jack answered with a laugh.

"Well I guess I'll ride over to see Twyla and Sammy. There's a fire in the stove if you boys are hungry."

Del got his mouth working at that. "I'll come out while you saddle up, there's something I want to talk to you about."

"No, need. No, need. I'm all saddled up already. We can talk when I get back." Wouldn't hurt him to worry about it for a while longer. 'Kinda like Barret', Will thought.

As Will rode toward Twyla's he organized his thoughts. He regretted he'd not explained why he was going to Iowa. That was plain rude. Thinking Cole was dead had crowded everything else out of his head. He regretted that he couldn't be the man she wanted and Del could, but nothing could be done about that. They needed to have a straight talk to clear things up and he had to make sure that she knew he would always be there if she needed him. Other than that he just had to see her and talk to her one more time.

As he turned off the road, he could see her standing in the doorway, a coffee cup in her hand. What was she thinking? he wondered.

Twyla was surprised to see Will riding toward the house. She was unaware that he had returned. They'd spent too many hours on the porch swing making plans for their future, she had to direct him somewhere else. She forced a smile as he reined in at the hitching post.

"Mornin' Twyla," Will said, softly.

Twyla could see the tension in his face. Did he already know? Maybe

Del had told him this morning. "Morning Will, care for some coffee with me?"

"That sounds good, Twyla."

She turned and went to the kitchen, quickly taking down a second cup and filling it. She heard Will take a chair at the table. As she turned, she noticed the hat under the chair and his slicked down hair. How many times had she seen him like this? She could feel a sting in her eyes, and fought back the tears, he was so damned dear to her. She handed him the cup and took the chair across from him. For a few seconds, neither said anything, but just looked at one another.

'I should have just ridden out,' Will thought to himself, as he looked into those green eyes. They made him want to hold her to him, to smell her hair and feel her body pressed against his. He mustn't do that. It would just hurt more in the long run.

"I just came to say goodbye, Twyla, and to see Sammy one more time."

She reached for his hand and he clasped hers gently. "I'm sorry to hear that, Will." She truly meant it though she knew it couldn't be. "Won't you change your mind? Make a life here with us?" she asked, quietly.

"It wouldn't work. Del's a good man, Twyla. He'll make a good husband and father for Sammy. I'm sure Jimmy will rest easy with your choice. I love you dearly, but I'm not the settling down kind. I'll always wonder what is on the other side of the mountain or around the next turn in the road."

Twyla shifted her eyes to the cup in her hand. She could feel the tears on her cheeks.

"You know about Del and me?"

"Well I'm not as dumb as I look, you know. If I could change into the kind of man you want, I would. I'll always love you and should I be ready to settle down some time, I hope I can find someone that reminds me of you. I sure hope you don't mind me a lovin' you until that time comes along."

"Oh Will, some-times you say things that just break my heart." She pushed her chair back and walking around the table, took his face in both hands and kissed him soundly. "You will always be my knight in shining armor."

Suddenly, he felt a sense of relief. He smiled, broadly. "Keep that up and I might turn into a store clerk and challenge Del to a duel for your hand."

"All you have to do is say so and I'll marry you, Will."

"That's good to know. Real good."

"I'm sorry about your brother, Will."

"He didn't die. They are going to be fine. I wish I could have taken you to meet them, they all would have loved you and you them. I should have told you where I was goin'."

"That's alright. Chief told us."

They sat, holding hands across the table, smiling. "Well I have miles to put on before nightfall, so I guess I better say goodbye." Reaching under the chair, he withdrew his hat and stood. "Is Sammy around?"

"No, he's over at Mom's."

"Tell him good-bye for me, then. Thanks for the coffee, Twyla." Turning, he walked out the door and mounting, rode out of the yard. He looked back and was surprised to see her standing in the doorway, crying. She didn't care how many bad men he had killed. If she were a man she would probably have done the same. She watched him until he rode out of sight. 'What have I done? Am I right or wrong?' She didn't know.

Returning to the ranch, he found Jack and Del waiting on the porch. They waved as he entered the yard. He could see the determined set of Del's jaw.

"Well boys, I've decided to head on out. Thought I'd like to see 'Frisco', and maybe Texas one more time. Maybe look up Rosella, if she is still around."

"Damn, Will. Why don't you stay here, at least until warmer weather?" Jack pleaded. "We just got together again."

"I've given it a lot of thinkin' and I figure the sooner the better. I'm just not ready to settle down just yet. Too many things to see and do."

"Does this have anything to do with me and Twyla? Because I can leave Will. It doesn't have to be you," Del asked, with concern. It had taken all his will-power to speak those words.

"Nope, we're nothing more than dear friends, Del. Really didn't realize it until I went home. The idea of hanging up the saddle and takin' a regular job just doesn't appeal to me."

Del inwardly breathed a sigh of relief. He thought that Will might be lying. It was the sort of thing a man like him might do, but he was not about to press the matter. Deep down, he felt a glow of pleasure, and a deep determination to be worthy of taking Will's place at Twyla's side.

An hour later, Dolly was packed and the three shook hands for the last time. He took one last look at the ranch and mounted.

"You figure to come back someday?" Jack asked.

"Oh sure, you'll see me again," Will replied. He wasn't at all sure of that as he rode down to the stream to Jimmy's rock. "Well, Partner, I have kept my promise to you. Del will do right by her and your son. Adios, my friend."

They watched Will ride out. Jack wanted to try to talk him into staying, but he had seen that all-to-familiar look on his face. His mind was made up. He'd seen it more than once before. When Will was walking down to fight Rooster came to mind.

Del wasn't entirely satisfied. He hoped that Will was truly leaving because of his desire to roam, but he couldn't understand how any man could leave Twyla. He knew that in many respects, he wasn't half the man Will was, but his love for Twyla was strong and true. He remembered how close he had come to stepping over the dead line. He was losing the best friend a man could have. Good luck, Will, he thought. May you find what you're looking for.

Entering the stables in town, Will saw Chief and John Henry working in one of the stalls. Hearing the horses, Chief looked up and seeing Will, dropped his shovel and hastened over. He noticed Rosebud, in tow, and took the rope from Will. Seeing the horses packed, he looked up at Will with concern. "You goin' huntin'?"

John Henry had joined them, and Will saw the puzzled look on his face. "No, I'm heading to California. Just stopped to leave Rosebud and to tell you goodbye and to thank you Chief, for keeping the horses in such good shape."

Chief nodded. Will had never seen him look so sad.

Both Chief and John Henry knew something of the relationship that had developed between Twyla and Del. The reason for Will's departure seemed obvious, but neither said anything about it. "I put new shoes on both horses while you were gone." John spoke with a sad voice. He was going to miss Will and that was for sure. The fact that Will was responsible for the change in Cap and the rest of the Baldon crew was making his life so much easier. But most of all, Will had been a good friend.

"You'll tell the rest of the folks goodbye for me, won't you? You two take care. It's been a real pleasure knowing you." He reached down and gripped their hands. Tipping his hat, he reined around and noticing Seth and Melinda watching from in front of the store, rode over to them.

"You headin' out, Will?" Seth asked.

"Yep. I hear California callin' my name," Will answered.

"Danged sorry to hear that, Will. We'll miss you around these parts."

"Would you fix me up some supplies? Here's a list."

"Be my pleasure, Will. Melinda just baked some pies. Have some on the house while I fill the order."

"Can't say I ever passed up a piece of pie. No time to start now." He tied the horses in the shade of the building and walked around to the pump. He slicked down his hair again before going inside and taking his accustomed chair, sliding his hat underneath it. When Seth had taken the supplies out and tied them on the gray, he joined Will at the table. They ate their pie in silence.

Seth was seething with indignation and finally he burst out. "Dammit Will, she's making an awful mistake."

"No she isn't. I don't want to settle down. I never have and I doubt I ever will. If I married her that wouldn't change. She wants her home and family here and that will never change either. She loves me as much as a home loving woman can love a roving man and knows that I will always love her and that's enough for us." Melinda, standing in the kitchen listened in silence. She walked out and resting her hands on his shoulders bent and kissed Will on the cheek. "I love you too, and don't you forget it."

"A man can't ask for anything more than that." He reached for his hat grinning, then he stood and swept it in wide arc, bowing to her. Suddenly the memory of the Love Sisters came to mind. He laughed delightedly.

He and Seth walked out onto the boardwalk and stood, neither wanting to end it. Will reached into his shirt pocket and took out several gold nuggets and handed them to Seth.

"That's too much, Will."

"Don't need it. Maybe you could buy something for Twyla on her birthday for me. You tell Cap that I said good-bye."

Melinda joined them and they all walked out to the horses. Will mounted. Looking down at Melinda, he could see the tears in her eyes as she stood in the circle of Seth's arm.

"You take care of yourself, Will," she managed to say.

"Sure, I'll do that. And you take care of Jack. He's a good man." With a tip of his hat to Seth, he reined away from the two.

Chief came out of the stable holding his knife in it's beaded sheath. He held it in both hands and extended it out to Will. "You take this. You are a warrior. I am too old to use this weapon. I will feel good knowing that you wear it. I think Buel would like you to have these things. He was a warrior and skinned many buffalo and maybe took a scalp or two. May it keep you safe. It is good for killing vermin." He smiled, his eyes glistening.

"I'll use it for that purpose. It's a beautiful gift. I'll wear it with pride, Chief." He hooked the loop on the sheath over the saddle horn. "You're a good friend. I thank you for all the knowledge you've shared. I'll try to make you proud." He reined around and rode out of town. This time he didn't look back.

Looking westward, he felt a small surge of excitement, as he wondered what awaited him beyond the mountains. He knew that he would always carry the memory of the folks at Willow Creek and that Twyla would always be there, in his mind, and in his heart, when he needed her.

He settled comfortably in the saddle and nudged Missy with his spurs. The horses stepped out eagerly as if they, too, were eager to get back on the trail. The familiar sounds of leather rubbing, bit chains and hooves, brought a smile to his lips. Maybe there's another Twyla out there waiting for me. Perhaps I'll find that special person and no longer have the desire to explore. He took a deep breath as he looked to the far break in the mountain range.

Smiling to himself, he took the harmonica from his shirt pocket. He lifted the eye patch up to his forehead and let the morning breeze cool his face. He thought of several happy tunes that he and Jimmy had made up, and he began to play.

31

1982

"Let's stop at the next rest area, that Pepsi is catching up to me," Cindy suggested.

"No problem," Earl replied. "I need to go too. Sure is pretty country, don't you think?"

"It's beautiful," Cindy replied. "I just hope that everything else is all we've heard. I must admit that I'm getting just a little tired of all this driving."

Ten minutes later Earl saw the rest area sign and turned in. There were no other cars. As he got out of the car he breathed in the smell of pine and fir trees. A warm breeze gently ruffled his long brown hair. Emerging from the restroom a few minutes later, greatly relieved, he noticed the plexiglass covered map on a rustic wall. "You are here" was indicated with a red arrow. He located Summit, which they had passed through an hour before and followed the road past the red arrow to the town of Landon. Another twenty-five or thirty miles, he thought. Could this be their future home? He had heard about the place from friends and he hoped that it lived up to its billing. He needed to get back to his clay and oils. He looked up as Cindy approached. "Another thirty miles, at the most." She was beautiful. He'd never get over the fact that she had chosen to marry him. Five years next July. She always brought a smile to his face. Sliding into the seat, he took her hand and kissed her fingertips before he started the car.

The road continued to climb for another mile, then started to descend. There was a sign there, that said, *Historical Marker 500 ft.*

"Let's take a look," Cindy suggested.

"I read your mind," Earl said with a laugh. "We haven't driven past one yet in the last five years."

Pulling off the roadway, they took in the view of the Willow Creek Valley. Five miles wide and fifteen long, with low escarpments stretching out into it like fingers on three sides and a long cliff to the south. They could see the sun reflecting off the buildings of a town, concentrated in the center of the valley and scattering outward. Getting out of the car they approached the marker which they read in silence.

"MIDPOINT STATION The original trail here was established in 1836 by trappers. By 1848 this became a stop on the stage route between Summit and Willow Creek. Later the route was extended to Landon. The springs were developed during those years and the troughs were in use until the end of World War One."

Forty-five minutes later they entered the town of Landon. The main street was wide, and lined with rustic storefronts. Large awnings covered the sidewalks almost to the curb. The main street extended seven or eight blocks and Earl noticed that almost all the buildings were occupied. There was a park across from the City Hall in the center of Main Street. The town was bustling with business and he had to pull off the main street to find a parking place. Cindy had spotted a real estate office and they headed in that direction.

Earl was pleased to see a number of antique stores and several galleries full of shoppers. They paused to look at some of the art work displayed in the windows. He was glad to see that it was up to his standards, as far as difficulty and technique. He would definitely have some competition.

At the real estate agency a small bell above the door signaled their entrance and a middle-aged man emerged from a back room. Earl had to smile. The man was wearing a red bandana instead of a tie, a brilliantly striped blue and white shirt and red cowboy boots. His large stomach hung over his belt, covering most of a football sized buckle. His pale blue eyes were squinted and his wide mouth was in a perpetual grin. A flowing handlebar mustache completed his fashion statement.

"Howdy folks. How can I help you, this fine day?"

"We're thinking of moving here and are looking for property that's not overly expensive. The house isn't too important, as we can remodel it ourselves if necessary. Our main concern is having a building large enough for a pottery and art studio. Something we could live in if necessary while the house is being fixed up," Earl explained.

"My name is Al, Al Jennings. You folks want something in town, or out in the country?"

"I'm Earl Stabler and this is my wife Cindy," Earl said as they all shook hands.

"We were thinking out." Cindy answered. "We'd kind of like to have a few animals. Maybe five acres, or so."

"That's good, because I don't have anything that fits your needs close to town, but I do have a piece of property about fifteen miles out. It comes with twenty acres. The house is over a hundred and fifty years old, and needs some fixin', but the core house was very well made, and the additions have been quality work. The property is vacant, so you can go out there and look it over. I realize it's a fair piece from town, but well worth the look. It also has a large barn that might fit your needs. If you're interested, I'll get the key for you. Where are you parked?"

"Across the street, between those two large buildings," Earl replied.

"Great. Just go to the stop sign and hang a left. Go two blocks and you'll come to Oak Street. Turn right and keep going. It will turn into the old Willow Creek road. You can't miss it. When you get to Willow Creek, turn left at the old mine building, cross the bridge and travel out about three miles. The house will be on left. Can't miss it."

A couple of miles out of Willow creek they noticed a large, two-storied house, on their left. The ancient trees were well cared for, and the house seemed to be in good condition. They slowed down to look at a small sign on the elaborate gate. "Baldon House, 1866." They passed several more houses along the road as well as drive-ways leading to houses set back, out of sight.

When they reached the end of the road they turned down the last drive as instructed and parked in the open farmyard. They sat in the quiet and let their eyes roam over the old ranch house and the large trees surrounding it. Earl took in the large barn, and was pleased. It was definitely big enough and the roof looked straight as did the roof on the house. Al was right though, it was pretty shabby.

Paint had peeled and the porch sagged. Windows were broken and wires coming in from the road looked frayed. Still, there was nothing that came to eye that couldn't be fixed. They got out of the car and went up on the porch. They turned to look at the view and it was wonderful, or it would be with a little tree trimming. Unlocking the door, they entered the living room and took in the large rock fireplace. The floors were worn, but were firm.

Cindy went into the kitchen and pictured it the way it should look. It had been enlarged and the windows looked out toward the cliff, a half-mile away. It was enough to take her breath away.

A second bedroom had been added in the back and a large old fashioned bathroom was located between it and the older one that had a second fireplace. Another half-bath was located off the laundry-room which was probably an add-on too.

"I love it, Earl. I just love it. I can see a large patio out this window, with arbors and a small pond. What do you think?"

"It's better than what I had expected but we need to check out the barn."

Together, they walked, hand in hand, around the detached garage and opened the large barn door. A pair of startled Owls flew out the back door that was half off its hinges.

"Did you see that? Owls!" Earl exclaimed.

"Awesome." Cindy replied.

Earl took in the large squared beams with mortise and tenon construction. Large square nails protruded from the uprights. Earl could picture the barn with a solid floor and skylights in the roof. Large windows, facing the front, would provide ample light. It was perfect.

After a half-hour of mentally renovating the barn, they re-entered the house. The door to the old dry-room behind the fireplace was open and Earl peered in. Puzzled, he looked at the opening at the far end of the small room.

"I'll be right back. I need my flashlight."

Returning, he shone the light through the small door and down in the hole to which it led. "Check this out. We have a root cellar."

Cindy peered over his shoulder and announced. "I'm not going anywhere near that until you get it cleaned out. It looks spooky to me and it's probably home to a hundred spiders."

Later as they walked farther out around the yard, they found a small fenced enclosure, almost completely overgrown with ivy. Stepping over the small fence, Earl pulled the ivy aside, revealing a small marble headstone. *Charles Lovelace, Died 1853. Killed by Indians.*

"Now that is something else!" Earl exclaimed. "A pioneer grave right in the front yard! I wonder who he was! Let's go back to town, Honey. I think we've found exactly what we've been looking for. What do you think?"

"I want it! I sure hope they're not asking too much for it," Cindy answered, with a worried look.

It was getting late and they were able to park right in front of the real estate office. Al who'd been waiting for them, met them at the car door. "What do you think? I realize that it's in a rough condition, but, believe me, the price is right. With a lot of sweat and a little money, it could be a real nice place."

A half hour later, the paperwork was well underway.

"By the way, Al, do you know any of the history of the place?" Earl asked.

"Well some," Al replied, "but if you really want to know about it, go across the street to the museum. Lilly should still be there. She knows about all there is to know." We can't do anything more tonight.

Lilly looked to be in her seventies. She was a handsome old lady and must have once been beautiful. Her green eyes sparkled to match her smile. She was small, with snow white hair piled neatly on her head and fastened with a yellow bow.

"My name is Cindy, and this is my husband Earl. We're in the process of buying the property out at the end of Willow Creek Road. Al, at the real estate office, said you might be willing to fill us in on its history."

"Oh I'm so pleased. Do you intend to live there? I mean, it is in poor condition."

"If you give me a pencil and a sheet of paper, I'll show you what we have in mind, so far." Earl took the paper she offered and began to draw a series of pictures of the place as they now saw it in their heads.

"It'll be just beautiful," Lilly replied, as she looked at the sketches. "My great-grandmother and grandfather would be so pleased."

"It belonged in your family?" Cindy asked in surprise. "Tell us all about it."

"I'm through here. If you have an hour, let's take a drive," she replied, with a smile.

"We have all the time in the world," Earl answered. "Where are we going?"

"To the cemetery." Lilly replied, with a laugh. "You must meet the family."

They all climbed into her old station wagon and Lilly started by explaining the grave site on the property as she drove along. "Charlie was the original builder of the house and barn. From what I've been able to research, he also owned a mine southwest of here in Colorado. I've been meaning to try to locate it but haven't gotten around to it yet. There's a map in the museum files. Maybe next year. His body was found in a cave under the floor of the dry room. He'd been shot by Indians, and had hidden there. He died of his wounds and no one knew what had become of him. The Indians never went near the place again. It was considered, *bad medicine.* She slowed down, as she neared Willow Creek and guided the car through the cemetery's white painted gates. She parked in the gravel under the spreading trees and they climbed out.

The rustic cemetery was about two acres in size, and had many fine old tombstones. It was without water, and the ground rustled as they walked through the covering of leaves that had drifted down from the aged trees. Only the roadside fence was wood. The rest was sagging wire that allowed them a view of fields and trees.

"We start in the back corner," Lilly said, as she led the way. "This is my great-grandmother, Twyla, and my great-grandfather Delbert Trenton.

Earl read the headstones; *Twyla Trenton, born 1845, died 1912 "Beloved wife and mother. Gone, but never forgotten. Delbert Trenton, born 1843, died 1900. Loving Father and Husband.*

"Over here are Twyla's parents Ken and Martha Pinkham. This is Seth, who was Twyla's little brother and his wife, Evelyn. The Comptons, Miles and Verna, were old-time residents. Their son Jimmy died in the Civil War. He was buried at Andersonville Prison in Georgia. The rumor was that he was the father of Twyla's son Samuel who was my grandfather. Twyla's little sister, Melinda married Jack Turner. They're over in the next row with two of their children, the other three moved out of the area.

"This man is somewhat of a mystery," Lily said, pointing to a gray stone. "Will Morgan was the person your property is named after. It has been called the Morgan Ranch for years although Charles Lovelace was the original owner. When we get back, I'll show you some clippings."

Earl looked at the small stone.

Will Morgan, born 1837 died 1914 R.I.P.

This is for Will Trenton, my father, who was named after Will Morgan. He died in World War I, and his body was buried in France. And here is my mother, bless her soul."

Earl read the dates. Lilly's father had been born in 1887 and died 1919. Her mother, Francine, was born 1890 and died in 1973.

"Oh, this might be of interest," she said, pointing to two headstones. "This is John Henry Hamner, the black man that owned and ran the stables. John Henry had been a slave and was left the business by his partner with whom he built the building on arriving in Willow Creek. Chief was a Lakota Sioux who lived in the stables for years helping with the work and doing other odd jobs around town, including being a great storyteller and town character. The local papers spoke very fondly of the two of them when they passed on. The museum annex is housed in the old stable building which is a marvel of the builder's skill and was moved from Willow Creek to Landon after a fire destroyed most of the town."

Back at the museum. Lilly opened a large scrapbook and carefully turned the pages. Her fingers caressed them as she searched for the items she wanted. She found the page she was looking for and turned the book so that they could read the entry. The first was from the Summit Journal, dated 1866.

Texas Gunfighters Wound Twigg
Hold town under siege for three days

Beloved Sheriff Twigg was seriously wounded this week by two Texas rowdies who proceeded to terrorize the citizens until the arrival in town of another gunman. Both gunmen were shot dead in the street outside Roger's Mercantile by the stranger who wore a patch over one eye and called himself Buck. He was offered a job as deputy but declined saying he was on his way to Willow Creek on business. Twigg is recuperating at home where he is taking applications for the job of deputy."

"Will Morgan was going by the name Buck at that time. It's a rather complicated story, but as you're staying, there'll be plenty of time later for me to try to explain it," She said with a laugh. She turned the book and leafed through several more pages. Pausing, she turned it around once more.

Nate Baldon of Willow Creek Dies
In Stage Mishap

Mr. Baldon, scion of the Baldon ranch family and leading citizen of Willow Creek was crushed by the wheels of the Summit stage this week. Ernie Walton, driver of the stage states that Baldon had stepped out of the stage on a personal matter and had his hand on a spoke when the horses shied and he became tangled in the wheel, much to his misfortune. The funeral was held in Willow Creek on Thursday.

"Nate was Twyla's first husband, "Lily explained and turned to the next page without turning the book around. The clipping fastened to the page read.

Visitor to Willow Springs Shot And Wounded
By New York Gunman

As Del Trenton, guest of the widow Baldon, was recovering from his injuries, the fleeing gunman was hunted down by a friend, Will Morgan, known hereabout as Buck, and Chief, a Lakota Sioux, who works for John Hamner, owner of the Willow Creek Livery. Justice was served on the spot. In describing the incident, Chief tells of meeting a Lakota hunting party who recognized Morgan, by his exceptional horses, as the person who handed out a similar justice to three scalp hunters who had been terrorizing the peaceful local Indians. It was told to him that the three were intent on stealing the grays when the aforementioned justice was dealt out with the customary forty-five.

Closing the book, she smiled and paused, trying to decide if she should tell them about the diary entry. They seemed so nice, and besides, they were buying the ranch.

"One of the last entries in my Great-Grandmother's diary before she married Del Trenton was: *I loved you too, Will. Goodbye until we meet again.* As far as I know, they did not see each other again for over thirty-five years."

"I remember seeing Mr. Morgan when I was a girl, but I don't have a very clear picture of him as I was quite young and interested in my own life. I remember the eye patch and he had a number of scars on his face. About the only other thing is a simply wonderful doll he gave me for Christmas. My father told me that he came back around 1906 and spent several years with my grandmother before her death. He was at her bedside when she passed on and committed suicide at her grave site two years later."

"Here is something else that you may be interested in," she added, as she escorted them to a glass display case. "This is the Colt revolver and Henry repeating rifle that belonged to Mr. Morgan. He donated the rifle when the museum first started. The revolver was donated by my father, after Mr. Morgan used it to kill himself." The antique Lakota knife and sheath were a present to Mr. Morgan from Chief and are extremely valuable.

Earl looked at the weapons, taking in their fine condition. Obviously, they had been well taken care of before coming to the museum. It was times like this that he wished objects like this could tell their story. He stared at them thoughtfully while the two women went on talking about the romance of the story.

"What's the story on the harmonica?" Earl asked finally, pointing to the mouth organ placed next to a silver case with a woman's picture in it and a small leather pouch.

"Oh that was Mr. Morgan's too. He always carried it from the years he was in the Civil War, until shortly before his death. He'd been imprisoned at Andersonville with Jimmy Compton, the boy who died there. I mentioned him at the cemetery. They had been close friends and had apparently owned it together. Jimmy was engaged to Twyla and carried that picture of her to war. It was kept in the leather pouch with the harmonica during their imprisonment. "We do have one picture of Mr. Morgan with Jimmy Compton there in the corner."

Earl bent down to get a better look at the two faded faces. One was boyish and young, the other was obviously Morgan if looks had anything to do with action. Tough looking man and handsome too, he thought. Cindy was taken with the picture of Twyla and couldn't get over how much Lily looked like her.

As they left the museum, Earl was thinking of Will Morgan. I wonder what he did during his thirty-five year absence? If he created so much lore in such a short period of time while he lived here, he must have left a mark wherever else he went. He felt the urge to start some research on the man. Yes, there has to be a story here. A man like Morgan didn't just disappear for thirty-five years.

PROLOGUE

The progress of the United States of the eighteen-fifties was threatened by an ever increasing tension among its members. As the decade drew to a close the increasing discord highlighted a number of clear divisions between the northern and southern factions of the country. Congressmen from the industrial north advocated a strong central government while those from the South believed that the rights of the individual states should supercede those of the Union. Fundamentalists in the North argued for the abolition of slavery throughout the nation, an action that would clearly be the ruin of the Southern slave-based economy. Representatives from the South argued, with more than a little justification, that in that case their participation in the union was entirely voluntary and they were entitled to abandon it at any time they chose. As the nation drifted closer to open conflict new territories in the west were pressured to take sides in these issues. New states, joining the Union, were being fought over in the halls of Congress as to whether they would be slave or free. Tempers flared.

After slaughtering several families of pro-slavers, the radical abolitionist John Brown and his followers attempted to incite a slave uprising by taking over the armory at Harpers Ferry, Virginia. The uprising was quickly put down by federal troops under the command of Lt. Col. Robert E. Lee of the 2nd U.S. Cavalry. On Dec. 2, 1859, while being marched to the gallows, Brown handed his guard a slip of paper with this ominous prediction.

"I, John Brown, am now quite certain that the crimes of this guilty land will never be purged away but with blood."

It was two years later that the firing on Fort Sumpter by southern forces heralded the beginning of the war that killed more American soldiers than World Wars One and Two, Korea and Vietnam combined.

In the beginning very few, if any, envisioned 620,000 dead and well over a million wounded. A few minor skirmishes and then a negotiated settlement were all either side expected. In this general belief, neither side was prompted to make plans for taking care of tens of thousands of prisoners. Unfortunately, the South was determined that settlement would allow them to secede, while the North was equally adamant that the Union would remain whole.

The North had a penal system in place along with the where-with-all for some expansion. The South had nothing in the way of adequate space for such an undertaking beyond large warehouses meant for cotton and tobacco. Once the North's naval blockade was established there was little extra money for their own army much less to create an adequate penal system. What the South needed was something that could be erected quickly and cheaply and could hold large numbers of prisoners. Stockades, enclosing large open plots of land in rural areas were the only viable solution to the problem. None of these were destined to reach the size and infamy of that located at Andersonville, Georgia.

Housing upwards of 45,000 prisoners during its fifteen months of operation, covering the year 1864 and the first three months of 1865, over 12,000 died. The lack of sanitation, relatively common on both sides, here, reached monumental proportions. The only water source for the entire prison was a small stream that flowed through the center of the prison rectangle at mid point. This stream passed through the Confederate camp before reaching the prison where no attempt was made to prevent raw sewage and kitchen garbage from entering the water. A long boxed slit-trench was erected inside the stockade that ran parallel to a portion of the stream, allowing sewage to drain into it as well. Additionally, the absence of a firm chain of command in procurement of supplies, and qualified and humane officers in charge of the prisons themselves allowed for an environment rift with inequity and abuse of power.

The South, however, was not to blame for all the strife suffered by the Union prisoners. The North drafted or conscripted men into their army but allowed those with means to hire someone to take their place in order to avoid active service. This soon became a very lucrative source of income for the gangs of New York City, made up primarily of immigrants from Ireland. Their practice was to accept money to substitute for a prospective soldier, then at the first opportunity, desert and repeat the procedure all over again. Hundreds of these captured New Yaarkers as they were called, ended up in southern prisons where they continued their gang life-style of beating, thievery and murder. Approximately five hundred found their way to Andersonville.

In time, a group of men captured from the Armies of the West, which had been conscripted from areas far from New York, joined forces and put a stop to the majority of these acts. They called themselves Regulators, and remained active throughout the war.

Unlike troops who fell honorably in battle to the cannon, gun and saber, most who died at Andersonville and its sister prisons in both the North and South died, unheralded, from disease or starvation. Some did, however, meet brutal death at the hands of fellow prisoners, and a few ended their suffering at the hands of compassionate friends.

ABOUT THE AUTHOR

George Meuser lives in Medford, Oregon, is a student of history and expert on Andersonville, the most gruesome prisoner camp during the Civil War between the States. George taught school for over twenty-five years and portrays the real men and women who fought to keep the Union together and sacrificed their own lives.

Made in the USA
Coppell, TX
26 July 2020